After the Crash

A Novel

MICHEL BUSSI

Translated from the French by Sam Taylor

NEW YORK   BOSTON

Copyright © 2012 by Presses de la Cité
Translation copyright © 2015 by Sam Taylor

Hachette Books
Hachette Book Group
1290 Avenue of the Americas
New York, NY 10104

www.HachetteBookGroup.com

Hachette Books is a division of Hachette Book Group, Inc.
The Hachette Books name and logo are trademarks of Hachette Book Group, Inc.

The Hachette Speakers Bureau provides a wide range of authors for speaking events. To find out more, go to www.hachettespeakersbureau.com or call (866) 376-6591.

The publisher is not responsible for websites (or their content) that are not owned by the publisher.

Printed in the United States of America

Published in hardcover by Hachette Book Group
First international mass market edition: December 2015

10 9 8 7 6 5 4 3 2 1
OPM

For Maluo, little dragonfly
born with this story

After the Crash

December 23, 1980, 12:33 a.m.

The Airbus 5403, flying from Istanbul to Paris, suddenly plummeted. In a dive lasting less than ten seconds, the plane sank over three thousand feet, before stabilizing once again. Most of the passengers had been asleep. They woke abruptly, with the terrifying sensation that they had nodded off while strapped to a rollercoaster.

Izel was woken not by the turbulence, but by the screaming. After nearly three years spent traveling the world with Turkish Airlines, she was used to a few jolts. She had been on a break, asleep for less than twenty minutes, and had scarcely opened her eyes when her colleague Meliha thrust her aged, fleshy bosom toward her.

"Izel? Izel? Hurry up! This is serious. There's a big storm outside. Zero visibility, according to the captain. You take one aisle and I'll take the other."

Izel's face bore the weary expression of an experienced flight attendant who wasn't about to panic over such a small thing. She got up from her seat, adjusted her suit, pulling slightly at the hem of her skirt, then moved toward the right-hand aisle.

The passengers were no longer screaming, and they looked more surprised than worried as the airplane continued to pitch. Izel went from one person to the next, calmly reassuring them: "Everything's fine. Don't worry. We're just going through a little snowstorm over the Jura Mountains. We'll be in Paris in less than an hour."

Izel's smile wasn't forced. Her mind was already wandering toward Paris. She would stay there for three days, until Christmas, and she was giddy with excitement at the prospect.

She addressed her words of comfort in turn to a ten-year-old boy holding tightly to his grandmother's hand, a handsome young businessman with a rumpled shirt, a Turkish woman wearing a veil, and an old man curled up fearfully with his hands between his knees. He shot her an imploring look.

"Everything's fine, honestly."

Izel was calmly proceeding down the aisle when the Airbus lurched sideways again. A few people screamed. "When do we start doing the loop-de-loop?" shouted a young man sitting to her right, who was holding a Walkman, his voice full of false cheer.

A trickle of nervous laughter was drowned out almost immediately by the screams of a young baby. The child was lying in a baby carrier just a few feet in front of Izel— a little girl, only a few months old, wearing a white dress with orange flowers under a knitted beige sweater.

"No, madame," Izel called out. "No!"

The mother, sitting next to the baby, was unbuckling her belt so she could lean over to her daughter.

"No, madame," Izel insisted. "You must keep your seat belt on. It's very important..."

The woman did not even bother turning around, never

mind replying to the flight attendant. Her long hair fell over the baby carrier. The baby screamed even louder. Izel, unsure what to do, moved toward them.

The plane plunged again. Three seconds, maybe another 3,000 feet.

There were a few brief screams, but most of the passengers were silent. Dumbstruck. They knew now that the airplane's movements were not merely due to bad weather. Jolted by the dive, Izel fell sideways. Her elbow hit the Walkman, smashing it into the young guy's chest. She straightened up again immediately, not even taking the time to apologize. In front of her, the three-month-old girl was still crying. Her mother was leaning over her again, unbuckling the child's seat belt.

"No, madame! No . . ."

Cursing, Izel tugged her skirt back down over her ripped tights. What a nightmare. She would have earned those three days of pleasure in Paris . . .

Everything happened very fast after that.

For a brief moment, Izel thought she could hear another baby crying, like an echo, somewhere else on the airplane, farther off to her left. The Walkman guy's hand brushed her nylon-covered thighs. The old Turkish man had put one arm around his veiled wife's shoulder and was holding the other one up, as if begging Izel to do something. The baby's mother had stood up and was reaching over to pick up her daughter, freed now from the straps of the baby carrier.

These were the last things Izel saw before the Airbus smashed into the mountainside.

The collision propelled Izel thirty feet across the floor, into the emergency exit. Her two shapely legs were twisted like those of a plastic doll in the hands of a sadistic child; her slender chest was crushed against metal; her left temple exploded against the corner of the door.

Izel was killed instantly. In that sense, she was luckier than most.

She did not see the lights go out. She did not see the airplane being mangled and squashed like a tin can as it crashed into the forest, the trees sacrificing themselves one by one as the Airbus gradually slowed.

And, when everything had finally stopped, she did not detect the spreading smell of kerosene. She felt no pain when the explosion ripped apart her body, along with those of the other twenty-three passengers who were closest to the blast.

She did not scream when flames filled the cabin, trapping the one hundred and forty-five survivors.

Eighteen Years Later

1

Now you know everything.

Crédule Grand-Duc lifted his pen and stared into the clear water at the base of the large vivarium just in front of him. For a few moments, his eyes followed the despairing flight of the Harlequin dragonfly that had cost him almost 2,500 francs less than three weeks ago. A rare species, one of the world's largest dragonflies, an exact replica of its prehistoric ancestor. The huge insect flew from one glass wall to another, through a frenzied swarm of dozens of other dragonflies. Prisoners. Trapped.

They all sensed they were dying.

Pen touched paper once again. Crédule Grand-Duc's hand shook nervously as he wrote.

In this notebook, I have reviewed all the clues, all the leads, all the theories I have found in eighteen years of investigation. It is all here, in these hundred or so pages. If you have read them carefully, you will now know as much as I do. Perhaps you will be more perceptive than I. Perhaps you will find something I have missed. The key to the mystery, if one exists. Perhaps . . .

For me, it's over.

The pen hesitated again, and was held trembling just an inch above the paper. Crédule Grand-Duc's blue eyes stared emptily into the still waters of the vivarium, then turned their gaze toward the fireplace, where large flames were devouring a tangle of newspapers, files, and cardboard storage boxes. Finally, he looked down again and continued.

It would be an exaggeration to say that I have no regrets, but I have done my best.

Crédule Grand-Duc stared at this last line for a long time, then slowly closed the pale green notebook.

11:43 p.m.

He placed the pen in a pot on the desk, and stuck a yellow Post-it note to the cover of the notebook. Then he picked up a felt-tip pen and wrote on the Post-it, in large letters, *for Lylie.* He pushed the notebook to the edge of the desk and stood up.

Grand-Duc's gaze lingered for a few moments on the copper plaque in front of him: CRÉDULE GRAND-DUC, PRIVATE DETECTIVE. He smiled ironically. Everybody called him Grand-Duc nowadays, and they had done for some time. Nobody—apart from Emilie and Marc Vitral—used his ludicrous first name. Anyway, that was before, when they were younger. An eternity ago.

Grand-Duc walked toward the kitchen. He took one last look at the gray, stainless-steel sink, the white octagonal tiles on the floor, and the pale wood cabinets, their doors closed. Everything was in perfect order, clean and tidy; every trace of his previous life had been carefully wiped away, as if this were a rented house that had to be returned to its owner. Grand-Duc was a meticulous man and always would be, until his dying breath. He knew that. That explained many things. Everything, in fact.

He turned and walked back toward the fireplace until he could feel the heat on his hands. He leaned down and threw two storage boxes into the flames, then stepped back to avoid the shower of sparks.

A dead end.

He had devoted thousands of hours to this case, examining each clue in the most minute detail. All those clues, those notes, all that research was now going up in smoke. Every trace of this investigation would disappear in the space of a few hours.

Eighteen years of work for nothing. His whole life was summarized in this *auto-da-fé*, to which he was the only witness.

11:49 p.m.

In fourteen minutes, Lylie would be eighteen years old, officially at least…Who was she? Even now, he still couldn't be certain. It was a one-in-two chance, just as it had been on that very first day. Heads or tails.

Lyse-Rose or Emilie?

He had failed. Mathilde de Carville had spent a fortune—eighteen years' worth of salary—for nothing.

Grand-Duc returned to the desk and poured himself another glass of Vin Jaune. From the special reserve of Monique Genevez, aged for fifteen years: this was, perhaps, the single good memory he had retained from this investigation. He smiled as he brought the glass of wine to his lips. A far cry from the caricature of the aging alcoholic detective, Grand-Duc was more the type of man to dip sparingly into his wine cellar, and only on special occasions. Lylie's birthday, tonight, was a very special occasion. It also marked the final minutes of his life.

The detective drained the glass of wine in a single mouthful.

This was one of the few sensations he would miss: the inimitable taste of this distinctive yellow wine burning deliciously as it moved through his body, allowing him to forget for a moment this obsession, the unsolvable mystery to which he had devoted his life.

Grand-Duc put the glass back on the desk and picked up the pale green notebook, wondering whether to open it one last time. He looked at the yellow Post-it: *for Lylie*.

This was what would remain: this notebook, these pages, written over the last few days . . . For Lylie, for Marc, for Mathilde de Carville, for Nicole Vitral, for the police and the lawyers, and whoever else wished to explore this endless hall of mirrors.

It was a spellbinding read, without a doubt. A masterpiece. A thrilling mystery to take your breath away. And it was all there . . . except for the end.

He had written a thriller that was missing its final page, a whodunit in which the last five lines had been erased.

Future readers would probably think themselves cleverer than he. They would undoubtedly believe that they could succeed where he had failed, that they could find the solution.

For many years he had believed the same thing. He had always felt certain that proof must exist somewhere, that the equation could be resolved. It was a feeling, only a feeling, but it wouldn't go away . . . That certainty had been what had driven him on until this deadline: today, Lylie's eighteenth birthday. But perhaps it was only his subconscious that had kept this illusion alive, to prevent him from falling into utter despair. It would have been so cruel to have spent all those years searching for the key to a problem that had no solution.

The detective reread his final words: *I have done my best.*

Grand-Duc decided not to tidy up the empty bottle and the used glass. The police and the forensics people examining his body a few hours from now would not be worried about an unwashed glass. His blood and his brains would be splashed in a thick puddle across this mahogany desk and these polished floorboards. And should his disappearance not be noticed for a while, which seemed highly likely (who would miss him, after all?), it would be the stench of his corpse that would alert the neighbors.

In the hearth, he noticed a scrap of cardboard that had escaped the flames. He bent down and threw it into the fire.

Slowly, Grand-Duc moved toward the mahogany writing desk that occupied the corner of the room facing the fireplace. He opened the middle drawer and took his revolver from its leather holster. It was a Mateba, in mint condition, its gray metal barrel glimmering in the firelight. The detective's hand probed more deeply inside the desk and brought out three 38mm bullets. With a practiced movement he spun the cylinder and gently inserted the bullets.

One would be enough, even given his relatively inebriated state, even though he would probably tremble and hesitate. Because he would undoubtedly manage to press the gun to his temple, hold it firmly, and squeeze the trigger. He couldn't miss, even with the contents of a bottle of wine in his bloodstream.

He placed the revolver on the desk, opened the left-hand drawer, and took out a newspaper: a very old and yellowed copy of *Est Républicain*. This macabre set piece had been in his mind for months, a symbolic ritual that would help him to end it all, to rise above the labyrinth forever.

11:54 p.m.

The detective glanced over at the vivarium, where the dragonflies were making their dirgelike rattles and hums. The power supply had been off for the last thirty minutes. Deprived of oxygen and food, the dragonflies would not survive the week. And he had spent so much money buying the rarest and oldest species; he had spent hours, years of his life, looking after the vivarium, feeding them, breeding them, even employing someone to look after them when he was away.

All that effort, just to let them die.

It's actually quite an agreeable feeling, Grand-Duc thought, to sit in judgment on the life and death of another: to protect only in order to condemn, to give hope in order to sacrifice. To play with fate, like a cunning, capricious god. After all, he, too, had been the victim of just such a sadistic deity.

Crédule Grand-Duc sat on the chair behind the desk and unfolded the copy of the *Est Républicain*, dated December 23, 1980. Once again, he read the front page: "The Miracle of Mont Terrible."

Beneath the banner headline was a rather blurred photograph showing the carcass of a crashed airplane, uprooted trees, snow muddied by rescue workers. Under the photograph, the disaster was described in a few lines:

The Airbus 5403, flying from Istanbul to Paris, crashed into Mont Terri, on the Franco-Swiss border, last night. Of the 169 passengers and flight crew on board, 168 were killed upon impact or perished in the flames. The sole survivor was a baby, three months old, thrown from the plane when it collided with the mountainside, before the cabin was consumed by fire.

When Grand-Duc died, he would fall forward onto the front page of this newspaper. His blood would redden the photograph of the tragedy that had taken place eighteen years earlier; it would mingle with the blood of those one hundred and sixty-eight victims. He would be found this way, a few days or a few weeks later. No one would mourn him. Certainly not the de Carvilles. Perhaps the Vitrals would feel sad at his passing. Emilie, Marc... Nicole in particular.

He would be found, and the notebook would be given to Lylie: the story of her short life. His testament.

Grand-Duc looked at his reflection one more time in the copper plaque, and felt almost proud. It was a good ending: much better than what had gone before.

11:57 p.m.

It was time.

He carefully positioned the newspaper in front of him, moved his chair forward, and took a firm grip of the revolver. His palms were sweaty. Slowly he lifted his arm.

He shivered, in spite of himself, when the cold metal of the gun barrel touched his temple. But he was ready.

He tried to empty his mind, not to think about the bullet, an inch or two from his brain, that would smash through his skull and kill him...

His index finger bent around the trigger. All he had to do now was squeeze and it would all be over.

Eyes open or closed?

A bead of sweat rolled down his forehead and fell onto the newspaper.

Eyes open. Now do it.

He leaned forward. For the final time, his gaze rested on the photograph of the burned-out cabin, and the other photograph of the fireman standing in front of the hospital in Montbéliard, carefully holding that bluish body. The miracle baby.

His index finger tightened around the trigger.

11:58 p.m.

His eyes were lost in the black ink of the newspaper's front page. Everything blurred. The bullet would perforate his temple, without the slightest resistance. All he had to do was squeeze a little harder, just a fraction of an inch. He stared into eternity. The black ink below him came into focus again, as if he were playing with the lens of a camera. This would be his final view of the world, before everything went dark forever.

His finger. The trigger.

His eyes wide open.

Grand-Duc felt an electric shock run through him. Something unimaginable had just happened.

Because what he was looking at was impossible. He knew that perfectly well.

His finger relaxed its pressure slightly.

To begin with, Grand-Duc thought it must be an illusion, a hallucination provoked by his imminent death, some kind of defense mechanism dreamed up by his brain...

But no. What he had seen, what he read in that newspaper, was real. The paper was yellowed by age, the ink somewhat smeared, and yet there could be no doubt whatsoever.

It was all there.

The detective's mind started working frantically. He had come up with so many theories over the years of the investigation, hundreds of them. But now he knew where to begin, which thread to pull, and the whole tangled web came apart with disconcerting simplicity.

It was all so obvious.

He lowered his pistol and laughed like a madman.

11:59 p.m.

He had done it!

The solution to the mystery had been here, on the front page of this newspaper, from the very beginning. And yet it had been absolutely impossible to discover this solution at the time, eighteen years ago. Everyone had read this newspaper, pored over it, analyzed it thousands of times, but no one could possibly have guessed the truth, back in 1980, or during the years that followed.

The solution was so obvious: it jumped out at you... but on one condition.

The newspaper had to be looked at eighteen years later.

2

Were they lovers, or brother and sister?

The question had been nagging at Mariam for almost a month. She ran the Lenin Bar, at the crossroads of Avenue de Stalingrad and Rue de la Liberté, a few yards from the forecourt of the University of Paris VIII in Saint-Denis. At this hour of the morning, the bar was still mostly empty, and Mariam took advantage of the quiet to clean tabletops and arrange chairs.

The couple in question were sitting at the back of the café, as they usually did, near the window, at a tiny table for two, holding hands and looking deep into each other's blue eyes.

Lovers?

Friends?

Siblings?

Mariam sighed. The lack of certainty bothered her. She generally had a keen instinct when it came to her students' love lives. She snapped out of it: she still had to wipe down the tables and sweep the floor; in a few minutes, thousands of stressed students would rush from the metro station

Saint-Denis–Université, the terminus of Line 13. The station had only been open for four months, but already it had transformed the local area.

Mariam had seen the University of Paris VIII slowly change from its rebellious beginnings as the great university of humanities, society, and culture into a banal, well-behaved suburban learning center. Nowadays, most professors sulked when they were assigned to Paris VIII. They would rather be at the Sorbonne, or even Jussieu. Before the metro station opened, the professors had had to cross through Saint-Denis, to see a little of the surrounding area, but now, with the metro, that, too, was over. The professors boarded the metro on Line 13 and were whisked off toward the libraries, laboratories, ministries, and grand institutions of Parisian culture.

Mariam turned toward the counter to fetch a sponge, casting a furtive glance at the intriguing young couple: the pretty blond girl and the strapping, spellbound boy. She felt almost haunted by them.

Who were they?

Mariam had never understood the workings of higher education, with its modules and examinations and strikes, but no one knew better than she what the students did during their break time. She had never read Robert Castel, Gilles Deleuze, Michel Foucault, or Jacques Lacan, the star professors of Paris VIII—at most, she might have seen them once or twice, in her bar or in the campus forecourt—but nevertheless she considered herself an expert in the analysis, sociology, and philosophy of student love affairs. She was like a mother hen to some of her regulars and an advice columnist to others, helping them through their heartaches with professional skill.

But despite her experience, her famous intuition, she could not fathom the relationship between the couple at the window.

Emilie and Marc.

Shy lovers or affectionate relatives?

The uncertainty was maddening. Something about them didn't fit. They looked so alike, yet they were so different. Mariam knew their first names: she knew the first names of all her regulars.

Marc, the boy, had been studying at Paris VIII for two years now, and he came to the Lenin almost every day. A tall boy, good-looking, but a little too nice, like a disheveled "Little Prince." Daydreamy, and somewhat gauche: the kind of provincial student who still didn't know how things worked in Paris, and who lacked the money to look cool. As for his studies, he wasn't a fanatic. As far as she understood, he was studying European law, but for the past two years, he had seemed very calm and thoughtful. Now Mariam understood why.

He had been waiting for her. His Emilie.

She had arrived this year, in September, so she must be two or three years younger than he.

They shared certain traits. That slightly low-class accent, which Mariam could not locate, but which was indisputably the same. And yet, in Emilie's case, the accent somehow seemed wrong; it did not fit her personality. The same could be said of her name: *Emilie* was too ordinary, too bland for a girl like that. Emilie, like Marc, was blond and, like Marc, she had blue eyes. But while Marc's gestures and expressions were clumsy, simple, unoriginal, there was a *je-ne-sais-quoi* about Emilie, a strikingly different way of moving, a kind of nobility in the way she held her head, a purebred elegance and grace that seemed to suggest aristocratic genes, a privileged education.

And that was not the only mystery. In terms of money, Emilie's standard of living appeared to be the very opposite of Marc's. Mariam had a knack for evaluating, in an instant, the quality and cost of the clothing worn by her students, from H&M and Zara to Yves Saint Laurent.

Emilie did not wear Yves Saint Laurent, but she wasn't far off. What she was wearing today—a simple, elegant orange silk blouse and a black, asymmetrical skirt—had undoubtedly cost a small fortune. Emilie and Marc might be from the same place, but they did not belong to the same world.

And yet they were inseparable.

There was a complicity between them that could not be created in only a few months at the university. It was as if they had lived together all their lives, perceptible in the countless protective gestures that Marc made toward Emilie: a hand on her shoulder, a chair pulled out for her, a door held open, a glass filled without asking. It was the way a big brother would behave toward a little sister.

Mariam wiped down a chair and put it back in position, her mind still churning over the enigma of Marc and Emilie.

It was as if Marc had spent the previous two years preparing the ground for Emilie's arrival, keeping her seat warm in the lecture hall, a table near the window in the Lenin. Mariam sensed that Emilie was a brilliant student, quick-witted, ambitious and determined. Artistic. Literary. She could see that determination whenever the girl took out a book or a folder, in the way she would skim confidently over notes that Marc would take hours to master.

So, could they be brother and sister, in spite of their social differences?

Well, yes. Except that Marc was in love with Emilie!

That, too, was blindingly obvious.

He did not love her like a brother, but like a devoted lover. It was clear to Mariam from the first moment she saw them together. A fever, a passion, completely unmistakable.

Mariam did not have a clue what this could mean.

She had been shamelessly spying on them for a month now. She had glanced furtively at the names on files, essays, placed on the table. She knew their surname.

Marc Vitral.

Emilie Vitral.

But ultimately, that did not help. The logical supposition was that they were brother and sister. But then what about those incestuous gestures? The way Marc touched Emilie's lower back... Or perhaps they were married. She was only eighteen: very young for a student to marry, but not impossible. And, of course, it was technically possible that they just happened to have the same name, but Mariam could not believe in such a coincidence, unless they were cousins or belonged to a more complicated kind of family, with stepparents or half siblings...

Emilie seemed very fond of Marc. But her expression was more complex, difficult to read. She often seemed to stare into space, particularly when she was alone, as if she were hiding something, a deep sadness... It was that melancholy that gave Emilie a subtle distance, a different kind of charm from that of all the other girls on campus. All of the boys in the Lenin stared hungrily at her, but—probably because of that reserve—none of them dared to approach her.

None except Marc.

Emilie was his. That was why he was here. Not for his courses. Not for the university. He was here purely so he could be with her, so he could protect her.

But what about the rest? Mariam had often tried talking with Emilie and Marc, chatting about any old subject, but she had never learned anything intimate. But one day, she was determined she would find out their secret...

She was cleaning the last tables when Marc raised his hand.

"Mariam, could you bring us two coffees, please, and a glass of water for Emilie?"

Mariam smiled to herself. Marc never drank coffee when he was alone, but always ordered one when he was with Emilie.

"No problem, lovebirds!" Mariam replied.

Testing the water.

Marc gave an embarrassed smile. Emilie did not. She lowered her head slightly. Mariam only noticed this now: Emilie looked awful this morning, her face puffy, as if she hadn't slept all night. Was she worrying over an exam? Had she spent the night revising, or writing an essay?

No, it was something else.

Mariam shook the coffee grounds into the bin, rinsed the percolator, and made two espressos.

It was something serious.

As if Emilie had to give Marc some painful news. Mariam had witnessed so many conversations like that: farewell dates, tragic *tête-à-têtes*, with the boy sitting alone in front of his coffee while the girl left, looking embarrassed but relieved. Emilie looked like someone who had spent the night thinking and who, by early morning, had made her decision and was ready to accept its consequences.

Mariam walked slowly toward them, the tray in her hands bearing two coffees and a glass of water.

Poor Marc. Did he have any inkling that he was already doomed?

Mariam also knew how to be discreet. She placed the drinks on the table, then turned and walked away.

3

Marc Vitral waited a few moments for Mariam to move away. Then he bent down over his backpack, which he'd left on the floor next to his chair, and took out a small cube wrapped in silver paper.

"Happy birthday, Emilie," he said cheerfully.

He handed her the package.

Emilie rolled her eyes.

"Marc!" she scolded him. "You've wished me happy birthday three times in the last week. You know I don't need all that..."

"Shhh. Open it."

Frowning, Emilie unwrapped the present. Inside was a piece of silver jewelry: a complicated-looking cross, with each arm ending in a little diamond shape, except for the top one, which featured a large circle surmounted by a crown. Emilie held the cross in her hands.

"You're mad, Marc."

"It's a Tuareg cross. Apparently there are twenty-one different kinds. One shape for each city in the Sahara. This one is from Agadez. Do you like it?"

"Of course I like it. But..."

Marc went on, unstoppable: "Apparently, the diamond shapes represent the four cardinal points. Whoever gives someone a Tuareg cross gives them the world."

"I know the legend," Emilie whispered softly. " 'I offer you the four corners of the world because you cannot know where you will die.' "

Marc smiled, embarrassed. Of course Lylie already knew all about Tuareg crosses, just as she knew about everything. There was silence for a moment. Emilie reached out for her cup of coffee. Instinctively, Marc did the same. His fingers moved toward hers, hoping they would touch. Suddenly, Marc's hand stopped dead. Lylie was wearing a ring. It was gold, beautifully wrought, and set with a pale sapphire; a magnificent antique, and undoubtedly worth a fortune. Marc had never seen it before. He stared at it in confusion for several seconds, overcome by the jealousy he always felt when confronted with something that seemed to distance him from Emilie. Finally he managed to stammer: "That...that ring, is...is it yours?"

"No. I stole it this morning from a shop in the Place Vendôme!"

Marc still felt floored and his eyelid fluttered slightly. The Tuareg cross he had given her had cost him all the money he'd earned from two days and three nights working as a switchboard operator for France Telecom, his student job, but it looked like cheap junk compared to that ring. And Lylie had already put the African jewel back in its canvas box, whereas the ring sat proudly on her finger.

He forced himself to swallow a mouthful of coffee, then said: "That...your ring...was it a birthday present?"

Emilie lowered her eyes. "Sort of. It's a bit compli-cated...Beautiful, though, isn't it?"

She paused, trying to find the right words.

"I'll explain it to you, don't worry, at least not about this ring..."

Emilie put her hand on Marc's.

Don't worry. At least not about this ring...

The words reverberated inside Marc's head. What did she mean? Lylie looked awful this morning, as if she had not slept all night, even though she was trying to smile at him. Suddenly, as if she had made an important deci-sion, her eyes lit up. She took a few sips of coffee then bent down over her schoolbag. She pulled out a notebook with a pale green cover and slid it across the table toward Marc.

"Now it's my turn, Marc. This is for you."

Marc felt another wave of vague anxiety rise within him.

"What is it?"

"Grand-Duc's notebook," Emilie replied instantly. "He gave it to me the day before yesterday, the day after my birthday. Well, actually, he left it in my mailbox, or got someone else to leave it there. I found it in the morning."

Marc cautiously touched the notebook with his finger-tips. His eyelid was fluttering again.

That notebook. Grand-Duc's investigation...Now he understood. Emilie had spent the last two days reading and rereading it. The eighteen-year investigation carried out by that mad old private detective. A lifetime's work. Emilie's lifetime. Almost to the day.

Some fucking birthday present!

Marc looked for clues in Emilie's expression. What truth had she discovered in the notebook? A new identity?

A calm acceptance of everything, at last? Or nothing at all? Only questions without answers...

Emilie was not giving anything away. She was too good at this game. She poured a few drops of water into her coffee, her little ritual, and drank it slowly.

"You see, Marc, he did give it to me in the end, just like he always promised. The truth. For my passage into the adult world."

Emilie laughed nervously. Still Marc did not pick up the notebook.

"And...?" he asked. "What does he say, in this notebook? Anything important? Do you... do you know now?"

Emilie looked away, out through the window, where small groups of students were crossing the Paris VIII forecourt.

"Know what?"

Marc began to feel exasperated. The words formed in his head but he did not say them aloud: *Know what that stupid detective was paid, for so many years, to find out! Know who you are, Lylie. Who you are!*

Emilie played distractedly with her ring.

"Well, now it's your turn. You need to read it, Marc."

Marc's mind was in turmoil. He picked up the notebook and heard himself say: "All right, little dragonfly. I'll read your damn notebook..."

He was silent for a moment, then added: "But what about you? Are you OK?"

"Yes, don't worry. I'm fine."

Emilie sipped her coffee again. She looked as if she were forcing herself to drink it.

"Did Grand-Duc leave a note?"

"No, nothing. But it's all in the notebook."

"And...?"

"It's better if you read it yourself."

"So where is Grand-Duc now?"

Emilie's eyes clouded over again, as if she were hiding something. She made a show of looking at her watch.

"Are you leaving already?"

"I don't have classes this morning, but you do. At ten o'clock. Constitutional European Law. You have a tutorial with the young and fascinating Professor Grandin. I really have to go."

Emilie poured the last drop of water into her coffee, drank the rest slowly, then bent down over her bag again.

"I...I have another present for you."

She handed him a little gift-wrapped package, slightly larger than a box of matches.

Marc froze. He was filled with foreboding.

"You mustn't open it now," Emilie continued breathlessly. "Only after I've gone. One hour later. Promise me? It's like hide-and-seek: you have to give me time to disappear. So close your eyes and count to, let's say, a thousand..."

Emilie seemed to be putting all her energy into convincing Marc that her request was just some foolish lovers' game, but Marc was not fooled.

"Promise?" Emilie insisted.

Resigned, Marc nodded. They looked at each other for a long time. Emilie blinked first.

"No, you won't do it. You're stubborn, Marc, I know you. You'll tear into it as soon as my back is turned."

Marc did not contradict her. Emilie lifted a slender hand.

That damn ring sparkled in the light.

"Mariam?"

The landlady reacted instantly, as if she had been watching them, just waiting for such a command. She stood in front of Marc and Emilie's table.

"Mariam, I have a favor to ask you. I want to leave this package with you. You must give it to Marc in one hour, and not a moment sooner! Even if he begs you, bribes you, or blackmails you. And, now that I think about it, you must send him off to his class in one hour, too—room B318!"

Mariam looked at the package in her hands.

"I'm trusting you with this, Mariam."

She had no choice. Emilie leaped up from her chair, shoved the jewelry box containing the Tuareg cross into her backpack, and kissed Marc chastely on the cheek. Her lips landed halfway between his cheek and the corner of his mouth. An ambiguous kiss, as if placed deliberately to taunt Mariam.

Emilie pushed open the Lenin's glass door and walked out onto the square in front of the university. In seconds, she was swallowed up by the swarm of passing students, vanishing like a ghost.

The door banged shut.

Mariam closed her fingers around the package. She would do as Emilie had asked, of course, but she did not like this game. Mariam had seen many couples break up: in such a situation, women could be amazingly determined and imaginative.

Emilie was one of those women.

This whole scene stank of a lie. Emilie had run away as fast as her legs would take her, and the gift she had left in Mariam's hand was a time bomb. Marc should never have let her leave like that. That boy was too naive, too trusting ... Mariam still couldn't decide if the girl who was fleeing from him was his sister, his wife, his mistress, or his friend; she could not figure out what connected the two of them; but she was certain that Emilie had only one goal in mind.

To break that connection.

4

Marc stared at Mariam as she stood behind the counter. The landlady had put Emilie's gift in her cash register, while shooting Marc an unequivocal look. There was no point getting his hopes up: nothing would happen before the hour appointed by Emilie. Female solidarity. In desperation, his eyes fell on Crédule Grand-Duc's pale green notebook. Emilie had known what she was doing. Marc was stuck here with an hour to kill before his first class of the day: a soporific tutorial with a young professor who spent half the time answering his cell phone. Emilie had trapped him.

The Lenin was packed now. A tall guy asked Marc if he could take the empty chair from his table. Marc nodded distractedly. The red and white Martini clock on the wall told him the time was 9:03 a.m. Marc had no choice, but all the same he hesitated even to open the notebook. His fingertips stroked the shiny cover.

An elderly professor, standing at the counter with a glass of beer and a copy of *Le Parisien* newspaper, was eyeing Marc's seat. He wasn't wrong—Marc had only one desire at that moment: to run out after Emilie and throw this damn notebook in the trash.

He looked through the window, as if he might spot her familiar outline amid the increasingly dense crowd; as if the swarm of humanity might stop moving and part like the Red Sea, so he could run after Emilie. His vision went blurred. His heartbeat accelerated. His throat tightened. He knew the warning signs so well: the tachycardia, the respiratory problems... He turned his gaze away from the square.

As soon as he did so, he began to breathe more easily.

His hands touched the pale green notebook again.

So Emilie had won, as she always did. He, too, was going to have to confront his past.

Marc took a deep breath and opened the notebook. Grand-Duc's handwriting was small and dense. Slightly jumpy, but perfectly legible.

Then Marc began to read.

Crédule Grand-Duc's Journal

It all began with a disaster. Before December 23, 1980, I doubt if anyone—or hardly anyone—had ever heard of Mont Terri. I certainly hadn't. Mont Terri is one of those little peaks in the Jura Mountains, on the border between France and Switzerland, a peak located inside a loop of the Doubs River. It is a mountain where cows are pastured, a long way from anywhere, with the nearest towns being Montbéliard on the French side, and Porrentruy on the Swiss side. Although it is not especially high—2,638 feet, to be precise—it is nevertheless not always accessible, particularly in winter, when it is covered with snow. Mont

Terri is known, above all, for having been a Franco-Swiss *département*—known as Mont Terrible—during the Revolution. Since then, it has been forgotten by everyone except the hundred or so people who live there. When the Airbus 5403 from Istanbul to Paris smashed into its southwest flank on the night of December 22–23, journalists opted to use the name "Mont Terrible," rather than Mont Terri. You have to look at it from their point of view: "The Tragedy of Mont Terrible" is a much better headline than "The Tragedy of Mont Terri."

Perhaps people still remember the accident today. Perhaps not. There are so many such disasters, and they are all alike. A few months before I began to write this, a Boeing 747 crashed near Tenerife in the Canaries, killing one hundred and forty-six people. The year after the tragedy of Mont Terrible, on December 1, 1981, a DC-9 from Ljubljana to Ajaccio crashed into Mont San Pietro, killing one hundred and eighty: the only air accident in Corsican history. But everyone has forgotten about that, apart from the Corsicans. Today, everyone remembers the crash at Mont Sainte-Odile…until the next crash takes its place in their memory.

At the time, in 1981, people were talking about a chain of disasters.

What a load of rubbish! All you have to do is look at the statistics. Trust me: I spent hours reading websites about plane crashes. They are staggeringly detailed, providing numbers of deaths plus other facts and figures about the moments before the final dive. This may seem unbelievable, but the statistics show that in the last forty years, there have been more than 1,500 airplane crashes, with more than 25,000 fatalities. A quick calculation reveals that this makes nearly forty crashes per year: almost one per week, somewhere in the world.

So it's not surprising that everyone has forgotten about the tragedy of Mont Terri back in 1980. One hundred and sixty-eight deaths are now just so many specks of dust.

At the time, I, too, didn't pay much attention to the Mont Terri disaster. That morning, I barely even registered the news. I was staking out criminals on the coast near Hendaye: a case involving the embezzlement of casino profits, against a backdrop of Basque terrorism...It was pretty dangerous stuff, but exciting: my specialty at the time. I had gone solo as a private detective five years earlier, after almost twenty years acting as a mercenary all over the world. I was nearly fifty years old, with a bad hip and a spine as twisted as a caduceus. Each week of stake-out, I put on over two pounds, which I would then take at least a month to lose. In short, being a private detective, even if it was rather a half-assed plan, definitely seemed to suit me just fine.

Like everyone else, I must have heard the news of the crash in the morning, or heard it on the radio, while I was doing surveillance in the parking lot of the casino in Hendaye. Back then, I had no idea that a few months later that accident would take over my entire life. Ironic, isn't it? If only I had known...

The Airbus 5403 from Istanbul to Paris crashed into Mont Terri on December 23, in the middle of the night. At 12:37 a.m., to be precise. No one ever found out exactly what happened that night. Until that point, it had been quite a mild winter, but on the morning of the 22nd, it had begun to snow—and it hadn't stopped. That night, there was a terrible snowstorm. Mont Terri is a bit like a stepping stone between the Swiss Jura and the French Jura. The pilot simply missed his footing. That was what people said at the time, anyway: everyone blamed it all on the poor pilot, who was burned to cinders like everyone else in the cabin. What about the black box? you may ask. All it revealed was that the plane was flying too low and that the pilot had ended up losing control. The victims' association and the pilot's family sought to find out more, without success. So the pilot was blamed, along with the snow, the storm, the mountain, fate, Murphy's Law, and sheer bad luck. There was a hearing, of course. The victims' families needed to understand. But the public didn't really care about that particular judgment.

The cabin was crushed at 12:37 a.m. It was the experts who calculated that afterward, because there were no witnesses except the passengers—and nothing could be learned from them—nor even a broken watch that might have indicated the time of the crash. Before Christmas, ecologists had been fighting to save every pine tree in the Jura Mountains. In a few seconds, the Airbus uprooted more trees than a century of Christmases. Those that were not torn from the earth were set on fire, in spite of the snow. The airplane plowed a motorway through the forest several thousand feet long before collapsing, exhausted. A few seconds later, it exploded, and continued to burn all night.

The first emergency services did not discover the burning fuselage until an hour later. The reaction to the disaster was very much delayed, as nobody lived within a three-mile radius of the crash site. It was the inferno that alerted the valley's inhabitants. And then the rescue services were hampered by the snow: the helicopters remained grounded, and the first firemen were only able to reach the blazing airplane on foot, by following its scorched path. The storm died down in the early morning, and for a few hours Mont Terri became the center of the world. There was even a trial, or at least an investigation, I think, into why the emergency services arrived so late. But not many people were interested in that judgment either.

Besides, the rescue workers must have thought that there was no point rushing: it was clear there could be no survivors. But firemen tend to be conscientious, even at 1:30 a.m., in the Jura Mountains, during a snowstorm. So, they searched anyway, if only so that they hadn't traveled all that way for nothing, and could do something more useful than warming their hands for a few minutes by the vast fire that had destroyed everything on that side of the mountain—the fire that had transformed the bodies of the one hundred and sixty-eight terrified passengers into ashes.

They searched, their eyes streaming from the smoke and the horror. It was a young fireman—Thierry Mouchot, from the Sochaux brigade—who found her. You may be surprised by this level of detail, so many years later, but trust me, it's all true. Later, I would spend several hours talking to him, encouraging him to spin out into eternity those few seconds, going back over all the details to the point of absurdity. That night, he did not realize at first what he had found. He thought it must have been a corpse—the body of a dead baby. But it was the only body of a passenger on the Airbus that had not been burned to cinders. The baby was very young—less than three months old. It had been ejected on impact, from the front left door of the Airbus's cabin, which had been partially blown open when the plane crashed into the mountainside. All of this was reconstructed afterward by the experts, proved in great detail during the inquiry, as they attempted to calculate which seats the baby and its parents had occupied on the plane. Have no fear: I will come back to this shortly. Please be patient...

Mouchot, the young fireman, was convinced that what he had discovered was a corpse: after all, the baby had been covered with snow for more than an hour. And yet, when he bent over it, he saw that the child—its face, its hands, its fingers—was hardly even blue. The body was lying about a hundred feet from the blaze. It had been kept warm by the protective heat of the burning cabin. The young fireman quickly carried out mouth-to-mouth resuscitation, exactly as he had been taught, followed by a very gentle cardiac massage. He could never have believed he would be able to save a newborn baby, particularly in conditions such as these.

The baby was breathing again, weakly. In the minutes that followed, the emergency services took care of the rest. Afterward, the doctors confirmed that it was the fire in the clearing, the heat produced by the molten cabin, that had saved the infant—a little girl with blue eyes, very blue eyes for one so young, probably European, to judge from her pale skin. She had been ejected far enough from the plane not to be burned alive, but close enough to benefit from the protection of the fire's warmth. What had consumed the other passengers, including the child's parents, had saved her life. That was what the doctors said to explain the miracle.

Because it truly was a miracle!

Most of the national newspapers finished their special

report on the disaster late that night; they could not wait
for the emergency services' verdict. Only one paper, the
Est Républicain, took the risk of waiting longer, of holding
the presses, of making its staff stay up even later, of sending out a general alert. A good editor's hunch, probably.
The *Est Républicain* had at its disposal an army of free-
lancers in every corner of the Jura Mountains, and they
hung about in front of hospitals, by police cars... News of
the miracle first began to spread at about 2:00 a.m. In its
edition of December 23, 1980, the *Est Républicain* was
able to use the headline on its front page: *The Miracle of
Mont Terrible.* Alongside the photograph of the burned-
out fuselage, the newspaper published a color photograph
of the baby being held by a fireman in front of the Belfort-
Montbéliard hospital. The brief caption told the story: *The
Airbus 5403, flying from Istanbul to Paris, crashed into
Mont Terri, on the Franco-Swiss border, last night. Of the
169 passengers and flight crew on board, 168 were killed
upon impact or perished in the flames. The sole survivor was a baby, three months old, thrown from the plane
when it collided with the mountainside, before the cabin
was consumed by fire.*

France awoke to the news of this tragedy. In every
household in the country, the orphan discovered in the
snow moved people to tears. That morning, the *Est Républicain*'s scoop was taken up by all the other newspapers,
all the radio stations and television channels. Perhaps you
can recall it now. The wave of hot tears that rained down in
an outpouring of national grief.

One detail remained. The newspaper had published
a picture of the miracle child, but not her name. It was
difficult, at two in the morning: they would have had to

get hold of Air France in Istanbul. That, at least, is what the editor must have thought. After all, the name of the miracle child was not so important. True, adding the blue-eyed orphan's name to the caption under her photograph would have increased the story's emotional impact, but "The Miracle Child of Mont Terrible" wasn't bad either. And it preserved part of the mystery until the baby's identification, which was due to be announced the following morning.

At the latest.

Now, let's see . . .

How long have I been searching for that child's name? Only about eighteen years . . .

5

October 2, 1998, 9:10 a.m.

Marc's concentration was broken by the raucous laughter
of five students sitting around a high table, about twenty
feet away from him. It looked as though the five boys were
passing around photographs: probably snapshots of their
latest night out, the kind of pictures they would keep all
their lives, hidden away somewhere, a memory half glorious, half shameful. Marc knew them vaguely—they all
belonged to one of the main associations that ran the university's social activities.

He looked up.

9:11 a.m., if the Martini clock was to be believed.

Mariam was talking to a girl dressed head to toe in
black. The landlady did not even glance at Marc.

He sighed, and started reading again.

Crédule Grand-Duc's Journal

So that is the precise moment when the mystery of Mont Terri
began. Maybe a few snatches of memory are coming back to
you now. I have reconstructed the events that followed with

metronomical precision, but I will spare you the hundreds of
hours I spent interviewing witnesses. I believe a summary of
the facts will prove sufficiently edifying.

The orphaned baby discovered by the young fireman
was placed in the care of the pediatric department of the
Belfort-Montbéliard hospital, and watched over by an
army of doctors. Léonce de Carville learned both pieces
of news—about the crash and the miracle baby—from the
radio, at six in the morning (Léonce always woke early).
With a single telephone call, he canceled his entire work
schedule for the day and headed instead to Montbéliard
by private jet. Fifty-five years old at the time, Léonce de
Carville was one of the hundred best known captains of
industry in France. An engineer by training, he had made
his fortune laying pipelines in every continent on Earth.
The de Carville business was subcontracted by the world's
largest oil and gas multinationals. The de Carvilles' success was due not so much to technological innovation in
the oil and gas pipelines they supplied, as to their ability to
install them in the most dangerous and complicated loca-
tions: underwater, under mountains, in seismic zones, and
so on. The business really took off in the 1960s, when the
de Carvilles invented a revolutionary technology to stabi-
lize oil pipelines in areas of permafrost, a technology the
company managed to export—in the middle of the Cold
War—to both Siberia and Alaska.

In the white maze of the Belfort-Montbéliard hospital,
Léonce de Carville wore that mask of dignity that would
impress everyone involved in the case.

"Follow me, please," said an eager nurse.

"Where is she?"

"In the nursery. Don't worry, she's doing fine..."

"Who is looking after her?"

"Um... Dr. Morange," the nurse answered, a little surprised. "He was on duty last night..."

Léonce de Carville did not have to say another single word to make his meaning clear.

"You are lucky, Mr. de Carville. Dr. Morange is one of our most renowned specialists. He's still here. You can ask him anything you like..."

Léonce de Carville's mouth cracked into what may have been a smile or a scowl. He walked on, determined and assured, and people quickly moved aside to let him pass.

The night before, the industrialist had lost his only son and his daughter-in-law. He had been the one, the shrewd CEO, who had pushed his son, two years earlier, into taking over the Turkish subsidiary of the de Carville business. It was an open secret that young Alexandre de Carville had been next in line to lead the multinational after his father's retirement. Alexandre de Carville had coped brilliantly with his baptism of fire in Turkey, where not only his scientific training but also his diplomatic and political skills were needed. He had had to deal with both a military regime and a democratic government, as the country went through a volatile phase. And he had been playing for the highest stakes: his ultimate objective was to win the biggest contract in de Carville history, something that would make the company's fortune for decades to come. Alexandre de Carville had moved to Turkey with his family to negotiate a deal for the Baku–Tbilisi–Ceyhan oil pipeline, the second longest in the world at over a thousand miles, stretching from the Caspian Sea to the Mediterranean. More than half of the pipeline would go through Turkey, ending at the little port of Ceyhan, on the southeastern Mediterranean coast, close to the Syrian border, where Alexandre de Carville and his family had set up a summer house. It was a long-term undertaking: for two years, negotiations had stalled. Alexandre de Carville had spent most of the year in Turkey, with his wife, Véronique, and their daughter, Malvina, who was six years old at the time. Following the news of her pregnancy, Véronique had not returned to France: her fragile health had led the doctors to advise against all travel. The child's birth had gone well, however: Lyse-Rose was born in the Bakirkoy, the largest private maternity hospital in Istanbul. Léonce de Carville and his wife, Mathilde, who had remained in France, had received an elegant card announcing the birth, together with a rather blurry photograph of their new granddaughter. But there had been no rush. The family reunion was scheduled for Christmas 1980. At the start of the Christmas holidays, Malvina de Carville had flown to France, as she did every year, one week before her parents. The rest of the family— Alexandre, Véronique, and little Lyse-Rose—were to arrive a few days later, on the night flight from Istanbul to Paris on December 23. In the de Carvilles' vast family mansion at Coupvray, on the banks of the Marne, everything was ready. In honor of her little sister, Malvina—an adorable, mischievous dark-haired girl who commanded an army of servants like a general—had ordered that the route from the entrance hall to Lyse-Rose's bedroom, including the great cherrywood staircase, should be decorated with pink and white pom-poms.

Malvina de Carville...

Allow me to digress for a few lines, so that I can

introduce you to Malvina. It's an important point, as you shall soon discover.

I don't think Malvina de Carville ever liked me very much. In fact, that is something of an understatement. The feeling is mutual. Even if I tell myself that she is not to blame for her madness, that without this tragedy she would undoubtedly have grown up to be a clever and desirable woman—well born, then well married—it does not alter the fact that, with her ever-increasing obsessions, she has always scared the shit out of me. Unlike her grandmother, she never trusted me; she must have sensed that I thought of her as some kind of monster. I promise you, I am not exaggerating. However adorable she may have been at six years old, a monster is what she became: ugly, embittered, uncontrollable. Anyway, that discussion is for another time. With a little bad luck, this notebook could end up in her hands, and God knows how that shrew might react!

So, let's talk instead about the thing that made her go mad: the so-called miracle, and what happened afterward.

In the Belfort-Montbéliard hospital, Léonce de Carville maintained his usual reserve. But, for once, those around him did not take it for coldness, but for modesty, humility, decency. He remained stoical, even when he was shown his granddaughter for the first time, sealed off from him by a wall of glass that rendered her screams silent.

"That's her," the nurse said. "The first crib, directly in front of us."

"Thank you."

His tone was sober, calm, composed. The nurse gave him some space. She had heard the news: Lyse-Rose was the only thing left in this poor man's life.

In that moment, the industrialist's faith must have been shaken—or dented at the very least. Of course, Léonce was not as fervent a Catholic as his wife, Mathilde. He had converted only out of consideration for his new family, so that his rational, scientific views would not upset them or the other good (and highly influential) Catholic families in Coupvray. But in such moments, it would have been difficult, even for the most rational of men, not to think of supernatural forces. Not to be torn between anger at a cruel God who had taken your only son, and gratitude and forgiveness toward a mean God who, perhaps out of remorse, had agreed to save your granddaughter. But only her.

Lyse-Rose cried silently inside her glass cage.

"It's a miracle," said Dr. Morange, behind him. The doctor was wearing a white shirt and a priest's smile.

He looked exactly the same when I met him, years later, and he told me everything that had happened.

"She's doing miraculously well. She is not suffering any aftereffects at all. We are keeping her in purely for observation, as a precaution, but she has already fully recovered. It is truly astounding."

Thank you, God, Léonce de Carville must have thought, despite himself.

It was at that moment that a nurse came to see Dr. Morange. There was a telephone call for him. Urgent, yes, and very strange. Dr. Morange left Léonce de Carville by the glass cage that contained his granddaughter.

Now that he was alone, the poor man could finally let his tears flow, thought the doctor, who—like everyone else in the world—loved a tragedy with a happy ending. He took the receiver from the nurse. "Hello?"

The voice on the line sounded as if it were coming from the end of the world.

"Hello, Doctor. I am the grandfather of the baby, the one from the plane. You know, the one that survived the crash, in the Jura. The switchboard put me through to you. How is she?"

"She's well, very well. I think she may even be out of here in a few days. Her paternal grandfather is already here. I could get him for you, if you like . . ."

There was a silence. In that moment, the doctor sensed that something had slipped beyond his control.

"Doctor . . . I'm terribly sorry, but you must be mistaken. *I* am the baby's paternal grandfather. And my granddaughter has no maternal grandfather. My daughter-in-law was an orphan . . ."

The doctor felt a strange tingling in his fingers. His brain seethed with possible explanations. A hoax? A journalist attempting to find out more information?

"We are talking about the plane from Istanbul to Paris that crashed last night? The miracle child? Little Lyse-Rose?"

"No, Doctor . . ." The doctor heard the relief in the other person's voice. "No, Doctor, I think there's been a misunderstanding. The baby that survived is not named Lyse-Rose. She is named Emilie."

Sweat beaded on the doctor's forehead. This had never happened to him before, not even in the operating room.

"Sir, I am terribly sorry, but that's impossible. The child's grandfather is here, in the hospital. Mr. de Carville is here right now. He has seen the baby and identified her as Lyse-Rose . . ."

There was an embarrassed silence on both ends.

"Do…do you live far from Montbéliard?" the doctor asked.

"Dieppe."

"Ah…Well, I think perhaps the best thing, Mr.…?"

"Mr. Vitral. Pierre Vitral."

"Well, Mr. Vitral, I think the best thing is for you to telephone the police station in Montbéliard. I believe they are currently trying to verify the passengers' identities. I'm afraid I can't tell you any more. But they will be able to provide you with the information you need…"

Suddenly, the doctor felt bad: he was acting like a cold-hearted bureaucrat, sending this poor, distressed man to the next office, just to get rid of him. He knew perfectly well that as soon as the man hung up, he would collapse, devastated, as if his granddaughter had been killed for a second time. But the doctor quickly told himself that this was not his fault. The story was ridiculous. The man must have made a mistake.

They both hung up, and the doctor wondered if he should mention this strange telephone call to Léonce de Carville.

Pierre Vitral slowly replaced the receiver. His wife, Nicole, was standing next to him, waiting anxiously.

"So, is Emilie all right? What did they say?"

Her husband looked at her with infinite tenderness. He spoke gently, as if he were to blame for the bad news he was about to give her: "They said the baby that survived is not named Emilie. She's named Lyse-Rose…"

For a long time, Nicole and Pierre Vitral did not speak. Life had been hard for both of them. Theirs was a marriage of two hard-luck stories, which they told themselves could turn into a positive thing, like when two negative numbers are added together. Together they had faced up to a lack of money, to the cruel blows of fate, to illness, to the trials of daily life. They had never complained. It's always the same: if you don't shout, you never get anything. As the Vitrals had never protested against life, life had never bothered to correct the imbalance that afforded them so much misery. Pierre and Nicole Vitral had both ruined their health—Pierre his back, and Nicole her lungs—in twenty years spent selling fries and sausages from a specially remodeled orange-and-red Type H Citroën van. They sold their wares on the seafront at Dieppe, and all the other beaches of northern France, following the calendar of events and festivals, as far as the region's generally inclement weather allowed. They had tempted fate by having two children, and fate had paid them back by taking one of them: Nicolas had died in a moped accident one rainy night in Criel-sur-Mer.

Bad luck had dogged the family's footsteps for many years, and then, for the first time—only two months before Christmas, 1980—they had finally won something: a two-week holiday in Gumbet.

Gumbet, as I imagine you are completely unaware, is in Turkey: a resort on a peninsula that extends into the Mediterranean, packed with four-star hotels. They would be staying in luxury, all expenses paid! They had won by pure chance: a lottery organized by their local supermarket. It was their son Pascal's ticket that had been drawn. There had been only one condition: the holiday had to be taken before the end of 1980. Unfortunately, it wasn't the best timing for Pascal and his wife, Stéphanie, who had just become parents for the second time. There was no problem with Marc, their eldest, because he was already two years old and could stay with his grandparents while they were away. But Stéphanie was still breastfeeding little Emilie, and in any case she had no desire to be away from her newborn daughter for two weeks. The tickets could not be exchanged, so either they had to take the baby with them, or they would not be able to go at all.

They went. They had never been on a plane before. Stéphanie was a young woman with laughing eyes who saw the world as a huge, crunchy apple, begging to be eaten. She and Pascal had thought it would be wrong to turn their backs on good luck, now that it had finally smiled on them. They should not have been so trusting; you should never trust a smile. Pascal, Stéphanie, and Emilie were supposed to land at Roissy on December 23, then spend a day in Paris so they could admire the Christmas lights. Another whim of Stéphanie's. She was an orphan, adored by the entire Vitral family. Her presence made them feel good. In truth, she did not need a trip to Turkey in order to be happy. Everything she wanted from life she could find in Marc and Emilie, her little darlings, their father, and their doting grandparents.

Pierre and Nicole Vitral were together when they heard the news. They were listening, as they always did, to the seven o'clock bulletin on France Inter.

Facing one another, on either side of the cluttered kitchen table. The two stoneware bowls—Nicole's filled with tea, Pierre's with coffee—remained there for a long time afterward, the whole scene frozen in the moment when life stopped in that little house on Rue Pocholle in Pollet, the old fishermen's quarter that lay like an island in the middle of Dieppe.

*

"Why Lyse-Rose?" Nicole Vitral suddenly yelled.

They lived in a street of semidetached houses. There were ten buildings in the cul-de-sac, each of them containing two dwellings. Everyone could hear everyone else. Nicole's shout alerted the whole neighborhood.

"Why would they say the baby was called Lyse-Rose? Huh? Who *told* them that was her name? The baby? She said her name to the firemen, did she? A three-month-old baby on that airplane, a little girl with blue eyes…That's our Emilie! She's alive. How can anyone say she's not? They're plotting against us because she's the only one who survived. They want to steal her from us…"

There were tears in her eyes. The neighbors began to come out of their houses, in spite of the cold. She collapsed into her husband's arms.

"No, Pierre, no. Promise me…promise me they won't take our granddaughter. She didn't survive that crash just for someone else to steal her from us."

In the little bedroom that adjoined the living room, two-year-old Marc Vitral, woken by his grandmother's cries, began to scream. He could not possibly understand what was happening, though, and he would not retain any memory of that terrible morning.

October 2, 1998, 9:24 a.m.

Marc stopped reading, and wiped the tears from his eyes.

No, of course he did not remember that morning. Not until he read this account of it.

There was something surreal about discovering each detail of the tragedy that had consumed his childhood in this way.

The noise and movement around him in the bar was making his head spin. The five guys from the student association got up and left, still laughing, and the glass door banged shut behind them. Marc breathed slowly, trying to calm himself down. After all, he already knew almost all of this story. His story.

Almost all.

The clock said it was 9:25 a.m.

And he had only just begun.

6

Malvina de Carville knocked on the glass with the barrel of her Mauser L110. The dragonflies barely stirred. Only the largest, with its sparkling red body and gigantic wings, attempted to raise itself an inch or two into the air before falling to the floor of the vivarium, where it lay piled up with dozens of other insect corpses. Not for a moment did Malvina de Carville think of switching on the oxygen in the tank or lifting the glass lid to allow the survivors to escape. She preferred to watch the creatures suffer. After all, she was not to blame for this massacre.

She hit the glass with her revolver again, harder this time. She was fascinated by the insects' despairing attempts to flap their heavy wings in that thin, deadly air. She stood watching them for several minutes. Let them all die, these dragonflies—what did she care? They weren't why she was here. She was here for Lyse-Rose. *Her* dragonfly. The only one that mattered. Malvina moved off into the room. Surprised by the living-room mirror, she found herself staring at her own reflection. A shiver of disgust ran through her. She hated that white-hair slide, the way her long, straight hair parted neatly in the middle; she hated her sky-blue wool sweater with its lace collar; she hated her flat chest, her skinny arms, her eighty-something-pound body.

People in the street thought she must be a fifteen-year-old girl, at least when they saw her from behind. She was used to seeing the shock in their eyes when they were confronted by her face. She was a twenty-four-year-old teenager, dressed as if she'd just been transported from the 1950s.

Fuck it. She didn't care.

They could all go screw themselves, all those people who'd been telling her the same thing for the past eighteen years, all those shrinks, supposedly the best in the country, whom she had exhausted, defeated, one by one. All those child psychiatrists, those nutritionists, those specialists on this and that. And her grandmother. She was sick of the tune they'd been singing to her all these years. Refusal to grow up. Refusal to age. Refusal to mourn. Refusal to forget Lyse-Rose.

Lyse-Rose.

She knew what they meant when they talked about mourning her, forgetting her. They might as well say kill her.

She turned and walked toward the fireplace. She had to step over the corpse. Not for anything in the world would she have let go of the Mauser in her right hand. You never knew. Although it didn't look as if that bastard Grand-Duc was going to get up any time soon. A bullet in the chest. And his head in the fireplace.

She grabbed the poker in her left hand and clumsily dug around in the hearth.

Nothing!

That shithead Grand-Duc had left nothing behind!

Increasingly annoyed, Malvina started to bang the iron rod around the fireplace, smacking Grand-Duc in the face and raising a cloud of black smoke. There had to be *something*: a scrap of paper that hadn't been burned, a clue of some kind . . . But no, she had to face facts. There was nothing here but tiny flakes of black confetti.

The storage boxes lay scattered over the floor, the dates written in red felt-tip pen on the side: 1980, 1981, 1982–83, 1984–85, 1986–89, 1990–95, 1996 . . .

All of them empty.

A blind, uncontrollable rage rose within Malvina. That piece of shit detective was really taking advantage. Was this what her grandparents had paid him for, for eighteen years? Not just his salary but all his expenses, his travel, his costs . . .

For a pile of ashes!

Malvina dropped the poker on the polished floorboards, leaving a black gash in the wood. It was their money that had paid for this bastard's house, in the ultra-chic Butte-aux-Cailles neighborhood. *Their money.* And for what, in the end? So that he could burn all the evidence before shutting his big fat mouth forever.

She tightened her grip on the Mauser.

Malvina de Carville felt no more compassion for Grand-Duc than she did for the dragonflies in the vivarium.

Less, in fact.

He had gotten what he deserved: shot through the heart in his own home, his eyes, nose, and mouth buried in the warm embers of his lies. He had known the risk he was running when he started double-dealing. Well, now he'd

lost. Why waste tears over that? The only thing she regretted was that he could no longer talk. But she wasn't going
to give up. She would not abandon her little sister. She was
there for her, always. Her Lyse-Rose, her little dragonfly.
She had to keep searching. She had to find something.

That notebook, for example. The book containing
Crédule Grand-Duc's notes. From what she had gathered,
it had a pale green cover. Where could he have hidden it?
Whom might he have given it to?

Malvina walked into the kitchen. Everything seemed
clean and tidy. A blue dish towel hung from a nail. Anyway, she'd already searched this room, and found nothing.
It was the same in every other room—Grand-Duc was a
meticulous kind of guy.

So, the house was a dead end. She needed to think.

Malvina considered the telephone call her grandmother
had received from the detective the previous evening. He
claimed to have found something—finally. After all these
years; on the very eve of Lyse-Rose's eighteenth birthday.
A few minutes before midnight, to be precise. He had mentioned an old newspaper, the *Est Républicain*, and a revela-
tion he had had, simply by opening it eighteen years later.

Yeah, right. The old bastard was clearly bluffing. It was
pathetic.

Her grandmother might have fallen for his lies, as she
always had, but not Malvina.

It was obvious to her that he had been playing for time.
His contract ended on Lyse-Rose's eighteenth birthday,
so the money would stop rolling in. The old bastard just
wanted to keep it flowing a while longer. Her grandmother, her head filled with years of religious bullshit,
was prepared to believe anything. She had always put too

much trust in that Grand-Duc, and he had known how to play her. Malvina noticed the copper plaque on the desk. CRÉDULE GRAND-DUC, PRIVATE DETECTIVE.

Even his name was stupid!

Yes, he'd known how to play them, her grandfather and her grandmother.

But not Malvina.

She was free. Clearheaded. She had been able to see through his double-dealing. Grand-Duc had always favored the Vitral family. He was on their side. He had always given Malvina funny looks, as if she were a circus freak. He was wary of her. But not wary enough...

Malvina gave one last look at the desk, then walked through to the entrance hall. Her sharp eyes noted the umbrellas standing in a tall vase, the long coats hanging from pegs.

She stopped in front of the framed montage of photographs above the hall window. A picture from the wedding of Nazim Ozan—Grand-Duc's partner in crime—and his fat Turkish bitch; another of Nicole Vitral, of course, with her huge tits bulging out of her ugly dress. Grand-Duc would no longer be able to ogle the Vitral woman's oversized mammaries as he put on his coat and picked up his umbrella before walking out into the street.

Distractedly, Malvina looked at the other photographs in the entrance hall. Shots of mountain landscapes—the Jura Mountains, probably. Mont Terri. Montbéliard.

She remembered. She had recognized the baby—her sister—when she saw her in the hospital there. She had been six years old. She was the only living witness.

Lyse-Rose was alive. Those bastards had stolen her sister.

They could say whatever they liked. Refusal to mourn and all that other crap.

She would never, ever abandon her sister.

Malvina shook herself. She had to do something. She went back into the living room, stepping over Grand-Duc's corpse again, then examined once more the fireplace, the vivarium, the desk. She had broken into the house, smashing the bedroom window, half hidden by hollyhocks. She had left her fingerprints all over the place. The police would come here eventually; a neighbor would alert them. She needed to be careful. Not for herself—she didn't give a shit—but for Lyse-Rose. She had to remain out of jail. So that meant erasing every last trace of her presence throughout the house. With luck, she might notice a detail that she had missed the first time. Maybe even that green notebook . . .

What might that bastard have written in his notebook? Had he really discovered something—the truth—in that newspaper, on Lyse-Rose's eighteenth birthday?

He was probably bluffing. But what if he wasn't?

Could she take such a risk?

No, she had to find that notebook . . .

He must have given it to the Vitrals . . . Yes, that was the kind of thing he would do. Give it to them, as some sort of birthday present. And if that were the case, then that pervert Marc Vitral would probably have the notebook now. He was probably reading it at this very moment.

7

A gorgeous female student, her brown hair cut short like a boy's, was devouring Marc Vitral with her big ocean-blue eyes. The kind of eyes that most men would have dived into without hesitation. Marc hadn't even noticed her.

The girl must have been even more intrigued by his reaction. The blond boy, lost in his sad thoughts, his eyes shining with tears, stared straight through her as though she were invisible. Men who did not notice her beauty were rare specimens and, naturally, she was only attracted to men who were inaccessible.

But Marc could not stop thinking about Grand-Duc's description of his parents, Pascal and Stéphanie. His only memories of them were old photographs. He lifted his hand and looked at Mariam. Thinking he was trying to persuade her to give him his present early, she looked disapprovingly at the clock.

"Mariam, could you get me a croissant? I haven't eaten anything this morning."

Mariam gave him a wide, reassuring smile.

A few seconds later, she carried the croissant over to him on a plate. The noise in the café was deafening.

Marc tore the croissant in half and shoved it into his mouth.

9:33 a.m.

He started to read again.

Crédule Grand-Duc's Journal

I think you will agree with me when I say that fate was being an absolute bitch to both the Vitrals and the de Carvilles. First it tells them that the Airbus has crashed, that there are no survivors, stealing from them the two generations on which they had built their hopes for the future. And then, a few hours later, it joyfully announces a miracle: the smallest, most fragile being on the entire aircraft has been spared. And they are even able to celebrate that fact, to thank God, to put aside the deaths of their other loved ones... But then fate plunges its dagger into their backs a second time. What if that miracle child, the flesh of your flesh, the fruit of your loins, is not yours after all?

On December 23, 1980, the police station at Montbéliard had been busy since dawn. The superintendent himself had taken charge—Vatelier, an experienced, dynamic policeman with a scraggly beard and battered leather jacket. Turkish Airlines had faxed over the passenger list at 7:00 a.m. Funnily enough, there had been two babies on the plane: two young French girls, born on almost the same date.

Lyse-Rose de Carville, born September 27, 1980
Emilie Vitral, born September 30, 1980

A strange coincidence, you might be thinking. But I have done some checking, and the presence of babies on airplanes is far from unusual. On the contrary, it is a common occurrence, particularly on long-distance flights during the holiday season. Even as the global economy expands, families still feel that same, age-old desire to be reunited around a Christmas tree, or a birthday cake, or a bride and groom, or a coffin.

So, two babies. How could Vatelier and his team know which one was the survivor? At first, the police team imagined that the investigation would be over quickly. There are many ways to distinguish one baby from another: the color of its eyes, its skin, its blood group, the contents of its stomach, its clothing, its belongings, its next of kin. With so much to go on, how difficult could it be?

Except that speed was of the essence. There were journalists banging on the doors of the police station: this story was a godsend for the media. Who could believe it: one surviving orphan, and two families? But the child's future was on the line here and you couldn't just leave it in the hospital nursery for months while you decided who its parents were. The investigation had to choose quickly, so that the baby could be delivered safely to its family.

At 2:00 p.m. on December 23, Léonce de Carville summoned a pack of highly paid lawyers to Montbéliard. He tasked them with shadowing Vatelier's investigation closely, verifying each detail as it came in.

In legal terms, it was a complex affair. But the Ministry of Justice took only a few hours to decide how the inquiry should be handled: the Montbéliard police would investigate, but the final decision would be made by a juvenile-court judge, after a hearing involving all the parties and witnesses. Behind closed doors, naturally. The deadline for the decision was to be the end of April 1981, so that the child's emotional stability would not be put at risk. In the meantime, the baby would be looked after by the nursery in the Belfort-Montbéliard hospital. The man chosen to lead the inquiry was Judge Jean-Louis Le Drian, a bigwig at the Paris High Court, author of a dozen works on abandoned children, the search for identity, adoption, and so on. He was the obvious choice.

By the next day, December 24, Judge Le Drian had somehow managed to cobble together a small working group, none of whom were any more enthusiastic than he was about the idea of working on Christmas Eve: Vatelier, the Montbéliard police superintendent; Morange, the doctor who had overseen the miracle child's recovery; and Saint-Simon, a policeman from the French Embassy in Turkey, who was in communication with them by telephone.

Afterward, they all told me about that surreal meeting in a large office on Avenue de Suffren, with an unbeatable view of the Eiffel Tower illuminated against a white winter sky. They were facing a cheerless Christmas Eve, without tinsel or presents, their children waiting for them around the tree while they considered the future of a three-month-old baby.

Judge Le Drian was in a difficult situation because he knew the de Carvilles slightly. He had met them once or twice at parties in Paris; the kind where hundreds of people crammed together into the splendid living rooms of Haussmannian buildings. I think I can imagine what he was thinking. At the back of his head, a little voice must have been whispering: *Let's hope that the kid is the de Carvilles' granddaughter, otherwise this is going to be awkward…*

A fifty-fifty chance. Heads or tails.

But at first it seemed that the coin was not going to fall the right way.

When I met Judge Le Drian, years later, he still looked the same as he had at the time of the inquiry—sharp, precise, dressed impeccably, with a mauve scarf that was a shade lighter than his purple tie—and I wondered how this besuited man was able to persuade traumatized children to trust and confide in him. The judge had filmed all the meetings. He gave me the tapes; he felt he could refuse nothing to the de Carville family. Those tapes enable me to give a very accurate, detailed account of the inquiry. As for the verdict… well, I will let you be the judge of that, so to speak.

"I will try to keep this as brief as possible," Le Drian began. "I'm sure we are all busy men. I will start with the information concerning Lyse-Rose de Carville. She was born in Istanbul, slightly less than three months ago. Only her parents really knew her, and Alexandre and Véronique de Carville took everything relating to Lyse-Rose with them on the Airbus. Her toys, her clothes, her medicines, her medical card, all their photographs of her. Everything was lost when the plane went up in flames. Saint-Simon, have you uncovered any other witnesses in Turkey?"

The nasal voice of the man from the Turkish Embassy crackled from the telephone loudspeaker that sat on the table: "Not really. Apart from a few Turkish servants who glimpsed Lyse-Rose through mosquito netting, the only eyewitness is her six-year-old sister, Malvina. You see..."

Le Drian sensed that already things were going wrong. Whenever that happened, whenever he felt events tumbling out of his control, he would stand up and pull down one end of his scarf so that the two ends were exactly the same length. Just a nervous tic. And of course, the damned scarf kept slipping to one side or the other, without the judge even being aware that he had moved his neck at all. Superintendent Vatelier watched the judge's mannerism, his smile barely concealed by his beard.

"I spent a long time talking to the de Carvilles," Vatelier said. "Well, mainly Léonce de Carville. They only know what their granddaughter looks like through some vague descriptions they were given over the telephone. Although they do possess a photograph of Lyse-Rose, taken at her birth, along with the letter they received containing the announcement..."

"What does this photograph show?"

"Not much." Vatelier scowled. "It's a picture of the mother breast-feeding the child, so you can only see Lyse-Rose from behind—her neck, one ear, that's all."

Judge Le Drian pulled nervously on the right-hand side of his scarf. Clearly, things were not looking good for the de Carvilles.

I apologize for skipping ahead, but I just wanted to mention here that in the weeks that followed, Léonce de Carville summoned several highly regarded experts who attested that the ear of the miracle child was identical to that of Lyse-Rose on her birth photograph. I have looked closely at the picture and the analyses, and my conclusion is that it would require a considerable dose of willful blindness to have any kind of certainty on the matter, whether for or against this supposition. Judge Le Drian clearly did not share the experts' bias and he continued to explore the baby's genealogy.

"What about Lyse-Rose's maternal grandparents?" he asked.

Vatelier, the police superintendent from Montbéliard, consulted his notes.

"Véronique, Lyse-Rose's mother, is the fourth of seven children. The parents, the Berniers, are from Quebec and they have eleven grandchildren. Véronique was already quite distant from her family when she met Alexandre in Toronto at a seminar on molecular chemistry. The Berniers seem to be supporting the de Carvilles, albeit not very loudly."

"OK. Let's keep digging on that side," said Le Drian. "In the meantime, shall we move on to Emilie Vitral? Apparently, she left more clues behind…"

"Yeah, I guess," Vatelier sighed, "although her medical card, her suitcase, her feeding bottles, and her bibs also went up in smoke with the plane. But here are the details: in the first two months of her life, her grandparents saw her five times, two of which were at the hospital in Dieppe in the week following her birth. They also saw her on the day the family left for Turkey, when Pascal and Stéphanie brought Marc to stay with the grandparents. The baby was fast asleep at the time."

The superintendent turned to Dr. Morange, who spoke for the first time: "I was present when the Vitrals saw the baby in the hospital at Belfort-Montbéliard. They recognized their granddaughter immediately."

"Of course," said Le Drian. "Of course. They were hardly going to say the opposite..."

The judge sighed wearily, and pulled on the left-hand side of his scarf.

"Well, we weren't about to put four babies in a lineup and make the grandparents pick out the right one, were we?" said Vatelier.

"Maybe you should have," Le Drian replied. "It would have saved us a lot of time."

With a shrug, the superintendent continued: "Just to make things even more confusing, the Vitrals do not possess a single photograph of their granddaughter. From what they tell me, Stéphanie had made a little photo album of her daughter, containing twelve pictures, and she took it everywhere with her. Presumably that, too, was destroyed in the fire."

"And the negatives?" the judge asked.

"The police force in Dieppe did a thorough search of the parents' apartment, but for the moment, they have not found anything. I imagine Stéphanie must have taken them with her."

Perhaps...

I, too, searched for those damned negatives. Can you believe it? Not one single picture of the baby! Anyway, there's no point in my prolonging the suspense, at least not in this particular instance. We never found them. Other than the theory that they had disappeared along with the plane, or that the Vitrals were simply making up the story about the album, I also wondered whether Léonce de Carville might be involved: he could have gone to Pascal and Stéphanie's apartment before the police arrived and gotten rid of any evidence that could compromise his position. I wouldn't put it past him.

Judge Le Drian's neck was beginning to sweat. This case was shaping up to be a legal minefield.

"All right," he said, "we've gone through almost everyone now. So what about the rest of the Vitral family...Is that a dead end, too?"

"Pretty much," said Superintendent Vatelier. "The child's mother, Stéphanie, was abandoned by her mother. She was raised in an orphanage in Rouen. She was only sixteen when she met Pascal Vitral on a café terrace and fell in love. So little Emilie—if she is the one who survived—has no living kin other than her grandparents, Pierre and Nicole, and her older brother, Marc."

Judge Le Drian stared out the window, above the lights of the Eiffel Tower, in search of a star that might guide them through this dark Christmas night.

The arguments and counterarguments went on like this for hours, and I could describe every detail. Not only do I have the films of the meetings, I have also gone through almost three thousand pages of notes accumulated by Judge Le Drian during the weeks that followed. And that's without even mentioning my personal research. Fear not, I will come back to these discussions in a moment, at least for what seem to me to be the most important points. But I think you must already be getting a sense of the investigators' difficulties.

Which side of the coin would land faceup? Heads or tails? I still don't know.

I am simply passing on all these clues to you. Now it's your turn to sift through them...

But I can hear you asking questions: What about scientific proof? Their clothes? Blood type? Eye color? And all the rest?

Don't worry, I'm coming to that.

You won't be disappointed.

8

October 2, 1998, 9:35 a.m.

Marc ate the rest of his croissant without even looking up at the clock, or at the beautiful student, or at Mariam. Around him, the Lenin was alive with noise and movement. And so, too, visible through the café's windows, was the square outside the university. Even if he had his doubts about Grand-Duc's revelations, Marc had to keep reading, storing away all the information he discovered.

Because this was what Lylie wanted...

Crédule Grand-Duc's Journal

Two weeks later, on January 11, 1980, Judge Le Drian convened a new meeting. Same investigators, same office in the same building on Avenue de Suffren...but this time, they met in the morning. The Eiffel Tower seemed to shiver in the fog, its feet covered by puddles that were slowly growing in the fine drizzle. Lines of tourists stood under umbrellas. This was the most visited monument in the world, and yet there was no shelter of any kind where people could wait, not even a simple glass roof.

Judge Le Drian was growing increasingly irritated. Influential whispers had reached his ears, making it clear that everyone he knew was strongly sympathetic toward the de Carvilles.

The judge was not stupid. He had gotten the message. But he could only act according to the facts at his disposal and he was hardly going to start fabricating false evidence.

Dr. Morange was concluding his report on the child's blood type. He had passed around photocopies of the medical analyses.

"So, to summarize, our miracle child has the most common blood type, A positive, along with forty percent of the French population. We have learned from the hospitals in Dieppe and Istanbul that both Emilie Vitral and Lyse-Rose de Carville are also, without any doubt whatsoever, A positive."

"Is there no way of extracting any more information from these tests?" the judge asked.

The learned doctor explained. "You have to understand: blood tests only allow us to eliminate the possibility of paternity, not to confirm it. We would only be able to assert a family connection if there was an unusual rhesus factor, or in the event of a rare genetic illness. But that isn't the case here. The science can't tell us anything about who this child's family is."

I can sense you wondering now, with all this talk of science: What about DNA and all that jazz? But let us not forget, this was 1980. Back then, DNA testing still seemed to be in the realms of science fiction. The first legal case to have been decided on the basis of a DNA test occurred in 1987. But don't worry, we will return to this issue; it was a question that had to be confronted eventually, but by then, the miracle child was much older, and the situation had changed completely.

Back in 1980, the experts on Avenue de Suffren managed as best they could. Dr. Morange showed his colleagues a series of pictures.

"These are models created by the lab in Meudon. We have applied computer-generated aging techniques to images of the miracle child, to see who the baby might resemble in five years, ten years, in twenty years..."

The judge glanced at the photographs and seemed irritated: "If you think I'm going to base my decision on something as crazy as that, you're dreaming!"

On that point, he was right. Or partly, at least. Objectively, the artificially aged child looked more like a Vitral than a de Carville, although it wasn't obvious, and the de Carvilles' lawyers had little trouble ridiculing the process. Eighteen years later, having witnessed the miracle child grow up, year after year, I can tell you that those aging programs are complete and utter crap.

"There remains the question of eye color," the doctor continued. "The only real distinguishing feature of this baby... Her eyes are strikingly blue for her age. The color can still change, darken, but all the same, this appears to be a genetic characteristic."

Vatelier took over: "Emilie Vitral had pale eyes that were already turning blue. All the witnesses we approached—the grandparents, a few friends, the nurses in the maternity hospital—confirmed that. Pale blue eyes like those of both her parents, her grandparents, and practically the entire Vitral family. The de Carvilles, on the other hand, are mostly dark haired with dark brown eyes. The same goes for the Berniers—I checked."

Judge Le Drian appeared to be at the end of his rope.
This was not good—not good at all for the de Carvilles.
Outside, the drizzle had turned to a downpour, but the stoic
tourists continued to wait at the foot of the Eiffel Tower,
hidden beneath a canopy of umbrellas. The judge stood up
and went to the light switch, bringing a little brightness to
the room. His scarf slithered to the right. He did not bother
to readjust it.

"Hmm, I see what you're saying," he said, playing
for time. "But really that's just one more presumption—
there's still no proof. Everyone knows that two parents
with brown eyes can have a child with eyes of any color
whatsoever."

"That's true," Dr. Morange admitted. "It's just a question of probability…"

And probability was not pointing toward the de Carvilles. I remember a few weeks later, *Science and Life*
magazine used the example of the "miracle child of Mont
Terrible" to explain why the science of genetics was incapable of systematically predicting an individual's physical
characteristics based on his or her ancestry. I have always
suspected that Léonce de Carville must have commis-
sioned that article, directly or indirectly—the timing of it
was just a little too convenient.

Next, the judge interrogated Saint-Simon, the Turkish
policeman, through the loudspeaker.

"So what about the child's clothing? Is it really so difficult to draw any conclusions from the clothes she was
wearing on the day of the crash?"

Calmly, Saint-Simon replied. "Gentlemen, let me remind
you of the clothes the child was wearing when she was
found. A cotton vest, a white dress with orange flowers,

and a beige wool sweater. We can be fairly certain that the clothes were bought in Istanbul, in the Grand Bazaar, the largest covered market in the world..."

Judge Le Drian did not let this opportunity slip: "The Vitrals were only on vacation in Turkey for two weeks, and they spent only two days in Istanbul. Logically, Emilie Vitral would have been wearing the French clothes she had brought with her for the journey. It seems highly improbable that her parents would have thought to dress her, a few hours before they went back to France, in clothes bought in Istanbul. If the child was wearing a vest, dress, and sweater bought in Turkey, then it seems to me that this baby must be Lyse-Rose de Carville. She was born in Istanbul, after all..."

Saint-Simon retorted: "Except, your honor, that the Turkish clothes worn by the baby were relatively cheap. I checked—they are completely different from the rest of the clothes I found in Lyse-Rose's closet in the de Carvilles' villa in Ceyhan. I will send you a detailed description. Lyse-Rose's clothes were all well-known brands, bought in the eastern district of Istanbul, in Galatasaray. Not in the Grand Bazaar."

Before he could launch into a sociological analysis of the various districts of Istanbul, Le Drian interrupted him: "OK, I'll look at the list. Vatelier, could you tell us about the ballistics report?"

Rubbing his beard, Vatelier gave the judge a wary look.

"The experts tried to reconstruct how and at what precise moment the baby was ejected from the plane. We know where each passenger was sitting. The de Carvilles were in the tenth row, on one side, toward the back of the cabin; the Vitrals were in the center of the Airbus, roughly level with the wings. So the two babies were more or less equidistant from the door that broke open on impact—the door through which the baby was ejected. All the experts agree on that point. I've sent you the files. They were able to reconstruct the point of impact in detail, the way the door twisted, and they all say that only a human being weighing less than twenty pounds could possibly have escaped alive."

"All right, Superintendent," interrupted the judge, who, that day, was sporting a mustard-yellow scarf that was not a particularly good match for his bottle-green jacket. "But since then, there has been the Le Tallandier theory. Unless I'm mistaken, the physics professor Serge Le Tallandier demonstrated the unlikelihood of a baby being ejected laterally. Meaning, in other words, that it is less probable that Emilie Vitral should have been ejected, because she was sitting in the center of the cabin. What is your opinion on that, Superintendent?"

"To be completely honest, Le Tallandier's calculations are so complicated that a mere policeman—even one from the forensics department—wouldn't dare to contradict him. But I should point out that Serge Le Tallandier was a classmate of Léonce de Carville at military school, and that he was also the advisor on Alexandre de Carville's dissertation at Mines Paris-Tech..."

The judge looked at Superintendent Vatelier as if he had just blasphemed.

"Are you attempting to discredit the opinion of a renowned expert who runs his own laboratory at the Polytechnique, the best military school in France?"

Vatelier smiled and said: "I am not attempting to discredit anyone, Your Honor. I have no competence in that field. But I can tell you that, when I talked to Le Tallandier's colleagues at the Polytechnique about his theory, they burst out laughing."

The judge sighed. Outside, the Eiffel Tower had completely disappeared in the fog. Hundreds of tourists had probably waited hours in the rain for nothing.

The weeks passed and the case seemed to be heading into a legal and scientific impasse that was of ever-decreasing interest to anyone except the two families involved.

The police persisted.

The journalists didn't care.

The general public, which had been so fascinated by the case in the days following the "miracle," quickly wearied of it as the uncertainty dragged on. The mystery seemed unsolvable, and everyone was bored by the experts' squabbling. As the furor died down, the police attempted to work discreetly, while de Carville's lawyers did their best to ensure that, as far as possible, the inquiry took place outside the public eye. It was clear that, if the case was decided purely by senior government officials, the judgment was likely to be in their favor. Judge Le Drian was a reasonable man, after all . . .

The *Est Républicain*, which had carried the initial scoop, was the last newspaper to continue providing a daily update on the case, although the updates became increasingly brief. The journalist who was writing about the investigation, Lucile Moraud, had spent decades covering the sleaziest stories in eastern France; she did not miss them. She soon found herself faced with a dilemma: What should she call the miracle child? It was impossible to remain neutral if you used either of the names, Emilie or Lyse-Rose, and circumlocutions such as "the miracle child of Mont Terrible" or "the orphan of the snow" or "the girl who lived" tended to slow down her prose, which she wanted to be simple and direct so she could appeal to her readership. Inspiration arrived in late January 1981. At that time, as I'm sure you will remember, a song by Charlélie Couture was playing constantly on the radio, a song that seemed eerily topical: "Like an airplane without wings..."

Infuriated by the slowness of the inquiry and the timidity of Judge Le Drian, Lucile Moraud convinced her editor to run, on January 29, a full front-page photograph of the "miracle child" in her glass cage in the pediatrics wing of the hospital. Below it ran a caption in bold lettering, consisting of three lines from the song:

Oh, dragonfly,
Your wings are so fragile,
As for me, my body is broken...

The journalist had hit the bull's-eye. Now no one could hear Charlélie Couture's hit without thinking of the miracle child with her fragile wings. For the French people, the orphan of the snow became "Dragonfly," and the nickname stuck. Even the families began to call her that. And so did I.

What an ass! Dragonfly...

I even went so far as to become interested in the insects themselves, and spent a fortune collecting them. When I think about it now...All of that, just because some shrewd journalist knew how to manipulate the sentiments of the masses.

The police were less romantic. In order to refer to the baby without implicitly siding with either family, they invented a neutral acronym that linked the beginning of one name to the end of the other. By crossing Lyse-Rose with Emilie, they created Lylie...

Lylie.

Superintendent Vatelier was the first to use this name in front of journalists.

And, let's be honest, it isn't bad. As with Dragonfly, the nickname Lylie stuck, a bit like an affectionate diminutive.

Not Lyse-Rose or Emilie, but Lylie.

A chimera. A strange being composed of two bodies. A monster.

Speaking of monsters, I think it is time I told you more about Malvina de Carville.

Léonce de Carville was a strong-willed, determined man, used to getting what he wanted in life. However, so far none of the evidence in this case was working in his favor, and he became frustrated, impatient. And so it was that he made two mistakes. Two very serious mistakes.

The first concerned his granddaughter Malvina. She was only six years old at the time: a lively child, and treated like a little queen. Naturally, it was always going to be difficult for her to get over the death of both her parents and possibly her little sister, too. But, supported by her family and an army of shrinks, she would probably have recovered, the way people do.

Except that she was the sole eyewitness, the only living being to have seen Lyse-Rose in Turkey, during the first two months of her life. Perhaps the only two months of her life.

Is a six-year-old girl capable of recognizing a small baby? Or of distinguishing it from another baby?

It was a question worth asking.

Against the affirmations of the Vitral grandparents, Malvina was the de Carvilles' sole asset, the only one capable of identifying Lyse-Rose. Léonce de Carville should have protected her; he should not have allowed her to testify; he should have thrown the police out of his home. He had the means to do it. Malvina should not have had to answer questions; she should have been left alone, sent far away from the turmoil to a special retreat filled with attentive caregivers and happy children. Instead of which, Malvina had to testify, over and over again, in front of judges, lawyers, police, experts. For weeks on end, she was shuttled from office to hearing room, from waiting room to courtroom, constantly surrounded by sinister-looking men in suits and muscled bodyguards. To protect her from journalists, of course.

Malvina systematically repeated the exact same words to every person she saw:

"Yes, this baby is my little sister."

"I recognize her. She is Lyse-Rose."

After a while, her grandfather didn't even have to encourage her to do it anymore. She grew certain of what she was saying; she no longer had any doubts. She could not possibly be mistaken.

The clothes she was shown were Lyse-Rose's. It was her face that she recognized. Those were her cries that she heard. And she was ready to swear it—before the judge, on the Bible, on the life of her favorite doll. At only six years old, she was strong enough to stand up to the Vitrals.

Since then, I have watched Malvina grow up. Well,

perhaps that is the wrong term. Let's just say that I have watched her grow older, becoming an adolescent, then an adult. I have seen the madness rise within her.

That girl scares me, I can't deny it—I believe she ought to be in a psychiatric hospital, closely watched at all times—but there is one thing I have to acknowledge: she is not to blame in the slightest for what happened to her. Her grandfather Léonce de Carville bears all the responsibility for that. He knew what he was doing. He deliberately used his own granddaughter. He knowingly sacrificed her mental health, against the advice of all the doctors and the pleas of his own wife.

And, what's worse, it did him no good at all.

Because Léonce de Carville made another mistake, perhaps even more serious than the first.

9

October 2, 1998, 9:43 a.m.

Lylie had not moved in the last thirty minutes. She was sitting on a marble balustrade on the Esplanade des Invalides. The cold of the stone was seeping into her legs, but she wasn't really bothered by it. It was a cold, dry day. Across from her, the dome of Les Invalides could hardly be distinguished from the almost monochrome white sky.

A dozen rollerbladers were practicing in front of her, indifferent to the weather. Almost as if they were trying to impress her.

The Esplanade des Invalides is mostly used to practice speed, slaloming, and jumping. The rollerbladers had put down two lines of plastic orange cones, and they were racing one another over a hundred yards. It was like a modern version of a medieval joust, with the fastest, or the last one standing, winning the heart of the watching princess.

Lylie liked watching the rollerbladers: their speed, their laughter, their shouts. The noise and the movement helped her to stay calm. This wasn't easy, as everything in her life seemed to be in a state of flux. She thought again about Grand-Duc's notebook. Had she been right to give it to Marc? Would he read it? Yes, of course he would, but would he understand it? Marc had a complicated relationship with Crédule Grand-Duc: the detective wasn't exactly a father figure to him, but all the same, he had, for many years, been one of the few masculine presences in Marc's life. And Marc was always so sure of things—his instinct, he called it. His convictions. Was he ready to accept a different kind of truth?

One of the rollerbladers was staring at her with black, hawk-like eyes. He was older than the others, maybe in his forties, with a thin, chiseled face and hair that was already beginning to go gray. He had won all his races hands down. He had taken off his leather jacket, and would lift up his T-shirt at every opportunity, revealing his muscular body.

Lylie had not even noticed him. She was thinking about Marc's present now, that macabre setup.

Was there any point to it?

Tears formed in the corners of her eyes. She had no choice: she simply had to distance herself from Marc, at least for a few hours, a few days; she had to do this without him, to protect him. Afterward, when it was all over, perhaps she would have the courage to tell him everything. Marc was so fond of her. But who was she?

His Lylie, his dragonfly. What she would have given to be known by a single, ordinary first name . . .

The silver-haired rollerblader brushed past Lylie. She jumped, startled abruptly from her thoughts. A smile played across her lips. In spite of the cold (it must have been less than fifty degrees Fahrenheit), the man had now taken off his T-shirt and was dancing bare-chested in front of her, his huge thigh muscles clearly visible through his skintight jeans.

He was staring at her shamelessly, appraising Lylie's body. His mating ritual seemed well practiced and there was no ambiguity as to his intentions: he was a sexual predator. She wondered how many times he had done this before, how many young women had fallen into his clutches.

Lylie held his gaze for a few moments, evaluating her seducer. Her expression was almost indifferent. She was used to the attention: her beautiful, slender body often attracted men's eyes, yet she felt surprised that they would look at her in that way, desire her. She felt as if she were transparent.

She returned to her ruminations. She should not give in to self-pity. Right now, the important thing wasn't her name. The important thing was to act, and to do so quickly and alone.

She was determined. Now that she had learned the truth, the awful truth, she had no choice. She had to accept that.

She had only found out yesterday and her life had been turned upside down in an instant. Everything seemed to have sped up now, but she had committed the irreparable act long before all this. Now she was caught in a vise and her options had been reduced to this: escape or be crushed.

The rollerblader wasn't giving up. He skated in wide circles, his eyes fixed permanently on Lylie. But she was thinking about Marc again. Trapped in that bar.

Trapped by her, and with another fifteen minutes to go. After that, she felt certain, he would try to call her. She picked up her bag and switched off her cell phone. She had to remain invisible, out of contact, at least for the moment. Marc would be against her plan. He would try to protect her, seeing only the risks, the danger.

She knew him well. He would call it murder.

*

Like a flight of swallows in the moment after a gunshot, the dozen rollerbladers suddenly disappeared toward Les Invalides, following their gray-haired leader, who had either grown weary or annoyed by the failure of his mating dance. The plastic orange cones, the jackets, the T-shirts... everything vanished in an instant, leaving behind nothing but the gray, empty tarmac.

Murder...

Lylie smiled nervously.

Yes, she supposed, that was one way to look at it.

A fatal and essential crime.

Killing a monster so that she would be able to live.

Or at least to survive.

10

October 2, 1998, 9:45 a.m.

Marc looked up. 9:45 a.m., according to the Martini clock.

Why was time passing so slowly? A strange foreboding rose within him. That present from Lylie, which Mariam had put in her cash register, that matchbox-size gift...it was a trap. A pretext. A decoy. The only point of this interminable hour of waiting was to give Lylie enough time to get away from him, to hide.

But why?

He didn't like this. He felt as if each second were taking Lylie farther away from him. Yet his eyes were still drawn back to the notebook. He could guess what was coming next—Léonce de Carville's second mistake. He had been there when it happened, he'd been told, a witness with tears in his eyes. If Grand-Duc's version matched the legend told in Rue Pocholle, he would enjoy reading it.

Crédule Grand-Duc's Journal

Léonce de Carville believed that money solved everything.

The inquiry had stalled. And even if the Minister of

Justice, in agreement with Judge Le Drian, had set a deadline of six months for the final decision, the wait was too
long for Léonce de Carville.

All his lawyers urged patience. The longer the inquiry
went on, the more likely he was to win it, they said, because
of his influence. Slowly but surely, the media, the police,
even Vatelier would fall into line. Without any definite
proof on either side, the case would boil down to a squab-
ble between the experts, and that meant the judge's decision would be final. The Vitral family had no influence,
no experience, no support. However, Léonce de Carville
evidently did not share his lawyers' confidence, no matter
how calm he appeared to be in public. He decided to deal
with the problem on his own, once and for all, in the same
way he always dealt with business matters: instinctively
and autocratically.

Around noon on February 17, 1981, he picked up his
telephone (this was not something he would delegate to
his secretary) and made an appointment to see the Vitral
family the following morning. Well, not the family, but
Pierre Vitral. Another big mistake on his part. Later,
Nicole would tell me the whole story, in great detail.
Triumphantly.

The next morning, in Dieppe, the Vitrals' neighbors in Rue
Pocholle were amazed to see a smart Mercedes parked in
front of Pierre and Nicole's house. De Carville entered,
carrying a black briefcase, like someone from a movie.

A caricature.

"Mr. Vitral, would it be possible for me to talk with you
in private?"

Pierre Vitral hesitated. His wife did not. Her reply was

unambiguous: "No, Mr. de Carville, that would not be possible."

Nicole Vitral was holding little Marc in her arms. She did not let go of him as she continued speaking: "You see, this is a small house and the walls are thin. Even if I went into the kitchen, I would still hear everything that was said. So would the neighbors, for that matter. There are no secrets here. But then, we don't *want* to keep secrets from each other."

Marc began to cry in her arms. She sat down on a chair and bounced him on her knees, making it clear that she was not going to budge.

Léonce de Carville seemed unperturbed.

"As you like," he said, smiling. "This won't take long. What I have to propose can be summarized in a few words."

He moved farther into the room, glancing at the small TV set in the corner, which was showing some American sitcom. The living room was tiny—thirty square feet at most—with orange Formica furniture, as if they were still living in the 1960s.

"Mr. Vitral, let us be frank. No one will ever know for sure which baby survived this airplane crash. Who is alive now—Lyse-Rose or Emilie? There will never be any real proof: you will always feel certain that it is Emilie, just as I will remain sure that Lyse-Rose was the one who survived. No matter what happens, our convictions will remain the same. That is human nature."

Up to that point, the Vitrals could only agree.

"Even a judge or a jury will never be sure," de Carville went on. "They will be obliged to make a decision, but no one will ever know if it was the right one. Essentially, it is a fifty-fifty chance—heads or tails. Mr. Vitral, do you really believe a child's future should be determined by the toss of a coin?"

The Vitrals gave no response. They were waiting for de Carville to make his point. Moronic laughter blared from the TV set. Nicole walked over, switched it off, then returned to her seat.

"I am going to be completely honest with you, Mr. Vitral. Mrs. Vitral. I have gathered information about you. Doubtless you have done the same for me."

Nicole Vitral felt a growing dislike for this man's self-satisfied smile.

"You raised your children with dignity. Everyone says so. It wasn't always easy for you. I heard about your eldest son, Nicolas—the moped accident, four years ago. I also heard about your back, Pierre, and your lungs, Nicole. I am sure that with a job such as yours . . . What I mean is, you ought to have found something else a long time ago. For your own sake, and for your grandson."

So that was it. Nicole was holding Marc too tightly and he cried out.

"What are you getting at, Mr. de Carville?" Pierre Vitral asked suddenly.

"I am sure you have already grasped my meaning. We are not enemies. On the contrary. We should be friends, in the interests of our Dragonfly. We should join forces."

Nicole Vitral stood up. Léonce de Carville did not even notice, so attached was he to his chain of thought.

"Let us be frank," he continued. "I am sure that you have dreamed of enabling your children, and your grand-children, to enjoy real vacations, to study in the best schools. Of giving them all that they desire. All that they deserve. A real chance in life. But a real chance has a price. Everything has a price."

De Carville was digging a hole for himself, but he was incapable of realizing it. Instead, he kept on digging. Horrified, the Vitrals said nothing.

"Pierre, Nicole, I don't know if our little Dragonfly is my granddaughter or yours, but I want to give her everything she could ever want, to satisfy her every desire. I swear I will make her the happiest girl in the world. In fact, I will go even further: I have a high regard for your family, and I would like to offer you financial help, so that you are better able to bring up your grandson, Marc. I am well aware how difficult this tragedy has been for you, as well as for me, and that you will be forced to continue working for many years in order to feed another mouth..."

Nicole Vitral moved closer to her husband. Her rage was building.

Léonce de Carville finally hesitated for a moment, then continued: "Pierre, Nicole, if you agree to give up any claim to the child, to Lylie, if you acknowledge that her name is Lyse-Rose de Carville, I solemnly undertake to look after you and Marc. You will be able to see Lylie as often as you like—nothing will change in that sense. It will be as if you are still her grandparents..."

The look on de Carville's face was imploring, almost human.

"I beg you to accept. Think of your future. Of Lylie's future."

Nicole Vitral was going to say something, but it was Pierre who responded first. His voice was astonishingly calm.

"Mr. de Carville, I would prefer not even to reply to

your question. Emilie is not for sale. Nor is Marc. Nor is anyone here. Money can't buy everything, Mr. de Carville. Didn't the death of your son teach you that?"

Taken aback, Léonce de Carville suddenly raised his voice. It was a rule of his never to remain on the defensive. Marc was now screaming in his grandmother's arms. The whole street must have heard what followed.

"No, Mr. Vitral! Don't start lecturing me, on top of everything else. Perhaps you don't realize how humiliating it has been for me, to come here and make this proposal to you. I have offered you a genuine opportunity to escape your situation, and you can't be bothered to take it. Pride is a wonderful thing…"

"Get out!"

De Carville did not budge.

"Get out of here right now! And don't forget your briefcase. How much is inside? What price were you offering us for Emilie? A hundred thousand francs? The cost of a nice car. Three hundred thousand—a bungalow with a sea view, for our retirement?"

"Five hundred thousand francs, Mr. Vitral. With more to come after the judge's decision, if you wish."

"Get the hell out of my house."

"You are making a mistake. You are going to lose everything. You know as well as I do that you haven't a chance of winning this battle. I have dozens of lawyers who are on first-name terms with the experts and the policemen in charge of this investigation. I am personally acquainted with half of the judges in the Paris High Court. That isn't your world. The game is rigged, Mr. Vitral, and you know it. The miracle child will be called Lyse-Rose, even if irrefutable evidence is found proving the opposite.

Lyse-Rose is the one who survived; it is a *fait accompli*. That's just how it is. I have not come here as your enemy, Mr. Vitral. I was under no obligation to offer you anything. I came here simply to help you."

Marc was still wailing in Nicole's arms.

"I told you to get the hell out of my house."

De Carville picked up his briefcase and walked toward the door.

"Thank you, Mr. Vitral. At least I have eased my conscience. And it hasn't cost me a penny!"

He left.

Nicole Vitral held Marc tightly. She was weeping into his hair. Weeping because she knew that de Carville had not been lying. Everything he had said was true. The Vitrals knew the workings of fate; they had faced up to it so many times. With pride. She also knew perfectly well that they had no chance of winning.

Pierre Vitral stood for a long time staring at the soundless television. At that moment, his back was not troubling him. He was suffering from something else, a different pain that blocked it out.

Pierre Vitral looked at the little television screen one last time. Finally, a glimmer of resistance appeared in his expression. Almost to himself, he mumbled: "No, Mr. de Carville. No, you won't win."

My own opinion of this incident, looking back at it years later, is that de Carville made a huge mistake that day. He awakened the Vitrals' anger. Without that, he probably would have won the case, and no one would have paid any attention. The Vitrals would have cried foul, and the world would have turned a deaf ear.

*

The Mercedes had not even left Pollet as Pierre Vitral took a newspaper from the cluttered cabinet shelf.

"What are we going to do?" his wife asked.

"We're going to fight. We're going to crush him."

"How? You heard him. And he's right..."

"No...No, Nicole. Emilie is not dead yet. He forgot something. Everything he said was true before...before Dragonfly, before Pascal and Stéphanie died. But not anymore! Because we are important now, too, Nicole. People are interested in us. We're newsworthy. Our names are in the newspapers, on the radio..." He turned toward the corner of the room. "And on TV, too. I bet de Carville never watches TV. He has no idea. These days, TV, newspapers, they're just as important as money."

"What are you going to do?"

Pierre Vitral underlined a telephone number in the newspaper.

"I'm going to start with the *Est Républicain*. They know the case better than anyone. Nicole, you remember that journalist who wrote all those articles about the inquiry?"

"Articles? The last one was barely five lines long!"

"Exactly. All the more reason to start with her. Can you find her name for me?"

Nicole Vitral put Marc on a chair in front of the television. From under the living-room table, she took a binder in which she had methodically collected every newspaper article about the Mont Terri crash. It took her only a few seconds.

"Lucile Moraud!"

"OK. We've nothing to lose. Let's see where this gets us..."

Pierre Vitral picked up the telephone and dialed the newspaper's main switchboard.

"Is this the *Est Républicain*? Hello, my name is Pierre Vitral. I'm the grandfather of the miracle child of Mont Terrible... Yes, 'Dragonfly'... I would like to speak to one of your journalists, Lucile Moraud. I have some important information to give her about the case..."

Pierre Vitral sensed a sudden urgency on the other end of the line. Less than a minute later, he heard a voice—slightly out of breath, and surprisingly deep for a woman's—that sent a chill down his spine.

"Pierre Vitral? This is Lucile Moraud. You have some news for me? Is it serious?"

"Léonce de Carville has just left my house. He offered us five hundred thousand francs to drop our claim."

The three seconds of silence that followed seemed interminable to Pierre. Then the journalist's husky voice broke the silence again, making him jump: "Do you have witnesses?"

"The whole neighborhood..."

"Jesus Christ... Don't move. Don't speak to anyone else about this. We're going to send someone over right now to interview you."

11

October 2, 1998, 10:00 a.m.

Ten a.m. exactly.

Marc had been reading with one eye on Grand-Duc's words and one on the clock.

He closed the green notebook and shoved it into his backpack, among his folders. He walked up to the counter of the bar with a satisfied smile. Mariam was busy rinsing glasses, her back to him. Marc pressed an imaginary bell on the countertop. "Ding-dong!" he said loudly. "Time's up!"

Mariam turned around and calmly dried her hands on a dish towel before folding it neatly and hanging it up.

"Time's up!" Marc repeated.

"All right..."

Mariam looked up at the clock. "Well, you don't waste any time! I bet you never overslept on Christmas morning, did you?"

"No, I didn't. But please hurry up, Mariam! You heard what Lylie said earlier: I have a class now..."

"You can try that with other people, not with me," said Mariam. "Anyway, here it is... your present."

She opened a drawer, picked out the tiny packet, and

handed it to Marc. He grabbed it eagerly and turned toward the exit.

"Aren't you going to open it now?"

"No. Imagine if it's something private. A sex toy, or some lacy lingerie..."

"I'm not joking, Marc."

"So why would you want me to open it in front of you?"

"Because I can guess what's in that package, smartass. And I'd like to be able to help pick you up after you fall."

Marc stared at Mariam, shocked.

"You *know* what's in this package?"

"Yes... Well, more or less. It's always the same thing. When..."

A customer standing behind Marc was drumming his fingers impatiently on the counter and staring at the row of Marlboro cigarettes.

"When what?"

Mariam sighed.

"When a girl runs away, giving herself an hour's head start. An hour's head start on the poor guy she's left sitting alone in my bar!"

Marc paid his bill. He thought fleetingly of the sapphire ring on Lylie's finger, of the Tuareg cross she had not fastened around her neck. He managed to shrug, as if unconcerned.

"See you tomorrow, Mariam. Same time, same table. Near the window. Save us two chairs, won't you?"

He picked up the package with a hand that he managed to stop shaking and left.

As she handed three packs of cigarettes to her next customer, Mariam watched Marc walk away. She had said too much. She was no longer so sure of herself. Marc and Emilie were a strange pair, not like any other couple she had seen before, but she was certain of one thing: that in the next few hours, Marc's future would be left up in the air and he would have a crucial decision to make. Would he make the right decision or the wrong one?

Marc disappeared into the square outside Paris VIII, his gray coat seeming to melt into the tarmac. For a moment, Mariam was distracted by the uninterrupted wave of passersby.

Marc was running away, buoyed up by his convictions. But the tiniest thing could turn his world upside down, Mariam thought, make every certainty in his life melt into air. All it would take is a single detail. A grain of sand. The beating of a dragonfly's wings.

Marc walked quickly away from the Lenin. He went up Avenue de Stalingrad, heading vaguely toward the Stade Delaune. The morning rush was beginning to thin out. There were more old people on the streets now, more mothers with young children, plastic bags hanging from the handles of their strollers. He walked another few minutes down the street and found himself almost alone. Hands trembling, he ripped the silver wrapping paper from the package and stuffed it into the pocket of his jeans. In his hand was a small cardboard box. He opened it nervously.

The object dropped into the palm of his hand.

Marc reeled.

For a few moments, his legs would not carry him. He stumbled backward, smashing into the cold metal of a lamppost. He took deep, slow breaths, trying to regain his balance.

Don't panic. Take your time.

The street where he stood was empty, but all he had to do was shout out, and someone would hear him, come to him. No. He had to think rationally.

In spite of himself, his breathing accelerated, his throat tightened. Always the same symptoms, ever since he was two years old. Marc was agoraphobic.

Breathe slowly. Calm down.

Contrary to what many people think, agoraphobia is not a fear of large spaces or crowds. It is, quite simply, the fear of not being able to be saved. The fear of being afraid, one might say. This kind of panic normally occurs in places where the person feels isolated—a desert, a forest, a mountain, the sea—but also in the middle of a crowd, an amphitheater, a stadium. It is just as likely to happen in a street crammed full of people as in a deserted street.

Marc was used to it. He knew how to deal with it, as long as the feeling wasn't too intense. He rarely had attacks these days. He was able to attend lectures in crowded rooms, to take the metro, to go to rock concerts, and so on.

He took a deep breath.

Little by little, his breathing went back to normal. He was still leaning against the lamppost, in spite of the pain the metal cylinder was causing his back.

Marc looked down at his hand.

He was holding a miniature toy.

An airplane.

A replica Airbus A300, quite heavy—it was made of metal—and painted a milky white, except for its tail, which was red, white, and blue. The kind of toy you could find on the shelves of thousands of little boys' bedrooms. Marc's hand shook. His fingers closed over the cold fuselage.

What did this mean?

Was it a joke?

A macabre gift to accompany his reading of Grand-Duc's notebook?

Ridiculous...

Marc needed to think. Was this really all there had been in the package?

Marc fumbled inside his jeans pocket, and smoothed out the wrapping paper. He cursed his stupidity. Folded up in the paper that he had torn so recklessly was a small white page with writing on it. Marc immediately recognized Lylie's handwriting. Leaning back, he read:

Marc,

I have to leave. Don't be angry with me. This is something I always promised myself. That I would go away, when I turned eighteen. Go far, far away...to India, Africa, the Andes... or maybe—why not?—to Turkey. Don't worry. There is nothing to fear. I'm used to airplanes now, after all! I am strong.

I will survive. Again.

If I had told you about my plan, you wouldn't have agreed. But if you take the time to think about it, I am sure you will realize that I am right. We can't go on like this, not knowing. That is why I have to distance myself, Marc—from you. I have to take stock. To cut away the dead branches...

Marc, don't try to find me. Don't call me. Don't do anything. I need space, and time.

I believe this: that one day, we will know who we are, and what we are to each other.

Take care of yourself.

Emilie

*

Marc's breathing accelerated again. He forced himself to quell the swarm of questions massing in his head.

He needed to act. Do something.

He opened his backpack and shoved the miniature airplane inside, along with the letter and the wrapping paper. He took a breath, then grabbed his cell phone. Because he worked for France Telecom, he had been able to get the latest, state-of-the-art model—with automatic memorization of phone numbers—both for himself and for Lylie.

Without thinking, he scrolled through the list of names, stopped on Lylie's, and pressed the green circle. The screen cleared. The phone seemed to ring forever.

He was used to calling Lylie and her not replying. The answering machine always clicked in after the seventh ring. He counted in his head as he waited. After the fourth ring, he knew she wasn't going to pick up.

"Hello, this is Emilie. Leave me a message, and I'll call you back when I can. Bye…"

Marc swallowed. The sound of Lylie's voice brought tears to his eyes.

"Lylie, it's Marc. Please call me, wherever you are. Please, please call me back. I love you. More than ever. Come back to me."

Marc hung up. He walked slowly up the Avenue de Stalingrad, turning over Lylie's words in his mind.

"Far, far away…"

"Take stock…"

"Cut away the dead branches…"

What did it all mean?

Marc was not stupid. Lylie's eighteenth birthday was just a pretext. This whole situation was connected to

Grand-Duc's notebook—the notebook that Lylie had spent all night reading. What had she discovered? What had it made her think?

"Know who we are, and what we are to each other..."

No! Marc did not share Lylie's doubts. Nothing in the world could shake his conviction. It was absolute.

Marc reached Place du Général-Leclerc. Rows of buses crossed into Rue Gabriel-Peri and Avenue du Colonel-Fabien.

What could he do? How could he find Lylie? Follow her footsteps? Read the whole of Grand-Duc's notebook, and guess what Lylie must have guessed?

Marc cursed. He stood motionless as the buses came and went in front of him. The idea that he could just sit there and read the rest of that one-hundred-page notebook in the hope that he might find a clue seemed ridiculous. He picked up his cell phone again and scrolled down until he reached the letter W.

Work.

Marc moved away from the noisy square where he had been standing.

"Hello? Jennifer?...Great! This is Marc. Sorry about this, but I'm in a massive rush. I need information, for personal reasons. The telephone number of a guy in Paris. Are you writing this down? He's called Grand-Duc. Crédule Grand-Duc. Yeah, I know, not exactly a common name. So you shouldn't have any problem finding him..."

Jennifer, who worked with him at France Telecom, was the same age as Marc and was studying applied languages. Marc was pretty sure that, given a little nudge, she would have fallen for him. While he waited for her response, the phone still glued to his ear, he admired the bell tower of the Basilica of Saint-Denis that stood out, high above the buildings that lined the streets in between.

"Yeah? You've got it? Fantastic!"

Marc scribbled down Grand-Duc's phone number and address. He said a quick thank you to Jennifer, then immediately started dialing the private detective's number. It rang for a long time before another answering machine clicked on. Marc cursed inwardly. Never mind—he had to lay his cards on the table. There was no time to lose.

"Grand-Duc? It's Marc Vitral. Listen, I have to speak to you as soon as possible. Or better still, see you in person. It's about Lylie. And your notebook—the one you wrote for her. I'm holding it right now. She gave it to me and I'm reading it. So if you get this message, please call me back on my cell. I'm on my way to your place now: I'll be there in forty-five minutes at the latest."

Marc quickly strode back toward the metro station. Grand-Duc lived at 21 Rue de la Butte-aux-Cailles. In his head, Marc envisioned all the main lines on the metro map. Line 13, toward Châtillon-Montrouge, would take him into the center, past Saint-Lazare, the Champs-Elysées, Invalides, Montparnasse...Grand-Duc's street must be toward Nation, on Line 6, between Glacière and Place d'Italie. So, he would have to change at Montparnasse. About twenty stations in all.

Marc took the stairs down into the metro and as he turned the first corner, he noticed a man sleeping on a dirty sheet alongside his dog, a thin yellow mongrel. The man was not even begging. Without even breaking his stride, Marc dropped two francs on the sheet. The dog raised its head and watched him walk past, a surprised look on its face. After two years of using the Paris metro,

Marc still gave money almost every time he saw a home-less person. He had formed this habit in Dieppe, where his grandmother always gave money to people who lived on the streets. She had taught him these fundamental prin-ciples as he grew up: solidarity with his fellow man; never to be afraid of poor people; never to be ashamed of giving. This was still part of his moral landscape now, in Paris, just as it had been in Dieppe or would be in any other city in the world he might visit. Lylie gently teased him for the amount of money his principles cost him. No Parisian would do that, she said. True, but he wasn't a Parisian.

The metro platform was almost deserted. Some good luck at last, thought Marc. Forty-five minutes on the metro, twenty stations...he would have time to read more of Grand-Duc's notebook, and that might help him to under-stand what was going on, to walk in Lylie's footsteps.

But five words haunted Marc: "Cut away the dead branches..."

What did she mean?

Cut away the dead branches.

The train entered the station. Marc got on board and took out the green notebook.

An idea had become lodged in his brain, and he couldn't stop thinking about it: What if the toy airplane had been nothing but a decoy, a form of misdirection? Lylie had not told him everything. What about that ring, for instance? The sapphire she was wearing: Where had that come from? There were too many unknowns.

What if Lylie did not intend to go far away, after all? What if she was still here, close to him, with another goal in mind?

To distance herself from him.

Why?

Because she was going to do something risky, something dangerous.

Because it was something he would not have agreed to.

Cut away the dead branches…

What if Lylie had discovered the truth and was now out for revenge?

12

Crédule Grand-Duc's Journal

The advantage of dealing with journalists from the regional press is that they rarely break stories before the Parisian press. Even when the events take place in their backyard, a Parisian newspaper is usually alerted before the regionals, arrives before them, and scoops the interviews with the main protagonists in time for the evening news. So, when a regional paper gets hold of a story with national appeal, it does not do things by halves. It milks the story for all it is worth.

Fifteen minutes after Pierre Vitral's telephone call, a journalist from *Informations Dieppoises,* the local weekly paper, was sent to their house in Rue Pocholle. The *Est Républicain* belonged to the same media group, so Lucile Moraud had opted for the fastest solution. The freelance journalist's mission was to extract the main story, take the first pictures, and fax everything over to the company's headquarters in Nancy. Lucile Moraud was already negotiating her scoop with the regional television channels, FR3-Franche-Comté and FR3-Haute-Normandie, aiming to squeeze the maximum number of sales out of

tomorrow's edition of the newspaper. The strategy was to
tantalize the public with a few details on television that
evening, so that they would want to read the full, exclusive
interview with the Vitrals on page 2 of the *Est Républicain*
the following morning.

The brief bulletins on regional television were taken
up that evening by the nationals. A team from TF1 even
caught Léonce de Carville on his driveway, in Coupvray,
before his lawyers had time to interpose themselves and
tell him to say nothing more. His words threw oil on the
media fire.

No, he did not deny it.

Yes, he had offered money to the Vitral family.

Yes, he was absolutely convinced that the miracle child
was his granddaughter, Lyse-Rose. He had acted out of
pure generosity toward the Vitrals, or pity—the two sentiments intricately interlinked to him. God, of course, had
been kind to his family. He could not behave otherwise.

The next day—February 19, 1981—he went even further, announcing live on the ten o'clock news: "If there
is any doubt about the identity of the child, if the truth is
uncertain, then obviously the judge is going to make his
decision based on the child's best interests. If it were possible, the baby would make the decision herself. And, if that
were the case, who could possibly doubt that this infant
would choose the future I am offering her, rather than that
offered by the Vitral family?"

Through working on this case, I have learned how the
media operates. It is like a giant snowball thrown down a
mountainside, and once it starts rolling, no one can control its direction or velocity. If you remember anything

at all about the "Dragonfly" case, then this is almost certainly the moment that would stick in your memory; the few weeks that preceded the judgment. Between February and March 1981, it was—with the obvious exception of the presidential election campaign—*the* dominant news story. France was divided in two. It was, in the crudest possible terms, a battle between the rich and the poor. So two unequal sides. If you split France in two along the line of the average salary, there are far more people below that line than above it, therefore the vast majority of French people supported the cause of the Vitral family. They made frequent appearances on television, the radio, and in the newspapers and it was sensational: a soap opera with an unscripted ending.

De Carville had to shoulder the role of the villain. Around this time, the American series *Dallas* had just started screening in France. Léonce de Carville did not resemble J. R. Ewing in any physical sense, but the parallel was unmissable. And, as in the series, there was every chance that the bad guy was going to win.

Suspense. Emotion.

Perhaps you were supporting one side or the other back then.

I wasn't. At the time, I couldn't have cared less about the "Dragonfly" case. In February 1981, I was still busy with the casino affair; I had moved from the Basque coast to the Côte d'Azur and the Italian Riviera. I spent my whole life in my car, on stakeout: a boring job with ever-diminishing returns. I do remember catching a brief glimpse of a TV program—some sort of reality show before such things were invented—late one night while I was relaxing in my hotel room. Nicole Vitral was being interviewed. It was

she who had increasingly taken over the family's dealings
with the media. Pierre Vitral may have set the machine in
motion, but it had left him behind and now he shunned the
cameras. Given the choice, he might well have called a halt
to the entire media circus and let justice take its course,
even at the risk of losing.

Nicole Vitral must have been about forty-seven at the
time. She was a young grandmother, not really beautiful
in the classical sense of the term, but undeniably what the
media might call a hot property. She radiated a sort of
infectious energy. Her cause was a crusade, and she was
its saint, its martyr, preaching with a disarming directness
and an inimitable Caux accent. She was sincere, honest,
moving, funny, and extremely telegenic. Her face—gaunt
and ravaged from years of working in the salty winds of
the Manche—did not stand up particularly well to close-
ups, but she was a strong woman. And as I sat in front of
my television screen that night, knowing nothing about the
case or this woman's crusade, I felt deeply aroused by her.
Physically, I mean.

I certainly wasn't the only one. She had those blue
eyes, sparkling with life, defying fate and all the misery it
had thrown at her. But most of all, she had those breasts.
Nicole Vitral always tended to wear clothes—low-cut
dresses or open-necked blouses—that showcased her generous bust. This had undoubtedly helped increase the sales
of sausages on the beach at Dieppe. And to spice things up,
she also almost always wore a cardigan or a jacket, which
she kept pulling shut to cover her exposed flesh. I have had
the opportunity to observe her on many occasions since
then, and it has become one of her nervous habits, a reflex.
You are talking to her and, inevitably, your eyes drift

downward, if only for the briefest of moments. Almost instantaneously, Nicole Vitral will reach for her lapels and wrap them around her, only for them to fall open again a few seconds later.

It is a strangely arousing routine that I have always found irresistible.

On television, the effect was even more perverse, because the viewer was given an almost godlike view: we could see the curtain of her jacket falling open to expose that opulent chest, and the cameraman slowly, suggestively zooming in toward it, while Nicole failed to notice this invasion of her privacy.

Nicole Vitral, with her unusual charms, and perhaps without even realizing it herself, had a troubling effect on millions of Frenchmen that February in 1981. And her charm worked on me, too, that night, although I would not meet her in person for another few months. In fact, she has had a troubling effect on me for the last eighteen years. She troubles me still, at nearly sixty-five years of age. My age, in other words, almost to the month.

As you will have guessed, the Vitrals' case suddenly became much more winnable. The best lawyers in France—at least those who had not already been hired by the de Carvilles—offered their services. Gratis, naturally. There was so much publicity surrounding the case, and public opinion was firmly weighted toward them. It was a godsend.

The first task for the Vitrals' new, influential, media-friendly lawyers was to wage a guerrilla war against Judge Le Drian. They suspected him of partiality because Le Drian and the de Carvilles belonged to the same world.

The Lions Club, the Rotary Club, the Freemasons, din-
ners with the ambassador... all of this was mentioned,
along with some rather unsubtle and ignoble insinuations.
Finally, the Ministry of Justice gave in to the pressure.
Judge Le Drian offered his resignation on April 1, and a
new judge was appointed: Judge Weber, a star of the court
in Strasbourg; a small, honest figure who wore glasses,
somewhere between Eliot Ness and Woody Allen; a man
whose integrity was never questioned afterward, not even
by the de Carvilles.

The hearing began on April 4. No matter what happened,
it would all be over within a month and the judge would
have to choose. The two parties had agreed to avoid any
compromise solution, so, the judge would definitively
not recommend a dual identity, or a shared-parenting
arrangement—school terms with one family, holidays
with another, that sort of thing. The hearing would not
give birth to a monster with two names. Whatever happened, Lylie would exist no longer. She would be Emilie
or Lyse-Rose.

Judge Weber simply had to decide who had survived
and who had perished. I have wondered about this question ever since: Has any other judge ever been given such
power, to kill a child so that another may live? To be at
once savior and executioner? One family would win, the
other would lose everything. It was better this way; everyone agreed.

Just make a decision.

Fine. But based on what?

I have been through the investigation file dozens of
times. I have read the hundreds of pages that Judge Weber

read. I have listened over and over again to the recordings
of the hearing: I was given access to the recordings years
later, thanks to the de Carvilles.

What a lot of hot air! Experts asserting one thing, and
another bunch of experts contradicting them. The hearing
came down to a battle of words between the experts called
by each side, none of them impartial. The impartial experts
had nothing to say. After days and days of questions and
statements, it boiled down to the same thing: the baby had
blue eyes... like the Vitrals. The Vitrals were leading on
points, but only just, and then at the last moment, the de
Carvilles' lawyers discovered a distant cousin with pale
blue eyes, so we were back to square one.

Judge Weber should have kept a coin in his pocket,
should have been weighing it constantly during those
interminable sessions in court.

Léonce de Carville's lawyers devoted all their time and
energy to erasing the memory of their client's disastrous
media outing, altering the way he was perceived by the
public. They were not wholly successful, but this strategy
did bring results. They launched public attacks on what
they called the "Vitral clan," which implicated not only
the family, but the neighborhood in which they lived, the
entire region.

At war with the clan, snubbed by public opinion, Léonce
de Carville ultimately stood alone, with his dignity, his
principles, his morality. His lawyers somehow succeeded
in making him look like the victim of a witch hunt, a noble
individual torn to pieces by the mob; they cast him in the
role of the tough but honest man, who had fought tirelessly
all his life to achieve success, never allowing himself to
relax, to be a grandfather, a "Papa."

This was the picture of Léonce de Carville that emerged from the hearing and was made public through the words of the watching journalists: the great man humbled and humiliated by a crowd of pygmies. Naturally, people began to doubt their convictions: What if, after all, de Carville *was* telling the truth? What if we have let ourselves be manipulated by the Vitrals' media circus, by the poverty that they displayed so immodestly, by Nicole Vitral's large breasts?

Léonce de Carville's lawyers knew exactly what they were doing.

The whole issue was heading inexorably toward a draw. In spite of the urgency, the possibility of extra time was looming, followed by a penalty shoot-out that might never end.

That was the situation when, on the last day of the hearing, the youngest of the Vitrals' lawyers entered the fray. Maître Leguerne is now a highly renowned and successful lawyer in Paris, with a three-story office on Rue Saint-Honoré. But back then, in 1981, he was a complete unknown. He was one of those lawyers working for the Vitrals for free. The moral being: defending penniless orphans and widows can end up earning you big bucks.

Leguerne had prepared his coup meticulously. He had asked Judge Weber if he could have the final word in the hearing, as if he were about to pull a crucial piece of evidence from his sleeve at the very last minute...

13

Saint-Lazare

A sudden noise made Marc turn his head. The doors of the
compartment opened and the crowd of people waiting on the
platform surged into the previously half-empty train. It was
not quite the sardine-like crush of rush hour, but all the same
the density of bodies forced Marc to stand up. His seat banged
shut. He stepped back into the corner, his back pressed against
the window, and settled into position with his legs slightly
apart so he could keep his balance. A man's hand, holding onto
one of the metal bars, jutted just under his nose, while with the
other hand the man held a paperback thriller, which he was
reading avidly. Marc turned away slightly, so he could keep
reading his own mystery. As the train shook him from side
to side, Grand-Duc's tiny handwriting danced before his eyes.

Crédule Grand-Duc's Journal

Maître Leguerne took the stand. There were about thirty
people in court that day—April 22, 1981—including the two

families, lawyers, various witnesses, and the police. Leguerne addressed himself first of all to the policemen in the room:

"Gentlemen," he asked, "was the miracle child wearing any kind of jewelry when she was discovered? A necklace, for example? Or a bracelet, perhaps?"

The policemen looked shocked. Superintendent Vatelier, sitting in the front row, coughed into his beard. No, of course not. As if the baby might have been wearing a bracelet around her wrist spelling out *Lyse-Rose* or *Emilie*... What point was this smartass young lawyer trying to make?

"All right," said Leguerne. "Mrs. Vitral, did little Emilie ever wear jewelry of any kind, such as a bracelet or a small chain?"

"None at all," Nicole Vitral replied.

"Are you certain of that?"

"Yes..." Nicole Vitral swallowed a sob, then continued: "Yes. We were supposed to give Emilie a bracelet for her christening, after the family came back from Turkey. We had already ordered it from Lecerf, in Offranville, but she never got the chance to wear it."

Nicole bent over, rummaged in her handbag for a few moments, then took out a long red jewelry box, which she held out for Judge Weber to see. She opened it and into her palm spilled a tiny silver chain.

A wave of emotion ran through the people in the courtroom, including the de Carville camp.

Emilie was engraved on the nameplate in italics—in a childlike, cheerful calligraphy—as well as the date of her birth: *September 30, 1980*.

As Nicole Vitral admitted to me afterward, this was a setup. The christening really had been booked for the following month, but no bracelet had yet been ordered. It was just a clever piece of theater, risky but effective. A preparatory move, before dealing the death blow.

The young lawyer then turned toward Léonce de Carville.

"Mr. de Carville, did Lyse-Rose have any jewelry—a bracelet, for example?"

De Carville shot a worried look at his lawyers but Judge Weber insisted: "Please answer Maître Leguerne's question, Mr. de Carville."

Léonce de Carville was about to open his mouth, but Leguerne did not give him time. Triumphantly, he pulled from his thick red file the photocopy of a receipt from the famous and extremely expensive jeweler Philippe Tournaire, on Place Vendôme.

Judge Weber confirmed the contents of the paper. The receipt made explicit mention of the delivery of a solid gold chain bracelet. It stated that the name "Lyse-Rose" and the date of birth—September 27, 1980—had been hand-engraved on the bracelet. The receipt was dated October 2, 1980—less than a week after Lyse-Rose's birth.

This proved nothing, absolutely nothing at all. But for the first time since the hearing began, de Carville was on the defensive, without a counterargument meticulously prepared for him by his legal team.

"Mr. de Carville," Leguerne continued, "did Lyse-Rose usually wear this bracelet?"

"How should I know? I sent it to my son in Turkey, just after Lyse-Rose's birth. But I imagine he would only put it on her for special occasions. It was a bracelet of great value."

"You imagine? Or you know?"

"I imagine..."

"All right. Thank you."

Maître Leguerne produced another photocopy from his red file—this time of a postcard sent from Ceyhan, in Turkey.

"Mr. de Carville, did you receive this card from your son about a month after Lyse-Rose's birth?"

"Where did you get that?" Léonce de Carville yelled.

"Did you receive this postcard?" the lawyer asked again, impassive.

"Yes, of course," de Carville admitted. He had no choice.

"'Dear Dad,'" Leguerne began to read. "I will skip over the details to the part that interests us. 'Thank you for the bracelet. You must have paid a fortune for it—it is magnificent. Lyse-Rose never takes it off...It is the only truly French thing she possesses'..."

Leguerne went silent, triumphant amid the general air of astonishment.

I never found out who betrayed the de Carvilles. Probably one of their domestic staff. Leguerne must have paid a handsome price for that postcard. Then again, everything is relative. However much he paid, you can be sure it was nothing like the value of a three-story building on Rue Saint-Honoré.

"This proves nothing!" one of the de Carvilles' lawyers shouted. "It's ridiculous! The bracelet could have been stowed away for safekeeping before the journey. It could have been torn from her wrist during the crash..."

Smiling, Leguerne asked: "Was a bracelet or any other kind of jewelry found near the Airbus, in that area of ground which was searched so diligently?"

Everyone in the courtroom was silent, including Vatelier, who was shocked at having been beaten to the punch in the investigation by an ambitious young man in a black robe.

"No, of course not. Isn't that right, Superintendent? Were there any signs on the baby's wrist of a bracelet having been torn from it? Was there even the faintest red mark?"

A well-timed pause.

"No. The doctors found no marks on her at all. Let us go further... Was there an area, a line, on the baby's wrist that was slightly paler than the surrounding skin? A little less suntanned? The type of mark that is usually left by a piece of jewelry that is never taken off..."

Time seemed to stand still.

"No, there was no mark of any kind. Thank you. I rest my case."

Maître Leguerne went back to his seat. Léonce de Carville's lawyers reiterated loudly and repeatedly that this *coup de théâtre* was nothing of the sort, that the bracelet's existence was insignificant. Leguerne did not reply. He knew perfectly well that, the more the opposing lawyers argued, the greater weight would be given to the question he had raised.

If the bracelet was unimportant, why had de Carville never mentioned it to the police?

In hindsight, this question about the bracelet looks no more or less important than any of the other evidence. Just one more doubt. But at that particular moment in the trial, the bracelet was transformed into a decisive proof against the de Carvilles' case. A new piece of evidence, something the courtroom had been waiting for since the hearing began. So, however tenuous, however slight, this new piece of evidence was enough to tip the balance.

Judge Weber looked at Léonce de Carville for a long time. The industrialist had lied. It was a lie of omission, admittedly, but a lie all the same. He had been caught red-handed. For that alone, in the absence of any more compelling reason, shouldn't the law take the side of the opposing party?

If in doubt...

As for the de Carvilles' bracelet, it would haunt me for many years to come. When I think now of how much energy I spent on searching for it, tracking its long journey... When I think of how close I came to getting my hands on it... But please forgive me, I am getting ahead of myself again.

Judge Weber's decision was announced a few hours later. The miracle child of Mont Terrible was Emilie Vitral. Her grandparents Pierre and Nicole Vitral became her legal guardians, as well as the legal guardians of her elder brother, Marc.

Lyse-Rose de Carville was dead, burned alive with her parents in the cabin of the Airbus 5403 from Istanbul to Paris.

Léonce de Carville's lawyers wanted to appeal, to take the case all the way to the High Court, but it was de Carville himself who refused. His role as the noble victim, the broken man, was no longer just a stance.

The two heart attacks he suffered the following year, with only a few months in between, which left him more or less a vegetable in a wheelchair for the rest of his life, seemed the logical conclusion to the affair.

14

"Hide Grand-Duc's body!"

Mathilde de Carville's tone brooked no argument.

Nevertheless, Malvina de Carville did attempt to protest.

"But, Grandma..." she said into the telephone.

"Hide his body now, I said! Doesn't matter where. In a closet, under a bed. We need to play for time. Anyone could come to his house. A neighbor, his cleaning lady, his mistress... Sooner or later, the police will turn up. I bet you've left fingerprints all over the place, haven't you, you little fool? You have to wipe them all away."

Malvina bit her lip. Her grandmother was right: she had behaved like an idiot. She was standing in the living room, just between the detective's corpse and the vivarium, where the insects were still dying. She knew she had to remove her fingerprints, but she could not stay here too long: she needed to tell her grandmother this.

He was on his way.

"Grandma, there's something else..."

On the other end of the line, Mathilde de Carville was

silent for a moment. She was holding the receiver with one hand while continuing to prune her roses with the other.

"What is it, Malvina?"

"Marc Vitral called Grand-Duc's house. About five minutes ago, if that. He left a message on the answering machine."

Mathilde de Carville cut a branch off with a precise clip of her shears.

"Marc says he wants to see Grand-Duc. He'll be here in half an hour. He's coming on the metro. It's about Lyse-Rose. And…and he says that he has Grand-Duc's notebook. Lyse-Rose read it yesterday. She gave it to him this morning…"

Another rose branch fell, cut off at its base. Wilted petals rained down over Mathilde de Carville's black dress.

"All the more reason to hurry, Malvina. Do what I told you to do—clean up every trace of your presence, and then get out of there."

"And then what, Grandma?"

For the first time, Mathilde de Carville hesitated. To what extent could she use Malvina? To what extent could she keep her under control? Without risking another mistake…

"Stay close by, Malvina. Marc Vitral doesn't know you. Hide in the street somewhere. Watch him, follow him. But don't do anything else. Telephone me as soon as you see him. You understand, don't you? Don't do anything other than what I've told you. And, most important, hide that body immediately!"

"I understand, Grandma."

They hung up.

The steel jaws closed and a severed branch fell to the ground.

Mathilde de Carville knew all about Malvina's hatred for the Vitral family. She was also well aware that her granddaughter was walking the streets carrying a loaded Mauser L110, and it was in perfect working order: that, unfortunately, had been confirmed in the most terrible way. Was it really reasonable of her to allow the possibility of Malvina and Marc Vitral meeting on Rue de la Butte-aux-Cailles, in front of Grand-Duc's house?

Reasonable!

Mathilde de Carville had banned that word a long time ago.

The simplest course of action would be to leave it up to fate, to God's judgment. As she always did.

Mathilde smiled to herself and continued pruning the roses with a surprising dexterity. Her long fingers had the strange ability to hold the branches, between the thorns, without ever being pricked, twisting them with a firm movement toward the sharp blades. Mathilde de Carville worked quickly, methodically, hardly even looking down at her hands, the way a dressmaker sews with her eyes elsewhere.

Her elegant black dress was dirty with soil, blades of grass and rose petals. Mathilde de Carville was unconcerned. She turned her face toward the vast park of the Roseraie villa. Léonce de Carville was sitting in his wheelchair, in the middle of the lawn, under the large maple tree. His head had fallen sideways. He was a hundred feet away from her, yet Mathilde could still hear him snoring. She thought about calling Linda, the nurse, to tell her to go and straighten his head, place a cushion under his neck...she could take him back to the house, too: it wasn't very warm anymore.

Then she shrugged. What was the point?

Her husband had sunk into this vegetative state nearly seventeen years ago. He had managed, with great difficulty, to recover from the first heart attack, but the second one had been too much. It had struck in the middle of the annual general meeting, on the seventh floor of their head office, near Bercy. The emergency services had managed to save his life, but his brain had been deprived of oxygen for too long.

Mathilde continued examining her plants while observing the shadow of the cross she wore around her neck as it moved over the ground.

God's judgment. Once again.

In the aftermath of the disaster on Mont Terri, her husband had wanted to do everything himself, as usual. And obediently, she had let him. After all, he was the powerful one, the one with all the right connections...

How wrong she had been. After the death of their only son, Alexandre, Léonce had lost his clarity of vision. He had made so many mistakes! The briefcase stuffed full of cash that he had offered to the Vitrals; the bracelet he had refused to mention to the police; poor little Malvina, dragged around by him for weeks so she could testify left, right, and center.

Not to mention the rest. The shameful secrets.

Mathilde felt nothing but contempt for her invalid husband. After all these years, the Airbus accident was practically the only thing for which she didn't blame him.

Mathilde's fingers flew from branch to branch. The roses' thorns offered no resistance and the stems fell one after another.

Of course, it had been his personal project, that famous Baku–Tbilisi–Ceyhan pipeline. Sending her only son to live in Turkey for months on end, with his pregnant wife, forcing their granddaughter to be born in a foreign country...And all for nothing. Now, in 1998, not one single length of that damn pipeline had been laid.

Léonce de Carville had gotten everything wrong.

She watched with disgust as the maple leaves fell onto her husband, dozens of them, covering his hair, his shoulders, his arms, piling up between his legs.

Mathilde chopped off one last branch and stood back, contemplating her work. The dozen rose plants had been pruned to within an inch of their lives. Mathilde remembered the advice given to her by her own grandmother: "You can never prune a rose too much; prune them as much as you can, and then prune them some more; fight the plant's desire to make you raise your clippers, and insist on pushing them lower. Always prune three inches lower than you think you need to."

The Roseraie villa dated from 1857: the year was still engraved in the granite above the porch. Mathilde knew that the roses had been planted that same year, and that the de Carville family had personally looked after them ever since. Dozens of people were employed by the family—to tidy the house, cook the meals, mow the lawn, polish the pots and pans, clean the windows, and guard the property—but for generations, the de Carvilles had looked after the rose garden themselves. Mathilde had been introduced to the art of gardening as soon as she was old enough to walk. In addition to looking after the rose plants, she had also planted a winter garden, not far from the villa. She took one last admiring look at the pruned plants and then, without even glancing at her husband, walked toward the greenhouse.

She thought again of Malvina's last words. So, Grand-Duc's notes, the legacy of his eighteen-year investigation, were in the hands of Marc Vitral...

The irony...

Should she use Malvina to recover the book? Should she continue lying to her, maintain the girl's illusions? All the evidence she had obtained since the accident, all that evidence provided by Grand-Duc...she had never mentioned any of it to Malvina. It would have killed her.

Mathilde entered the greenhouse and stood there for a long time, as she did every morning, inhaling the wonderful blend of aromas. This was her haven. Her life's work. It was here, in this greenhouse, that she felt closest to God, to His creation. It was here that she was best able to pray, much more so than in any church.

Malvina...

Her poor, mad granddaughter.

That, too, was her husband's fault. She remembered what a lovely little girl Malvina had been at six years old. She remembered her laughter on the staircase, the cunning hiding places she found in the garden, her wonder-filled eyes as she sat with her grandmother and leafed through the herbarium...But what could she do for Malvina now, apart from lie to her? Put her in a psychiatric hospital? Malvina's obsession was the only thing that made her get up in the mornings, made her dress, eat: Lyse-Rose was alive, she had survived, in spite of the judge's decision eighteen years earlier, and she alone, her big sister, could bring her back to life, even after all these years.

Bring her back to life with a Mauser L110 in her hands...

Mathilde de Carville bent down near a bunch of Kaffir

lilies, one of the last plants to flower in autumn. Every year, Mathilde managed to keep them alive in her greenhouse until December; it was a matter of great pride to her, the bouquet on the table on Christmas Eve, a mixture of rose lilies and Kaffir lilies. Mathilde maintained a tight control over the level of water in the soil: adequate moisture was the secret to her lilies' radiance and longevity.

Her mind wandered once again to Malvina, her own weapon of vengeance. Well, someone had to defend the de Carvilles' interests. Why not Malvina?

Things were going to change in the coming hours and days. Now that Lylie had read Grand-Duc's notebook, Malvina was no longer the only time bomb walking the streets. Grand-Duc's birthday present had been a poisoned chalice. The film of her life. All the family secrets revealed in a hundred pages.

Two families. Twice the pain.

Enough to make Lylie go mad, too—mad with rage.

Mathilde moved farther into the greenhouse. The "Red September" asters in her winter garden were losing their last petals, a few purple sunbeams clinging to the golden core...

A curious image suddenly entered Mathilde's mind. Almost like a dream, or a premonition. She pictured Lylie entering the Roseraie, armed with a revolver—a Mauser L110—her finger poised on the trigger. She was walking softly across the lawn.

And Lylie would have good reason to seek revenge, if Grand-Duc had told all in his notebook. Mathilde smiled to herself. One question nagged at her. Would the finger on that trigger be adorned with her ring? The pale sapphire ring with inlaid diamonds...

Gradually, the image faded. Under her breath, Mathilde whispered: "Happy birthday, Lylie."

If only she had known, she would never have hired Crédule Grand-Duc to carry out his stupid investigation.

Mathilde walked on, turning back to check that she was still alone. She was. No one was watching her through the windows of the greenhouse. She leaned over her secret garden and pushed aside the irises to reveal a few discreet stems and the small yellow flowers of the greater celandine. Mathilde enjoyed looking at the four golden petals, arranged in a cross—"swallow-wort," as it used to be called—but she preferred the celandine's other side: the four petals concealed a fatal poison, perhaps the most toxic plant of all, with the unique concentration of alkaloids concealed within its sap.

Her guilty pleasure. Her little weakness.

God forgive her.

She turned around and left the greenhouse. Léonce de Carville was still sitting there, motionless except for the regular trembling of his body. A dead tree, with a twisted trunk.

Mathilde's gaze took in the entire property: the rose garden, the villa, the park...

Perhaps all was not yet lost. Their name, breeding, honor.

Lyse-Rose.

She was starting to think like Malvina.

One last hope did remain: that telephone call from Grand-Duc the night before, the last call he made before his death. He claimed to have discovered a new piece of evidence that called into question all his previous convictions. He told her this eureka moment had come two days earlier, in the final minutes of his contract, supposedly as he was reading the *Est Républicain*.

Was she naive enough to believe him? Was she stupid enough to be taken in by such an obvious bluff?

Grand-Duc had not wanted to say any more; he said that he wanted to check a few final details. She thought again about Malvina and her Mauser. Grand-Duc had acted like someone out of a detective novel, the kind of witness who withholds information in search of a reward, but ends up with a bullet through his heart instead.

And yet, in spite of everything, Mathilde could not help believing Grand-Duc's last words.

A way out. A final hope.

And, as always in this case, fate hung in the balance. For one family to be given hope, the other must be offered despair.

15

Miromesnil.

Champs-Elysées–Clemenceau.

The stations rushed past. With each one, the compartment became emptier. The train would speed up abruptly, only to slow down almost immediately, like a blind sprinter.

A pretty girl got on at Invalides. For a moment, Marc thought it was Lylie, with her slender figure and her blond hair. But only for a moment. The metro was crawling with pretty blondes. And neither chance nor his whining messages on Lylie's answering machine would help him find her. The only thing that would help was an attentive reading of this notebook.

Crédule Grand-Duc's Journal

An official letter containing Judge Weber's decision was delivered to the Vitrals' mailbox, on Rue Pocholle, on the morning of May 11, 1981. The previous night, Dieppe's vast seafront had been transformed into the scene of one gigantic party. Everyone had sung, drunk, laughed, danced barefoot on the grass. Dieppe, the Red City, the workers' port, the town devastated by the gradual closure of all its factories, had celebrated the election of François Mitterrand to the French presidency the way other towns celebrate Bastille Day. Finally, the Left was in power. Finally, there were Communists in the government. *Change*: the word was on everyone's lips. The grand old lady of French seaside towns had donned her ball gown for one night only, and it suited her to perfection.

Pierre and Nicole Vitral took part in the celebration, in their own way. They had been waiting for this—fighting for it, marching in support of it, distributing pamphlets—for a generation. Their van stayed open almost all night, selling champagne and cider along with their usual fare of crêpes, waffles, and other snacks. But the Vitrals had not been able to abandon themselves wholly to the city's joy. They were waiting for the judge's letter, the final decision; they still feared that the de Carvilles would appeal, that some last-minute development would arise. They had not wanted to celebrate such an incredible victory until the official document was in their hands and they could hold little Emilie (who was still being kept at the nursery in Montbéliard) in their arms.

They didn't dare believe it.

But, then again, who—even in Dieppe—had truly believed that the Left would win the election?

It was about eight in the morning when Pierre opened the judge's letter. His hands were trembling. He had slept for only two hours that night. Judge Weber's letter left no room for doubt. The name of the sole survivor of the Mont Terri crash was Emilie Vitral. Her paternal grandparents were now her legal guardians. They could go to Montbé-liard to fetch her that very morning.

In Pollet, there was still plenty of champagne and food to be shared around. The celebrations would continue.

The tenth and eleventh of May, 1981, were the most wonderful days of their lives.

Mathilde de Carville waited until darkness fell before she approached the Vitrals' van. She had watched patiently while the last customers were served. She had also made sure that Nicole Vitral was alone: her husband was in Pollet, for the district meeting—as he was every Wednes-day evening. He was thinking seriously about running for local office. It was a warm May night, though windy, as always.

Mathilde de Carville made her move on May 13, 1981, exactly two days after the euphoria. It is not easy for me to write impartially about her, as you will soon understand. If the portrait I paint of her does not seem objective, you must at least believe in my sincerity.

Mathilde had trusted in her husband all the way through the hearing; in her husband and in God. Until that point, she had never had cause to complain about God—or her husband, for that matter. Born into an aristocratic family in Angers that had moved to the chic Parisian suburb of Coupvray, she was a gracious, intelligent, humane young woman, with a dash of malice à la Romy Schneider. In her early twenties, Mathilde was admired, envied, courted... but not for long. She put her trust in God, fell in love with the first man heaven set in her path, and swore eternal fidelity to him. This was Léonce, a brilliant, ambitious, and penniless young engineer. Little by little, the engineer destroyed every gracious and humane impulse Mathilde had in her. But if God had willed it thus . . .

With Mathilde came a dowry of inestimable value: her family name. Mathilde de Carville. A name redolent of privilege and noble blood. Léonce took his wife's name, which is, of course, rather unusual. In order for a husband to do that, you need a genealogical tree that goes all the way back to Saint Louis. So, Mathilde gave her husband her name, along with the several million francs in French treasury bonds that he needed to found the de Carville company. Léonce's industrial genius did the rest: hence the company's commercial success, the huge profits, the legal patents, the subsidiaries all around the world. Up to that point, Mathilde must have believed that her name had been wisely invested.

When God took her son, Alexandre, from her in that plane crash, Mathilde did not doubt. That might seem strange to you, but years of experience have taught me that misfortune tends to intensify religious belief rather than shake it. Divine injustice causes not revolt, but submission, just as punishment leads to obedience. Mathilde took the veil and atoned for her sins—only God knew what they were. She trusted in God's justice, and in the justice of men.

However, when Judge Weber decreed the death of her granddaughter, Mathilde doubted for the first time. Not in God, of course, but she lost her belief in the justice of men. Her belief in her husband, too.

Her faith changed. It was no longer simply contemplative, passive, submissive. Mathilde had now become aware that she was God's representative on Earth, that her faith was her strength, her weapon. It gave her direction, a divine mission. She knew she had to act.

I know where this kind of thinking can lead. All over the world, people are busy killing each other on behalf of gods that never asked them to do a thing. I had a taste of that in another life, before I became a private detective.

Happily for Mathilde, her transformation went smoothly. She simply believed that some men were deaf to the word of God, and that the reason the Almighty had given her so much money was not to undermine His decision, but so that she might use it to change the order of things.

Filled with these new convictions, Mathilde de Carville made two decisions. The first was that she would go to see Nicole Vitral, that May evening on the seafront in Dieppe; a meeting that Nicole Vitral still remembered in astonishing detail when I met her twenty months later.

Nicole Vitral was instinctively cautious when she saw Mathilde de Carville arrive. The two women had seen each other, sized each other up, during the hearing. Now everything had changed. Nicole Vitral knew her rights. Emilie was her granddaughter. No one, not even a de Carville, could take that away from her. For that reason, and that reason only, she agreed to hear what Mathilde de Carville had to say.

Mathilde stood in front of the Citroën van. Nicole, standing inside the vehicle, was a good seven inches taller than she was. Mathilde's voice was emotionless.

"Madame Vitral, I will get straight to the point. Some bereavements are harder to bear than others. As I'm sure you will realize, Judge Weber's verdict was like a death penalty for us. In giving life to one child, he has killed another."

Nicole Vitral looked irritated, as if all she wanted to do was close the metal shutter and leave it there.

Mathilde raised her voice slightly: "No, no, please hear me out. You see, today, so soon after the verdict, we don't realize what it will be like. You have a baby to look after. Lyse-Rose is still fresh in our memory. But in five, ten, twenty years? Lyse-Rose will never have existed, never have played, never have gone to school. Emilie will exist; she will live. The crash will be forgotten, and so will the agonizing doubt. She will be, forever, Emilie Vitral, and even if she wasn't really Emilie Vitral, that is who she will become. No one will care anymore about what happened just after her birth."

A gust of cold wind made the orange-and-red canvas awning flap noisily against the van. Nicole Vitral felt embarrassed, ill at ease, but she did not interrupt.

"Nicole... May I call you Nicole? Yes, some bereavements are harder to bear. I will never have a gravestone where I can leave flowers, no slab of marble with her name engraved on it. Because if I did that, Nicole, if I grieved for Lyse-Rose as if she were dead, if I prayed for her soul, I would be a monster! Because I would be burying someone who is, perhaps, alive..."

"Here we go!" said Nicole Vitral coldly.

"No, Nicole, you don't understand. Hear me out before you judge me. I do not want to take Emilie away from you. It's all quite simple from your perspective. If she really is your granddaughter, then everything has worked out perfectly. If she is not yours, then you will raise her like an adopted child. The uncertainty no longer matters to you. But for me, that uncertainty, that doubt..."

"What is your point?" Nicole demanded. She had grown in confidence since this case began, through her dealings with the media, the lawyers, the police. In the same loud voice, she said: "Do you want the child to call you 'granny'? To phone you from time to time? You want to invite her on the first Sunday of each month for biscuits and tea?"

Mathilde de Carville did not bat an eyelid.

"There is no need to be cruel, Nicole. Lyse-Rose is dead. But inevitably, you must be feeling the same way I do. That sweet little baby you love so much, you will call her Emilie, but deep down, you will never know. Neither of us will. Life has trapped us."

Nicole sighed. "All right, go on. What do you want?"

"All I want is to be able to help this child. If she is Lyse-Rose, then my conscience will be clear. If she is Emilie, well... good for her."

Nicole Vitral leaned over the counter and stared at Mathilde de Carville. "What do you mean by help? You mean seeing her?"

"No... I think it's better if she doesn't know about me. I don't know if you intend to tell Emilie about this business at some point, but I believe it would be better for her if she remained unaware of it for as long as possible. I have no desire to watch her as she comes out of school in the afternoons. To see her grow up through a windshield, hoping to spot some resemblance to my son. That is not my style. I couldn't bear it."

Mathilde gave a strange, uncharacteristic laugh.

"No, Nicole, the rich have more radical ways of easing their conscience."

"Money, you mean?"

"Yes, money. Don't get on your high horse, Nicole. I'm not trying to buy the child, like my husband did. This is not a bribe or a negotiation. It is simply a gift, to her. I ask for nothing in exchange."

Nicole was about to reply but Mathilde did not give her time.

"Don't refuse, Nicole. You have Emilie—you've won. I am not trying to buy you. I am not buying anything. Just think about it: why refuse Emilie this money, this windfall?"

"I haven't refused it," Nicole said coldly. "Nor have I accepted it." She spoke more quietly: "What you are proposing is ... complicated."

"Open a bank account in Emilie's name. That's all you have to do ..."

Nicole Vitral's lips trembled.

"And afterward?"

"Emilie will receive one hundred thousand francs per year, paid into that account. Until she is eighteen years old. This money will be for her use only: for her education, her hobbies, to give her the best possible chance in life. Of course, it will be up to you to manage that money during those eighteen years. You may do as you like. I am simply giving you the means ..."

For several seconds, Nicole Vitral was silent. She felt herself being rocked by the sound of the shingle, swept endlessly back and forth by the ebb and flow of the waves.

Ebb and flow. For and against.

Finally, she said: "I will open the account, Mrs. de Carville. For Emilie. Because if I didn't do that, I might feel guilty. She might reproach me for it afterward. Pour your money into it if you want ..."

"Thank you."

"... but we will not touch it!" Nicole almost screamed. "Emilie will be educated exactly like her brother, Marc, and we will pay for it ourselves. We will make sacrifices if we have to, but we will do it. When she is eighteen, Emilie can do what she wants with that money. It will be up to her. You understand?"

Mathilde de Carville gave a faint, wry smile. "You are cruel, Nicole. But I thank you, all the same." After a second's hesitation, she continued: "May I ask you a second favor?"

Nicole Vitral gave an exasperated sigh. "I don't know. Make it quick. I'm about to close."

Mathilde took out a royal-blue jewelry box from the pocket of her long coat. She opened it, took a step forward, and placed it on the counter. Nicole stared helplessly at the pale sapphire in the ring.

"It is a very old tradition," said Mathilde calmly. "For their eighteenth birthday, the girls in our family always receive a ring set with a stone the color of their eyes. It has been like that for generations. I am wearing a ring given to me by my mother more than thirty years ago. Sadly, I will never have the chance to do the same for Lyse-Rose."

Nicole Vitral finally looked up. "I'm probably being stupid, but I don't understand..."

"I am leaving this ring with you. Take care of it. Perhaps in three years, or in ten years, simply by spending time with Emilie, you will guess. You will know instinctively if she is your granddaughter or not. If that happens, and if, deep in your heart, you are certain that the granddaughter you have brought up is not of your own blood, I think you will keep that secret to yourself..."

She took a breath, her eyes glistening. "And it will probably be better that way, for the girl at least. But if that does happen—if, through the years, you find evidence or simply come to feel certain that she is not your granddaughter—then please, on her eighteenth birthday, give her this ring. No one but the two of us will know what it means. But that way, for you and for me, justice will be served."

Nicole Vitral was going to refuse, to give back the ring, to tell this woman that her idea was ludicrous, sick, but Mathilde de Carville did not give her the chance. Without even waiting for a reply, she turned around and walked away, her long dark coat melting into the twilight.

The royal-blue jewelry box remained where it was, on the counter.

16

October 2, 1998, 11:08 a.m.

Malvina closed the window behind her. Then she unrolled the dish towel, which she had used to wipe every surface in the house, from her hand and shoved it into her jacket pocket. Surely no one would notice that a dish towel from Grand-Duc's kitchen drawer was missing.

Proud of herself, she crept slowly through the small garden, so that no one on the street would see her. She waited for two cars to pass, hidden behind a corner of the house, then—when the coast was clear—she stepped over the low stone wall and out into the street. It was fine: no one would ever know that she had entered Grand-Duc's house. She wasn't stupid, in spite of what people might think. She turned around. One last detail was bothering her. From the pavement, if you looked carefully, you could see the broken pane in the lower right-hand window. She had smashed it in order to open the window and let herself in. She shrugged. It wasn't important.

She walked quickly down Rue de la Butte-aux-Cailles. She could not stay out in the open. The Vitral boy might arrive at any moment.

She took a car key from her pocket and pressed the red button that unlocked the vehicle's doors remotely. Her car was so small, she could find a parking space almost anywhere in Paris—in this case about fifty feet from Grand-Duc's house. It was not the most discreet of cars, but Vitral had no way of knowing it was hers.

Malvina hid as well as she could, hunching down in the driver's seat of her Rover Mini. There wasn't much space, but if she kept her head low, a passerby might think the car unoccupied. Malvina, on the other hand, commanded a clear view of the entire street—through the windshield and in the rearview mirror. Assuming Vitral came from the Corvisart metro station, he would walk up from the end of the road without passing the Mini, but she would be able to see him. Perfect.

She wriggled around until she was able to get her hand on the Mauser L110. She put it under the driver's seat, within easy reach.

Only one thing still bothered Malvina: there were too many people about, particularly in that bakery about fifty yards away. Too many witnesses, although most of them were not close by. She remembered her grandmother's words: "Watch him, follow him. But don't do anything else. Telephone me as soon as you see him." Malvina's hand crept under the seat and touched the Mauser, as if to check that it was still there. The feel of the cold metal reassured her. Given that she was twenty-four years old, was she still obliged to obey her grandmother?

Marc walked on autopilot through the endless corridors of Montparnasse station, his eyes seeking out signs for Line 6.

Lylie had been wearing that ring, with the pale sapphire,

the color of her eyes. So Nicole must have given it to her for her eighteenth birthday, two days ago. His grandmother had respected the terms of the agreement with Mathilde de Carville. She had not mentioned it to anyone. Not once. Not even to Lylie.

But she had given her the ring.

Marc now knew what that meant, what a terrible confession it represented for his grandmother.

He had to call her, talk to her. Right now, though, finding Lylie was his priority. With his free hand, he typed out a short text: *Lylie, call me back FFS!*

He decided he would send her another text in an hour if she didn't reply, that he would keep pestering her until she gave in.

Where could she be? He thought again of the miniature airplane in his bag. Was she being serious about going far away? It was possible... Now that she was eighteen, Lylie had the financial means to go anywhere she liked. She could even stay there for years.

Weaving between his fellow travelers, Marc went over in his mind the last words he had read in Crédule Grand-Duc's notebook. Lylie's bank account. Mathilde de Carville's gift. The old woman had known what she was doing. As the years passed, Marc had become convinced that it was simply the money that had created that gulf between him and Lylie, giving rise to those abnormal feelings, the unnatural attraction that could not possibly exist between a boy and a girl who shared the same blood.

The money explained it all. And yet, deep within him, a voice had always whispered that, ultimately, the money made no difference.

The voice was right. Because now he had the proof that

his grandmother felt the same way he did, even if she had never said anything about it.

Lylie was wearing the de Carvilles' ring.

His grandmother had confessed the truth when she gave it to her. Lylie was not his sister. They were free.

Marc felt uplifted by a kind of euphoria. He hopped onto the train heading toward Nation. Five stations until Corvisart, and then a short walk to Rue de la Butte-aux-Cailles, where Grand-Duc lived.

Time to read a few more pages...

Crédule Grand-Duc's Journal

This is the point where I make my entrance. At last!

Crédule Grand-Duc, private detective.

I took my time, didn't I? And undoubtedly missed all the action. In fact, therein lay my problem.

Mathilde de Carville entered my office, in Belleville, on Rue des Amandiers, the day after her meeting with Nicole Vitral. She wore nothing but black, as if she had poured all of her sadness into her clothing. I think that meeting with Nicole Vitral took a lot out of her. She had made the decision herself, without consulting her husband. Mathilde felt humiliated by her trip to the seafront at Dieppe, but she had understood that it was a necessary sacrifice if she was to have any hope of persuading Nicole Vitral to give way. Nicole Vitral had to feel more powerful than her rival, otherwise she would never have agreed to open a bank account in Lylie's name.

Never again, Mathilde must have sworn after that meeting; never again would she humiliate herself in such a way. She had eased her conscience, but it had cost her dearly:

much more than a check for one hundred thousand francs per year. So, after that meeting in Dieppe, Mathilde's heart had frozen. By the time she entered my office, she was not much more than a polite, well-dressed ice cube.

She walked toward me.

"I have heard a lot about you, Mr. Grand-Duc..."

She introduced herself. Vaguely, I made the connection with the case that had dominated the television and radio coverage for several weeks.

"I have been told, Mr. Grand-Duc, that you are discreet, tenacious, patient, and meticulous. Those are the very qualities I am seeking. My proposition is very simple: I want you to go over every minute detail in the Mont Terri case file, one by one. And to find more information, if there is any."

Back then, although I was only one of many private detectives in Paris, I was beginning to earn something of a reputation for myself. Over time, I had solved every case that had been given to me: the casino affair on the coast, plus a few others. Like a boxer who has fought only nobodies and therefore won every match, I had never tasted failure, and thus I believed myself invincible. I had no idea why this woman had chosen me. But, after all, why shouldn't she? It didn't really matter: I was not going to let this opportunity slip away.

Mathilde de Carville came closer. I remained seated. I am not a big man. At a rough guess, I would say she was nearly two inches taller than I. I sat up straight in my chair and put on a serious expression.

"This is a complex case, madame. A case that cannot be rushed. It will take time..."

"I have not come here to bargain with you, Mr. Grand-Duc.

You can take or leave my offer. I do not think I will have much trouble finding another detective, but I also believe you will accept my terms. Beginning today, you will receive one hundred thousand francs per year, for eighteen years, until Lyse-Rose, my granddaughter, if she is still alive, becomes an adult. The end of September, 1998, in other words. The thirtieth, not the twenty-seventh, as that is what the judge decided."

One hundred thousand francs a year! Multiplied by eighteen! There were so many zeroes, I couldn't even count them. They lined up in my mind like pearls on a necklace. Eighteen years of guaranteed salary. It truly was an offer I could not refuse...

Except that...Even if my stupid first name, Crédule, means "naive" or "gullible," I still needed more details.

"What exactly do you require of me, madame, in return for such a handsome salary? Would I have to pay you back if I hadn't found anything after eighteen years?"

"Mr. Grand-Duc, you are not under any obligation to get results. However, I do demand that you do everything you can to solve the mystery. I want no stone left unturned: every clue, every theory, must be thoroughly investigated. I am offering you enough time and money to ensure that is the case. If any evidence exists proving the identity of the survivor of the Mont Terri crash, I want you to find it. And let me be perfectly clear, Mr. Grand-Duc: I want to know the truth, whether or not it is to my liking."

I felt as though I were standing on the edge of a cliff.

"And you think that such an investigation will take... eighteen years?"

"You will be paid for eighteen years. Consequently, you have eighteen years to discover the truth. I do not expect you to devote yourself exclusively to this case during that time. I am simply providing you with the necessary means to solve it: time and money."

"What happens if I discover the truth after five months?"

"Do you really not understand, Mr. Grand-Duc? Have I not been sufficiently clear? You will be paid for eighteen years, no matter what. This will be a gentlemen's agreement. All I demand is that you do everything in your power to discover the identity of the survivor. That is all that matters to me."

She leaned down toward me, the wooden cross hanging from her neck suspended in the air just above my nose.

"Of course I reserve the right to break our agreement at any moment, if I have the feeling that you are not upholding your end of the bargain. If I sense you are taking advantage of the situation. But that won't happen, will it? I have heard you are a man of honor..."

No contract...Can you imagine? I seemed to be dealing with a mad old woman who didn't know how to spend her vast fortune. It was a miracle. But how far was she prepared to go?

"I'll have to go to Turkey," I said. "Perhaps for a long time."

"In addition to your salary, all your expenses will be paid..."

Dare I risk asking for more?

"I...I don't speak Turkish. It will be difficult on my own..."

"If it is necessary to the investigation, you may hire employees. Their expenses will also be paid."

I had my own reasons for asking the question. Already, I was planning—at least to begin with—to work with a guy I knew from a couple of months I'd spent in Central Asia. Nazim Ozan was the only person in France I knew who spoke Turkish, and whom I trusted, more or less.

Mathilde de Carville wrote me a check—for the then vast sum of one hundred thousand francs—and left my office looking as gloomy as she had when she arrived. I felt as if I had won the jackpot, without even having bought a ticket.

For the first time, my names seemed to fit. I was credulous to believe that this investigation would be my springboard to fame and fortune. And, for three days, I celebrated my good luck like a Grand Duke, spending as much as I liked, safe in the knowledge that my extravagance would not cost me a centime, because I could claim it all as expenses.

How could I possibly have imagined, in that moment, that I had fallen into a bottomless pit? That the light that had attracted me was leading me toward the void?

17

Rue Jean-Marie-Jégo climbed steeply, rising by about a hundred and fifty feet, until it reached Butte-aux-Cailles: a picture-postcard little street that made you feel you were walking up to a village square, with its church, its town hall, its bar, and its *boules* pitch shaded by plane trees. All this in the middle of Paris. Marc knew vaguely that Butte-aux-Cailles was supposed to be one of the few remaining Parisian "*quartiers*"; he had come here one evening for a drink at the Temps des Cerises. A bourgeois faux-hippie student—the kind that Marc loathed: probably the son of a diplomat—had explained to him that this hill was protected from the property developers because the underground limestone quarries made the construction of tall buildings impossible. The one thing Marc had retained from that conversation was that it cost an absolute fortune to buy a house here.

Marc climbed one last set of steps and came out on top of the hill. Still holding tight to the handrail, he picked up his phone and sent another text to Lylie.

The same as before: *Lylie. Call me back FFS!*

Afterward, he checked his messages. Nothing.

There weren't many people around on Rue de la Butte-aux-Cailles, with the exception of customers at the bakery, which was apparently the only place open on the street. The restaurants still appeared to be empty. Marc walked past the houses until he reached number 21. There, he found a small, one-story building, set in the middle of a pretty little garden, about sixty square feet in area. It was the kind of tiny house that would have looked ridiculous in the French countryside, but here, in the center of Paris, it was the pinnacle of luxury. A detached house, a bungalow, with a little garden of its own. Even bearing in mind the one hundred thousand francs per year he had been paid by Mathilde de Carville, such a house seemed beyond Grand-Duc's means.

The pale green shutters were closed. Just in case, Marc rang the bell, situated between the slightly rusted yellow mailbox and the security gate, which needed a new coat of paint.

No reply.

He waited a minute, and rang again. Still nothing. Puzzled, he ran his hand through his hair. Grand-Duc was not at home. He took a closer look at the house, and the garden, searching for inspiration. He walked back to the street.

And then he found it.

On the right-hand side of the house, the corner of one of the window panes was broken. With a bit of luck, he might be able to get his hand through, grab the handle, and open the window. Marc looked around: no one in the street was paying him any attention. He jumped over the low stone wall and went over to the window. He put his hand on the frame and, to his great surprise, it opened. The window had been merely pushed shut.

For a moment, Marc was taken aback by this strange confluence of circumstances, this curious lack of security in a private detective's home. But only for a moment. A second later, he was inside Grand-Duc's house.

The bastard's in, thought Malvina. She had watched Marc Vitral as he walked toward the house and climbed over the wall. Now I've got him, she thought, and he's carrying a backpack. Surely Grand-Duc's notebook must be inside. It was all working out. Malvina attempted to move a little. Her neck, which she had twisted below the steering wheel, was hurting, but she didn't care. She wouldn't mind staying in this position for hours and wearing a neck brace for the rest of her life if it meant she could catch Vitral on his way out, take that damn notebook off him, and rip out its lie-filled pages one by one. She wanted to point her gun at Vitral and make him talk, too. She would find a way. When the time came, she would make the rules.

The smell of smoke and ashes hit Marc instantly, catching in his throat. Marc coughed. He found himself in a little outbuilding, a sort of storeroom containing various gardening and DIY tools. He pushed the door open, climbed up three concrete steps, and opened another door. This took him directly into what must be Grand-Duc's living room.

The stench of smoke was much stronger here. Marc coughed again. His eyes were drawn toward the large fireplace just in front of him. One thing was obvious:

an enormous quantity of paper had been burned in that hearth. He noted the empty storage boxes on the floor. Clearly, Grand-Duc had been tying up some loose ends.

Before Marc had time to analyze the situation, a strange noise made him freeze. Behind him, to his right, there was a sort of muffled rattling, a succession of short jolts, like the jammed mechanism of a mechanical toy. Marc turned around. To his shock, he discovered a huge vivarium filled with dragonflies, most of them lying inert on the damp floor. He moved closer. The only one still able to fly was the largest, with a red and gold thorax, and even it was struggling. As if it had noticed this new presence in the room, the insect was weakly flapping its wings. The sound Marc had heard was its wings hitting the glass wall. For a few moments, fascinated by the dragonfly's desperate movements, Marc did not react. And then he thought: a dragonfly. A prisoner. Almost dead, like all the others in the glass cage. Without any further thought, Marc removed the glass lid that covered the vivarium and leaned it against the nearest wall. Instantly refreshed by the influx of oxygen, the Harlequin dragonfly took only a few wingbeats to escape from its prison. Marc watched it fly, hesitantly at first and then majestically. The dragonfly flew higher and higher, before coming to rest on the ceiling light.

Marc's heart raced. He felt the most intense, almost childish, joy at having saved the insect.

His dragonfly.

He would never have guessed that Grand-Duc collected them. But why would he let them suffer like that?

Marc made a more detailed examination of Grand-Duc's office. Everything was perfectly neat and tidy:

pencils, notepaper, the strange little wine bottle (empty), the glass. There was something odd about this orderliness: as if Grand-Duc had wanted to tie up everything relating to the case. The burned papers. The sacrificed insects. And his testament, of course: the pale green notebook, which Grand-Duc must have finished writing the night of Lylie's eighteenth birthday.

So, what had happened? Why was the detective not here?

Marc could sense an odd feeling of urgency in this house, as if someone had left in a hurry; the bottle that had not been put away, for instance; that broken window, which had been pushed shut. And that smell, too. Not the smell of smoke from the fireplace, but another one, insidiously concealed by the first.

Something was not quite right here…

Suddenly, Marc's face lit up. For there was no mystery about Grand-Duc's last thoughts: all Marc had to do was turn to the last page of the notebook and read the final lines of his confession.

Marc concentrated on the words. The last page of Grand-Duc's notebook contained only about twenty lines. As always, the detective's handwriting was small and regular. ·

Now you know everything.

Today is September 29, 1998. It is twenty minutes to midnight. Everything is ready. Lylie is about to turn eighteen. I will put my pen back in the pot on my desk. I will sit at this desk, unfold the December 23, 1980, edition of the Est Républicain, *and I will calmly shoot myself in the head. My blood will stain this yellowed newspaper. I have failed.*

All I leave behind me is this notebook. For Lylie. For whomever wishes to read it.

In this notebook, I have reviewed all the clues, all the leads, all the theories I have found in eighteen years of investigation. It is all here, in these hundred or so pages. If you have read them carefully, you will now know as much as I do. Perhaps you will be more perceptive than I. Perhaps you will find something I have missed. The key to the mystery, if one exists. Perhaps...

For me, it's over.

It would be an exaggeration to say that I have no regrets, but I have done my best.

Slowly, Marc reread the last line: *I have done my best.* For a while he was paralyzed, attempting to suppress the feeling of intense unease that was rising within him. He went back a few lines and read again:

I will calmly shoot myself in the head. My blood will stain this yellowed newspaper. I have failed.

Marc looked up.

Grand-Duc had planned to commit suicide.

So why was there no trace of his blood on the desk? No newspaper? No gun? Clearly two days earlier, between 11:40 p.m. and midnight, Grand-Duc had decided *not* to kill himself after all...But why? Why undertake so much rigorous preparation, only to give up on the idea at the last minute?

Had he lost his nerve? Had he decided to carry out the act somewhere else, at a later time? Or had he lied in this journal...about his sacrifice? And what about the rest? Or had he discovered something, at the last minute? A glimmer, a clue, one last lead...

Marc read the final lines of the notebook again.

Grand-Duc had left no clue behind. Only one thing was sure: he was not sitting dead at his desk with a bullet in his head.

Marc closed the notebook and coughed again. The smell was getting worse. Another mechanical whirring made him turn his head. A dozen or so dragonflies were now flying through the air; the removal of the vivarium lid must have saved their lives. Those insects were tougher than they looked. Marc smiled, and thought of Lylie, *his* dragonfly, the only one he truly wanted to save. And he would, even if it meant trapping her with a glass lid. Marc could feel his mind becoming muddled, the insects fluttering before his eyes like the imaginary flies that precede a dizzy spell.

He stood up. He needed to move about.

Jesus Christ, what *was* that smell?

He took a few steps forward. The closer he got to the kitchen, the stronger the smell became. The kitchen was clean, tidy...even the trash had been emptied. But the stench seemed to be coming from that tall, narrow cabinet next to the sink.

Slowly, cautiously, Marc opened the door.

Almost immediately, the corpse fell to the floor next to his feet with a muffled thud.

It was stiff. Like a wax model.

Marc recoiled, pale with horror.

The body lay on the floor in front of him. There was a dark red stain on the shirt.

Crédule Grand-Duc.

Dead. Just as he had said he would be in the notebook.

Except that it would be fairly unusual for someone to shoot himself in the chest, then hide the gun, clean up the blood, and lock himself in a closet.

Marc took a step backward.

The detective had not committed suicide. He had been murdered.

18

Keeping her head down low inside the Rover Mini, Malvina de Carville picked up her telephone.

Her call was answered immediately.

"He's here," Malvina whispered. "Vitral is in Grand-Duc's house."

"That's to be expected. You didn't leave any trace?"

"No, Grandma. Don't worry. I even cleaned up Grand-Duc's hair and bits of skin from the fireplace."

She gave a high-pitched laugh. Her grandmother always treated her as if she were an idiot.

"Grandma?"

"What?"

"He might find Grand-Duc's body. I hid it, but it...it smells really bad..."

She sensed her grandmother thinking at the other end of the line.

"Grandma?"

"Yes," Mathilde de Carville replied finally. "Well, if he finds it, too bad. In fact, it might be for the best. He broke into the house; he will have been seen by witnesses. He'll leave fingerprints all over the house. Perhaps it's the best thing that could have happened."

Malvina shivered with pleasure. Her grandmother was right, as always. Marc Vitral was going to regret entering that house.

"Grandma? He's carrying a backpack. I think Grand-Duc's notebook must be inside. Do you think I..."

Mathilde's voice was cold. "No, Malvina, don't do anything. Just follow him, that's all. You must not do anything, especially in broad daylight. Do you hear me?"

"Yes, Grandma. I understand. I'll call you back."

Under the passenger seat, Malvina weighed the Mauser in her hand. Yes, her grandmother was almost always right. But not this time...

A few dragonflies buzzed around Grand-Duc's corpse.

Marc retched. He could feel himself panicking, but he had to get a grip on it: he could not afford to have an agoraphobic fit now, in this house.

Should he call the police?

Marc thought quickly. He had entered Grand-Duc's house through a broken window. He had left his fingerprints everywhere. It was not a good idea. Most important, the police would spend hours questioning him in the local station, and he couldn't allow that to happen. Not now. Lylie needed him.

He looked down at the corpse. He was no pathologist, but it seemed clear that the murder had occurred recently. The rigidity, the smell...it all led him to believe that the body had been here for only a few hours. Marc thought again about Grand-Duc's last words in his notebook. His planned suicide. How was that connected to this crime?

What had he discovered that had made someone want to seal his lips forever?

A dragonfly flew down and buzzed under his nose. He waved it away irritably.

The timing did not fit. Grand-Duc had been killed a few hours ago, not two days ago, on Lylie's birthday. Marc looked around the living room again, at the desk, the fireplace, the vivarium.

The whole thing was surreal. The dragonflies were waking from their apparent death one by one and flying around the room. They kept colliding with windows, drawn to the flashes of daylight that pierced the closed shutters.

Marc decided to check the other rooms in the house. He found nothing suspicious, but at least the methodical search enabled him to calm down, to breathe almost normally. He went into the hallway, and immediately the blood began to thunder through his veins again. The wall of the hallway was covered with photographs. Nazim Ozan, Lylie, views of Mont Terri...

Suddenly he froze, his eyes glued to one particular picture: his grandmother. For some reason, Grand-Duc had kept a photo of Nicole in the hallway of his house. In the photograph, she looked much younger—not even fifty. She was standing on the beach, in Dieppe. Marc's heart was beating hard, half in anger, half in shock. In his mind, his grandmother had always looked the way she looked now: a woman of sixty-five, faded by years of sacrifice. He had practically no memory at all of this smiling, ample-breasted woman with an almost seductive gleam in her eyes.

He turned away. He had to get out, quickly. Agoraphobia...he could feel an attack coming. He thought confusedly that before leaving Grand-Duc's house, he should get a cloth and wipe everything he had touched: the vivarium lid, the desk and chair, the door handles, the window ... But he didn't want to, didn't have the time.

He just had to get out of there. Escape the putrefied air of this house and breathe fresh air again.

What did he have to fear, after all? He hadn't killed Grand-Duc. The detective had been dead for several hours. He had been a long way from Butte-aux-Cailles at the time of the murder.

Marc climbed through the open window, taking deep breaths.

Yes, he could forget about cleaning the house. There were more urgent things to consider.

Finding Lylie, first and foremost.

He also had to call his grandmother, in Dieppe. To try to understand. To discover why Grand-Duc had been murdered.

He did have an idea, as far as the last question was concerned. An idea that was directly related to his next destination.

As Marc left, he did not notice the dragonflies escaping through the open window behind him, flying away toward the horizon.

Malvina watched Marc Vitral approaching in the side mirror of her Rover Mini. He didn't have a clue, the dickhead. Malvina's hand slid under the seat, fumbled around, then found the Mauser L110. A few feet more, and he would be within range. She would shove the gun barrel into his gut, and he would have no choice but to hand over his stupid backpack, with that shit-for-brains detective's notebook stashed inside.

After that, she would see. Maybe she would let him off lightly: just shoot off one of his balls. Or both...She hadn't decided yet.

He was only about thirty feet away.

Malvina lifted her head and tightened her grip on the revolver. A few old people were chatting outside the bakery at the end of the street. She didn't care. Those senile bastards were too far away—they wouldn't have a clue what was going on. She turned toward the pavement, just to make sure.

One second later, she froze.

Three kids were sticking their tongues out at her. They could only have been four or five years old. Their fat, snotty-nosed faces were watching her through the window, as if she were playing hide-and-seek, crouched down between the steering wheel and the driver's seat. *Peeka-boo, we see you!*

A schoolteacher came along and grabbed the three jokers. Malvina sat up straight. Stupid little brats!

She realized a whole kindergarten class was walking past her car, at least thirty kids, on their way to the cafeteria or the playground.

Marc Vitral smiled politely at the children and their teacher as he passed them in the street, then walked quickly away, lost in his thoughts, without even a second glance at the Rover Mini parked by the side of the road.

"Hello, Grandma? It's Malvina. I missed him, Grandma..."

"What do you mean, you missed him? Marc Vitral? You mean you shot at him and..."

"No, I didn't even do that. I didn't have time."

Malvina de Carville heard her grandmother give a sigh of relief.

"All right, Malvina. What is he doing now?"

"He's walking to the metro. Shall I follow him?"

"Don't move a muscle, Malvina."

"But..."

Was her grandmother crazy?

"But Grandma... what about Grand-Duc's notebook?"

"I told you: don't move!"

Malvina knew she could still follow Marc, Mauser in hand, trap him in one of the metro's passages, take the backpack from him, throw him onto the tracks...

"Come home, Malvina. Come back to the Roseraie. It's better this way."

"But I can still get him, Grandma. Believe me, I can..."

Her grandmother's voice was both gentle and firm, as it was when she would read the Bible to Malvina before bedtime.

"Malvina, listen to me. Vitral has undoubtedly read Grand-Duc's notebook. His first reaction was perfectly logical: he went to Grand-Duc's house. He must have found the detective's corpse there, so his second reaction will be equally predictable."

Malvina did not understand. What point was her grandmother trying to make?

"Come home, Malvina. Marc Vitral will come to us, here in Coupvray. He will come to the Roseraie."

Malvina cursed her own stupidity.

A little black dot grew larger in her rear-view mirror, moving in and out of sight. After performing a few loop-de-loops, the handsome red-and-gold dragonfly landed on the hood of the blue Rover Mini.

19

Marc paused for a moment. He leaned against the chrome handrail that divided the steep staircase leading down to Boulevard Blanqui. The cold steel numbed his hand.

Marc had worked out his journey: Line 6. Change at Nation. Then Line A4 of the RER train, toward Marne-la-Vallée, getting off at Val-d'Europe, the penultimate station. He would be in Coupvray within an hour, at the most. He would have no trouble getting hold of the de Carvilles' address: all he had to do was call Jennifer, his colleague, as he had when he needed Grand-Duc's address.

There was no need to let the de Carvilles know he was coming. There would be plenty of people there to answer his questions. He doubted whether the old grandfather in his wheelchair or the queen mother left the property very often. They probably never even went shopping. They paid people to do that kind of thing. They paid people to do every kind of thing.

Marc smiled to himself. What a surprise his visit would be! After all, he and the de Carvilles were working toward the same goal now: proving that Lylie was not his sister, that Vitral blood did not flow through her veins. Surely they could find some common ground.

Marc shivered as he thought again of Grand-Duc's corpse.

He grabbed his cell phone and called his grandmother's number in Dieppe.

Once again, he got the answering machine.

For a long time now, he had called his grandmother "Nicole." It was his way of answering the question that had puzzled him during his first ten years of life: should he call her "Mother" or "Grandma"?

"Nicole? It's Marc. Have you heard from Lylie? Recently, I mean. Since this morning. Call me back, please—it's very important." He paused for a second, then continued: "I know I don't actually remember this, but you were very beautiful when you were fifty. I love you..."

Marc's left hand tightened around the cold metal of the rail. The fingers of his other hand danced lightly over the telephone's keyboard.

The phone rang. Seven times.

"Lylie... Where are you, for God's sake? Answer me! Call me back! Don't go, Lylie. I've just left Grand-Duc's house. He didn't commit suicide. He's... He... I think he must have discovered something. I can find out what it was, too. I will discover it. Call me, Lylie."

The platforms of the metro were practically empty at this time of day. Marc stared across at a large billboard ad for tourism in the Emirates, losing himself in the mysterious landscape shown on the poster. A few seconds later, the train appeared, sinking into the golden sands, in front of the Oriental palace, under the stars of a thousand and one nights.

Crédule Grand-Duc's Journal

So I was hired for an eighteen-year investigation. Can you imagine? For eighteen years, this case has been stuck in my brain, like a piece of mental chewing gum, chewed for so long that it has lost all its flavor. Beware, reader, that the gum does not become glued to your own thoughts, massaged by your imagination, stretched out by your logic—because you may never get rid of it.

The first few months of the investigation were extremely exciting. Despite the very generous deadline, I was filled with a sense of urgency. I read all the inquiry documents—hundreds of pages—in less than two weeks. During the first two months, I interviewed scores of witnesses: the firemen who attended the Mont Terri crash; all the medical staff from the Belfort-Montbéliard hospital; Dr. Morange; the de Carvilles' friends and relatives; the Vitrals' friends and relatives; the police, including Superintendent Vatelier; the lawyers, including Leguerne; the two judges, Le Drian and Weber; and who knows how many others...

I was working fifteen hours a day, hardly sleeping at all. I was thinking about the case when I fell asleep and it was still buzzing around my head when I woke up. It was as if I wanted to solve the case as quickly as possible, or to please my client by demonstrating my zeal for the job, so she would give me a contract for life.

In fact, my motives were not so calculated. I was genuinely fascinated by the mystery, and was convinced that I could discover something new; some clue that everyone had overlooked. I accumulated notes, photographs, hours of recordings. It was madness...I couldn't have known, then, that what I was actually building was the foundations of my own neurosis.

After a few weeks of analyzing all the evidence, I became fixated on finding out about one thing in particular. At the time, it seemed like a brilliant idea.

The bracelet!

That damned gold bracelet, given to her by her grandfather, which Lyse-Rose de Carville must have been wearing when the plane crashed. The piece of jewelry that had tipped the balance away from the de Carvilles in the mind of Judge Weber; the decisive grain of sand in the scales of justice; Maître Leguerne and the Vitrals' lethal weapon. I had become convinced that this lethal weapon was a double-edged sword. Without that bracelet, the balance of probability fell toward the miracle child being Emilie Vitral. But if the survivor was Lyse-Rose, there was no reason why the delicate bracelet might not have broken during the plane crash. And if the bracelet had been found, somewhere in the vicinity of the plane…in that case, the situation would be reversed and the bracelet would provide irrefutable proof that Lyse-Rose was the miracle child.

I am a patient, stubborn, meticulous man. When it comes to work, I can be completely obsessive. So, even though I knew that the police had searched the site around the burned Airbus for hours, I decided I would begin that search again. Armed with a metal detector, I spent seventeen days on Mont Terri in late August 1981, raking over every inch of forest. There had been a storm the night the plane had crashed. The bracelet might have fallen into the snow, become buried in the muddy earth. It's not difficult to imagine that a policeman sent to search the area in such conditions—his fingers freezing, his feet soaked—might not be especially zealous.

I was.

Not that it did me any good.

I will spare you the list of beer cans, coins, and other worthless pieces of junk that I discovered. I was basically doing the job of the man who looks after Mont Terri as part of the Haut-Jura nature preserve. His name is Grégory Morez. A good-looking man with designer stubble and wolfish eyes, his face craggy and tanned as if he climbed Mount Kilimanjaro every weekend. We ended up becoming friendly.

I brought down three trash bags from the mountain, filled with all kinds of rubbish, but not a bracelet in sight.

To be honest, I wasn't really disappointed. I had suspected this might happen. But as I've told you, I am a stubborn man. I was simply obeying Mathilde de Carville's orders to leave no stone unturned, taking it one step at a time.

What I really believed was, if the bracelet had fallen somewhere near the miracle child on the night of the tragedy, it was perfectly possible that someone—a fireman, a policeman, a nurse—might have found it and simply kept it as a souvenir. Or maybe someone local had come to scavenge around the scene of the crash, after the plane had stopped burning. The bracelet was made of solid gold, valued at the time at exactly eleven thousand five hundred francs, according to the receipt. It bore a hallmark from Tournaire, on Place Vendôme, and was the kind of object that could make people greedy. And, of course, no one could possibly have imagined how important that damned bracelet would become afterward.

My idea was very simple: to bombard the local region with small advertisements offering a lucrative reward for information that would lead us to the coveted trinket. The reward had to be considerably more than the object itself was worth. With the agreement of Mathilde de Carville, I gradually increased the size of the bait. We began at twenty thousand francs…This kind of fishing required patience, time, and dexterity, but I was confident that the fish would eventually bite. If the bracelet had been found, if it was hidden away in a drawer, jealously guarded by a casual thief, one day or another it would resurface.

And I was right. On that point at least, I was right.

My other main occupation during the first six months of my investigation was what I liked to call my Turkish vacation. Altogether, I must have spent nearly two and a half years in Turkey, and most of that time was during the first five years.

I was accompanied by Nazim Ozan, who had agreed, without a moment's hesitation, to partner me in my investigation. At the time, he was working, often illegally, on building sites. He was nearly fifty, and had had his fill of being a mercenary in the world's most dangerous countries, surrounded by fanatical maniacs. And, most important, he had found love. He lived in Paris with a somewhat plump but still very lovely woman called Ayla. Like Nazim, she was of Turkish origin. God knows why, but the two of them were inseparable. Ayla was a powerful and fiercely jealous woman, and I had to spend hours negotiating with her whenever I wanted Nazim to come with me to Turkey. And, once we got there, he had to call her every day. I don't think Ayla ever understood anything about the case itself. Worse still, I'm not even sure she believed us. But she didn't hold it against me. She even insisted that I be a witness at their wedding in June 1985.

In spite of Ayla's objections, I generally did take Nazim with me when I went to Turkey, where he acted as my interpreter. In Istanbul, I always stayed at the Hotel Askoc, on the Golden Horn, near the Galata Bridge. Nazim stayed with some cousins of Ayla, in the district of Eyup. We would meet in a café across from my hotel—the Dez Anj, on Ayhan Isik Sokak. Nazim took the opportunity to drink raki after raki, and attempted to initiate me into the pleasures of the hookah.

As I said . . . my Turkish vacations.

I have to admit, I think I have always been slightly cynical about the arts and traditions of the rest of the world: the idea of exotic foreign lands and so on. I suppose you could call it a sort of racism, but it's an unbiased racism, a general skepticism toward the whole human race. I imagine it dates back to my former job as a mercenary—an armed garbage collector charged with emptying the world's filthiest trash cans, or a door-to-door dynamite salesman, if you prefer.

I'd had my fill of Turkish life within a week of being there. The incessant ringing from the minarets, the endless bazaar in the streets, the veiled women, the prostitutes, the smell of tea and spices, the crazy taxi drivers, the constant traffic jams all the way to the Bosphorus . . . In the end, the only Turkish thing I could bear was Nazim's mustache.

Anyway, I'm sure you've had enough of my amateur anthropology. I just wanted to demonstrate that my "Turkish vacations" were nothing of the kind, and I am serious when I say that I took refuge in my work. At least for the first few months, Nazim and I worked like madmen. We spent hours interrogating merchants in the Grand Bazaar, trying to find out who had sold the clothes worn by the miracle child. A cotton vest, a white dress with orange flowers, and a beige wool sweater...Can you imagine? The Grand Bazaar in Istanbul is one of the biggest covered markets in the world, with fifty-eight streets and over four thousand shops...Most of the vendors jabbered away in English or French, attempting to ignore Nazim's translation so they could address themselves directly to me, as if there were a watermark of the French flag on my forehead.

"A baby, my brother? You are looking for clothes for your baby? I have everything you need. Boy or girl? Tell me your price..."

Four thousand shops, with two or three times as many merchants, spotting the Western fool at a hundred paces. But I held firm. I spent more than ten days pacing that maze, and ended up with a list of nineteen shops that sold all three items—the cotton vest, the white dress, and the wool sweater—in exactly the same style as the miracle child's...And none of the vendors remembered having sold those clothes to a Western family.

It was a dead end.

Thankfully, there was still a great deal to be learned about Lyse-Rose and her parents, Alexandre and Véronique de Carville. The official inquiry has based its analysis of Lyse-Rose's identity on two things: the photograph taken from behind, received in the mail by the de Carville grandparents, and Malvina's testimony. So we had to start all over again in Turkey, in their coastal residence

in Ceyhan. I was reasonably optimistic. Surely, in three
months of life, Lyse-Rose must have been seen by quite a
few people.

I quickly became disillusioned.

Apparently, Alexandre and Véronique de Carville were
not very sociable, and tended to avoid contact with the
indigenous population. They were the kind of people who
remain cloistered in their white villa with its view of the
Mediterranean. They even had their own private beach.

To be more honest, it was Véronique who really lived
like a nun—Alexandre worked in Istanbul most of the
week. They occasionally had friends around—colleagues,
French people—but only before Lyse-Rose was born. Once
Véronique had given birth, she became a lot less interested
in social gatherings. I was only able to find seven people—
two couples who were friends with the de Carvilles, plus
three business clients—who had been invited to the Ceyhan villa after Lyse-Rose's birth. Each time, Lyse-Rose
had been asleep, and all the guests could remember was a
tiny baby covered in sheets who woke at regular intervals.
Only one client, a Dutchman, had seen Lyse-Rose awake,
and then only for a few seconds. Véronique had retired
from the party to breast-feed her daughter and she could
not do that in front of the Dutch industrialist. I did manage
to find the man in question—a sales manager for the Turkish subsidiary of Shell—and he told me that he would be
as incapable of recognizing Lyse-Rose's face as he would
her mother's tits.

At the Bakirkoy maternity hospital in Istanbul, where
Véronique de Carville gave birth, more than thirty babies
are born each week. It is a very chic private clinic, and

I was welcomed with astonishing obsequiousness. The pediatrician, the only doctor to have looked after Lyse-Rose, had examined her about three times and pointed out to me that he saw more than twenty newborn babies every day. From a notebook, he provided me with Lyse-Rose's birth information. Weight: seven pounds, two ounces; length: nineteen inches.

Did the child cry? Yes.

Were the eyes open? Yes.

Other remarks: None.

Distinguishing features: None.

Another dead end.

Véronique de Carville must have been bored out of her mind in her villa. There were a few staff members at her disposal. I managed to find a gardener—rather old, and a bit too nearsighted for my liking—who had seen Lyse-Rose lying in the shade of a palm tree one afternoon... covered by mosquito netting. His description of her was consequently vague.

I am not going to give you a detailed list of all the hazy, half-assed, or completely useless witness statements that I accumulated during those months. Leave no stone un-turned, Mathilde de Carville had told me. Obediently, I did exactly that. After all, one coherent witness was all I needed.

At the Ataturk airport in Istanbul, a flight attendant remembered tickling a baby under the chin on December 22, just before the Airbus departed for Paris.

"One baby, or two?"

"Just one."

At least, that was what she thought; she wasn't sure about either the date or the flight. But she was sure there had been only one baby.

That damn flight attendant sowed another doubt in my overcrowded brain. What if there had been only one baby on board the plane?

After all, how could anyone be certain about who was actually sitting in the Airbus that night? The passenger list was known, but what if one of them had failed to board? A baby, for example? Maybe even Lyse-Rose. A delay, a last-minute holdup, a kidnapping ... I invented various scenarios in which Lyse-Rose might never have boarded that Airbus, in which she might still be alive now.

The theory was utterly insane.

But it wasn't the only one. For instance, wasn't it rather strange that there was so little tangible proof of this three-month-old's existence? So few witnesses, no friends to cuddle her, no babysitter to look after her, no photographs. Practically nothing. It was as if that baby had never existed. Or, to be more precise, it was as if someone had wanted to hide her ...

The longer I worked on the case, the more paranoid I became. What if Lyse-Rose had not caught the flight because she was already dead? An accident at home? An incurable illness? A crime? But if that were true, then Alexandre and Véronique de Carville had taken their secret to the grave with them.

Perhaps only Malvina knew. And she had lost her mind.

My theories made Nazim laugh when I recounted them to him at the Dez Anj café. He soaked his mustache in his raki.

"A crime? You're losing it, Crédule!"

Between puffs on his hookah, he brought me down to earth.

"Listen, this kid didn't live in a dungeon for three months. She must have gone out occasionally. So maybe some passerby, some tourist saw her. Maybe they accidentally filmed her . . . You never know."

"What do you mean?"

"Well, you've got money. Why don't you run some ads in the Turkish newspapers, with the photograph of the miracle child—the one taken by the *Est Républicain*?"

Nazim was right! His idea was genius. We bombarded the Turkish press, explaining what we were looking for and what we were offering in exchange: a fortune in Turkish currency.

Early on the morning of March 27, 1982—I will always remember that date—I found a letter waiting for me in my cubbyhole at the Hotel Askoc reception desk. It had been hand-delivered. The letter was brief. It contained a name—Unal Serkan—and a phone number. But, most important, it contained the photocopy of a photograph.

I ran across Ayhan Isik Sokak like a madman, almost getting myself crushed by the flow of vehicles. Nazim was waiting for me at Dez Anj.

"What's up, Crédule?"

I shoved the photo into his big, hairy hands. His eyes widened. He stared at the picture in shock, just as I had a few minutes earlier.

The picture had been taken at a beach.

In the foreground was a dark-haired woman, clearly Turkish, suntanned and perfectly proportioned, posing in a bikini. In the background, you could make out the hills of Ceyhan and, surrounded by greenery, the walls of the de Carvilles' villa. About ten feet behind the woman in the swimsuit, next to the legs of another woman, was a baby lying on a blanket. A tiny baby, only a few weeks old. Nazim stared speechlessly.

The baby was Lylie—our Dragonfly, the miracle child of Mont Terrible—without any doubt whatsoever. Same eyes, same face...

Pascal and Stéphanie Vitral had never gone to Ceyhan during their vacation in Turkey. They had never even been within a hundred miles of the town. There could be no doubt—finally we had the proof we were looking for.

The miracle child found in the snow on Mont Terri was Lyse-Rose de Carville.

October 2, 1998, 11:44 a.m.

The phone beeped, just once, almost inaudible amid the din from the underground train.

It was not a call to his cell phone, but a ringtone informing him that he had a message on his voice mail. A missed call.

Marc's trembling hand reached into his pocket.

20

As Ayla Ozan sliced the grilled mutton meat it fell in thin slivers onto the stainless steel countertop. Her mind was elsewhere. This did not make her any less competent at her job; in fact, if anything, she was better at making kebabs when lost in her thoughts than when she wasted her time chatting and joking with customers.

The line was beginning to lengthen, as it always did just before lunch. Her little take-out restaurant on Boulevard Raspail had plenty of regulars.

Although Ayla's face did not show it, she was worried. Deeply worried. She had not heard a word from Nazim in two days now. This was not like him at all. The meat continued to slide down under the blade of the carving knife. Ayla imagined stroking the blade over the back of Nazim's neck, his temples. She loved cutting her giant's hair. Her hand was trembling slightly; she never trembled when she shaved Nazim.

Ayla was not the type to be easily scared. She had seen other people full of fear when she fled Turkey for Paris with her father after the coup d'état of September 12, 1982.

At the time, her father had been one of the central figures in the Demokratik Sol Parti, and they had only just managed to escape the clutches of the army. Thirty thousand arrests in only a few days. Almost her entire family had ended up behind bars.

She had arrived in Paris without luggage, without friends, without anything at all. She had been thirty-eight years old, spoke practically no French, and had no qualifications.

Yet she had survived. You can always survive, if you really want to.

She had opened one of the first kebab shops in Paris, on Boulevard Raspail. Back then, French people had no desire to eat grilled meat in that way, outside, in front of other people, surrounded by flies and the city's pollution. Her customers were Turks, Greeks, Lebanese, and Yugoslavs. That was how she had met Nazim.

He came in every lunchtime. She couldn't miss him with his big mustache. It took him almost a year—three hundred and six lunchtimes exactly: Ayla had counted—to ask her out for dinner. They went to a Turkish restaurant (but a chic one) on Rue d'Alésia. Since then, they had never been apart, or hardly ever.

Married, for life.

Ayla shivered, in spite of herself.

Always together, or nearly always.

The only thing that ever took Nazim away from her were those damn trips to Turkey with Grand-Duc, for that stupid case involving the rich kid who had died in a plane crash. A private investigation funded by billionaires. Ayla picked up three hot foil packets stuffed with kebabs and yelled: "Number eleven! Number twelve! Number thirteen!"

The customers raised their hands, like schoolchildren

or people lining up at the welfare office, holding up their tickets. Ayla only had one pair of hands: she couldn't go any quicker. She opened a package of frozen french fries and threw them into boiling oil.

She had thought all that shit was over and done with. Thanks to her restaurant—if you could really call it that— she had managed to put aside a bit of cash, day after day. She had built up a nice little nest egg now.

She was too old to be carrying bags of meat, burning her fingers on the fryer. She dreamed of returning to Turkey with Nazim, being with her family once more. She had almost enough money now. She had done the calculations over and over again. She had spotted a little house on the coast, near Antakya—a bargain. The weather was always good down there. She and Nazim still had plenty of years ahead of them; their best years.

So what the hell could that jackass be up to now? What stupid plan had Grand-Duc got him mixed up in?

Three more sheets of foil. She wrapped the kebabs like presents.

Number fourteen. Number fifteen. Number sixteen.

"Just one last time, I promise," Nazim had told her. He had gotten all excited again when Crédule called him two days ago. His eyes had sparkled like a child's and he had taken her in his arms, lifted her up like a feather. Nazim was the only one who could do that.

"We're going to be rich, Ayla. We only need to sort out one last thing, and we'll be rich!"

Rich? Who cared about that? They already were rich: had almost enough to buy the house in Antakya.

"Is this really the last time? You promise?"

Ayla's hands were trembling. The carving knife deviated

from its usual straight line, mangling the meat into an inedible mush.

The more she thought about it, the more frightened she became. This silence. This sudden absence of news. Even when he went to Turkey, Nazim called her every day. And Crédule wasn't answering his phone either. She had been calling for the past two days. Yes, the more she thought about it, the harder it was to bear the passing minutes. She had a bad feeling about this. Were it not for these last customers, she would have run up to Butte-aux-Cailles like a madwoman and banged on Grand-Duc's door. In fact, that was exactly what she was planning to do, once she had closed the shop.

Number seventeen. Number eighteen.

She was well aware that Nazim was no angel. He had even confessed to her some of the terrible things he had done over the years. He had told her when they made love, when she let him rub his mustache all over her body, when she laughed, shivering, as he tickled her breasts, her thighs, her pussy, with his bristly upper lip... Afterward, when he had come, he told her everything. He couldn't help himself. He had never hidden anything from her. She knew the names and the places; she knew where Nazim had hidden the evidence. She was his life insurance. An investigation funded by billionaires... It was better to take precautions when the money was flowing too easily, because there would always come a time when you had to be accountable for what you had done.

That was another reason she wanted to leave, to go to Antakya. So that Nazim could leave all this shit behind.

Number nineteen.

She sighed. No, Nazim was no choirboy. Without her, he would be incapable of making the right choice, of distinguishing between good and evil.

21

The train slowed down as it came into Place-d'Italie, shattering the darkness with a thousand sparks. Marc grabbed his cell phone and put it to his ear

"Marc, you are incorrigible! I asked you not to call me, not to try to get hold of me or to look for me. I told you: I made an important decision the day before yesterday. It was very difficult and painful, and it took me a while, but in the end I made it all by myself. You won't understand what I'm going to do. Or you won't agree with it. I know how you feel, Marc. I know you mean well. Don't take that the wrong way—it's meant as a compliment. I admire your moral sense and your devotion. I know you would accept anything, forgive anything, if I asked you to. But I don't want to ask this of you. I wasn't lying when I talked about a journey in my letter. Departure is set for tomorrow, and it's a one-way trip. Nothing can stop this now. That's just how it is. Take care of yourself."

Marc had to fight the urge to hurl the phone at the door of the train. The network functioned only intermittently on the metro. Lylie had called him... and his phone had not rung. She had gotten his voice mail...

He was trembling. What had she meant?

"Departure is set for tomorrow..."

"A one-way trip..."

"Nothing can stop this now..."

Was it possible?

Marc found it hard to imagine such a thing.

So dark, so macabre.

Not Lylie!

And yet, the more he thought about it, the more the message between the lines seemed to become clear.

A one-way trip.

The miniature airplane. The decision made on her eighteenth birthday.

It all fit.

Lylie had decided to put an end to all her doubts, her obsessions, her past.

She had decided to kill herself.

Tomorrow.

Lylie threw the kebab, in its foil packet, in the trash can near the lake. She had barely touched it. She wasn't hungry.

She walked over to the water's edge. Montsouris, supposedly the biggest park in Paris, was also, she thought, the most sinister. At least in October. The bleak, filthy waters, the skeletal trees, the view over Avenue Reille, with its gray buildings of various heights, like a concrete hedge trimmed by a blind gardener.

The park's ducks had flown south a long time ago, and the stone lovers, shivering on their marble plinth, looked as if they would rather just get dressed and go home.

Lylie walked alongside the lake. It was strange, she thought, how your mood could transform a place. As if your surroundings instinctively mirrored what was in your head. As if the trees, sensing her pain, had lost their leaves in sympathy.

Lylie had switched off her phone again. A few minutes earlier, she had given in and called Marc. He had left her so many messages, had sounded so worried; she owed him that at least. It had been a relief when she got his voice mail. She was not up to answering his questions right now.

Lylie headed toward the Allée de la Mire and sat on a bench. The children's laughter, coming from the little playground, made her turn her head.

Two toddlers were playing there, watched by their mother, who was sitting on a bench, reading a blue-and-white paperback.

Twins. The little girls were wearing the same beige trousers, the same red button-up jacket, the same shoes. It was impossible to tell them apart. Nevertheless, every time their mother looked up at them, she addressed each one directly: "Juliette, don't stand up on the swing"; "Anaïs, don't push your sister on the merry-go-round"; "Juliette, you're supposed to go down the slide, not up it," and so on.

The little girls sometimes held hands and sometimes separated as they rushed from one ride to the next, as if they were trying to mix up their identities. Which one was which? Lylie followed their progress the way you follow a card trick. She lost each time, incapable of guessing, after a few moments, which one was Juliette and which Anaïs. All their mother had to do was look up for half a second and she knew instantly: "Anaïs, tie your shoelaces!"; "Juliette, come over here so you can blow your nose."

Lylie watched, enthralled, and felt a strange emotion rise within her. The girls were identical in every way, and yet they both knew who they were: Anaïs was not Juliette; Juliette was not Anaïs. Not because they felt different, but simply because their mother could tell them apart, she knew their names, and she never got them mixed up.

Lylie stayed there, watching them, for a long time. Finally, the girls' mother put away her book, stood up, and called: "Juliette, come down from the jungle gym. Anaïs, hurry up with the rope ladder. We're going home. Daddy is waiting for us."

The mother gently stroked her swollen belly. She was a few months pregnant.

Twins? Another little girl?

Lylie closed her eyes. She saw a baby, only a few months old, screaming alone on a mountaintop. Its scream was lost in the vast forest, muffled by the falling snow.

Unable to stop herself, Lylie burst into tears.

22

Dugommier.

Daumesnil.

Still no phone coverage.

Marc had not yet recovered from the shock of Lylie's message. He felt worried, helpless.

What else could he do but rush blindly on, almost randomly, through the tunnels beneath Paris? In desperation, he opened Grand-Duc's notebook to see if it held any more clues. All he could do was keep reading, in the hope that he might eventually find Lylie.

Crédule Grand-Duc's Journal

Léonce de Carville had his first heart attack while I was in Turkey, on March 23, 1982, only a few days before Unal Serkan delivered the photograph of Lyse-Rose de Carville, taken on the beach.

There was no connection between the two events.

To be perfectly honest, I didn't really care about Léonce de Carville's coronary. I had met him several times, as part of my investigation, and I think he regarded me as some kind of expensive bauble that his wife had bought. In truth, I think he also hated the fact that his wife had taken such an initiative—hiring me—without consulting him. I was the living proof that his bulldozer approach to the case had failed. He deliberately dragged his feet when it came to providing me with information for my investigation, drip-feeding it to me via his overworked secretaries. So perhaps you will understand why I didn't burst into tears when he fell, stricken, on the lawn of the Roseraie. After all, his wife was the one writing my checks, not he.

I know you don't care about any of this. What interests you is the photograph taken on Ceyhan beach. You want to know what happened next. I'm getting to that...

Unal Serkan was one slippery customer. I had already spoken to him several times on the phone, offering him a fortune—two hundred and fifty thousand Turkish lira—in return for the original negative of the photograph. This had been going on for weeks now. I could tell Serkan was after more money. He wanted to see how high he could push the bidding.

Finally, he agreed to meet me on April 7, early in the morning, on Avenue Kennedy, at the foot of Topkapi over-looking the Bosphorus. He was a small, fidgety guy whose eyes pointed in different directions—one toward Europe and the other Asia. Nazim came with me to translate. Serkan wanted a deposit of fifty thousand pounds. If I said no, he would sell the picture elsewhere.

Elsewhere? Who would want it? The Vitrals? Did he think we were stupid?

I didn't agree, obviously. He was not getting a single penny from me unless he handed over the negative. He, too, refused to budge an inch. We almost came to blows, right then and there, in front of the statue of Ataturk. Nazim had to separate us.

Going back to the hotel, I had a strange feeling. Not as if I had just made a mistake. Quite the opposite, in fact. As if I had dodged a bullet.

I called France and asked to be sent all the newspapers and magazines that had published articles about the Mont Terrible tragedy. They arrived three days later, on April 10. After less than an hour, I had the explanation I was looking for. The hideous blue vase on my bedside table exploded against the vermilion rug hung on the wall.

Unal Serkan had not taken much trouble. On January 8, 1981, *Paris Match* had published a series of photographs of Lylie, lying in her crib at the Belfort-Montbéliard hospital nursery. In one of them, Lylie was in exactly the same position as she was in the photograph of the beach in Turkey, supposedly taken one month earlier—leaning slightly to the side, her right leg bent, left arm under her head.

Unal Serkan's photograph was a fake, and not even a good one. He had simply replaced the sheets in the crib with a beach towel of the same color and texture. All he had needed after that was a picture of his girlfriend.

I wanted to tear down every rug I could find from the walls of that room. I spent two hours pacing around and, gradually, I began to calm down. In the end, I wasn't even angry with Unal Serkan. It had been a clever idea, and undoubtedly worth a try. It might easily have worked. Who wouldn't want two hundred and fifty thousand Turkish lira in return for a simple photomontage? I never saw Unal Serkan again. I had bigger fish to fry.

*

I spent the next few weeks in Turkey dreaming up other theories, which Nazim found increasingly woolly and unconvincing. He was right. It was probably due to the hookah. I had ended up developing a taste for it, in spite of my misgivings. The hookah, raki, and the inevitable keyif; afternoon tea served on a silver platter, in carved glass beakers, so hot it burns your lips as you refresh yourself between increasingly insane questions.

"Nazim, what if Lyse-Rose wasn't Alexandre de Carville's daughter?"

"What if she wasn't?" Nazim sighed, blowing on his tea. "How would that change things, Crédule?"

"It would change everything! Think about it: what if Alexandre de Carville wasn't the father. What if Véronique had taken a lover and that lover had blue eyes! That would change all the variables in terms of genetics, her eye color, all the little resemblances we're looking for. Don't you think?"

"A lover, Crédule?"

Nazim gave me an amused, mischievous look with his dark brown eyes. It was exactly the kind of look that Ayla must have fallen for.

In books and films, investigating adulterous affairs is portrayed as being one of a private detective's most boring chores. But to be perfectly honest, spying on other people's sex lives is one of the best parts of the job. I had no difficulty discovering that Alexandre de Carville was not exactly a model of virtue. I had suspected as much. A young, rich, powerful man living in a city where the harem is an age-old tradition, with a wife who stayed at home and looked after the children almost three hundred miles from where he worked . . . It was hardly a surprise.

Over time, I managed to turn up half a dozen extramarital adventures undertaken by the handsome Alexandre. Curiously, women seem to confess quite easily to affairs when their lover is dead; even more so when the wife is dead, too.

Alexandre de Carville was not afraid of clichés. He had humped his secretary on his glass desk at the company headquarters in Istanbul. I saw them both—the glass desk and the secretary—and they were both equally cold and elegant. He also had a three-month affair with a very hot and very young local girl who wandered around the streets of Galata in a miniskirt, her navel exposed, under the searching gaze of black-veiled women. She had taken him to nightclubs. I found her; she is married now. Two kids. She's still not wearing a veil, but she's not wearing miniskirts anymore either. I'll skip over Alexandre's adventures in hammams, with belly dancers, and with various prostitutes and escorts, often in the company of business clients. According to my research, his most faithful lover was Pauline Colbert, a single French businesswoman, who claims to have been the last person to have had sex with Alexandre de Carville, on December 22, 1980: the very day he flew out with his family on the Airbus 5403. It was clear to me that the fact of having made a man come several times, as she was eager to specify—less than twenty-four hours before he was burned to a crisp was deeply exciting for her in retrospect. She had an ordinary face, but a sexy body, and I got the impression that it wouldn't have taken too much effort on my part to persuade her to add a private detective to her tally of conquests.

First question: Was Véronique de Carville aware of her husband's escapades?

Answer: How could she not have been?

Second question (the most important): Did she pay him back in kind?

I never found any proof of that. Everything seemed to suggest that Véronique was fairly depressed, living almost alone with her daughters, Malvina and then Lyse-Rose. She did not, as I have already mentioned, have many visitors. I interrogated her entourage in an attempt to identify any possible lovers, potential fathers for Lyse-Rose. There was the gardener's son, a kindhearted Adonis who would work shirtless in the garden under Véronique's window. He was the type who would certainly have appealed to a depressed Westerner, a sexually frustrated woman reading *Lady Chatterley's Lover* beneath the covers, but he never confessed anything of the sort to me, and besides, he had extremely dark eyes, which would not have been particularly helpful from a genetic point of view.

I concentrated my search on blue-eyed men living in the vicinity of the de Carvilles' villa in Ceyhan. There were not many of them. I found three altogether, one of them reasonably credible: a handsome ponytailed German who rented out paddleboats nearby. I took pictures of him, and over the years I would compare those photos to Lylie's face, looking for any resemblance. Thankfully nothing stood out. It would have been hard to explain to Mathilde de Carville that she had paid me a fortune only to learn that Lyse-Rose had survived the crash and that she was not their granddaughter—not even a de Carville—but the daughter of a German who made a living renting out paddleboats.

Meanwhile, in France, the reward offered for information about the bracelet had gone up to forty-five thousand francs, and still no one had taken the bait, not even a hoaxer such as Unal Serkan. Then again, it was not particularly easy to replicate a solid gold bracelet with a Tournaire hallmark.

Still, leaving no stone unturned, I continued to offer my harebrained theories to Nazim, over tea and a hookah.

"Nazim, what if the crash wasn't an accident?"

It was lunchtime, and the Dez Anj café was crammed with tie-wearing Turks sipping their raki during the hour of prayer. Nazim was so startled, he almost knocked the tray out of the waiter's hands.

"What are you suggesting, Crédule?"

"Well, if you think about it, the actual cause of the accident has never been ascertained. The snowstorm, pilot error...it's easy to blame those things, don't you think? But what if there was another cause?"

"Go on. Like what?"

"A terrorist attack, for instance."

Nazim's mustache trembled.

"Against whom? The de Carvilles?"

"Why not? An attack aimed at their family, and Alexandre, the sole heir. It's not such an absurd idea, really. Alexandre was working on a high-risk project, the Baku–Tbilisi–Ceyhan pipeline, which goes straight through Kurdistan. Alexandre was negotiating directly with the Turkish government while the PKK was carrying out attacks all over the region..."

Nazim burst out laughing.

"The Kurds! Oh, come on...You in the West see terrorists everywhere. The Kurds! A bunch of peasants..."

"Nazim, I'm serious. The Kurdistan Workers Party was not at all happy at the prospect of seeing all that black gold flowing straight past them without any of it ending up in their territory. They must have been even less happy at the thought of the de Carvilles' bulldozers invading Kurdistan, surrounded by Turkish army tanks..."

"OK, Crédule, I can buy that. But it's a long way from being angry about the pipeline to deliberately crashing an Airbus with Alexandre de Carville on board. And anyway, how would that change things, if there'd been a terrorist attack against the de Carvilles?"

"It might be more complicated than that. What if Lyse-Rose was kidnapped before the Airbus took off? Or what if the de Carvilles knew about the attack beforehand and sent doubles to take their place..."

Nazim laughed again, even louder, then gave me a hearty slap on the back and ordered two more rakis. We spent the night watching boats in the Golden Horn and talking endlessly about the case. As I think back on it, these were easily the most enjoyable moments of the investigation. Those first months, in Turkey. My happiest memories. After that summer in 1982, my stays in Turkey became fewer and farther between.

On November 7, 1982, however, I was in Turkey once again. I had been there for two weeks. I heard the news three days later from Nazim. Mathilde de Carville had not even thought to warn me. Pierre and Nicole Vitral had been the victims of an accident, in Le Tréport, just before dawn on Sunday morning. Pierre never woke up. Nicole was still hovering between life and death.

From our perspective in Istanbul, the story of an accident was hard to believe. Was it just my profession warping my judgment, or was there more to it than that? In my room at the Hotel Askoc, I suddenly felt afraid. For the first time, I realized that continuing to work on this case for the de Carvilles, for eighteen years of my life, meant effectively losing those years... and possibly losing the years that would remain to me afterward.

But still I continued.

October 2, 1998, 11:52 a.m.

Nation.

Marc looked up. Sweat was running down his back.

This was where he had to change trains.

He found himself on the platform, notebook in hand, hyperventilating. He walked over to the nearest bench, closed the notebook, and opened his backpack. He was in shock.

The seventh of November, 1982.

That date was stamped on his memory. He had read it so often in the years since, engraved on his grandfather's gravestone, because he'd had nothing else to do while his grandmother stood there weeping. She went to the cemetery every day. When he didn't have school, Marc would go with her, pushing the stroller in which Lylie slept. It was a long way, and they had to walk up a steep hill, with Nicole coughing constantly...

The seventh of November, 1982.

Marc walked in a daze through the corridors of the metro, searching for directions to Line A. Gradually, his breathing returned to normal and he was able to think. The map of the RER network unfurled inside his head. He would go to Vincennes, Noisy-le-Grand, Bussy-Saint-Georges...

He slowed down. It was not a good idea to go too fast, to allow himself to be sucked into the spiral of events: Grand-Duc's notebook and its revelations; the detective's murder; Lylie's disappearance. His grandparents' accident.

He was not stupid. He could not simply walk into the lion's den like this. Not without taking some precautions at least. He examined his mental map of the metro. Yes, it would make much more sense to go the other way, toward La Défense. It was only one station more and would take only a few minutes longer. That way he would have time to safeguard what he had learned.

Less than two minutes later, Marc found himself in the crush of people at the Gare de Lyon. He let himself be carried along by the human whirlwind, past posters advertising the latest films: *The Horse Whisperer, Saving Private Ryan*...

The latest books and concerts.

Marc barely turned his head.

A poster for Charlélie Couture, in concert at the Bataclan. He thought about Lylie.

Oh, dragonfly,
Your wings are so fragile,
As for me, my body is broken...

Marc took out his telephone. Finally, he had coverage. He dialed Lylie's number.

It rang seven times, as usual.

Answering machine.

"Lylie, wait. Wait for me. Don't do anything stupid! Call me back. I'm on this. I'm going to find..."

Find what?

No hesitation. Just keep going.

Marc reached the mainline departures area. The orange TGV trains were lined up like sprinters. The luggage-storage facility was located to the right, behind the newspaper kiosk. Marc opened a heavy steel door and shoved his backpack inside the gray locker. He was not going to turn up at the Roseraie, the de Carvilles' lair, with Grand-Duc's notebook in his possession. The detective had given it to Lylie, not to the de Carvilles, and there must have been a reason for that. Marc would meet the de Carvilles, talk to them, negotiate. After that, he would make a decision.

He had to enter a code. Five numbers. Without thinking, Marc typed: *7 11 82.*

The locker door swung shut with a thud. Marc exhaled. He went to a stall selling sandwiches and bought a ham sandwich and a bottle of water.

He had made the right decision. It was better to keep the notebook elsewhere, for the moment, even if he was desperate to read the next part: Grand-Duc's version of his grandparents' accident.

Marc had been four at the time and had only vague memories of it. Grand-Duc's words were far from ambiguous, however: ". . the story of an accident was hard to believe. Was this just my profession warping my judgment, or was there more to it than that?"

Marc had to know. He did a sudden U-turn, walked back to the locker, and typed in the code.

7 11 82.

His hands trembling, Marc rummaged through the bag and took out the notebook. He skimmed the pages, glancing at the words: ". . . meant effectively losing those years . . . possibly the years that remained . . . But still I continued."

This was where he had stopped reading.

Marc grabbed the next five pages between his fingers and ripped them from the notebook. His grandparents' accident, as narrated by Grand-Duc. Then, shutting the locker door, he rushed back into the maze of the Gare de Lyon.

23

Nicole Vitral walked slowly along the Rue de la Barre. When she reached the crossroads near the Sévigné school, she stopped and coughed. A nasty, hacking cough. She still had to climb the whole of Rue de Montigny before she reached the Janval cemetery. More than half a mile. Never mind—she would take her time. Now that she was retired, this was practically all she had to do each day: visit her husband's grave, then buy bread at Ghislaine's on her way back, plus some meat every other day. Her legs were not as strong as they used to be.

Nicole braved the first part of Rue de Montigny: this was the steepest section. She had just passed the swimming pool when a van overtook her, then parked in front of her, with two wheels on the pavement.

The cheerful face of Sébastien, one of the town councilors, appeared at the window.

"We're going up to the school, Mrs. Vitral. Do you want us to drop you off at the cemetery on the way?"

Sébastien was one of the youngsters at the town hall. Well, he was in his forties. But he was a Communist, and proud of it. Nicole Vitral had watched him grow up. He was a good guy: an activist, and stubborn as a mule, but also mature and likable. With men like him in it, the Party still had a bright future, she thought, no matter what people said on television. They would win the next local election, she was sure of it.

Nicole did not need to be asked twice and got into the front seat of the van. Sébastien was accompanied by Titi, who was employed by the council as a gardener. Nicole had watched him grow up, too. He may not have been the sharpest knife in the drawer, but he was very adept at looking after the flower beds, and he contributed greatly to the prosperity of the local bars.

"You're still fighting fit, by the looks of it, Mrs. Vitral!"

"Not really…You should make the bus go past the cemetery, Sébastien, for all the old widows like me…"

The town councilor smiled. "That's not a bad idea. I'll add it to the agenda. So, how's Marc doing in Paris?"

"Fine, fine…"

Nicole's thoughts went back to the message Marc had left on her answering machine that morning. What could she say to him? Of course she knew where Emilie was; she had guessed the irrevocable act she was about to perform. She had prayed so often, through the years, that this would not happen. Life could be cruel sometimes.

Titi's loud voice woke Nicole from her thoughts. His breath already stank of booze.

"That Marc…Is he still following Emilie around? He never even comes back to play rugby on Sundays with the team anymore. Mind you, it's no great loss—I know he's your grandson and all, Nicole, but seriously, the guy has butterfingers…"

Titi laughed loudly.

"Shut your face, Titi," said Sébastien.

"It's all right." Nicole smiled.

She looked behind her. In the back of the van were boxes containing hundreds of leaflets.

"Still fighting the good fight, Sébastien?"

"Always! Chirac may have dissolved the Right in the Assembly, but we're still waiting for things to change, aren't we? Even with our comrades in government!"

"What are the leaflets about?"

"We're trying to save the commercial port. They want to take away our trade with West Africa, which is pretty much all we have left. Bananas, pineapples, that sort of stuff. If we lose that, the town will die. There's a protest march in Rouen on Saturday."

Titi elbowed Nicole in the ribs. "But even if we lose the bananas and pineapples, we'll still have your peaches, won't we? Eh, Nicole?"

Sébastien sighed. Nicole gave him an understanding look.

"Well, I can't promise anything about the march," said Nicole, "but if you bring me a box of those leaflets, I'll go door-to-door for you in Pollet. There are still a few people in Dieppe who know me and may listen to me..."

Titi almost jumped out of his seat. "That is totally true, Nicole! I used to love watching you on TV back in the old days. I was fifteen. I used to get so turned on watching you try to hide your big titties!"

"Jesus, Titi, shut the fuck up!" shouted Sébastien.

"What do you mean?" Titi asked, taken aback. "I was just saying. Nicole's hardly going to think I'm trying to pull her at her age. I was just paying her a compliment."

Nicole gently touched Titi's arm. "It's all right, Titi. I wasn't offended. In fact, I liked hearing you say that."

During the brief silence that followed, Nicole could not help thinking about Emilie. She wished she could be with her now. Not so she could try to change her mind, just to be there for her. Nicole knew that this would be the end of Emilie's innocence. The taste of death would remain with her forever, the memory. The remorse.

The van came to a halt.

"Here we are," said Sébastien. "The cemetery. Shall I bring you the box of pamphlets tonight?"

"That's fine."

"You'll really be helping us out, Nicole. You should stand for election, you know..."

"No, that was Pierre's thing, not mine. That was his plan. He wanted to stand in 1983."

Embarrassed, Sébastien said nothing for a moment. Then: "I remember. It was a terrible loss. Jesus, what a waste! Actually..." He hesitated. "The...the van, the Citroën, did you keep it?"

Nicole smiled resignedly. "Yes. I still had to work. And there were Emilie and Marc to look after."

"The best fries on the Côte d'Albâtre!" said Titi. "Believe me, Nicole, I didn't go to your van just because of your tits!"

Sébastien laughed, and Nicole smiled nostalgically. Her blue eyes still retained their sparkle.

"That van is still in our garden. And now there's no one there to ask me to move it so they can play. It's just gathering rust..."

Nicole opened the door.

"Well, I'd better let you lads get back to work!"

Titi helped her get down. They watched her as she crossed the empty parking lot.

Nicole pushed open the iron gate.

Marc would call back. Soon, probably. Maybe he would even come to Dieppe. What would she tell him? Should she give their impossible love affair a chance?

She had to decide. To speak or to say nothing. This was urgent, she knew: she had to make a decision today.

Nicole closed the cemetery gate behind her.

She would ask Pierre for his advice. He always made the right choices.

24

A delicate ray of sunlight greeted Marc when he got off
the RER train at Val-d'Europe. It was the first time he had
set foot in the new town, which had opened a few months
earlier. He was amazed by the vast circular square of
Place d'Ariane. He had been expecting to find a modern,
high-tech city, along the lines of Cergy or Évry. Instead
he found himself in the center of a Haussmannian square,
just like those in Paris's established arrondissements,
except that the square was not a hundred years old. It was
not even a hundred days old. New imitating old, and quite
convincingly, too.

Cranes towered above him, above the gutters and fake
gargoyles. A sign announced: *Arlington Business Park*.
The unfinished glass towers in the business district already
towered over the fake "old" square by a hundred feet or so.
Far away, beyond the bypass, Marc could see the peaks
of Disneyland: the highest tower of Sleeping Beauty's castle; the red rocks of the miners' ride; the dome of Space
Mountain... The effect was surreal.

Which was undoubtedly what the planners had hoped for.

A snippet of conversation from an evening at Nicole's house in Pollet rose to the surface of his memory. It had been a few months ago, after they had watched a news report on television about the new town created by the Disney consortium. The new shopping center had just been opened. In the kitchen, Nicole had cursed: "It's already bad enough people taking their kids to Disneyland and making that capitalist rat Mickey even richer. But giving them land so they can build towns in France…it's unbelievable!"

Lylie had been clearing the table. As always, she had known more about the subject than the rest of the family.

"But it's a kind of utopia, Grandma. Did you know Walt Disney had dreamed of creating an ideal city in Florida, called Celebration? No cars, no segregation, everything under a climate-controlled dome…But he died before it was built, and his successors changed the project. Val-d'Europe is only the second city in the world to be built by Disney. The only one in Europe. The newest town in France, with twenty thousand inhabitants…"

"A utopia! Are you kidding?" Nicole replied. "Private schools. A golf course. Houses costing three million francs…"

Lylie did not respond. Marc was sure she would have liked to defend the concept: the urban planning, the green spaces, the architectural challenges, the carefully thought-out transportation system. But Lylie, as always, remained silent. She had simply smiled as she picked up a dish towel to help Nicole, and had contented herself by talking to Marc about it, briefly, later that evening. Everyone knew that the de Carvilles lived in Coupvray, one of those pretty villages close to Val-de-Marne, whose French traditionalism had been so perfectly integrated into the American project at Val-d'Europe, sending house prices rocketing even higher. A marriage of tradition and modernity.

Marc walked on. The area had been designed with pedestrians in mind, and in that sense it could not be reproached. Coupvray was less than a mile away. He reached Place de Toscane, and smiled at the sculpted fountain, the cafés and terraces painted the color of raw sienna. He had never been to Italy, but this was exactly how he would have imagined a Florentine or Roman square, even in winter.

In spite of the fact that the town was designed for pedestrians, there were not many about. Marc was now crossing through the golfing district, with its English-style cottages. Bow windows, green and purple wood, forged iron. Marc felt as if he were crossing a picture postcard of Europe.

The sight of some more classical-looking (albeit expensive) houses told him that he was approaching Coupvray. He noticed a series of familiar signs: village hall, school, Louis Braille's birthplace. Jennifer had given him the de Carvilles' address: Chemin des Chauds-Soleils, a cul-de-sac on the edge of the village, in the middle of Coupvray Forest. Coupvray had been built in a bend of the Marne river, encircled by woods. The canal from Meaux to Chalifert formed a sort of border to the village, a straight line providing a shortcut for vessels navigating the Marne. It made this bucolic paradise, only a few miles from the French capital, even more picturesque. There were three fishermen sitting on the low stone wall overlooking the canal. A brown sign read: *Ecluse de Lesches*. This seemed like the perfect spot to sit down and rest. And to read the five pages of Grand-Duc's notebook that he had torn out and put in his pocket.

Marc had not felt brave enough to read them on the RER, with strangers eyeing the words over his shoulders.

Not this part of the story. His part.

Crédule Grand-Duc's Journal

I spent that Sunday—November 7, 1982—in Antalya, on the Mediterranean coast, a place where the sun shone three hundred days of the year. I was at the residence of a high-ranking official from the Turkish Home Office. I wanted to check again that no one had seen anything in Ataturk airport on December 22, 1980. The idea wasn't so far-fetched: a CCTV camera, some kind of incident… the airport had been full of soldiers at the time and one of them might have noticed something. I wanted to send a questionnaire around the barracks. The official thought I was crazy, of course. After weeks spent chasing him, he had finally given in and consented to see me at his beach house one weekend when all the bigwigs of Turkish national security would be there. Nazim was not with me, for once: Ayla had insisted he go home. He had fallen ill, if I remember correctly… This was extremely inconvenient for me, as I needed an interpreter to explain what it was that I wanted, and it was especially difficult as the others were there to relax in the sun with their wives and were not remotely convinced by the urgency of my requests. Then again, neither was I.

As I've said, I learned about the accident in Le Tréport three days later, from Nazim. Since then, I have talked with Nicole about it a great deal, and she told me the details. That weekend, the three towns of Le Tréport, Eu, and Mers-les-Bains had organized their "Festival of the Sea," as they did every year. Thousands of people came to eat *moules-frites*, walk through the town, and go for boat rides. Pierre and Nicole worked at the festival every year, as they did most of the local festivals. Apart from the summer months, they were dependent on weekends such as this in order to make ends meet. They left Marc and Emilie with neighbors and went off to spend the night in their orange-and-red Citroën van. They parked the van in strategic spots, as close to the beach as possible, and within an hour of arriving, they were serving up fries, crêpes, waffles, and other snacks. They usually worked until late at night. Festivals in the north of France often go on until dawn, in spite of the climate. In order not to lose time or money, Pierre and Nicole would sleep for a few hours on a mattress in the cramped space between the gas oven and the refrigerators before starting work again on Sunday morning. It was a hard life, but in one weekend like that, they could make more money than they would in ten normal days.

On Sunday, November 7, 1982, Pierre and Nicole Vitral closed up their van at about three in the morning. They would never open it again. It was a man walking his dog along the seawall who alerted police. The smell of gas was detectable even outside the van—or, rather, the smell of methanethiol, the sulfur-based product that is added to butane, which is colorless and odorless. The firemen smashed open the back door of the van with an ax and discovered two bodies inside. The butane had been escaping since at least 5:00 a.m., in a confined space. Pierre Vitral was no longer breathing. The firemen did not even try to resuscitate him; they could tell when someone was dead. But Nicole Vitral was still alive. She was transported to Abbeville. It was fifteen hours before the doctors could announce definitively that her life had been saved. Her lungs were permanently damaged.

The inquiry did not take long. There was a hole in one of the gas pipes leading to the ovens. The accident was stupid and all too predictable. The insurance company lived up to the industry's reputation for compassion and generosity: according to them, sleeping in the van, between the butane bottles and the still-warm ovens, was madness; the equipment was ancient, though it had been given the all-clear by health inspectors; and the insurance company's experts found other defects that allowed them to justify not paying a single centime to Nicole Vitral.

All that remained to her was the van—with a back door and a plastic pipe that needed replacing—and two children to bring up single-handedly.

It was perhaps this incident that brought me closer to the Vitrals. Pity? Yes, you could call it that. There is nothing wrong with pity.

Yes, pity. But also suspicion.

From the moment Nazim told me what had happened in Le Tréport, I did not believe that it was an accident. It is true that fate is like a playground bully, always picking on the weakest, but still...there are limits. In the weeks that followed, I met with the de Carvilles' lawyers. Some of them, not especially proud of their clients' behavior, confessed to me that, just before his second heart attack, Léonce de Carville had asked them a purely theoretical question: What would happen if Nicole and Pierre Vitral died? Would little Lylie remain a Vitral and be placed with a foster family, or was an appeal possible? In that hypothetical context, what would be the likelihood of the baby being given to the de Carvilles?

It was a delicate, not to mention rather morbid, question. The lawyers did not agree, but the general consensus was that, if the Vitrals died and Lylie was still under two years old, a new verdict was not impossible. "This is purely hypothetical," they said, but it would be feasible not only to raise doubts about the identity of the child, but also to question her best interests. Surely it would be better, in those circumstances, to give the young orphan to the de Carvilles rather than casting around for a foster family.

I will say no more about that. Make of it what you will.

If Mathilde de Carville was crazy enough to hire a private detective for eighteen years, her husband, notably less patient, was certainly capable of hiring an assassin. Putting a hole in a gas pipe, in a van that did not lock properly, would be easy for anyone who didn't possess too many scruples. I have never believed that Mathilde could have been aware of such a plot, never mind been behind it; her religious beliefs would not have allowed it. But Léonce de Carville had no such moral qualms. He never recovered from his second heart attack, twenty-three days later. It is possible to see some element of cause and effect at work here. Nicole Vitral survived. Perhaps Pierre Vitral's death played on his conscience. And that death was entirely pointless because it made no difference to the fate of Lyse-Rose.

That is all I know. Léonce de Carville is a vegetable

now, and his secrets will never be revealed. But would you give him the benefit of the doubt?

October 2, 1998, 12:40 p.m.

The benefit of the doubt...

Marc had been only four at the time of the accident, and remembered almost nothing about it. All he recalled was the terrible sadness of the adults in his life, and his own desire to protect Lylie at all costs, to hold her hand tightly, never to let her go.

His grandmother had never given him many details of his grandfather's death, but he understood that. These things are not easy to talk about. Grand-Duc's account was much clearer than any of the snippets of information Marc had been able to glean through the years.

Marc watched the three fishermen sitting across from him: though quite young, they sat motionless, and looked as if they were about to fall asleep. Where was the fun in waiting hours for a fish that never took the bait? Maybe they were simply waiting for the end of the world, in this little bit of heaven.

The benefit of the doubt...

Did the Devil live here, in this little bit of heaven?

Marc delved into the depths of his memory. Without knowing exactly why, it seemed to him that Grand-Duc's narrative had set off some kind of alarm in his brain. A jigsaw piece that did not fit; an anomaly.

There was something not quite right about what he had read.

He tried to concentrate harder. He felt increasingly certain that the detail was something he had learned by heart;

that the memory was undoubtedly there, somewhere in his brain, but that it could only be brought to the surface by finding a trigger: a word, some kind of starting point.

He kept trying, but without success. All he could be sure of was that this detail was something that was tidied away in his bedroom, among his belongings, in the house on Rue Pocholle. He felt certain that if he searched that room he would find what he was looking for.

Was it urgent? Where did it fit with everything else? Lylie's one-way trip...

Dieppe was only two hours away by train. And he had to talk to Nicole in any case.

But all that could wait.

He turned over the last torn-out page and read it.

25

Crédule Grand-Duc's Journal

One month after the tragedy in Le Tréport, Nicole Vitral was once again serving customers from her food truck. She had no choice. Many people found it strange, even morbid, that she continued to work in that coffin on wheels, in that battered metal death trap that had carried away her husband, her feet treading the same floor where he had taken his last breath.

Nicole would reply with a smile: "People keep living in the same houses where their loved ones died, don't they? They sleep in the same beds, eat off the same plates, drink from the same glasses... Those objects are not responsible for the deaths. My van is just an object like any other."

I realized, years later, that Nicole actually loved her job; she enjoyed serving people fries on the Dieppe seafront, just as she had done for years with Pierre, even if the smoke from the frying aggravated her lungs, making her cough endlessly. Pierre had fallen asleep in this van and never woken up; Nicole, alone now, felt less so here than anywhere else. Except for the Janval cemetery, perhaps.

It was around this time, in the summer of 1983, that I

drew closer to Nicole and her grandchildren. I met Nicole for the first time one morning in April. Marc was at school, and Lylie was asleep.

Nicole stood in the doorway in front of me.

"Crédule Grand-Duc," I introduced myself shyly. "I'm a private detective. I'm investigating…"

"I know who you are, Mr. Grand-Duc. You've been hanging around in the area for months. News travels fast here, you know."

"Oh…I see… Well, at least that should save us some time. Mathilde de Carville hired me to investigate this case…"

"I hope she's paying you well at least."

"I can't complain on that score…"

"How much?"

Nicole Vitral's eyes shone fiercely. She was playing a game of cat-and-mouse with me. Why lie about it?

"One hundred thousand francs. Per year."

"You could have gotten more. Much more."

She was wearing a low-cut blue-gray sweater. The V-neck offered a magnificent view. I was extremely turned on. Without moving an inch, she demanded: "What do you want from me?"

"I'd like to be able to see Lylie. To talk to her. To watch her grow up."

"Is that all?"

I sensed that this negotiation was going to take a while. I didn't know where to look: at her sparkling eyes, or down below, in the valley between her breasts. Unthinkingly, Nicole pulled up the V of her sweater.

"I have nothing to hide," she said. "You may be surprised to learn this, but I want to know the truth, too. Have you found out anything?"

I hesitated. Did I have the upper hand now? Not for long: her sweater quickly slid down again.

"I have followed lots of leads, most of them dead ends. But I have also discovered a few troubling details..."

Nicole Vitral appeared to hesitate. Her eyes surveyed Rue Pocholle.

"Did Mathilde de Carville make you sign any kind of confidentiality clause?"

"Not at all. She is just paying me to find out the truth."

"Well, I don't have any money to pay you, but Mathilde de Carville is generous enough for both of us."

Smiling, she pulled up the V of her sweater again.

"Quid pro quo? Come in and have a coffee, and you can tell me all about it while I wait for Lylie to wake up."

Nicole Vitral trusted me. God knows why.

I knew I was playing a dangerous game. If I did discover something important, my position between the two widows (or quasi-widow, in the case of Mathilde de Carville) would not be easy to maintain, even if I managed to stay neutral. And that became increasingly difficult; it was not much of a contest between the simple modesty of the Vitral family and the contempt of the de Carvilles. Léonce de Carville had water in place of muscles, Malvina had steam in place of a brain, and Mathilde an ice cube in place of a heart. I was their employee, their faithful hound, but my sympathies lay with the Vitrals, without any doubt whatsoever.

Marc and Lylie were adorable children. I got into the habit of visiting them quite frequently, at least once a year for Lylie's birthday. Sometimes I took Nazim with me to Dieppe, and he scared them with his big mustache. But, most of all, I was fascinated by Nicole: her energy, her sense of humor, her stubborn determination to raise Marc and Lylie by herself. She had held firm to her promise and had not touched a single centime of Mathilde de Carville's money, which lay in Lylie's bank account, steadily accumulating zeroes.

Nicole was determined and true to her word. An incredible woman. And just like that, the months, the years rolled by.

I, too, was faithful to my pilgrimage. This is more important than you can possibly imagine. Every year, around December 22, I returned to Mont Terri. I slept in a nearby rental cottage, in Clairbief, on the banks of the Doubs River, and I spent my time on the mountainside, at the crash site. I stayed there for at least a few hours each time, thinking, walking, reading over the notes I had taken. As if the place might finally reveal its secret to me...

I always went alone, without Nazim. I came to know every path, every stone, every pine tree. I felt I had to tame that wild mountainous area, that I should take the time to listen to it, to get to know it beyond the immediate trauma of the crash. As I had done with the Vitrals.

You probably won't believe this, but...it worked! The mountain confided in me. It took exactly three years. On my fourth pilgrimage there, in December 1986, it revealed its secret to me: by far the most disturbing secret I discovered in eighteen years of investigation.

That day—December 22, 1986—I was surprised, at the top of the mountain, by a sudden, violent storm. To get back down, I would have had to walk for at least two hours in the rain and lightning. So I decided to look for shelter. I knew that the young trees, which had been planted shortly after the crash, would offer me no protection.

I walked blindly for about half a mile. Finally, I found myself staring at the most unbelievable sight. I was soaked through, and to start with, I thought I must be hallucinating. I kept going, through the mud, the vision before me growing clearer and more real.

I no longer noticed the driving rain. My heart was pounding. I kept going until I reached the

Marc swore.

The torn-out page ended halfway through the sentence.

Irritated, he kicked at the gravel beneath his feet. The fishermen looked up disapprovingly. The rest of the sentence would be on the next page of the notebook, in the locker in the Gare de Lyon.

Marc shoved the pages into his pocket and stood up, furious with himself and furious with Grand-Duc's convoluted story. Why couldn't he just write things down instead of stretching them out as if he were penning a thriller?

He crossed a bridge over the canal. The Chemin des Chauds-Soleils was the first street on the right as you entered the village and, like everywhere else, it was quiet. More of a path than a street, in fact, disappearing into darkness as it wound through the forest. Marc walked on cautiously. Who were the de Carvilles, really? Victims of fate, as he was? Lylie's true family, as he hoped? But also, perhaps, the people who were responsible for the murder of his grandfather.

Enemies or allies? Or both?

There were a few cars parked in the cul-de-sac, all of them expensive-looking. Mercedes, Saabs, Audis. All of them large and powerful—with one exception: a blue Rover Mini. Marc froze.

He had seen this car. Recently.

But where?

Marc had spent most of the day underground in the metro. The only time he had been outdoors was here, in Coupvray. And...

At Grand-Duc's house.

He felt a hand on his shoulder and something metallic digging into his lower back. Possibly a gun.

A harsh voice demanded: "Looking for something, dickhead?"

26

Oddly, Marc did not feel an attack coming on. He had none of the usual symptoms: no breathlessness or palpitations. All he noticed was a slight acceleration in his pulse.

Don't panic.

Turn around.

Chemin des Chauds-Soleils was utterly deserted. The shadows of tall trees from the adjoining properties swayed over the pale gray gravel. Marc turned around very slowly, raising his hands so that his attacker would know he was not about to offer any resistance.

"Don't get smart with me, Vitral."

Marc squinted. A girl, less than five feet tall and weighing no more than ninety-eight pounds, stood in front of him. She was dressed as if she had just come home from boarding school, but her face was that of a thirty-year-old woman.

Malvina de Carville.

Marc had never met her, never even seen a photograph of her, but he knew it had to be Malvina. She was aiming a revolver at him, a strange fury in her eyes. Marc's brain struggled to make sense of all this new information. So, the blue Rover Mini, parked a few yards away, had, one hour earlier, been parked in Rue de la Butte-aux-Cailles, and it belonged to Malvina de Carville. Which meant she had been at Grand-Duc's house a few hours earlier...carrying a revolver...

Had she killed Crédule Grand-Duc? And would Marc be next?

Malvina stared at him, examining him from head to toe.

"What the fuck are you doing here, Vitral?"

There was something almost comical in Malvina's tone, like the high-pitched yelp of a tiny poodle warning visitors away from its master's house. But Marc knew he should not allow himself to be lulled into a false sense of security. This girl was capable of anything. She could easily laugh as she put a bullet between your eyes. But even knowing this, Marc couldn't quite manage to take her seriously. And bizarrely, considering the situation, he felt no symptoms whatsoever: no fear, no panic.

"Don't move, Vitral. I said, don't move!"

Smiling, Marc walked a couple of feet toward her, his hands still raised.

"Stop looking at me like that!" Malvina yelled, as she retreated. "You don't fool me with your bravado. I know everything about you. I even know that you're sleeping with your sister. Don't you think that's disgusting, fucking your own sister?"

Marc smiled again. He couldn't help it. The insults sounded false coming from Malvina's mouth. She was like those eight-year-old boys at the leisure center in Dieppe, who swore in order to cover up their shyness.

"Surely, from your point of view, it's *your* sister I'm sleeping with."

Malvina appeared to be surprised by this reply. After a few seconds, she came up with a response: "That's right. It's my sister you're fucking, because she's too beautiful to be a filthy Vitral pig. But Lyse-Rose won't need you anymore, not now that she's eighteen..."

Malvina's insults had no effect on Marc. They seemed unreal. He did not even feel the need to defend himself, to deny that he was fucking Lylie. Instead he continued along the path, not allowing himself to betray the slightest hesitation. The girl pointed the Mauser at him more aggressively.

"I told you not to move."

Marc kept walking, without turning around.

"Sorry, but I didn't come here to speak to you. I want to see your grandmother. This is the right house, isn't it? The Roseraie?"

"Keep moving and I'll kill you, cocksucker."

Marc pretended not to hear. Was he right to trust his instinct, to assume the absence of agoraphobia meant this girl was not really dangerous? Or would he end up like Grand-Duc, shot through the heart? Sweat ran down his back. He stopped in front of the huge gate to the Roseraie.

"What are you doing, you prick? I told you already: I'll kill you!"

Malvina scampered after Marc, like an excited child, then stood in front of him, the Mauser still aimed at his chest. Again, she looked him carefully up and down.

"Looking for something?" Marc asked ironically.

"You didn't bring your bag. Are you hiding something? Under your shirt, perhaps?"

"Oh, you want me to strip, do you?"

"Keep your hands in the air, dickbreath!"

"Ah, I see... You want to undress me yourself. Rub your little hands all over my body..."

Malvina hesitated. Marc wondered whether he might have gone too far. Malvina's finger was tightening on the Mauser's trigger. On that finger, Marc saw a silver ring set with a beautiful translucent brown stone, like the color of her eyes, but more luminous. Malvina continued to examine him. She was undoubtedly looking for Grand-Duc's notebook: he had been right to take precautions.

He forced himself to be cruel: "Sorry, Malvina, I prefer your sister."

Ignoring Malvina's reaction, he walked forward and pressed the intercom button. He now had no way of seeing what the mad girl was doing behind his back.

"You little shit, I'm going to..."

A woman's voice crackled over the intercom, interrupting Malvina:

"Yes?"

"It's Marc Vitral. I've come to speak to Mathilde de Carville."

"Enter."

The gate opened. Malvina hesitated, as if embarrassed now to be found pointing a gun at Marc. Then her eyes flared and she barked at him: "Didn't you hear her? She told you to go in. What are you waiting for?"

Marc had known it would be a luxurious property, one of the most lavish in this wealthy enclave, but even so he was impressed by the vastness of the tree-filled park, the flower beds, the climbing roses. How big was this place?

Three acres? Four? He walked along the pink gravel path, his armed guard stalking him five feet behind.

"Can't believe it, can you, Vitral? How big and beautiful the Roseraie is. The biggest park in Coupvray. From the second floor, you can see the entire bend of the Marne. Now do you realize what Lyse-Rose missed out on all these years?"

Marc suppressed the urge to slap her. Malvina had shot so many poison darts at him that, inevitably, one or two had found their mark. Marc could not help comparing the Parc de la Roseraie to his grandmother's garden in Rue Pocholle. Ten by fifteen feet. With the Citroën parked there, they had not even had a garden at all. Farther off, close to the greenhouse, a squirrel flashed past, glancing nervously at the visitors.

"Now that you see what you deprived her of, I hope you feel some remorse."

Remorse?

Marc could still hear Lylie's laughter in his ears. The happy shouting of children when Nicole drove off in her Citroën to work on the seafront, leaving Lylie and Marc to play hopscotch or ball in the little garden.

Three steps. Malvina overtook him, the Mauser still aimed at his chest, and opened the thick wooden door.

Marc followed her inside.

Was he mad, going in like this, of his own free will? He had come here alone, and no one else knew where he was going. Malvina pointed him down a wide hallway. They climbed three more steps. Paintings of bucolic landscapes adorned the walls. Fur coats hung from forged iron hooks. An oval mirror at the end of the hallway gave the illusion that it went on forever.

Malvina gestured with the Mauser to the first door on the right: a heavy door with red moldings. They went in.

Marc found himself standing in a large living room. Most of the furniture was covered with white sheets, presumably intended to protect it when it was not in use. Directly across from him was a wall entirely covered by bookshelves. In the opposite corner was a white grand piano, a Petrof, one of the most expensive models on the market. Marc knew how much it must have cost.

Mathilde de Carville stood in front of him, tall and straight-backed, her only adornments being the cross that hung around her neck and a few incongruous mud stains on the lower part of her dress. Next to her, her husband slept in his wheelchair. Indifferent. A tartan blanket was spread across his lap, covered by a few yellow leaves. The black widow and the paralytic... it was like being trapped in a bad horror movie.

Mathilde de Carville did not move. She merely smiled at him strangely.

"Marc Vitral. What a surprise. I never thought for a minute that you would come here one day..."

"Neither did I."

The smile grew slightly wider. Malvina moved away and stationed herself next to the piano.

"Put down your gun, Malvina."

"But Grandma..."

Mathilde de Carville gave her granddaughter a stern look. Pointedly, Malvina laid down her weapon on the piano. It was obvious that she was desperate to pick it up again.

Marc could not help staring at the piano. Of course the de Carville family would have a piano. He could have guessed that, even without having set foot inside their house. No member of the Vitral family was musical. Neither his parents nor his grandparents had ever played a musical instrument. There were not even many records in the house on Rue Pocholle. And yet, from her very first months in Dieppe, Lylie had always been spellbound by sound, all kinds of sounds…in nursery school, she had been fascinated by musical instruments, and it had seemed logical when, at the age of four, she joined the local music school. It was practically free. Her music teacher had been full of praise for her, Marc remembered proudly.

"A nice model, isn't it?" said Mathilde de Carville. "It's genuine. Ordered by my father in 1934. You surprise me, Marc. Are you interested in the piano?"

Marc, lost in his thoughts, did not reply. When Lylie turned eight, her music teachers became more insistent. She was one of their best and most passionate students. She happily played every instrument that was handed to her, but her favorite was the piano. She ought to practice more regularly, her teachers said; she ought to be playing her scales every day, at home. The teachers quickly dismissed the Vitrals' first objection to this, that they didn't have enough space for a piano: there were some excellent models available, designed specifically for small apartments. And then there was the question of cost. A decent piano, even a secondhand one, would have cost Nicole several months of her salary. It was unthinkable. Lylie had not protested when Nicole explained to her that it was beyond their means…

A squeaking noise made Marc jump. Behind him, Malvina was sliding the Mauser across the lacquered wood of the Petrof.

"Leave that gun where it is, please, Malvina," Mathilde de Carville commanded calmly. "I played, too, Marc, when I was younger. Not well, however. My son, Alexandre, was much more talented than I. But I don't suppose you came here to talk about music…"

"You're right," Marc said. "I'll get to the point. I came here to talk to you about Grand-Duc's investigation. I am not going to hide anything from you. He gave me his notebook. Well, in fact, he gave it to…" He hesitated, then went on: "He gave it to Lylie, who gave it to me this morning and insisted I read it."

"But you came here without it?" Mathilde de Carville interrupted. "Very prudent, Marc. You do not trust us. But you need not have worried. As far as the notebook is concerned, I never asked Crédule Grand-Duc for any sort of exclusivity. It is a good thing that Lylie now knows the truth. Doubt is better than false certainty. Anyway, I think I have a good idea what that notebook contains. Grand-Duc was a faithful employee."

Marc watched Malvina's distorted reflection in the polished wood of the Petrof, then feigned surprise: "*Was?*"

Mathilde did not hide the irony in her reply: "Yes, *was*. Grand-Duc was under contract to me for eighteen years. But that contract ended two days ago."

Marc cursed inwardly. Mathilde de Carville was trying to manipulate him. Of course she knew about Grand-Duc's death. He had been killed by her granddaughter. Possibly on her orders…Marc's hands were shaking. What was he doing here, with this bitter old witch and her mad, murderous offspring? Not to mention the ancient vegetable in his wheelchair. What good could possibly come from this situation?

Marc stepped forward, to give himself confidence. He had nothing to lose...he may as well say what he had come here to say.

"All right, I'm going to be honest with you. For eighteen years, our families have held tightly to their convictions. The de Carvilles claim that Lyse-Rose survived; the Vitrals say it was Emilie. And the judge said that, too."

Marc exhaled, searching for the right words.

"Mrs. de Carville, I have grown up with Lylie over the past eighteen years, and I have become certain of one thing." Marc hesitated again, then went on: "Mrs. de Carville, Lylie is not my sister! Do you understand? We do not share the same blood. I believe it is Lyse-Rose who survived the crash."

The Mauser made a sharp snapping noise as it fell onto the piano. Malvina's eyes shone with surprise and happiness, as if Marc had suddenly become their ally. A spy who had taken off his mask and revealed his true identity.

He was one of them!

Mathilde de Carville, on the other hand, did not move a muscle. For a long time she was silent, then she said simply: "Malvina, take Grandpa outside."

"But Grandma..."

There were tears in her eyes.

"Do as I tell you, Malvina. Take Léonce for a walk in the park."

"But..."

This time, Malvina could not hold back her tears. She left, pushing the wheelchair in front of her, while her grandfather continued his long sleep.

27

October 2, 1998, 12:55 p.m.

Lylie reeled dangerously. This bar stool, with its narrow legs, seemed to have been designed specifically to tip over whenever the person sitting on it had had a little too much to drink.

It won't be long, thought Lylie.

She brought the tumbler of gin to her lips. It didn't burn so much now. She no longer felt anything but the swaying of the stool.

She was the only woman in the bar—Barramundi, on Rue de Lappe. It was the kind of bar you did not enter alone, even during the day, unless you had something very specific in mind. While the guys in the bar pretended not to be interested in her—continuing to drink their beers and their glasses of wine, scratching at their lottery cards, and watching sports endlessly on the television—she could feel their eyes on her bare thighs, creeping up her back, toward the nape of her neck . . .

To forget.

Lylie downed the rest of her gin and turned to the barman, a placid man with a single tuft of gray curly hair on top of his head.

"What else do you have?"

She had already tried vodka and tequila. For the moment, her favorite by far was vodka. But she was still at the beginning of her learning curve; she had never touched a drop of alcohol before her eighteenth birthday. And even on her birthday, she had drunk only one glass of champagne. Now she was making up for lost time.

"Perhaps you should quit while you're ahead, miss. Don't you think you've had enough to drink?"

What was he talking about, this baldie with his stupid lock of hair? Didn't he realize she was eighteen now? Lylie was about to shove her ID card under his nose, but the bastard had already turned his back on her.

A man wearing a gray suit and a floppy tie was standing by the bar about thirty feet away from her, staring into a glass containing some brownish liquid. He was the only man in the bar not to have undressed her with his eyes. Lylie leaned toward him, gripping the counter as she balanced precariously on her stool.

"Hey, you! What are you drinking?"

Floppy Tie sat up a little bit.

"Just a scotch..."

"I want that, too! Hey, garçon, that's what I want."

The bartender, unruffled, frowned with his right eyebrow. "Are you sure, miss?"

"It's all right, Jean-Charles," said Floppy Tie. "This one's on me."

Jean-Charles frowned again, this time with his left eyebrow. The man must have trained for years to attain such mastery of his eyebrows, Lylie thought.

"Let's make this the last one, then. I don't want any trouble."

The scotch drinker, whose stool-balancing technique was far better than Lylie's, somehow managed to sidle up alongside her without leaving his seat. He was not there to console her, not at all. To him, the bar was an island, and he had been here since his ship sank, surviving on liquor and conversations with other shipwreck victims: swapping tales of storms and messages in bottles.

"So what is a nice girl like you doing in a place like this, Miss...?"

"Dragonfly. Miss Dragonfly."

The man seemed to have only just noticed that the girl he was chatting up possessed the beautiful, slender body of a model, and that the entire bar was watching their little mating ritual.

"Nice name, that...Dragonfly. I'm Richard...I'm a college professor, in Boieldieu, in the twentieth arrondissement, so as you can probably guess, I'm..."

Lylie reached out to pick up her glass of scotch. She sipped it and pulled a face. Clearly, nothing was going to taste as good as vodka. Realizing that she was completely uninterested in his tales of academia, Richard changed the subject.

"So...a pretty girl like you... You don't look like a pro. How is it possible that you're here, when you're so pretty, I mean?"

Lylie leaned toward Richard.

"Come here, you."

Suddenly grabbing hold of his tie, Lylie pulled him toward her until her mouth was close to his ear.

"I'll tell you, Mr. Floppy Tie. I'm not pretty at all. This is just a disguise."

Richard looked dazed. "Huh?"

"My thighs, my breasts, my mouth, my skin . . . all those things that guys look at and want to touch . . . it's just a disguise, you see, made of latex. Like a wet suit . . ."

"You . . . are you . . ."

"I'm not joking. Everyone thinks I'm beautiful, but the truth is, inside, I'm a monster!"

"Uh . . ."

"Cat got your tongue? I'm telling you, I'm like a snake. I have several skins. I'm like those monsters on TV, the ones that look like humans on the surface but underneath they are ugly reptilian things. You know what I'm saying?"

"Not really. I don't watch much television, you see. I'm a professor . . ."

A pull of the tie, and the man shut up.

"I'm going to tell you something else. Something worse. I'm not alone: there are two of us inside this skin. Can you believe it? Two of us in the same body."

"Well . . . I think it's . . ."

"Don't say a word. It's better like that. I'm going to have to leave in a few minutes. You know where I'm going? I'm going to do something bad. Something I really don't want to do. Something that disgusts me. But I have to do it . . ."

Richard clung to Lylie's shoulder; it was either that or he would fall off his stool. His arm was pressed against Lylie's breast. As he brought his lips closer to hers, he stammered: "Why? No one has to do anything they don't want to do. Perhaps I could help you . . . take off your disguise, so I could see underneath. See you and your friend . . ."

Richard grew bolder. Lylie still had hold of his tie, so he did not have much room to maneuver, but he managed to slide his right hand under her skirt. Lylie did not bat an eyelid.

"It's too late. You can't do anything for me, nobody can. I'm going to kill someone who has done nothing to deserve it... That's just how it is."

"All right, all right... but there's still time. A few minutes. You should show me your other skin, before you leave... if you want me to believe you..."

The man's right hand climbed higher up Lylie's thigh, while his left hand brushed against her breast. The bartender frowned with both eyebrows at the same time and slammed a glass down on the countertop.

"Easy, Richard. Take it easy with the kid. Take your hands off her. Don't you think you've had enough hassle with that kind of thing already?"

Richard hesitated. Lylie pulled harder on his tie, half choking him.

"Hey, are you listening to me? I'm telling you I'm going to kill an innocent person!"

Lylie leaned farther forward. This time, it was too much for the stool, and she collapsed in a heap on the floor.

Richard reached down to help her up.

"Don't touch me!" she screamed. "Take your filthy hands off me! Piss off!"

28

October 2, 1998, 1:11 p.m.

Mathilde de Carville pulled apart the curtains and looked through the window to see if her granddaughter was doing what she had been told to do. Marc gazed after her, out through the fine mesh of the white net curtains, to the vast green and ocher park. The Roseraie seemed to be permeated with the cocooned ambience of an old film, with its antiquated bourgeois decor and pastel tones, all of it slightly out of focus. In the distance, Malvina was pushing her grandfather along the pink gravel path. The old man's head seemed to have fallen to one side during the walk on the uneven path, and his neck was now twisted. His open eyes were staring up at the white sky, or perhaps at the treetops, at the slowly falling leaves of the large maple tree. Malvina did not bother to fix her grandfather's position.

Mathilde waited a few seconds longer, then slowly let the curtain fall. The room was once again plunged into a dim half-light, in which the white silhouettes of the sheet-covered furniture and the white lacquered wood of the Petrof glowed like frozen ghosts. Mathilde de Carville turned toward Marc.

"Marc... May I call you Marc? I think my age makes it

permissible. As you have come to visit me, Marc, I would like to ask you a question. One simple question. When you saw Lylie, in the past few days, after her eighteenth birthday, was she wearing any new jewelry? A ring, for example?"

Marc was standing near the piano. His fingers danced over the keyboard without touching any of the keys.

Why lie?

"Yes, she was wearing a ring. A pale sapphire…"

Mathilde de Carville did not smile. She showed no sign of triumph or jubilation. Marc found that strange.

Marc's hand stroked the piano. The Mauser was still there, on the white wood, about three feet from his fingertips. Marc looked through the window, attempting to spot Malvina in the park, but the curtain revealed nothing but a line of pale light.

"She's mad," Mathilde de Carville's voice announced calmly. "My granddaughter has gone almost completely insane. I assume you realized that."

Marc did not reply, so Mathilde continued: "What about you, Marc? What do you think?"

Marc waited.

"About madness, I mean. What do you think?"

Marc let his fingers dance over the ivory keys.

"I am talking to you, Marc," the cold voice insisted. "I am talking *about* you. As a little child your brain, just like Malvina's, had to deal with all the uncertainty, the doubt. What had happened to your little sister? Was she alive? Dead? Are you in a better state than Malvina, when all is said and done?"

Marc looked up, but still did not speak.

"It's torture, isn't it, Marc? All those years. Not knowing what to feel about the girl you love more than anyone else in the world. Is it a chaste brotherly love? Or something more passionate and carnal? How must it feel to grow up with all that uncertainty?"

Her voice had changed. It had grown louder, more threatening. Mathilde de Carville moved toward the piano.

"In order to survive, we rationalize our feelings, don't we, Marc? Through all those childhood years, little Marc sought the affection of Emilie, his adorable little sister... and then little Marc grew up, and the doubt began to seem like an opportunity. Why not take advantage of it? Bury little Emilie and fall in love with Lyse-Rose, the rich and beautiful de Carville heir..."

Mathilde de Carville's fingers crept toward the revolver.

"I suffered, Marc. My God, how I suffered. I atoned for my sins, all those years. I don't even know what my sins were, but I atoned for them anyway. My vengeance has a bitter taste, Marc, believe me."

Marc coughed. It was the only sound he seemed to be able to make. Mathilde now stood only a couple of feet away from him. What vengeance was she talking about?

Suddenly, Mathilde de Carville turned away and walked toward the bookshelves on the other side of the room. She picked up a thick-spined book, the title of which Marc could not see, and opened it. From inside its pages, she extracted a lavender-blue envelope.

"Grand-Duc grew close to you, Marc. He even became a family friend. But don't be fooled: he was still my employee. He would file a report for me almost every week... at least in the early years. After five years of investigation, there were practically no new leads to follow. After eight years, there were none at all."

The image of Grand-Duc's corpse flashed through

Marc's mind. Mathilde placed the blue envelope on the piano, next to the revolver.

"None at all...except for one. The last one. The only one. This was in 1988..."

Mathilde turned around again.

"Marc, we aren't in any rush. May I offer you something to drink?"

Marc hesitated. Everything that had happened to him, everything he had found, since he arrived at the Roseraie, seemed to have been prepared, calculated, as if his arrival had been expected. This dimly lit room. The white piano with the Mauser on top of it. The disappearance of Malvina and Léonce into the garden, or elsewhere.

"Yes...sure," Marc said, in spite of his misgivings.

"Herbal tea? I have some excellent varieties, grown in my own garden."

Marc nodded. Mathilde de Carville was gone from the room for a long time, leaving Marc alone, next to the blue envelope and the Mauser. This was, clearly, her intention. A form of slow torture. Mathilde's revenge. Marc tried to slow his breathing, examining himself for the first signs of agoraphobia. While he had not sensed any danger at all in the company of the armed monster Malvina, this scene with her grandmother was having quite the opposite effect. He was beginning to feel the familiar tingling as the blood rushed through his veins.

Mathilde returned, carrying a small tray on which sat two cups. She poured hot water into both, and handed one to Marc with a saucer.

"Drink, Marc."

Marc hesitated. Mathilde smiled at him. "I'm not going to poison you!"

He took a sip. The liquid scalded his lips.

"I will not prolong your suffering any longer, Marc," said Mathilde de Carville.

He drank some tea. It tasted good.

"At the beginning of this decade," she went on, "as I am sure you are aware, it became possible to find out the truth. All that was needed was a simple DNA test. It was infallible. In return for a lot of money and a few drops of saliva or blood, there were laboratories in England that could give you the results within a few days. It took me several years to make the decision. The Catholic religion does not fit particularly well with this form of science. I hesitated for a long time, but finally I decided to have the test done three years ago, when Lylie was fifteen. It was Grand-Duc's final mission, in a way. He took care of everything. He had connections with forensics specialists in the police force and I provided him with the money. The way we did it was not strictly legal. He got hold of a sample of Lylie's blood on her birthday. I gave him mine, some from my husband, and some from Malvina. It was so simple."

Marc felt his legs give way beneath him. He took another sip of herbal tea. The more he drank, the more sour the taste became. He remembered Lylie's fifteenth birthday, of course. Grand-Duc had been invited, as he was every year, and he had given her a glass vase. The vase was so thin—or perhaps it was already cracked—that it shattered as soon as Lylie held it. She cut her index finger. Grand-Duc had stammered his apologies while he picked up the broken pieces of glass.

Would Grand-Duc confess to this subterfuge in his notebook? Marc would find out soon. His throat was burning.

Right now, he wanted only one thing: to tear open that blue envelope and read what was inside.

Mathilde de Carville smiled at him strangely again.

"Marc, the results are inside that envelope. I have known them for three years now. I am the only one who knows them. You have helped me by coming here, Marc. Now you can take this envelope with you."

Marc took a last sip of tea. With trembling hands, he grabbed the blue envelope. Mathilde de Carville's face creased into a triumphant grimace.

"But you must not open it, Marc! You must take this envelope to Nicole Vitral. This is between me and your grandmother. If anyone else deserves to know the truth, after all these years, it is she."

A long, frosty silence filled the room. Marc put the envelope in his pocket.

"How do you know I won't open it as soon as I leave here?"

"You are a good, obedient child, aren't you? I don't think you would betray your grandmother. This letter is for her."

"Those are your rules. Why should I follow them?"

"You'll follow them, Marc. Of course you will. Because you are already convinced that you know the answer written inside this envelope."

Marc gasped. His throat and stomach were burning.

"What do you have to fear, Marc? Isn't this what you wanted? For Lyse-Rose to have sur ived, for Emilie to be dead. Nicole will be sad, of course, but I am sure her grandson's happiness will console her."

Marc could feel the symptoms of a panic attack overcoming him. He could not control his breathing and he felt as if the herbal tea was consuming his stomach. Mathilde de Carville gave a horrible laugh.

"What are you hoping for, exactly, Marc? To marry Lylie? Do you want her to become Lyse-Rose de Carville? Do you wish to be my son-in-law? A white wedding at Notre-Dame? My husband might find it difficult to escort his granddaughter up the aisle, but we could work something out. And what about afterward? Would you come with Lyse-Rose to drink coffee on Sundays, to play chess in the park, while I discuss waffles and fries with your grandmother? What a shame, Marc. What a waste..."

Marc tried to grab hold of his cup, but it fell from his hands and smashed on the carpet, splattering the legs of the piano.

"Give that envelope to your grandmother, Marc. If she wishes, she may let you read the DNA test results afterward. And tell her that I have no regrets, in particular about the money I spent. I am at peace with myself."

Marc's eyesight grew blurred and his veins felt as if they were on fire. His legs, like two towers weakened by an inferno, collapsed beneath him and his hands grasped at the Petrof's keyboard, slowing his fall with a sinister clash of discordant notes.

29

Ayla Ozan stood in front of number 21 Rue de la Butte-aux-Cailles. Standing on tiptoes, she tried to see as far as she could into the garden. Nothing moved. The pale green shutters were all tightly shut. Ayla rang the bell several times, but nobody answered.

Finally, she turned around and walked down the street, desperately searching for some kind of clue. She had often been to Grand-Duc's house; she would make dinner while Crédule and Nazim worked on the case, talking late into the night. She would listen to them sometimes, but she always ended up falling asleep before they did, on the sofa, warmed by the fire in the hearth, watching the dragonflies in the vivarium, lulled by the sound of her men's voices: the love of her life and his best friend. Where could they have gone? With no one answering the door at Crédule's house, and no news from Nazim, she knew that something was very wrong.

Ayla passed a bar, Le Temps des Cerises. She thought about going in, to ask for information. Crédule sometimes came here for a coffee. She stopped, aware that the way she

was walking did not look very natural. Before leaving her
kebab shop on Boulevard Raspail, Ayla had taken a large
kitchen knife, the sharpest she could find, and wrapped it
in a plastic bag before sliding it down her leg, under her
wide trousers. It was too long to fit in her backpack. She
felt she needed a weapon, just in case... She could not rid
herself of the feeling that Nazim was in danger.

Ayla looked down Rue de la Butte-aux-Cailles. There
were very few people around. Mothers and children. Customers at the bakery.

Suddenly, she froze. Her heart thudded beneath her
long winter coat.

Crédule's black BMW X3 was parked on the street, a
short distance from his house. She could find no trace of
Nazim's blue Xantia, though. Nazim had gone to Crédule's house; if they had left the house together, why the
hell would they have taken the filthy, dented old banger
rather than the BMW? Especially Crédule, who was so
fastidious.

Ayla walked slowly around the area. She took Rue
Samson, Passage Boiton, Rue Jean-Marie-Jégo, and Rue
Alphand, her leg unnaturally straight due to the knife
secreted in her trousers. She thought about the possibility of the plastic bag giving way at any moment, the sharp
steel slicing open her leg...

"Are you looking for something?"

A man with a dog was staring at her, the type of nosy
do-gooder who didn't like strangers hanging around the
place. Particularly a Turkish woman who kept gazing at
parked cars.

"I...I'm a friend of Crédule Grand-Duc. He lives at 21
Rue de la Butte-aux-Cailles. That little house, just before

Le Temps des Cerises. He isn't home, but his car is parked nearby. A black BMW. You...Have you by any chance seen another car, a blue Xantia?"

The man looked at her as though he belonged to the immigration department. He consulted his dog.

"Rusted bumpers? Dried flowers attached to the rear-view mirror? A Turkish flag hanging in the back window? Is that the one?"

The man seemed pleased with himself. Ayla nodded and gave him her most dazzling smile, even though he seemed more interested in his dog than in her Ottoman charms. The mongrel was clinging affectionately to Ayla's legs.

"The Xantia was parked here for a few days," the man said finally, "but it hasn't been here since yesterday."

The knife was digging into Ayla's leg painfully. If that stupid dog kept pressing against her, he would soon end up with his head cloven in two, like a kebab. She bent down to free herself from the dog's affections, while simultaneously attempting to adjust the position of the knife. The man watched her even more mistrustfully. He was slimy, but he could prove useful. Ayla smiled and caressed the dog, so that neither of them would feel jealous.

"Do you mind if I ask you something else? You seem to know the area very well. Did you happen to see anything new or suspicious recently, in the last few days ? A stranger, perhaps? Another car that didn't belong here?"

The man stared at her, amazed by her insolence. Instinctively, he pulled at the dog's leash, but he could not resist the temptation to show off.

"Actually, there was something. A blue Rover Mini, fairly new. The owner was hanging around practically all morning: a young girl with the face of a middle-aged woman. She looked rather shifty to me. Is that the person you had in mind?"

Ayla Ozan's face suddenly went white. Of course, she knew who the man was talking about. Nazim had told her many times about Malvina de Carville: her unusual appearance, her capricious nature, that car—the Rover Mini—given to her by her wealthy grandmother. Nazim had also told her that the girl had gone utterly insane after the plane crash.

Insane and dangerous.

Ayla panicked.

"Right. Yes. Well, thank you..."

What could she do now? Go to the police? Put out a missing persons report? They would ask her questions if she did and she would have to tell them everything she knew—about the case, about the de Carvilles, about Nazim. He had only been gone for two days. If she talked to the police, he would end up in jail. Nazim would never forgive her...

The man with the dog was walking away, although he kept glancing back at her. No, she would have to deal with this on her own. She knew a great deal about the de Carvilles. She had not forgotten any of Nazim's postcoital confessions. Ayla felt a shiver of anxiety and excitement. She thought again of Nazim's body, of his mustache tickling her skin. She wanted so desperately to be held by him now. To be kissed by him, greedily.

She had only one lead: Malvina de Carville. She touched the cold steel of the blade. Ayla was alone, but she wasn't stupid. The de Carvilles lived near Marne-la-Vallée; it would be easy enough for her to find them. She had shared a bed with a private detective for twenty years. She could do this.

30

October 2, 1998, 1:17 p.m.

Marc walked through the dark hallway. Mathilde de Carville had not accompanied him; she had merely opened the door for him, leaving him alone with his doubts. His agoraphobia was gradually diminishing, his breathing returning to normal. The burning effect of the herbal tea was fading, too, as if his body's pores were opening up to the outside air. Passing the large oval mirror, Marc caught a glimpse of his wild-eyed reflection. He hurried on.

Down three steps, past the heavy oak door. Get out of here, as quickly as possible.

Marc's legs could hardly bear his weight and his thoughts were jumbled. Should he open the blue envelope and read the DNA test results? Or should he wait until he was in Dieppe? Perhaps Mathilde de Carville was trying to trap him...

The fresh air hit his face, and Marc took long deep breaths while he tried to order his thoughts. In front of him, not even a shadow moved in the Parc de la Roseraie. The suffocating atmosphere of the place reminded him of an old people's home. Or a lunatic asylum.

Marc walked toward the gate. To his left, behind the red-leafed maple tree, he saw Léonce de Carville. He was asleep, alone, head to the side, abandoned by Malvina de Carville in the middle of the lawn.

Think, Marc told himself. Concentrate.

He had three urgent mysteries to solve, all of them linked, in one way or another, to a crime. First, the murder of Grand-Duc, a few hours earlier. Everything led him to believe that Malvina de Carville was the guilty party. Next, the murder of his grandfather—because it certainly was a murder—fifteen years ago. Marc had to try to discover an anomaly in Grand-Duc's account, a lost memory that he felt sure he would find in his childhood bedroom in Dieppe. Last, there was Lylie. The "one-way trip" she had talked about. Was she running away? Seeking vengeance? Planning to kill herself?

Were these three things connected? Without a doubt. If he solved one problem, the other two would be solved as well.

A crunching of gravel. Behind him.

"Where are you going, Vitral?"

Malvina.

Marc turned around.

"I'm off. Your grandmother kindly told me everything I wanted to know..."

"Bullshit! You didn't learn a thing. Grandma may look impressive, but all she does is ramble on."

Marc sighed.

"I'm the only one who knows the truth," Malvina boasted. "I was in Turkey. All the others died in the crash, but not me. I took an earlier flight. Follow me, Vitral!"

Marc watched her, incredulous.

"I said follow me! Look, I'm not even carrying a gun anymore. You said earlier that Lyse-Rose is alive, that Emilie Vitral was the one who died in the crash, didn't you? So, follow me."

Marc did not move.

"Come on, Vitral. Come with me. I promise, you'll find this interesting."

Oh, well. Why not?

Giddy as a small child, Malvina raced back up the driveway, opened the oak door, walked down the hallway, then climbed the wide staircase. Intrigued, Marc followed her. When they reached the next floor, Malvina turned to face him and placed a finger to her mouth. Almost in a whisper, she said: "The room to the right is mine. Don't get your hopes up—I'm not taking you there. On the left, though, that is Lyse-Rose's room. Follow me..."

Malvina opened the door.

To his shock, Marc found himself in a little girl's bedroom. It was all there. The little pink bed, covered in cuddly toys; the curtains printed with giant giraffes; a terry-cloth towel laid out on an oak changing table; an armoire decorated with pastel-colored flowers. Arrayed on a shelf were a music box, a night-light, and more cuddly toys: a blue elephant, a tiger, a gray-and-white rabbit. On the floor, there was a huge play mat, cluttered with rattles and other toys.

"Grandma decorated this bedroom eighteen years ago, for Lyse-Rose's return from Turkey. We have kept it like this ever since, in case Lyse-Rose comes back to us. She could arrive at any moment, you know!"

Malvina stepped nimbly over the toys and opened the

door of the armoire. Inside, the shelves were crammed with clothes: dresses of every size, beautiful little shoes. A tiny pink fur-lined hat fell to the floor.

Smiling impishly, Malvina turned to face Marc and kept talking, like a little girl telling a grown-up about her doll's house: "I look after the room now. I'm sure Grandma would throw away all these things if I let her. Could you believe it? All these beautiful toys and clothes tossed in the trash? I know you understand. Of course, Lyse-Rose is a big girl now, but it'll really be something when she finally comes back here and discovers this room, won't it?"

Marc stepped back, overcome by a welter of contradictory feelings.

"Are you looking, Vitral? Come closer. You love Lyse-Rose, don't you?"

Almost against his will, Marc took a step forward.

"Look. Even her presents are here!"

Marc felt even more ill at ease.

"Can you see, Vitral? These are all Lyse-Rose's Christmas and birthday presents, since her first birthday."

Malvina pointed to gift-wrapped boxes strewn in piles across the room.

"I could tell you what they all are. I know them by heart. The biggest box, there, on the bed, was the present for her first Christmas with us. Grandma and I went shopping for it together. I was six years old. I still remember the toys in the shop windows..."

She moved closer to Marc and whispered in his ear: "Can you guess what it is?"

Marc shook his head, half moved, half horrified.

"It's a teddy bear. A huge teddy bear. Bigger than she

would have been. It's orange and brown, and it's called Banjo. I came up with the name myself. Banjo is her friend, and he's been waiting for her all these years. Hang on, I'll introduce you..."

Marc put his hand to his face. This weirdo was going to end up making him cry with all her crazy fantasies. Malvina carefully opened the large box and pulled out an enormous teddy bear with a dreamy expression on its face. Malvina placed Banjo on the bed, propped up by two pink cushions.

"Hello, Banjo!" she said cheerfully. "I'm going to tell you a secret. You won't be alone much longer. You won't believe this, but...Lyse-Rose is coming home!"

This is like Sleeping Beauty's room, Marc thought. Piles of toys; clothes that have stiffened during the long wait for the dead child's return. Like a museum devoted to an absence.

"In the other boxes," Malvina continued, "there are dolls, of course, and books, because I know she loves to read. For her tenth birthday, in that box over there, there is a violin. I don't know if that was a good idea, but we already had a piano. There's some jewelry over there, for her thirteenth birthday, and a watch, too. There are some records, but they're probably a bit old-fashioned now. Britney Spears, Ricky Martin, that kind of thing. The big parcel over there was for her sixteenth birthday: it's a stereo. And then the last one, for her eighteenth birthday, is in this envelope. Can you guess what it is?"

Marc shook his head again.

"It's a trip. Do you think that's a good idea? Do you think Lyse-Rose will be brave enough to catch a plane again?"

A storm was raging inside Marc's head. He could

strangle this crazy bitch right now, suffocate her under her cuddly toys, just to make her shut up.

"I have to admit, my favorite present is still the first one. Banjo, the teddy bear. Isn't he beautiful? When we first got him, I was a bit jealous. I loved him so much, I wanted to keep him for myself. But Grandma wouldn't let me. I'm sure Lyse-Rose will adore him, too. What do you think?"

Marc looked at Malvina, wondering how to respond. The child's bed with its pale pink sheets was the same shape and color as a granite gravestone. A child's grave. This room was a burial chamber. These presents, piling up year after year, were offerings to a martyr.

"You're very quiet, Vitral. You look like you're in shock. I suppose you're realizing just how much Lyse-Rose missed out on. I can't even imagine the kind of crap she must have received at Christmas at your house!"

He should slap her, at least. Hurt her physically, and then get out of here.

"Come here, Vitral, there's one last thing I want to show you..."

Marc readied himself for the worst. Malvina walked over to the armoire, opened a drawer, and took out a book, bound in pink cloth and decorated with flowers and pom-poms.

"It's Lyse-Rose's birth book," Malvina whispered. "Come on, I'll let you look at it. Just be careful."

Reluctantly, Marc took the book in his hands, opened it, and turned the pages.

MY FIRST NAME: *Lyse-Rose*
MY OTHER NAMES: *Véronique, Mathilde, Malvina*
MY DADDY: *Alexandre*

MY MOMMY: *Véronique*
I WAS BORN ON: *September 27, 1980, in Istanbul, Turkey*

More details followed, increasingly haunting...

MY HOME: *A photograph of the Roseraie*
MY BEDROOM: *A drawing of the room in which Marc stood—a child's drawing, probably done by Malvina when she was younger*
MY FAVORITE CUDDLY TOY IS CALLED: *Banjo*
MY BEST FRIEND IS: *My sister, Malvina*

Marc turned the pages in a trance. He was face-to-face with the phantom of an imagined life.

MY HAND: *A painted imprint of a baby's hand. But whose?*
MY FAVORITE COLOR: *Blue*
MY FAVORITE ACTIVITY: *Listening to music*
MY FIRST BIRTHDAY: *A photograph of Lylie cut from a magazine—Paris Match or something similar—had been clumsily glued in the middle of a de Carville family photograph. They were eating at a table on which sat a picture of a cake covered in candles, also taken from a magazine.*
MY FIRST VACATION: *The same photograph of Lylie had been stuck in a field filled with gentians, with mountains in the background. Malvina was posing next to her sister, looking radiant. She was eight years old, and the flower stems came up to her waist.*

Marc closed the pages. He couldn't take any more. Malvina grabbed the book from his hands.

"Seen enough, have you? I'm going to put this away."

From the living-room window, Mathilde de Carville watched Marc stride down the driveway. He was practically running away.

Malvina could not resist, of course: she had to show him the bedroom. She had forgotten about her grandfather, abandoned him in the middle of the lawn as if he were a cheap toy. Serves him right, thought Mathilde.

Marc was going to his grandmother's house, in Dieppe, in too much of a hurry to open the envelope, too frightened to disobey her orders. Poor little Marc... he wouldn't be disappointed when he read the DNA test results.

Marc opened the gate and disappeared from sight, swallowed up by the trees of Coupvray Forest.

Mathilde paced thoughtfully around the silent room. She had not told Marc Vitral everything. She had not told him about Grand-Duc's phone call, the night of Lylie's birthday—his final discovery, the one that would change everything. Grand-Duc claimed to have finally uncovered the truth. A different truth. And all he had done was look at an old newspaper.

Mathilde de Carville's fingers brushed against the white keys of the piano.

Had Grand-Duc been bluffing?

She would soon find out. She had asked one of the secretaries at the company's headquarters to send her a photocopy of the *Est Républicain* dated December 23, 1980. She would receive it that evening, in all likelihood, unless the secretary was an imbecile. She had asked for it to be hand-delivered. All she had to do now was wait a few hours, and then she would know if Grand-Duc had lied, or if the mystery was solved at last.

Mathilde de Carville sat down on the piano stool, her hands flat in front of her. She had not played for years. The piano had grown mute, useless, like everything else in this house.

Yes, it would all be over in a few hours.

The silence was broken by three sharp notes. *Do. Fa. Sol.*

It would all be over, except for Malvina.

No matter what that notebook contained, no matter what Grand-Duc had discovered, no matter what Marc Vitral read in that blue envelope, Lyse-Rose would continue to live forever, in the sick imagination of her sister. She would live as a doll lives in the mind of a little girl. Except that this particular little girl was carrying a Mauser L110, and she was capable of killing anyone who told her that the baby in her stroller was merely a lifeless toy, a corpse.

31

Marc walked quickly down Chemin des Chauds-Soleils. It crossed his mind that the path must have been named before the trees in Coupvray Forest grew so high that they cut out the sunlight. The "Path of Hot Sunlight" might have been better renamed "The Path of Cold Shadows." It was with relief that Marc left the forest and entered the village of Coupvray, with its gray church tower, its triangular sign warning drivers to slow down for schoolchildren, and the shy ray of sunlight that pierced the cloudy sky above.

He slowed down and checked his cell phone. Still no messages. Without breaking stride, he called Lylie. He cursed as the answering machine clicked into life.

"Lylie, it's Marc. We have to talk. As soon as possible. Call me back. I've just left the de Carvilles' house. That's right, you heard me. This is important, Lylie. Don't do anything rash until you've talked to me. I love you."

Marc arrived at the canal. The fishermen were still there. The river flowed idly by. Marc scrolled down the list of numbers on his phone.

Nicole.

The phone rang twice, then a familiar, croaky voice answered: "Hello?"

Marc sighed with relief. "Nicole, it's Marc. Did you get my message?"

"Yes, I did. I've just gotten back from the cemetery. I was going to call you, and answer your questions, although I don't think I can tell you anything you don't already know. You must have seen Emilie more recently than I have. You see, I..."

"Nicole, I'm in Coupvray. I've just left the de Carvilles."

Silence. Orpheus returning from the underworld. Without Eurydice.

"Nicole...Mathilde de Carville gave me an envelope for you. It's a DNA test, done in 1995. Grand-Duc stole Lylie's blood."

Nicole's broken voice echoed in his ears, imploringly: "Marc, you can't believe a word they say. Not after..."

Marc interrupted her: "It's for you to open, Nicole. That's what she told me."

Another long silence. All Marc could hear was Nicole's husky breathing.

"Marc, do you have the envelope on you?"

"Yes."

"Describe it to me."

Though he had no idea why his grandmother was asking this, Marc obeyed: "It's a normal-size envelope. Pale blue. Like the kind of letter you'd get from a hospital, or laboratory..."

"Have you opened it?"

"No. I promise, I haven't..."

"Don't open it, Marc, whatever you do. Mathilde de Carville was right about that, at least. You must come straight to Dieppe. It was crazy of you to go and see the de Carvilles. Come to Dieppe now, as soon as you can."

Nicole coughed. She seemed to be finding it difficult to talk. She cleared her throat, then continued: "Marc, things are never as simple as they appear. Don't believe anything the de Carvilles might have told you. They don't know everything. Far from it. Get here quickly. I just hope it won't be too late."

Marc felt as if he were drowning in icy water, being dragged irresistibly to the bottom of the canal.

"Too late for what, Nicole? Too late for whom?"

"Don't waste any more time, Marc. I'm waiting for you."

"Nicole..."

But she had hung up.

Standing behind a concrete pillar, away from the crowds in the Gare de Lyon, Marc checked the paper timetable that he always kept in his wallet.

Paris–Rouen: 4:11–5:29
Rouen–Dieppe: 5:38–6:24

He had more than an hour before he needed to catch his train to Saint-Lazare. That gave him enough time to finish reading Grand-Duc's notebook before he arrived in Dieppe. While he walked toward the metro, Marc attempted to remember the final words he had read on the torn-out pages. The detective was on Mont Terri, where he went every year. There had been a storm, and he was looking for shelter. And then...

The train appeared. A young woman carrying a guitar

on her back got on before Marc, smiling radiantly at him as he let her pass. The top of the case rose up above her head like some kind of Bigouden headdress. Marc affected a blasé indifference, like that transmitted by most underground travelers in the world's big cities. He stood at the end of the railcar, leaned against the window, and concentrated on Grand-Duc's story.

Crédule Grand-Duc's Journal

...I no longer noticed the driving rain. My heart was pounding. I kept going until I reached the hut in front of me. It was a simple shepherd's cabin, and even though the roof was full of holes, it would offer me some protection. But it was not the cabin that had caught my eye—it was the little mound of stones next to it, about one foot high and two feet wide. A small wooden cross had been planted in the earth in front of it. At the base of the cross, in an earthenware pot, there was a plant, a yellow winter jasmine that had not even withered.

You can imagine why this disturbed me. I was looking at a grave. A tiny grave.

I tried to rationalize my discovery. It was probably just a dog that the shepherd had buried. Or a sheep, or a goat, or some other animal.

The rain kept falling. I took refuge in the hut, but the rain came through the gaps in the roof so I had to lie pressed against the wooden wall to keep dry. I could not help thinking that the grave next to the hut, while it was undoubtedly the right size for a small animal, was also the right size for a human baby.

As I waited for the storm to pass, I examined the cabin.

It was unfurnished, but there was a long flat tree trunk that could be used as a bed in an emergency. A gray blanket, covered in holes and rolled into a ball, lay on the ground next to it. A pile of gray ashes, in a sort of cavity dug into the earth, suggested that someone had made a fire here, a few days or possibly a few weeks earlier. Further evidence that the cabin had been used as a squat by local adolescents was provided by the empty beer cans and cigarette butts scattered over the floor. The smell, a mixture of earth and piss, was only just bearable.

It was over an hour before the storm died down. By then, night had fallen, but my years of mountain pilgrimages had taught me to expect the worst, so I always carried a flashlight with me. I left the hut and shone the beam directly on the grave. It was drizzling. I advanced cautiously: Were these just the final few drops before the rain stopped completely, or was it the beginning of another storm? The halo of light broke through the darkness. The cross was made from two twigs tied together with string—and the string, I noticed, did not look very old. A year or two at the most.

I directed the flashlight beam at the plant. I was no expert, but it seemed unlikely to me that winter jasmine would be a perennial, particularly in these temperatures. Which meant that someone had placed the pot in front of the grave not so long ago. No more than a few months.

It was difficult for me to find out anything more that night. The temperature was dropping rapidly and I knew it would take me at least two hours to descend Mont Terri by flashlight. Nevertheless, I stayed where I was. I moved a few of the stones, attempting to see what they were concealing. But the answer, apparently, was nothing. Just earth.

Either that, or I would have to come back with a spade and start digging. I wasn't about to do that with my bare hands.

But you know me by now…you know I was never going to give up that easily. I removed the stones, one by one, with one hand, while the other held the flashlight. After ten minutes, I switched hands. I felt like a grave robber. A sort of zombie, out to recruit a corpse, preferably on a dark and stormy night. Any dead body would do: a dog, a goat, a baby…

But I found nothing, apart from stones and mud. Blindly, I piled the stones up in a mound again.

It was past midnight by the time I reached my BMW, and it took me another hour, driving at fifteen miles per hour, before I arrived at Monique Genevez's cottage, on the banks of the Doubs. The storm had returned, even stronger than before, and what was falling from the sky now was sleet rather than rain. I was soaked, muddy, numb with cold. My fingers were bleeding. It took me ten days to get over the cold I caught that night…And all that for a few stones. A dog's grave. A dog that I had not even managed to exhume. This case was driving me crazy. To calm myself before I went to bed, I drank three glasses of Mrs. Genevez's Vin Jaune.

The next day, I went to see Grégory Morez, the nature preserve employee with lumberjack shoulders and the face of a Hollywood idol. He had spent years driving all over Mont Terri and its environs in his Jeep, so presumably he would know about the cabin and the grave.

Morez seemed surprised by my question and was disappointed not to be able to give me a satisfactory response.

Yes, he knew about the cabin: local teenagers would go there occasionally, and he would do his best to chase them away. He had never paid any attention to the grave, but he thought it was probably that of a dog. It was common, in the Jura Mountains, to bury dogs under piles of stones.

I thought about going back up Mont Terri with a spade, so I could dig up the grave. But the weather that day was even worse than the night before: the air was colder and sleet was still falling heavily from the sky. Was it really worth the two- or three-hour walk? I had already spent quite a long time scratching at the earth beneath the grave, and found nothing. Could there really be any connection between that hut, that pile of stones, and my investigation?

No, of course not.

In the end, I drank a coffee in Indevillers, the closest village to the mountain, and waited half an hour—in vain—for the weather to clear up. By the end of the morning, it was snowing. I went straight back to Paris.

Yet another dead end in my investigation, I thought. Another theory that would have made Nazim howl with laughter if I had told him about it.

Can you imagine? Climbing a mountain to dig up a dead dog?

I didn't yet know it, but that day—December 23, 1986— I had made a mistake. It might have been the only mistake I made during the entire investigation, but my God, it was a big one! I can find plenty of excuses for myself— the snow, the cold, my tiredness, bad luck, the prospect of Nazim's sarcasm—but what would be the point in that? I, the stubborn and meticulous Crédule Grand-Duc, gave up that morning. I lacked the requisite courage; I did not keep going until the end. It was the only time that happened, believe me. But it was also the only time I could not have afforded to let it happen.

But I am getting ahead of myself again. Forgive me.

So, this was in 1986, and the reward for the bracelet had now risen to sixty thousand francs. Still no takers. Obstinately, I kept searching, suppressing the first signs of weariness in myself by methodically planning out what I should do next. I went to Quebec for a while, to meet Lyse-Rose's maternal grandparents—the Bernier family, in Chicoutimi—though it yielded me nothing.

One of the items on my planning list was to get closer to the Vitrals. It was also my pleasure. Lylie was nearly six, Marc was eight. I spent June 21, 1986, in their company. It was the annual World Music Day in France, and Lylie played two pieces on the piano with the Dieppe Orchestra, on a specially constructed stage on the seafront. Looking adorable in her pretty green dress, Lylie was by far the youngest musician in the group. Afterward, we ate fries at Nicole's van. There were a lot of people around that night. Nicole was even more radiant than usual, so proud of her talented granddaughter. So beautiful, too, and almost happy, for the duration of a Chopin sonata. I could not help staring at her, though she didn't notice, as her gaze was fixed on the stage. Not once was her stained jacket pulled across to hide the magnificent plunge of her cleavage.

A short while later, we sat on the grass, while Lylie ate a crêpe balanced on my knee. She asked me what my name was.

"Crédule."

"*Crédule-la-Bascule!*"

That was what she named me, that night. Crédule the

Seesaw. Does she still remember that? I was a private detective, an ex-mercenary, but for that little girl, I was just a playground ride.

As for Marc, he wanted to go home as soon as possible. It was the quarterfinal of the World Cup that evening: France versus Brazil. There was no need for Marc to say anything, though, as I didn't want to miss the match either, and the prospect of watching it with Marc gave me great pleasure. Nicole agreed to let me take him home to Pollet while she stayed on the beach with Lylie.

What a night...

Marc and I hugged, ecstatic, when Platini equalized, just before halftime, after Stopyra had discreetly stamped on the Brazilian goalkeeper; Marc grabbed my knee when Joël Bats saved Socrates's penalty, fifteen minutes before the end; we both screamed at the television set when that bastard referee did not whistle for a foul on Bellone, in the penalty area, during overtime. And when Luis Fernandez scored the last penalty in the shoot-out, we went out together, onto Rue Pocholle, and partied with the neighbors for hours.

1986.

Crédule-la-Bascule.

France in the semis against the Germans!

I acknowledge that this does not really add anything to the account of my investigation. But, to be honest, what else is there to tell?

Certainly, in 1986, it didn't seem likely that there would be anything else.

32

October 2, 1998, 1:41 p.m.

From her observation post, Ayla Ozan commanded a view
of the entire property. She was deep in the Coupvray Forest. From Chemin des Chauds-Soleils, she had followed a
path that wound up between trees. Now, hidden behind a
trunk, she was able to see all the comings and goings at the
Roseraie.

At that moment, there was no movement around the
de Carvilles' house. Even the old man, sitting limp in his
wheelchair in the middle of the lawn, looked like some
kind of modern sculpture. The only thing that was missing, to complete this illusion, was ivy crawling up his legs
and lichen on the wheels of his chair. Ayla had inspected
the woods and paths all around: there was no sign of the
blue Xantia anywhere. She'd had no difficulty spotting
Malvina de Carville's Rover Mini, however, as it was
parked practically in front of the Roseraie. The same car
that had been seen in Rue de la Butte-aux-Cailles a few
hours earlier.

So, neither Crédule nor Nazim was here. Ayla was
unsure what to do next. Wait here, just in case? Ring the

doorbell and pay a visit to the de Carvilles? Find that Malvina girl and make her talk, discover what she had been doing at Grand-Duc's house? More important, find out if she had seen Nazim?

Ayla could still feel the cold blade of her kitchen knife against her leg. Oh, yes, she would enjoy a little woman-to-woman chat with Malvina. The dead leaves rustled quietly under her shoes. She tried to think clearly. Getting in contact with the de Carvilles was probably not such a great idea.

The more she thought about it, the more certain she became that she ought to go to the police. Just tell them that she had not heard from her husband, Nazim Ozan, in two days. The police could send out a missing persons report. Perhaps it wasn't too late. Perhaps they wouldn't ask her too many questions. And if they did ask, and if she believed that it would help them find Nazim, then yes, she would tell the police everything she knew. Without a second's hesitation.

Her testimony would help Nazim, when it came down to it. He was not the only guilty party. She would tell the police that. They would understand. Nazim would understand, too. All that mattered, right now, was finding him.

Ayla looked over at the Roseraie again. What she wanted was for Malvina to come out. She would trap her, put the knife to her throat, and tell her that if she did not talk, she would kebab her. The girl would blab; she might be crazy, but she wasn't suicidal.

But Ayla still hadn't seen any sign of her, apart from the car. She had already been waiting here for an hour.

That was it. She had to go. She had to inform the police.

Ayla stood up.

*

The gun blast exploded in her ears.

Instinctively, Ayla dived to the ground. She landed on a thick bed of leaves. She breathed out. She wasn't hurt. She estimated that the shot must have been fired less than fifty yards away.

Had someone really tried to shoot her, or was she just panicking? Hunters? There must be plenty of them in a posh place like this.

She could shout out: "Hey, I'm here!"

That way, the hunters would know not to shoot in her direction.

Or the killer would know exactly where to shoot.

Or she could crawl down to the path, a few hundred yards away. Down there, she would be safe, as there were houses all around.

Ayla didn't move. She waited, listening for any noises. The adrenaline pumping through her body reminded her of the time she had fled Turkey with her father, hidden for hours under the false floor of a van. She could still remember the sound of boots on the boards above her, when they stopped at the border, her father's hand covering her mouth.

The forest was silent, except for the leaves blowing in the wind.

She waited for ten, twenty minutes, all of her senses alert.

There was nothing. The forest was calm. All was peaceful.

Quietly she stood up, scanning the shadows near the trees.

There was nobody around.

She had probably just heard a random shot. The trees

might have made it echo, so that it sounded louder and closer than it had really been. Yes, she was definitely too nervous. She needed to go to the police now, as quickly as possible.

She took a step, slowly, still unable to shake her suspicions. She put her hand out to the nearest tree.

The bullet was lodged in its trunk.

Ayla's hand went tense on the rough bark. She suddenly felt cold.

Whoever it was had been aiming at her.

Ayla heard the next shot barely one-tenth of a second before she felt the bullet tear into her shoulder. She collapsed to the ground, banging her clavicle and sending another howl of pain through her body. Involuntarily, Ayla screamed. She rolled around on her stomach, incapable of turning over. Her whole upper body was rigid, paralyzed by the pain. In vain, Ayla tried to stand up, using her one good arm. Like a three-month-old baby.

She scrabbled with her legs, trying to find a foothold so she could crawl away. But all she found was a pile of dry leaves that slid beneath her flailing feet.

Pain pinned her to the ground, but she knew she had to get away.

She heard footsteps moving closer. The sinister crackle of broken leaves.

And then nothing.

He was here. It was over.

Ayla was no longer in pain. The only sensation she could feel was the gentle caress of the dead leaves cushioning her face, her neck, her arms. She wanted to die with this feeling, this caress. Now it was no longer the leaves tickling her bare skin, but Nazim's mustache. His big mustache, so tender and soft. She thought about the house in Antakya, the one she wanted to buy with Nazim...their house, in their country, the country she had fled with her father, so long ago...

The silence was broken by the sound of a revolver being loaded. Ayla made one last effort to turn over, to see him. Her murderer.

She pushed with her good arm.

But her last wish was not granted.

In the very next instant, she was shot in the back of the neck.

33

October 2, 1998, 2:40 p.m.

Concorde. He had to change here.

Marc put the notebook back in his bag. The smiling girl with the guitar on her back was getting off here, too. They walked side by side through the passageway, almost touching, embarrassed, as people are when they find themselves standing close to a stranger.

Curled up on the cold floor of the corridor, a woman appeared to be praying to some god of the underworld. There was no child or animal with her; she was not playing music or displaying a cardboard sign; all Marc could see was a face hidden between her knees and an empty plate. Everyone walked past her or stepped over her. Without thinking, Marc dropped a coin from his pocket into her saucer. Guitar Girl gave him a surprised look, the sort of look that meant Marc had, in her eyes, just gone from "dickhead-too-busy-to-smile-at-someone-in-the-metro" to "more-interesting-than-I-thought."

A few yards farther on, the passage divided in two. Marc, still lost in his thoughts, turned to the right, following the signs for Line 12, toward Porte de la Chapelle.

Guitar Girl went left, toward Line 7, in the direction of La Courneuve, slowing down a little to watch the tall, sad-looking boy disappear into the distance.

Madeleine.

They were entering one of the busiest stations in Paris. It was not quite rush hour, but it was getting close. The crowds on the platforms and in the trains suddenly became more dense. It was impossible to read with so many people packed tightly around him.

Saint-Lazare.

The train emptied with dizzying speed. Marc watched, amazed, as people raced through the corridors of the station: some even sprinted, pushing past their slower neighbors, running up the empty staircases two steps at a time rather than taking the packed escalators, moving into top gear whenever a long, straight corridor gave them the chance. Were these people running so fast because they were late for something important, or did they do this every day, simply out of habit, the way other people might jog around a park?

Marc had once read about a man, one of the greatest violinists—a Russian name that he couldn't recall—who, one day, had played down in the metro for several hours. No posters, no official announcements; he just sat there anonymously and took out his violin. And while his concerts all over the world were always sold out, with people paying hundreds of francs for the privilege of hearing him play, that day in the metro, almost nobody stopped to listen to him. All those men in suits did not even slow down as they ran past on the way to their train, and yet—that weekend, perhaps, or even that evening—they would run to make sure they arrived on time at the concert of a famous musician they would not want to miss at any price.

For the first time that day, Marc gave himself a break. He walked calmly to the main concourse, where thousands of people stood waiting, motionless, staring upward, like a crowd at a concert waiting for a rock star to appear. Except that their eyes were not drawn to spotlights on a stage, but to words on a screen indicating which platforms the trains would depart from.

The Paris–Rouen train was one of those whose platform had not yet been announced. Marc crossed the entire concourse, slaloming through the masses, and sat down in the station bar, where he ordered an orange juice. The waiter took his money right away, as if he were afraid Marc might run away with the glass in his hand. Marc picked up his phone, and swore when he looked at the screen. Lylie had called.

The call had come when he was underground, of course, as if Lylie were tracking his progress on a screen, waiting until he was out of reach.

Marc listened to her message. It was barely audible.

"Marc, this is Emilie. What on earth were you doing at the de Carvilles' place? Listen, you have to trust me. Tomorrow, it will all be over, and I'll explain everything to you then. If you love me as much as you say you do, you will forgive me."

For a moment, Marc did not move, the telephone still clamped to his ear.

"Trust me . . . Forgive me . . ."

Wait until tomorrow?

No way. Lylie was hiding something from him: the

"one-way trip" that only he could prevent her from taking. Marc tapped at the keys on his phone and listened to her message again. There was something about it that intrigued him. ·

"Marc, this is Emilie..." He pressed the phone to his right ear and blocked his left ear with a finger. He needed to hear the message clearly, which wasn't easy in this noisy station.

He listened to the message for a third time. He was no longer paying any attention to Lylie's words, but to what he could hear in the background. The sound was quite distant and muffled, but this time he was almost certain that he was right. Nevertheless, he listened to it one last time, just to be sure. And there it was again: behind Lylie's voice, he could distinctly hear the sound of ambulance sirens.

Marc put the telephone back in his pocket and tried to think as he drank his orange juice. He could find only two possible explanations. Either Lylie was standing close to an accident, or she was near a hospital. It was a clue, in any case. The first he had found.

There was no point trying to find the location of a recent accident in Paris; Lylie would not stay there, and it would be impossible to locate. But, if the second theory were true, there was a chance. Doubtless, he would be faced with a score of addresses in Paris. But it was worth trying.

He was haunted by another question: Why a hospital? What had Lylie done? The first image that came to mind was of her being injured, carried on a stretcher to the emergency department, a swarm of nurses buzzing around her...

The one-way trip. Lylie had attempted suicide. She had not waited until tomorrow.

*

For the third time that day, Marc called Jennifer, his colleague at France Telecom. As fast as she could, she sent him eighteen texts containing lists of all the one hundred and fifty-eight hospitals in central Paris.

For more than half an hour, Marc talked to a series of switchboard operators. All the conversations went the same way:

"Hello. Has a young woman by the name of Emilie Vitral been admitted to your hospital today? No, I don't know which department... Accident and Emergency, maybe?"

The shortest calls lasted a few seconds, the longest a few minutes. The response was always more or less identical: "No, sir, we have no one here by that name." When he reached the twentieth number on the list, Marc stopped. It would take him forever to call all one hundred and fifty-eight hospitals and he realized he could be wasting precious time, chasing after a highly tenuous clue: the sound of ambulance sirens in the background of a phone message. They might simply have been speeding past as Lylie made the call.

By now, the waiter had asked him three times if he wanted anything else. Marc asked for another orange juice just to keep him at bay. Was this how Crédule Grand-Duc had felt all those years? As if he were following a lead that he knew, right from the beginning, would probably go nowhere? Navigating his way through a dark and stormy night with nothing more than a match?

Marc looked up at the departures board. Still no platform listed for Paris–Rouen. Everything was going too fast. Those siren screams... That blue envelope in his pocket, which he could open, in spite of Mathilde de

Carville's orders and the promise he had made to Nicole...
And this notebook, with Grand-Duc's narrative keeping
him on tenterhooks...

Crédule Grand-Duc's Journal

By 1987, the reward for the bracelet had gone up to
seventy-five thousand francs. That was a fortune back
then, even for a piece of jewelry from Tournaire. As for my
investigation, it was stagnating. There were no new leads,
so I just kept plugging away at the old ones, rereading the
same old files a dozen times.

I went to Turkey for a few weeks, for appearance's sake.
The Hotel Askoc, the Golden Horn, the carpet sellers,
twilight over the Bosphorus... the whole "Lylie Mystery
Tour." I also went back to Quebec, to see the Berniers, in
temperatures of minus fifteen. Still I learned nothing new.

And, of course, I returned to Dieppe. Twice, I think—
once with Nazim and once without. Those are good memories, at least. I will tell you about them for that reason, and
also because it is important to help you understand Lylie.
Her psychology, I mean. Her environment, determinism,
nature versus nurture, and all that crap. I will give you the
details, and you can judge for yourself. This is important if
you wish to form your own opinion.

It was March 1987. The weather was awful. From what
Nicole told us, we gathered that it had been like that for the
past two weeks in Dieppe: forty-mile-an-hour winds and
lashing rain. There was not a cat to be seen anywhere on
the seafront. Nicole coughed at the end of every sentence,
her lungs making her suffer.

Nazim was happy. He enjoyed going to Dieppe. He liked rain. He liked Marc, too, even if Marc was a little scared of him. Like me, Nazim did not have children. But at least he had a wife. The lovely Ayla, with her curves and her kebabs. When it came to soccer, Nazim was, naturally, a supporter of the Turkish national team. Marc made fun of him: a few years earlier, Turkey had lost 8–0 to England in a World Cup qualifier. "Were they playing foosball?" Marc joked. Nazim wanted to prove to Marc that he was not bitter about this, so he brought him a Galatasaray shirt worn by the club's left winger, Dündar Siz. The name Dündar Siz undoubtedly means nothing to you. Try translating it into French... You see now? Yes, Didier Six. The French player must have acquired Turkish citizenship in order to help Galatasaray win the championship the following year. Didier Six... How could Didier Six be anyone's idol? The guy was a one-trick pony. He always did the same move, faking a shift to the outside then cutting in on the inside. Worst of all, he shot the ball straight into the goalkeeper's arms from the penalty spot in Seville in 1982, during the semifinal of the World Cup against West Germany. He was playing for Stuttgart at the time, the traitor. People have been executed for less than that!

So anyway, five years later, the best present Nazim could find to give to Marc was a Dündar Siz jersey. The shirt of a traitor living in exile under a false name! What a wonderful example for a young boy to follow. Marc, being young and naive, put the shirt on without asking any questions.

As for little Emilie, she put on a fluorescent purple raincoat, with a hood that swallowed up her whole head so that only a few blond hairs emerged, and went out into the rain and the wind. Her boots were the same color as her raincoat. She jumped in puddles and went chasing after cats. Nicole was almost in tears when she told me why.

At seven years old, Emilie was already a good reader. And she was a big fan of Marcel Aymé's *Contes du Chat Perché*, with its talking animals.

"Can you believe it, Crédule?" Nicole said. "At seven years old!"

There cannot have been more than twenty books in their little household, and this was the only book for children. But I'm sure you are wondering what this has to do with chasing after cats... Well, Emilie loved the story about the farm cat who, to annoy everyone, would spend its day washing itself, continually rubbing its paw behind its ear—thereby invariably attracting rain for the following day. In the book, it pours with rain for weeks on end, purely because of the actions of this wayward cat, so in the end, the farmer decides to get rid of it. It is saved just in the nick of time by the book's heroines, Delphine and Marinette. So it seemed perfectly logical to Emilie that the reason Dieppe had been deluged for the past two weeks was because the local cats were also continually rubbing their paws behind their ears. Consequently, there was only one solution: she must persuade the cats to wash themselves in a different way. All the cats in Pollet. Imagine that, in a fishing district... Emilie spent hours sidling up to them, winning their trust, then gently explaining to them that her grandmother Nicole was unable to work because of their actions. And of course they, too, were suffering, because they couldn't bask in the sun they loved so much.

Emilie tried to persuade Nazim and me to help her catch the cats. There were some who wouldn't listen to her—strays, mostly—so she wanted us to frighten them.

"Come on, Crédule-la-Bascule! Come on, Mustache Man!"

She took us by the hand, tried to drag us out into the pouring rain. Nazim laughed loudly, but stayed inside with his coffee. So did I. Only Marc did as she asked and went outside with her. When he came back, his clothes were soaking and as transparent as the shirt of Dündar Siz, isolated on the left flank at the Parc des Princes.

On December 22, 1987, I went on my yearly pilgrimage to Mont Terri. I arrived in the evening, and left my luggage at the rental cottage on the banks of the Doubs. The owner, Monique Genevez—an adorable woman with a Franc-Comtois accent so strong that it almost reminded me of a Canadian's—always reserved the same room for me: number 12, with a view of Mont Terri. She also kept back some Cancoillotte cheese for me, allowing it to age for at least a month in advance, so that I could eat some with a bottle of Arbois wine. My investigation was getting bogged down and I was turning into a nervous wreck, so I felt I deserved a few compensations.

Before I had even parked my car that day, Monique was out of the house yelling at me excitedly: "Mr. Grand-Duc, there's someone here to see you!"

I looked at her, speechless.

"He's been here for two hours," she told me. "He called several times last month. He wanted to see you. I told him you would be coming here, as you always do, on the afternoon of December 22. I think it must be related to your investigation."

Surprised and excited, I rushed into the living room. A

man in his fifties, wearing a long dark winter coat, was waiting for me. He stood up and came over to me.

"Augustin Pelletier. I have been wanting to meet you for several months now, Mr. Grand-Duc. I saw one of your small ads in the *Est Républicain*. I had imagined that the investigation into the Mont Terri accident had been closed a long time ago, so I was surprised to discover you were still working on the case. I hope you might be able to help me . . ."

I had been hoping for the opposite—that he would be able to help me—but never mind. Augustin Pelletier seemed like a sensible sort to me: a solid, responsible businessman, not a teller of tall tales.

I sat next to him, in the entrance hall of the cottage. Through the window, you could see the whole mountain range, including Mont Terri. It was not yet covered with snow.

"I will do my best, Mr. Pelletier. This is rather unexpected . . ."

"It's a long story, Mr. Grand-Duc, but I will give you the short version. I am looking for my brother, Georges Pelletier. He disappeared many years ago. The last sighting of him was in December 1980. At the time, he was living as a hermit on Mont Terri, in a little hut, not far from the site of the crash."

34

October 2, 1998, 3:09 p.m.

Marc looked up. The information on the departures board took a moment to come into focus.

Paris–Caen. Platform 23.

Many of the people around him on the concourse suddenly rushed toward Platform 23, like so many colored grains of sand pouring through the slender neck of an hourglass. Marc had read somewhere that more than a thousand people could be squeezed inside a train. The average population of a large village... When you thought about that, the density of the crowd packed together in the station hardly came as a surprise: all it took was two or three trains to be delayed and you would have several thousand people standing around, waiting.

The platform for Paris–Rouen was still not indicated, so he had time to read a few more pages of the notebook. Had Grand-Duc really found a witness to the Mont Terri crash?

Crédule Grand-Duc's Journal

The clouds were coming from Switzerland. This was quite unusual. After years of experience, you see, I was becoming something of an expert regarding the climate of the Haut-Jura.

"Georges is my younger brother," Augustin Pelletier explained. "He was always more fragile than I. A complicated person. We were very different. He was only fourteen when he started running away from home. We were living in Besançon at the time. He hung around with one of the local gangs, and the police kept bringing him back to my parents. In the end, Georges was placed in an institution for two years."

I drummed my fingers on the armrests of my chair. I wondered where this story was leading.

"Don't worry, I will get to the crash, Mr. Grand-Duc," Augustin told me hastily, obviously noticing my impatience. "At sixteen, Georges left home for good. I will spare you the details. He slept in the street. Alcohol. Drugs. He was a dealer, too, though he never did anything too bad. My parents gave up on him, and I did, too. At the time, I had a job, a wife who didn't want me to get involved... I'm sure you can imagine what it was like. It's not easy to invite a junkie to your Christmas party.

"I managed as best I could," he went on. "I kept in touch with Georges indirectly, through the social services and the police. But Georges did not want our help. Every time I offered a helping hand, he would slap me in the face. Metaphorically, if you see what I mean..."

I saw, but I didn't care.

"I'm getting there, Mr. Grand-Duc. I was generally able to keep myself informed about Georges, although there were periods of time when he would disappear completely. For one or two years at the most. But in May 1980, I lost track of him for good. Georges was forty-two at the time, although he looked closer to sixty. I have not received any information about him for nearly eight years."

He was losing me. "Mr. Pelletier, I don't quite see what this has to do with me, or with the Airbus accident."

"Bear with me. I was very worried. I asked the other homeless people in Besançon about him. In the end, I found out that Georges had left for the countryside. He'd had enough of city life, and of certain unsavory characters in Besançon. Other dealers, the police... Apparently, the last anyone had heard, he was living in a hut on a mountain somewhere near the Swiss border. Mont Terri. Or Mont Terrible, as everyone was calling it back then, because of the accident. I spent months searching for him, but without success. After that, I more or less gave up hope of ever seeing him again. My wife was perfectly happy with that situation, of course, but when I saw your ad, I started thinking. I thought: why not? If someone is still trying to work out what happened in that place, on that night, then maybe he will also find some trace of my brother..."

My hands gripped the armrests of my chair like a captain at the helm of a three-master. I gazed through the window at the mountain peaks now lost in the mist. Was it possible that Georges Pelletier had been sleeping in that cabin on the night of December 22, 1980? Was it possible Georges was something I had never even dared hope for in seven years of investigating the case: an eyewitness to the crash?

Perhaps this Georges had been the first person to appear on the scene... Perhaps he had found Lyse-Rose's bracelet, lying next to the miracle child... Perhaps it was he who had dug that small grave...

"Did Georges have a dog?"

Augustin looked dazed. "Umm...well, yes. A small brown mongrel. Why?"

I was already taking notes on the back of a brochure.

"What kind of cigarettes did he smoke?"

"Gitanes, I think. I'm not sure, though."

"What size were his feet?"

"I think about ten or eleven."

"What brand of beer did he drink?"

"What brand of beer? I have no idea...Sorry, Mr. Grand-Duc, but why are you asking me all these questions? Have you found Georges? Is he...dead? Did you find his body?"

We needed a moment of calm.

Monique Genevez was the perfect hostess, bringing us tea and a local variety of Speculoos cookies, thicker and longer than the Belgian ones. Augustin did not touch them but I ate enough for both of us, while I told him all about my discovery the previous year: the hut, the cigarette butts, the grave. Augustin Pelletier seemed almost disappointed that I had not discovered any concrete evidence regarding his brother. Dunking my cookies in the tea, I reassured him: I could not promise that I would find his brother, Georges, even less that I would find him alive, but I could assure him that I would devote every ounce of my energy into look-ing for him over the coming months. I was not lying. He was my only potential witness and I was willing to scour the earth for him. Augustin's journey from Besançon had proved to be a good investment. He now had a private detective working on his behalf, with all the costs paid for by Mathilde de Carville. He left me his business card.

I only slept a few hours that night, partly because of my excitement, but mainly because of the bottle of Arbois wine that I drank to celebrate this news, washed down with a few glasses of my landlady's excellent Vin Jaune.

I left at dawn the following morning, fully equipped with a spade, a rake, a sieve, and other useful tools. I had decided to turn grave robber for the day, just to check if it really was Georges's small brown mongrel buried under the pile of stones. I also took test tubes and waterproof bags so that I could send cigarette butts and beer cans to a friend who worked in the police forensics department. As I was passing the nature preserve headquarters, Grégory Morez waved me over. He had a good laugh. "Jesus, Crédule! Not exactly traveling light, are you?"

Grégory... Apart from hosting the rare visit from groups of schoolchildren, he probably spent most of his time seducing the students who worked at the reception desk. That was the impression he gave, anyway. The bastard seemed to grow more handsome with each passing year, his hair turning a distinguished salt-and-pepper while the students remained exactly the same age each year. He left the side of a pretty young blonde who was making eyes at him and came toward me.

"Listen, I'm going to take pity on you. I'll give you a lift in the Jeep. You'll have to walk the last mile or so, but it'll save you a couple of hours. Julie, I'll be back in twenty minutes. Stay here if you want to hear what happened next that night in Spitzberg..."

Morez dropped me off at the end of the path and, with a wink, turned the Jeep back toward his headquarters and the pretty blonde. On the way up the mountain, I had questioned him about Georges Pelletier. He hadn't heard of the man, but then again, that wasn't too surprising. It had been seven years ago, after all. While I walked, I tried to sift through my memories from the previous year: the cold rain, the flashlight beam, the stones piled on the grave.

I found the hut easily enough. The weather was much warmer than it had been the year before, and I was sweating. Winter sunlight gilded the treetops and bathed the mountaintop in almost springlike warmth, although the primroses, daffodils, and gentians were as yet barely visible.

I felt the same excitement I had on my first stakeout. It was a long time since this investigation had yielded any new clues. I began with the hut. Nothing seemed to have been moved since the previous year. Of course it was perfectly possible that no one had visited in the interim. Wearing gloves, I picked up samples of the detritus that lay scattered over the ground. Sometimes I had to scratch at the mud to unearth half-buried objects: cigarette butts, beer cans, scraps of paper. All of this could help my search for Georges Pelletier, even if it had been seven years since he last stayed here.

I went outside. Now it was time for the most difficult part of my task: the grave. I stood in front of the pile of stones. The little wooden cross was still there but, beneath it, the winter jasmine had withered and died. So, nobody had left flowers here since the previous year. But why? Why would someone have brought flowers every other year, but not this one? It was very hot. I took off my sweater, but even in just a shirt, I was still sweating.

I leaned closer to the stones, and suddenly I sensed that something was wrong. It was strange, but I could not shake the conviction that these stones were not piled up in the same order as I had left them. They had been moved.

I tried to reason with myself. How could I be so sure? It had been night when I last saw this place, and pouring rain. And I had replaced them haphazardly...

And yet... This was more than a feeling. I was *sure* someone had been here. I had a very precise image in my mind of the shape of that pile of stones, and my memory was almost photographic. Those stones had definitely been moved.

But I knew I was not going to find the answers to my questions without getting my hands dirty, so I began to remove the stones, very carefully, one by one. That took over half an hour. Thankfully my grave robbing did not seem so macabre in the daylight. I stopped several times to have a drink of water.

When the last stone had been laid to the side, I picked up my spade and began to dig, taking great care all the while. I did begin to wonder what was the point of it all. Why was I going to such great lengths just to dig up a dead dog? What else was I expecting? The skeleton of a human infant?

I dug for nearly an hour. The sun sank toward the west and the cooling shadows of the pines fell over the grave. The hole I had dug was more than three feet deep now. I had removed the cross and dug under that, too. Stubbornly, I kept going for another half an hour.

But finally... nothing!

Not even a single bone from a dog, goat, or rabbit.

Nothing at all.

So that mound of stones, that cross, and that withered plant had been placed over virgin earth? I collapsed, exhausted and disappointed. All that effort, for no reward. I drank some water and did some thinking. Now, in the shade, drenched with sweat, I began to feel slightly cold, so I walked around for a bit, conversing with the pine trees. Suddenly, I laughed at my own stupidity.

No, of course I had not dug this hole for no reason! It would have been far more disappointing, for me and the investigation, if I *had* found an animal's bones under the grave. That really would have been a dead end. How would it have helped me if I had dug up the bones of Georges's dead dog?

An empty grave, on the other hand...that offered all kinds of possibilities. I wiped my forehead, then took out the cheese sandwich that Monique had prepared for me. In fact, as I thought about it, I realized there were only two possible explanations.

First, it could be a symbolic tomb, like the shrines you find at the side of a road where people have died in a car crash. That was plausible...The family of one of the victims of the Airbus 5403 might have decided to perform a similar gesture. To construct a place of pilgrimage, an empty tomb, because they had no body to bury inside it. But in that case, why build it here, over a mile from the actual crash site? Why dig this rectangular grave, the exact size of a three-month-old baby? There had been only two babies on the Airbus. Who had planted this cross, piled up these stones, watered the jasmine all those years? A member of the Vitral family? A member of the de Carville family? But who? And when? And why?

Then there was my second theory. There had been a skeleton under the stones. Someone had come here every year to pay tribute to a loved one, to leave flowers by the grave, quietly, in secret. But this year, the mysterious person discovered that the grave had been searched. The secret was out, or soon would be. So, this person could see only one solution: exhume the body. Remove the stones, empty the grave, fill in the hole, and replace the stones.

Because the stones had been moved, I was certain of that.

This second theory raised as many questions as the first one. Why go to so much trouble? Why be so careful? Certainly not if it were a dog's grave—only a madman would act in such a way. Georges Pelletier? No, that made no sense at all...

I felt serene, calm. This latest development, with all the questions it raised, was exactly what I had been waiting for. I would have plenty of time to explore my theories. I rummaged in my bag and pulled out the sieve. It was made of wood and nylon, the kind of sieve used by gold prospectors. I wanted to go through this earth with a fine-tooth comb. If even the smallest piece of bone remained—whether it was from a dog, a baby, or a dinosaur—I would find it.

I spent five hours sieving the mud. I am not kidding. Even an archaeologist could not have been more patient.

The reward for my stubbornness came that afternoon. As you can see, I was really putting the work in to earn my one hundred thousand francs. In the sieve, after all the earth had passed through the holes and the smallest stones had been moved to the side, I was left looking at a tiny piece of gold, shining in the sunlight. Oval-shaped, and no more than two millimeters long, it was a link from a delicate golden chain.

"What do you want, asshole? My photograph?"

Marc looked up from the page, suddenly brought back down to earth. The din of the station contrasted markedly with the silence of the pine forest he had been reading about.

Like most of the people around him, he turned to stare at the source of the demented cry, but it was just some hysterical girl insulting her neighbor. The other passengers shrugged and went back to their own lives. Marc, however, kept staring, his eyes riveted to the young woman.

He had recognized her voice, and his heart had plummeted. About thirty yards away, standing in front of an automatic ticket machine, Malvina de Carville was yelling at the man behind her.

There could be no doubt about it. This was not a coincidence. She had followed Marc here.

35

The motorcycle stopped on Chemin des Chauds-Soleils, just in front of the Roseraie. The rider jumped nimbly to the ground, removed his helmet, tousled his long black hair, and pressed the intercom.

"Yes?"

"Package for Mrs. de Carville. Special delivery. It's urgent, apparently."

"She's not available right now. Just leave it in the mailbox."

"I have to hand-deliver it to her."

"Well, you'll just have to wait, then. She can't be disturbed for the next ten minutes."

The motorcyclist sighed. "I can't wait. Who is this?"

"I'm Linda. The nurse."

"Well, that'll do, I guess," the deliveryman said after a moment's hesitation. "I can trust you. Will you give the envelope to Mrs. de Carville?"

"I think I can manage that…"

The motorcyclist laughed, then said: "Listen, Linda, what is going on here? I've seen ambulances, fire engines, police cars. It was hell getting across the Marne. Did they find a serial killer in the village or something?"

"You're not far off, actually! They found a woman's body in Coupvray Forest, close to our house. She'd been shot, apparently. They still don't know if it was an accident or a murder. Can you imagine? A murder in Coupvray!"

"Well, at least it'll liven things up round here..."

Linda went and collected the large padded envelope. She was not sure if she should call Mathilde de Carville. Her boss was in the greenhouse, and Mrs. de Carville hated being disturbed when she was gardening. That greenhouse was like a temple to her, and gardening a sacred act that Linda had no desire to profane. Yes, she decided, the envelope could wait. Linda put it next to the telephone on the desk in the entrance hall.

She did not want to leave Léonce de Carville on his own for too long. Above all, she did not want to get behind schedule. She still had to wash him, put his pajamas on, give him his dinner, and change his drip. If she worked quickly, she could be done by 6:00 p.m. Then Linda could pick up her baby early, and enjoy his company for a little while longer than usual...

She pushed the old man's wheelchair into the bathroom. This was her least favorite part of the day. She laid him down flat on the bench. When she had done that, she exhaled and pressed a button. The body was raised up to the level of her waist. The whole bathroom was automated, equipped with the latest and most expensive devices. It was as good as any hospital. Better, even. She had nothing to complain about in that regard: Mathilde de Carville had provided her with everything she needed to do her job properly.

Linda began to undress the old man.

When she turned him over to unbutton his shirt and slide his inert arms through the sleeves, Linda almost had the impression that he was reacting, trying to help her. Three days ago, she had even felt certain that he had smiled at her. Voluntarily. She knew this was impossible. At least according to the doctors. The patient was incapable of recognizing a voice or a face or a sound, of telling one day from another. So, the idea that he might try to help her slide his arm through a sleeve...

Linda removed his trousers, and then his soiled underwear. A few maple leaves fell to the bathroom floor.

The doctors are wrong, thought Linda.

She had been looking after Léonce for almost six years now— two hours in the morning and three in the afternoon—and she had become convinced that he was more than just a digestive tract on wheels.

Linda ran warm water from the tap, then rubbed soap onto the glove. She always began his daily wash with the genital region, then the lower part of his body. Linda's baby, Hugo, was seven months old now. She could tell the difference between a real smile and the mere twitch of a muscle.

She rubbed the glove along his left leg. In fact, Linda actually liked Léonce, even if everyone else in this sinister mansion hated him. His wife. His granddaughter, that horrible girl Malvina. She had heard so many bad things about Léonce de Carville: that he had been a tyrannical boss, capable of firing hundreds of workers—in Venezuela, Nigeria, Turkey—with just a snap of his fingers. An unscrupulous man. A hard man. But she didn't care. To her, Léonce was nothing worse than a life-size rubber doll, a defenseless old man. A poor, fragile creature whose only source of protection, care, and tenderness in this world was herself. He was just like her baby.

The two of them understood each other. The old man and the nurse. They were together for five hours a day. No doctor in the world could perceive the connection between them, even less so Mathilde and Malvina de Carville. But Léonce could still communicate, in his own way.

She heard a door bang.

Linda's gloved hand froze on the old man's flabby stomach. It was the front door. And yet Linda was sure she had closed it. She removed the glove and went out into the entrance hall.

There was nobody there. It had probably been just a gust of wind. That was not unusual: the Roseraie was a huge building with more than twenty rooms, and there was always a door or a window left open somewhere. Linda went back to the bathroom. Léonce was waiting for her. He needed her. As with her little Hugo, he should not be left alone.

Linda had made a mistake. Lost in her thoughts about Hugo and Léonce, she had failed to notice something important. She did not look at the desk in the entrance hall.

The padded envelope was no longer there.

Linda had finished washing her patient and had dressed him in clean pajamas, as she did each day. She refused to put an adult diaper on him, something even the most expensive hospitals did. It was a messy choice, but Linda didn't care. It simply meant she had to change his pajamas and his sheets every morning.

She put the old man on the special bed in his room, next to the bathroom. A new door had been installed so that the wheelchair could be rolled through. The bed was also the best and most up-to-date model available, entirely operated by means of electronic switches. In medical terms, Léonce de Carville was better off here than he would be in any nursing home. At least he would be able to die in luxury. Alone, but in luxury. Mathilde de Carville had been sleeping in a separate room on the first floor for years now.

Linda removed a feather pillow from the bed and set it on a nearby chair. Then she took a larger white pillow and slipped it behind Léonce's back so that he could sit propped up while she fed him. She looked at her watch. She would give him dinner in less than an hour.

She checked one last time that the old man's torso was firmly strapped to the bed. His eyes were wide open now, staring as they always did after he had been washed, only blinking occasionally. Linda had heard about a paraplegic who had written a book simply by blinking. Incredible! What if Léonce could do the same thing? What if the doctors were wrong and his brain did still work? What if there was something he wanted to tell her? The only problem was that she did not understand his way of communicating. What was going on inside that head?

Linda had also been told that Léonce de Carville was an extraordinary man. One of the richest and most powerful in France. And he had built up his fortune from nothing, constructing factories all over the world. He had commanded an empire. It was probably because of that power that he had become so hated. People were jealous. Now that he could no longer defend himself, the weaklings were getting their revenge. And yet those weaklings owed everything to him. The Roseraie, for example.

Linda placed a monitor—the same kind mothers use to check on their babies—on Léonce's bedside table. She always put the other monitor in the kitchen while she was preparing his dinner. That way, she felt reassured. She knew it was slightly ridiculous—what could possibly happen to him while she was away?—but she did it just the same.

As she left the bedroom, Linda took one last glance at the old man. His eyes were still wide open. A genius who had begun with nothing, brought back to square one.

The shadow crept silently behind Linda's back, then hid between the wall and the staircase. Linda could have seen it if she had turned her head that way. But she didn't. She walked straight to the kitchen.

Linda prepared the old man's dinner herself. His soup. She made a point of always using fresh ingredients: vegetables, ham, and many other ingredients that she would find at the market in Marne-la-Vallée, which she peeled, chopped, and mixed together by hand. Léonce spat up half of it and crapped out the rest, but Linda would not compromise her standards. And, for the past month, she had been making twice the usual quantity. She deliberately made too much soup, so that she could take half of it home to Hugo. She got home just in time for his supper, so it was perfect timing. She had not mentioned this fact to Mathilde de Carville, but surely the old woman wouldn't begrudge her a couple of leeks, three potatoes, and a slice of ham!

Linda put the baby monitor next to the blender and began peeling carrots. She liked this moment of silence. It reassured her.

The shadow moved past the kitchen and pushed open the door to Léonce de Carville's bedroom. Cautiously, it entered. Linda saw and heard nothing.

The old man stared at the advancing figure, his eyes wide open. He looked petrified, as if he understood the figure's intention. The shadow hesitated. The look in the old man's eyes seemed unreal, almost menacing. But the shadow's hesitation lasted only a second or so. It moved forward again. It felt no pity for the inert body of the old man, only hatred and contempt.

The shadow noticed a pillow sitting on a chair near the bed. It smiled. The perfect solution. Quick, silent. The shadow walked toward it. The old man's gaze remained fixed on the open door. The shadow felt relieved. So, the man's apparent fear was merely an illusion. Léonce de Carville had not recognized the intruder; he no longer recognized anyone or anything. Under the intruder's feet, the floorboards creaked quietly.

The blade of Linda's knife hung suspended in the air. The nurse had distinctly heard a noise in Léonce's bedroom. A creak. Still holding the knife, Linda went out into the hallway and headed toward the old man's room. The creaking noise could not have been made by Léonce, after all.

Her fingers tightened around the knife handle. This afternoon was taking a strange turn. First, the shooting in the forest. Police everywhere. Then the motorcycle messenger, with the envelope. The door banging earlier, and now this creak in the bedroom of a man who could not move.

Linda held the knife out in front of her, her entire arm trembling. This house had always frightened her, like a haunted house from a horror film. Usually, she managed to avoid thinking about it, but she had always felt uneasy here. Her legs felt like jelly beneath her and she shivered.

Still holding the blade in front of her, Linda entered the bedroom. Léonce de Carville was staring at her. His gaze was empty, but so was the rest of the room—there was nobody there. The tension left Linda in a burst of nervous laughter. This house and its family of weirdos were driving her crazy! She had to find another job elsewhere. There was no lack of rich families to choose from, here by the Marne. It would be tough on the old man, but she would just have to forget about the strange tenderness she felt toward him. She had Hugo to think of now.

Time to get back to work, Linda thought; she had to finish making the soup, and then she'd go home.

The shadow heard the sound of the blender in the kitchen, and sighed with relief. It had been careless before. Impatient. This time, the nurse would not hear a thing. Cautiously, it opened the door of the piano room, where it had been hiding, and went back to the old man's bedroom. It picked up the pillow from the chair, then laid the soft fabric over Léonce de Carville's face. He did not react at all. It was so easy. Too easy. How long would it take to suffocate a paraplegic? There would be no way of knowing when all the life had left this body, as it would not kick out or struggle. Should the pillow be held over the old man's face for a minute? Two? Three?

The intruder did not count the seconds. It merely waited as long as possible.

Suddenly, the impossible happened. Impossible according to the doctors, anyway. Léonce's arm suddenly stiffened. Was this the final twitch of a dying body? A hopeless attempt to save itself? The intruder kept pressing down. Léonce's left arm went into spasm. It jerked across the bedside table, knocking off the glass and the carafe, which fell to the floor and smashed.

Linda screamed.

This time, she knew she was not hallucinating—she had definitely heard the sound of breaking glass coming from the bedroom. Without stopping to think, she grabbed the kitchen knife again and rushed into the bedroom.

Broken glass and pools of water at her feet.

But there was nobody else there. Nobody except Léonce de Carville, his eyes still wide open, his skin white, and his mouth twisted like the mask from *The Scream*.

He was not breathing.

Linda recognized death when she saw it. She had been working with old people for nearly twelve years now.

He was dead. Suffocated.

The pillow was still lying on the bed.

In that moment, Linda felt no sadness or pity for the dead man in front of her. In that moment, the only emotion she felt, overpowering all the others, was fear.

36

On the concourse of the Gare Saint-Lazare, Malvina de Carville calmed down as quickly as she had lost her temper. Grumbling, she walked away from the line for the ticket machine. The man behind her shrugged and nobody paid her any more attention.

Nobody except Marc.

So, Malvina de Carville had followed him. This mad bitch had decided to tail him all the way to Dieppe, had she? Right now, though, he had the advantage, because they were in a public place. She couldn't do anything with so many people around. He had to seize his chance.

Marc jumped up, shoving Grand-Duc's notebook into his backpack. Without waiting for a response, he handed the bag to the waiter and said: "Could you look after this for a few minutes? I'll be back. Be careful, though, it's very precious . . . it contains my entire year's course work."

Too shocked to speak, the waiter clutched the bag to his chest. Marc was gone before he had time to protest.

Malvina was standing about a hundred feet away. She seemed to be hesitating between lining up for another ticket machine, joining the intimidatingly long line for the manned ticket counters, and not buying a ticket at all. Her back was to him. Marc could not believe his luck.

He slalomed through the passengers, heading straight for her. He felt an almost animal need to release the pressure that had built up inside him. His fingers grabbed her wool sweater and he almost lifted her off the ground. Marc was a foot taller than Malvina and twice as heavy. He dragged her unceremoniously toward a vending machine, away from the densest part of the crowd.

Malvina smiled. She did not look very surprised.

"Can't keep away from me, can you, Vitral?"

"What are you doing here?"

"Take a wild guess..."

Marc moved his hand toward Malvina's neck. It was a slender little neck and his fingers could easily go around it. He pulled Malvina closer to him. None of the other passengers was paying any attention to them—they probably looked like a couple embracing before they said good-bye.

"Did you follow me? How did you know I was going to Saint-Lazare?"

"It's not exactly rocket science, Vitral. Where would poor little Marc go if he was upset? To his loving grandma, of course!"

"All right, so you're very clever. But listen, I'm warning you now, if I see you on the same train as I'm taking, I will throw you out the door." Marc tightened his grip. "Understood?"

Malvina was having trouble breathing but the smirk still didn't leave her face.

"Do you understand?" he demanded again.

Malvina was choking. Marc wondered how far he could

go. He wasn't panicking now. His hatred for this girl seemed to give him an almost superhuman power.

But he did not have long to consider this question, because almost immediately he felt the barrel of a gun pressing between his legs. Instinctively, he loosened his grip.

"Stay close to me, Vitral," Malvina whispered, "so people will think we're lovers. That way, they won't see my Mauser aimed at your balls. But take your hands off my neck right now."

Marc looked out into the vast concourse. Nobody was taking any notice of them. They might be brother and sister. Perhaps that wasn't far from the truth.

"Where's your bag?" Malvina hissed.

"I don't have it, sorry. I suppose you want me to take off all my clothes again. In front of everyone . . ."

Marc was clumsily playing for time. Inwardly, he cursed his own stupidity. He had known this crazy bitch was armed.

"Well, maybe you should strip. Why not? You're not bad-looking. Not very bright, but cute. And, under the circumstances, you have to do as I say."

Drops of sweat clung to the back of Marc's neck. Malvina's left hand stroked his thigh, while her right hand continued to press the Mauser against his crotch. She withdrew the gun barrel a few inches and her fingers caressed the bulge in his jeans. She pressed more tightly against him. "Move and I'll shoot."

The image of Grand-Duc's corpse flashed through Marc's mind. A bullet in the chest. She wasn't bluffing. This madwoman was perfectly capable of shooting him in the middle of a crowded train station.

"Why aren't you going hard, Vitral?" Malvina asked. "Don't you find me attractive?"

Marc had run out of sarcastic rejoinders. The girl's fingers crawled over him like a lizard. Clumsily, she caressed his cock, her tiny hand applying too much pressure.

"Can't get it up, eh? Maybe you just prefer my sister."

Marc tried to take deep breaths. He wanted to push this crazy bitch away from him, even if it meant risking his life. Maybe she wouldn't dare shoot, after all.

"Cat got your tongue, Vitral? Don't pretend you're not turned on by my sister. It's all right, I'm not jealous. I know how beautiful she is, and how ugly I am. We're like beauty and the beast, the two of us."

With her left hand, Malvina caressed Marc's balls. Or, rather, she kneaded them, like bread, as if this were the first time she had ever touched a man's genitals.

"Still no erection, I see...Shall I tell you why I'm not jealous? Can you guess?"

Apparently, Malvina was a quick learner. Her fingers were stroking him more gently now. Marc felt violated. He'd had enough. He was going to have to push her away, shove her against the station wall. As if Malvina had read his thoughts, she pressed the gun against his testicles once more. He grimaced with pain.

"Don't you understand? Listen to me: if I'm a monster, it's not Lyse-Rose's fault, it's yours. It's the Vitral family's fault. You're the ones who stole my sister. I used to be as pretty as Lyse-Rose, you know. And I would still be as pretty now, and as tall, and as sexy. But I refused to grow up—that's what the doctors said—because your family took my little sister away. We would have had the same hairstyles, worn the same clothes, the same makeup...

Maybe we would have shared boyfriends, too. But you stole all that from me, Vitral. So who should I try to look beautiful for? Tell me! Who?"

Malvina's hand released its grip on his penis. She leaned in close to his ear and whispered: "Have you fucked my sister? Come on, you can tell me . . ."

What should he say? Was Malvina even expecting a response?

Her fingers began probing and stroking him again.

"You're a handsome boy, Vitral. I bet you get a lot of girls, don't you? I bet you could have any girl you wanted. So why do you have to screw my sister? Are you a pervert, or what?"

The Mauser pressed harder against his crotch.

"I'll kill you if you don't get a hard-on soon, Vitral. Lyse-Rose is going to come home now. To our house, I mean. To her true home. All this craziness is over. It was that little bitch Emilie who died in the plane crash: you told me so yourself. You're not going to steal my sister from me a second time."

It was time to stop thinking and act. Even if he couldn't move, Marc could still provoke Malvina. He forced himself to speak, his voice soaked in irony.

"So you're looking for a little sister, are you?"

It had been so long since Marc had spoken that Malvina seemed surprised. She even backed away from him slightly.

"Believe me, Malvina, you have plenty of little sisters. And little brothers, for that matter. There are probably dozens of them, scattered all over the Bosphorus. Your dad, Alexandre, put it just about all over Turkey before he died in that crash. From what I've heard, Daddy Dearest had no problem at all getting it up."

The Mauser was no longer touching him. Malvina's face had collapsed. Marc kept going: "You weren't that young—you probably remember, don't you? All those floozies your dad fucked in Istanbul. In his office. All over the place. Do you remember your mom crying? Do you remember her fucking other men? Men with blue eyes..."

Malvina seemed to be shrinking with every word.

Marc went for the kill: "Chances are, Lyse-Rose is not even your sister!"

Malvina screamed. Everyone in the concourse must have turned to watch. Her little hand crushed Marc's testicles. Marc collapsed, stunned by the pain.

Malvina hid the Mauser in her pocket and disappeared quickly into the crowd.

37

October 2, 1998, 4:13 p.m.

Marc walked through the fifth car of the train. He still had not found a free seat. He hated the Paris–Rouen train, particularly on a Friday evening. It seemed as if the train company sold twice as many tickets as there were seats.

His balls still ached, although the pain had dulled now. He had stayed on his knees for almost ten minutes in the station concourse, surrounded by concerned faces.

"Are you all right? Looks like she got you right where it hurts..."

Their tone was half worried, half amused. How were people supposed to react when faced with a guy bent double because the girl he had been embracing had just crushed his balls?

Marc had collected his backpack from the waiter and limped as quickly as he could to the platform for his train, which had finally been announced.

In the seventh car, Marc gave up looking for a seat. The train was a double-decker, so he sat on a stairway between the two floors. He was not the only one: other steps were already occupied by a mother with three children, a businessman going through some reports, and a dozing teenager. It was an uncomfortable place to sit, but it was better than standing up.

Marc wedged his backpack between his knees and checked his phone again. Still no message.

He called Lylie's number. Straight to voice mail.

"Lylie, this is Marc. Please answer me! Where are you? I listened to your last message, and I could hear ambulance sirens in the background. It's driving me crazy. I've been calling all the hospitals in Paris, trying to find you. Please call me back."

So far Marc had contacted about twenty hospitals—the largest ones. He had to keep going. He decided to do this for half an hour, then read some more of Grand-Duc's notebook.

It was the same story, over and over again: "Hello, madame. Has a young woman by the name of Emilie Vitral been admitted to your hospital today? No, I don't know which department... Accident and Emergency, perhaps?"

The train was so noisy that Marc could hardly hear what the receptionists were saying. Not that it varied very much.

There was no Emilie Vitral listed in their registers.

After thirty minutes, he had contacted another twenty-two hospitals. They were mostly private clinics and specialized medical centers now. He began to despair. There was no way he was going to find Lylie this way. Not before tomorrow, anyway...

He had to think. He had to find a way to make all of the pieces of the puzzle fit together. First of all, he had to finish reading Grand-Duc's notebook. He should have time for that before his train reached Dieppe. There were only about thirty pages left.

Marc put away his cell phone then took out the pages that he had previously torn from Grand-Duc's notebook. The back of the last page was blank. Marc grabbed a pen from his bag and scribbled:

WHERE IS LYLIE?

Then, below this, in a small, cramped hand, he added:

In a hospital? One-way trip?

He underlined the last phrase and added three exclamation marks.

Suicide?

Murder?

Revenge?

Without thinking about why he did it, Marc underlined the word "Revenge." Then he wrote:

WHO KILLED GRAND-DUC?

Malvina de Carville

For a few seconds, Marc sucked on his pen, then added a question mark after her name. The train was shaking, so his handwriting was far from neat, but at least he could read it. That was all that mattered.

Then, feverishly, he wrote:

Why didn't Grand-Duc kill himself three days ago?

What did he discover that night, just before midnight?

What could he have discovered that would make someone want to kill him?

MY GRANDFATHER'S ACCIDENT—WHAT IS WRONG WITH GRAND-DUC'S ACCOUNT?

Search your old bedroom in Dieppe. Take your time. It will come to you.

Marc read through what he had written. The number of question marks made him give a wry smile. And he hadn't finished yet. He touched the blue envelope in his jacket pocket.

DNA TEST. MYSTERY SOLVED?

Open the envelope?

Should he betray his promise to Nicole in order to find the solution?

No. That would not get him anywhere. Marc already knew what the envelope contained. Lylie was not his sister. Lylie was Mathilde de Carville's granddaughter. Malvina's sister. Everything pointed to this: from Grand-Duc's investigation to the ring that Lylie had been wearing that morning. And his feelings for her, of course . . .

TALK TO NICOLE

Marc added a final question mark, for good measure.

The train was due to arrive in Dieppe at 6:24 p.m. Less than three hours . . .

When it stopped at Mantes-la-Jolie, nearly half of the passengers got off, freeing up seats. Marc got up and sat near the window in the lower part of the train. He was still in some pain, but the extra leg space helped to ease his discomfort. Malvina was nowhere to be seen, and he was grateful for that small mercy, although there was no way of knowing if she might be on board. Marc sighed and took out Grand-Duc's notebook.

Crédule Grand-Duc's Journal

The tiny gold link was sent, carefully wrapped in a plastic bag, to the best forensics laboratory in France, at

Rosny-sous-Bois. The cigarette butts and beer cans were sent there, too. I still had friends in the police, and I had Mathilde de Carville's money. There was nothing illegal about it. Not very illegal, anyway. It was just a parallel investigation.

I got the results eight days later. The link I had found in the grave was definitely made of gold. That was the only certainty, however. The smallness of the sample made it impossible to tell whether the link had come from a baby's bracelet or any other kind of jewelry. It might even have come from a dog's name tag! There was also no way of knowing when or where it had been manufactured.

But still, a gold link from a piece of jewelry... it deepened the mystery. Why would that link have been buried in a grave marked by a pile of stones? Who could have buried it there?

The reward for information leading to the discovery of Lyse-Rose's bracelet, meanwhile, had risen to seventy-five thousand francs. It was a ludicrous sum, particularly for a bracelet that would, I very much hoped, be missing a link from its chain. But by that point, the prize seemed entirely theoretical. I had long ago given up hope that anyone would claim it.

I was wrong. The line would dangle in the water for another two years, but a fish would finally bite. A big fish. But be patient for a while longer, and I will tell you all about that. In terms of suspense, I don't think you really have anything to complain about: an interminable year for me is summarized for you in a few pages.

The cigarette butts and other debris found in the hut on Mont Terri were not particularly useful. After seven years, that was to be expected. Dozens of teenage drinkers and lovers must have spent nights in that cabin since Georges Pelletier stayed there in 1980.

So we were back to square one: I had to find Georges Pelletier. I spent many nights in Besançon, talking to homeless people and winning their trust. I realize this might seem quaint: a few drunks and tramps, sleeping on the streets of a small provincial town, sharing their stories around the campfire. Believe me, it was nothing like that! Living on the streets of Besançon is extremely tough. Imagine sleeping on a mattress made of damp cardboard during winter in the coldest town in France. There is no metro there. And the train station is closed at night.

I only spent about ten nights with them, between January and March 1988, and I thought I was going to die of the cold. I would go back to my hotel room in the early morning and spend three hours in a hot bath before I would feel normal again. Now do you believe me when I say that I was still earning that money the de Carville woman gave me after seven years of the investigation? As to whether my hard work was worth it . . . I'll let you be the judge of that.

Georges Pelletier's former neighbors and fellow junkies told me that he had reappeared after December 23, 1980. He was alive and well when he came down from the mountain, so clearly the Airbus had not crashed into him. He had not been wearing a bracelet around his wrist, and he was no more talkative than he had been before he went to Mont Terri. He had stayed in Besançon for six months, doing the usual things—drug dealing, shoplifting—then had fled to Paris before the police could nail him for anything. Or before his brother found him. According to his street friends, Georges was more wary of his brother's charity than he was of going to prison.

I will add just one more detail. Georges Pelletier's dog did not come back from the mountain with him. But Augustin was wrong about the size of his brother's mutt: it was not a little mongrel, but a very large Belgian shepherd. Certainly too big to fit in the tiny grave next to the cabin. Unless he chopped it up into pieces. But why would he do that? Why not simply dig a bigger hole?

As I'm sure you've guessed, I did not give up. All I had to do now was pick up Georges's scent in that concrete jungle of lunatics and lost souls that people call Paris. Nazim and I spent three months there, working full-time on the investigation. Small ads in the papers; talking endlessly to the police and social services; more nights spent on the streets, with a flashlight and a photograph of Georges; an evening in Augustin's living room, everyone smiling politely around the Christmas tree, just so that we could ask him to provide us with the most recent photograph of Georges that he could find.

It was good, methodical work. I am a pro, after all.

Nazim and I managed to follow Georges Pelletier's tracks as far as a man called Pedro Ramos. I met this man in June 1989 at a fairground in Trone, standing in front of the Tagada ride.

"Georges worked for me for two seasons," Pedro told me, while keeping an eye on his ride. Hysterical teenage girls and boys paid five francs each to have their bottoms bruised for two minutes on a whirling bench.

"I didn't ask him for his CV. I knew he'd be off when the season was over. He wasn't lazy, and he was clean when he came to work. I couldn't have cared less what he did with his time off."

"When was the last time you saw him?" I asked.

Pedro did not even have to think about it. He just waved his hand commandingly at a girl in a pink dress who was working the till. Her head changed color in time with the neon lights.

"Autumn 1983. Mid-November, to be exact. After the Saint-Romain fair, the last fair of the season. In the train station at Rouen. We had all packed up for the winter and everyone was going their separate ways. Pelletier knew where to find me if he wanted to work the following season, but he never turned up. That's pretty normal in this line of work. Two seasons is not bad at all, really. I never saw him again."

Another dead end.

I asked Pedro Ramos a few more questions, but I didn't learn anything of substance. The trail ended in the train station at Rouen. Not very far from Dieppe, when you think about it. Not far from the Vitrals...

A coincidence? Probably.

I hung around the fairs during the months that followed. Nazim enjoyed that. Some weekends, Ayla came with him. After all, Mathilde de Carville was paying for the rides: the ghost trains and the tunnels of love. It would be a long, long time before we learned anything new. Years.

38

"It's a wedding!"

Judith's little hands gripped the iron bars of the fence that surrounded the playground.

"No, silly, that's not a wedding! Look, they're all dressed in black. That means somebody's died..."

The procession moved slowly away. Judith was not convinced by what her friend Sarah was telling her. Sarah was always making stuff up. And Judith knew that when people wore nice clothes and walked in neat lines down the street, when the bells rang as they came out of church... that meant a man and a lady had just gotten married. She'd been to lots of weddings—at least two—so she knew all about them.

"It's a wedding, Sarah!"

Sarah, annoyed, shook the iron bars. "No, it's not, it's a dead person! They're going to put him in a hole in the ground. They did the same thing to my grandmother."

"I don't believe you!"

"So where's the bride, then?"

"We missed her. She must have gone past already."

"Don't be silly! Today is Friday. Nobody gets married on a school day. But when you die, it doesn't matter what day they bury you."

Judith had to admit that this made sense.

"And people at weddings aren't that old," Sarah went on. "Can't you see how old they all are?"

"Not all of them!"

"Yes, they are."

"No! Look. She's not old. Miss! Miss!"

Lylie was startled from her daydream. She saw two very cute girls, about five years old, standing behind an iron fence, wrapped up in hats, coats, gloves, and scarves.

"Miss, is that a wedding or a dead person?"

Lylie smiled. It was striking, the contrast between the happy shouts coming from the playground and the funereal silence of the procession. She crouched down so that her face was level with the girls'.

"It's a funeral," she told them.

"Told you!" Sarah gloated.

Judith pulled a face. Three other kids came over to see what all the fuss was about.

"Who was the dead person?" Sarah asked.

"I don't know," Lylie said. "I just happened to be passing. I came from that big white building over there. I have to go back there, actually."

"But why are you sad if you didn't know them?" Judith asked.

"What makes you think I'm sad?"

"Your eyes are all red. And why else would you follow a dead person when you could go to the park or go shopping?"

There was now a whole crowd of children watching Lylie from behind the fence.

"You're right, I am sad," Lylie whispered into Judith's ear. "But don't tell anyone, will you? What's your name?"

"Judith. Judith Potier. What's your name?"

"I don't know."

Judith bit her lip, as if worried she had said the wrong thing. She looked thoughtful for a moment. This was almost certainly the first time she had met someone who didn't have a name.

"Is that why you're sad?"

39

October 2, 1998, 4:39 p.m.

The train stopped at Vernon. Marc watched the passengers disembark and walk along the platform. There were no tearful farewells or happy reunions, just a dozen busy people rushing off to their homes. When the train started up again, the platform was empty and the cars were already lining up to leave the station parking lot.

The sun had not yet set behind the hills on the horizon. Marc drew the curtains so he could read Grand-Duc's notebook without the glare of sunlight in his eyes. The detective had now been investigating the case for ten years. Marc's memories of the events described were no longer vague and imprecise. He had his own personal version to set alongside Grand-Duc's.

Crédule Grand-Duc's Journal

In September 1991, Emilie Vitral was about to go to secondary school. I have not mentioned Emilie very much so far in this account, but it is important to understand how she changed during those years, to the point where Nicole

Vitral would finally yield and Mathilde de Carville would triumph, in her way.

Emilie was about to turn eleven. I think she always liked me. And the feeling was mutual. I think she liked my gruff, solitary side. Kids tend to enjoy talking to adults who don't say very much.

For her, I was Crédule-la-Bascule.

I think Marc was fascinated by me, too. Not only because I knew a lot about soccer but mainly, I think, because of my job. Private detectives hold a sort of glamour for young boys. I would tell him tall tales, and Nicole would laugh at my exaggerations and inventions. And while we enjoyed this time together, I would watch Emilie closely.

Secretly, I was hoping to see some kind of physical resemblance. If only she could have woken up one morning and suddenly looked as if she belonged to one family or the other. All I wanted was something definite; it didn't matter to me which side won.

But there was nothing. The color of her eyes still favored the Vitrals, but that was all.

Not all resemblances are physical, however. Nicole Vitral did her best to hide it, at least to begin with, but over time it became obvious: in Rue Pocholle, Emilie was so different from those around her that you might easily have believed she had been left next to the burning Airbus by extraterrestrials. For a start, she loved school. She was first in her class every year, while Marc struggled to achieve mediocrity. Emilie loved music. Emilie loved art. Emilie loved stories. She quickly consumed all the records, pictures, and books she could find in the Vitral home. There were a reasonable quantity of these, but they were there almost out of obligation, rather than any personal need, the way people keep a bicycle or a set of lawn balls in the garage. Just in case.

Emilie grew up different; you could see it from a million miles away. She became adorable, adoring and adored, but she was suffocating. The mobile library would stop in Dieppe every Tuesday evening and little Emilie would clean it out, so desperate was she for new literary and artistic experiences. She would ask her grandmother about Roald Dahl, Igor Stravinsky, Rudyard Kipling, Sergei Prokofiev, and dozens of other foreign names that meant nothing to Nicole.

It is not unusual for one person in a family to stand out from the rest. That is what I told myself. The flower that flourishes surrounded by weeds. The autodidact from a poor state school. The French version of the American Dream. The gifted youngsters who climb every ladder, without any helping hands, without a safety net below, to graduate from the best universities. Reaching so high, from so far below, yet remaining proud of their origins. Because that domestic prison in which they grew up marks them forever as different from all the "sons of" who surround them, the well-born children from the poshest Parisian arrondissements, the clones from Lycée Henri IV. Their background is the fuel that drives them onward, forward, upward. Their standards. And that is what they become: the standard-bearers for their families, their neighbor hoods. And how proud their families and neighbors are of them. The kids who made it. Is that why the poor have so many children? To increase their chances of a winning lottery ticket?

Anyway, that's enough of my half-assed ode to social

determinism. All I wanted to say was that Emilie flour-ished. The little girl with the big talent, protected by her family. And by Nicole in particular. But you have to imag-ine the nagging doubt that lay just below the surface of Nicole's pride and admiration.

Did Nicole have the right to be proud of her grand-daughter? *Was* she her granddaughter? Ten years after the Airbus tragedy, the Vitral family was still living in its shadow. If this girl really was Emilie Vitral, Nicole's own flesh and blood, then yes, it was wonderful—a true miracle. But what if she were Lyse-Rose de Carville, erro-neously sent to live with a poor family, in a very different world from the one that was her birthright? What if she were being stifled by her environment? What if she did not belong there?

"It's normal," Nicole would say to me sometimes. "A child raised by her grandmother. Alone. There's bound to be a difference, a gap between us."

And she was right. Partly.

At eleven years old, when she finished primary school, Emilie became more demanding. Well, no, that's not true: Emilie never demanded anything. But she expressed her desire to see farther than the end of Rue Pocholle. She wanted to discover new places, do new things. Most of all, she wanted to advance in her piano playing. Not because she was talented, or because her teachers were encourag-ing her, but simply because it was something she wanted to do. Or, more accurately, something she needed to do.

The dilemma was a simple one. Emilie could not con-tinue to progress as a musician unless she was able to practice every day. But that meant having a piano at home.

Emilie did her best to persuade her grandmother. She took measurements in the living room, and she knew that there was—just—enough space for a piano. And it would look nice. You could even put a vase on top of it.

But then there was the price.

A good piano would cost about thirty thousand francs. Say twenty thousand for a secondhand one.

Nicole tried to explain the reality to Emilie: "A piano! My poor Lylie, it's already difficult enough for me to clothe you and feed you. I had to work every Sunday in May and June just so we could go on vacation to Saint-Quay for a week, and I still don't know how I'm going to pay for your school things. And now I have to pay for your music lessons, too, because they're not free anymore. So, darling, you can see why it's not possible..."

Emilie could see. She understood, and she did not complain. She was almost preternaturally mature. At least, she appeared to understand. She went to her room, and through the thin dividing walls Nicole heard a tune, played on the plastic recorder that they had bought for Marc. It was the only instrument in the house. Nicole recognized the song, a hit at the time: "Leidenstadt" by Goldman.

Her heart ached.

When Marc came home from his rugby practice, he found his grandmother in tears on the sofa. Marc was thirteen years old. He did not know how to react. He could hear Emilie playing the recorder. It sounded nice. And a bit sad...

Nicole patted the cushion next to hers on the sofa. Marc sat down and she hugged him tightly.

"You mustn't be jealous of Emilie. Ever."

Of course not, Marc thought. Why would he be jealous?

"You have to keep behaving the same way toward her. She will always be your little sister...Even if I treat you differently. You're a big boy now, Marc. I think you're old enough to understand."

Treat them differently? What did she mean?

Nicole stood up, and so did Marc. She was smiling again, or pretending to. She asked Marc to help her move the sofa.

"I need to check if we really *can* fit a piano in here."

The purchase, in cash, of the brand new Hartmann-Milonga piano barely made a dent in the pile of money that had accumulated over the years in Emilie's bank account.

And Emilie was right: it did fit in the living room, between the sofa and the television, even if it was a tight squeeze.

Everything followed from that. Music courses in Paris, first of all, lasting a few days. Then longer stays in the capital. Then concerts, and tours, in France and abroad: London, Amsterdam, Prague. Records and books were bought for Emilie. And clothes, of course. Why should Emilie be deprived of the latest fashions? It was only human. She deserved the best. Nicole no longer felt able to deny her anything. Just in case...

Now you understand Mathilde de Carville's strategy. She had known what she was doing, right from the start. The bank account she opened for Emilie was a cuckoo's egg left in a sparrow's nest. Now that it had hatched, the bird that emerged was big enough to kill the nest's other inhabitants.

A gulf opened up between Emilie and Marc. I mean, a gulf in material terms. I will talk more about the other

differences between them later on in this account. Emilie
could ask for anything she wanted, no matter how silly or
how costly. Nothing was too much for her, whereas Marc
had to make do with hand-me-downs and secondhand
things. The neighbors' clothes. His grandfather's bicycle.
Rugby boots from his older teammates.

Emilie had insisted that she wanted to pay for Marc's
things, too, at first. It was her money, after all, as Nicole
had explained to her. But on this point her grandmother
refused to budge. For her, it was a question of honor. She
had made a moral commitment with Mathilde de Carville.

A line in the sand.

Not one centime of the de Carville money would be
spent on her grandson.

This may seem strange, I grant you. But how would you
have acted, in Nicole's place? The decision is not as easy
as it seems. Yes, Mathilde de Carville knew exactly what
she was doing, that evening in May 1981, when she gave
the cuckoo's egg to Nicole Vitral. Along with the sapphire
ring.

Yet there is an unexpected moral to this story. As far as
I was able to tell, the cuckoo's egg did not actually hatch.
Marc was not jealous. Ever. And his attitude had nothing
to do with the desire to obey his grandmother. Jealousy
was simply not in his nature. He was happy for Emilie, and
that was all.

And there was another miracle, perhaps more curious
still: in spite of all the gifts she received, all the gold and
sweetness that enriched her life, Emilie was not transformed into a spoiled brat. She remained the same lively,
humble, happy, straightforward girl she had always been,
never feeling the slightest scorn for the cramped living

room, the tiny houses of Rue Pocholle, the gray sea, and the hard pebbles beneath her bare feet.

Emilie grew up. She had the Vitrals' blue eyes and the de Carvilles' refined tastes. The kindness of the Vitrals... and the money of the de Carvilles.

Go figure...

Marc looked up from the notebook. There were tears in his eyes.

The train sped past the ponds of the Poses. Barges loaded with sand floated the other way back up the Seine. He saw it all again: the recorder, the sofa, the piano with Emilie sitting at it, playing Chopin, Berlioz, Debussy. He did not know any of the music, but it moved him all the same. Emilie sitting straight-backed, her fingers moving constantly over the keys. The piano was silent now. Still in the living room in Dieppe, but covered in a thick layer of dust. Marc remembered Lylie's clothes, too. How could he forget them? Her dresses and skirts, becoming more beautiful with every year.

How could he have been jealous?

Nobody ever understood that. Not Grand-Duc, not Nicole, and certainly not Mathilde de Carville.

The train stopped at Val-de-Reuil, the station in the fields, a long way from the town. Marc hesitated. He would be in Rouen in fifteen minutes. He took out his cell phone. There was time for him to call a few more hospitals. He tried three—without success. No one by that name had been admitted. Oh, well. Marc no longer believed in this line of inquiry. More than anything, he wanted to finish reading Grand-Duc's notebook.

His adolescence, narrated by a private detective. As if his own diary had been written by someone else.

40

October 2, 1998, 4:48 p.m.

Nicole Vitral walked slowly toward the stall at the end of the fishing port.

"What do you have today, Gilbert? Nothing too expensive."

"Sole," the fishmonger replied. "Straight from the boat that came in last night. Just one?"

"Two."

Gilbert's eyes goggled like the eyes on one of his dead fish. "Two? Is Emilie home? Marc? Or do you have a lover?"

"It's for Marc, you idiot!" said Nicole.

"All right, I'll give you a nice one, then. How is he?"

Nicole gave an evasive answer, something banal, then paid for the fish.

"Thank you, Gilbert. I'll be round to bring you some leaflets from the town council later this week. About the future of the port."

The fishmonger sighed. "Not more of that rubbish! Those councilors should be worrying about us shopkeepers, instead of the dockers. We'll be the first to go bust, believe me, even before the fishermen . . ."

Nicole had already turned to go. Gilbert Letondeur
was the best fishmonger in Dieppe, but he was also a
right-wing asshole, in league with the shipowners and the
Chamber of Commerce and Industry. Nicole knew that her
view of things was rather black-and-white, but that's just
how she saw things. Dieppe, for her, could be divided into
two opposing camps. And, in spite of the van from which
she had sold fries on the seafront, she had never aligned
herself with the forces of capitalism. A traitor!

Doubly a traitor, in fact, because she ate the enemy's
fish.

She walked on, toward the seafront. She was glad for
the dry weather, the calm wind. The seafront was a hive
of activity and color, covered with white canopies, each
draped with a foreign flag—for ten days every two years,
Dieppe played host to the International Kite Festival.

The sky was already full of multicolored objects in all
shapes and sizes, some floating motionlessly high above,
some circling and swooping. Looking up above her, Nicole
spotted a Chinese dragon, an Inca mask, a gigantic blue
cat...

She watched them and felt a wave of nostalgia. Back in
the 1980s, Dieppe had been the first port in France to stage
a kite festival. Since then, the event had been replicated on
every windy beach in northern Europe. Nicole had been
there with Pierre for the first two festivals, in 1980 and 1982.
How joyful it had been. And lucrative, too. Their daughter-in-law, Stéphanie, had been heavily pregnant during
the first festival, but she had still helped them on the first
weekend. Pierre, her doting father-in-law, and her husband,
Pascal, had had to persuade Stéphanie to sit down and rest.
Emilie had been born a few days later, on September 30.

And then there had been the Airbus crash...and then the trial, and the verdict. Pierre Vitral had lived through one more festival, in 1982, before falling asleep for the last time on November 7, in Le Tréport. The festival had become part of Nicole's life, a symbol reminding her that life and death hung by a thread, at the whim of the wind. Nevertheless, Nicole continued to work on the seafront during the festivals that followed, without Pierre to help her. She had no choice: the kite festival was the biggest earner on her calendar.

Marc and Emilie were too young to remember all this. For them, the festival was always like an early Christmas: something they looked forward to for weeks ahead of time. It gave Marc the opportunity to impress his little sister with his kite-handling skills. He had been given a kite in the shape of a giant red-and-gold insect by a neighbor. It had a long, beribboned tail and transparent paper wings. Marc called it "Dragonfly," of course. Some people— fools—still called Emilie by that name sometimes. Some of the shopkeepers in Dieppe, for instance.

Emilie would run from stand to stand, sampling all the different countries. Peru, China, Ethiopia, Mongolia, Ecuador, Yemen, Quebec...The kite as a tight cord linking all the children of the world: all they needed was a bit of a breeze, nothing else.

The art of taming the sky, purely for the fun of it.

Flying ever higher. No passengers. No crash. After 1980, Nicole had never been able to look at the sky in the same way.

Little Emilie would run for miles. Japan, Mali, Colombia. She would come back to the van, her eyes ablaze. All the world's tribes meeting here, in her backyard. "Grandma, have you seen, have you seen it all?"

                                *

Nicole left the seafront almost in tears. For the first time in her life, Emilie would miss the kite festival this year.

She went into the baker's.

"A baguette, Nicole?"

"Yes, please. And a Salammbô, too."

"Really? Is Marc back?"

A Salammbô was Marc's favorite cake. Or, at least, it had been when he was ten years old. Nicole knew it was ridiculous to continue trying to make her grandson happy with the same things that had lit up his childhood. But it made *her* happy, and Marc was always polite about it.

Nicole looked at her watch. He would be here in two hours. She walked toward the ferry bridge that separated Pollet from the rest of Dieppe, and thought again about their telephone conversation. Mathilde de Carville had given Marc the DNA test, with instructions not to open it, because it was for Nicole.

That cow!

Nicole had to wait for a while, as the ferry bridge was lifting up to let a ship pass. Nigerian flags. Bananas? Pineapples? Exotic hardwoods?

What did Mathilde de Carville think—that she was the only one to have thought about a DNA test? That Crédule Grand-Duc was her lapdog? That he had taken Emilie's blood without her grandmother noticing?

The line of cars lengthened in front of the bridge. The combination of sea air and gasoline fumes made Nicole cough. That de Carville woman was not as cunning as she imagined. And Grand-Duc was not the bastard he pretended to be. He had ordered two DNA tests. Two blue envelopes. One for each grandmother.

Nicole looked up at the Chinese Dragon kite, waving high above the roofs of the seafront. She smiled. In the middle drawer of her chest of drawers, under lock and key, she had kept the blue envelope given to her by Grand-Duc. The results of the test comparing her blood to Emilie's. It would, of course, confirm the results that Marc was carrying with him, comparing Emilie's blood to Mathilde de Carville's.

Finally, the ferry bridge lowered into place and the cars began to move again.

Nicole had opened the envelope in 1995. So, she, too, had known the truth for the past three years.

She needed to talk to Marc about this. Tonight. She could still save a life. If she waited any longer, it would be too late. She should have acted before, of course, but that was easier said than done.

She thought about the test result.

A relief? Yes, perhaps. As long as she could accept losing everything else.

41

October 2, 1998, 5:11 p.m.

The train sped along the coast of Deux-Amants, crossed
the railway bridge at Manoir-sur-Seine, and passed through
the station at Pont-de-l'Arche. Marc did not even notice the
cold of the window against his forehead. He switched on
the reading light above his head.

Crédule Grand-Duc's Journal

The early years of the 1990s were dead years. There were
more trips to Turkey and Canada, and my annual pilgrimage to Mont Terri. Nazim even staked out the cabin for
days at a time. But we never found anything new.

This was the beginning of my depression, I think:
between 1990 and 1992. The end of my illusions.

Nothing was happening on the Georges Pelletier front
either. He had just vanished. The reward for the bracelet
had stopped going up, and was stuck at seventy-five thousand francs. After all, what was the point in going any
higher?

I had not worked on the case at all for almost three

weeks when I received the telephone call from Zoran Radjic. The small ads, offering seventy-five thousand francs for the bracelet, continued to appear in a dozen newspapers every week, paid for in advance by automatic withdrawal.

"Crédule Grand-Duc?"

"Yes..."

"My name is Zoran Radjic. I read your ad about the reward for a missing gold bracelet. I think I have information that might be useful to you."

I was wary, of course, after being conned by that Turk years earlier.

"Do you know where it is?"

"Yes...I think so."

In spite of myself, I was excited. Credulous, as ever.

We met a few hours later, in a bar—l'Espadon, on Rue Gay-Lussac. We both ordered a beer. Zoran Radjic looked every bit the local con man. With his weasel-like face, furtive eyes, and slicked-back hair, he looked so obviously shady that you wondered how he managed to achieve anything.

Was it possible that this man might actually deliver the only piece of useful evidence we'd had? A bracelet taken from Mont Terri twelve years earlier. All the other details—eye color, musical talent, the grave next to the cabin—were nothing compared to this. If I could only get my hands on that damn bracelet, I'd be home free: the miracle child ejected from the airplane would, without any doubt at all, be Lyse-Rose de Carville.

"Go on," I told him, wishing to give away as little as possible.

"I saw your ad yesterday. I don't read the papers very often..."

Zoran was playing with his silver signet ring.

"Yes..."

"This goes back to 1983 or '84. The guy who showed it to me wasn't in the best of health. A junkie, you know? Back in those days, I used to help people out when they were in the shit... Well... to be honest, I used to deal drugs, too. And this guy was desperate for a fix. I sort of knew him. He'd been hanging around in the area for a while. He was flat broke, so he wanted to swap some jewelry for his next fix. It was a bracelet. Gold, according to him."

He played casually with his signet ring. I wasn't going to fall for his stalling, so sat back and waited for him to continue.

"I'm guessing you'd be interested in the guy's name..."

"I know his name," I said. "What I'm looking for is evidence. Or, better still, the bracelet itself. The seventy-five thousand francs is for the bracelet. Anything else... we'll negotiate."

The signet ring disappeared into his right hand. He made a fist.

"OK, I'll play along. We might not be talking about the same guy, after all. How much for the name?"

And there it was: the ring reappeared in his left hand. How did he do that?

"Ten thousand," I said. "Assuming it's the right name."

"No way. How do I know you're not going to fleece me? I give you the name, you tell me it's the wrong one, and then you piss off. And I've been had."

Maybe this guy was not as stupid as he looked.

"Fair enough. Have you a pen?"

"Yeah. Why?"

"I'll write the name on my coaster. You write the name on yours. If the two names are the same, you've won ten thousand francs. Then we can move on to the next step."

He grinned. The signet ring had somehow been moved to his right hand again. "Cool. I like this sort of game."

We both hunched over our coasters, hiding what we were writing from the other with our hands.

We turned the mats over at the same time.

Georges Pelletier. On both coasters.

I felt a shiver run down my spine. So, Georges Pelletier had offered the bracelet to this crook. It was all coming together.

But I was still cautious. I had spent five years wandering around Paris, searching for Georges Pelletier. Word spreads fast among lowlifes. So perhaps it wasn't so surprising that he knew the name of the man I was looking for.

"All right. The ten thousand is yours. I'll write you a check."

Radjic pulled a face. A check? He was strictly a cash-only kind of guy.

"Did you see the bracelet?"

"Yes. How much for the info?"

"Ten thousand, if I believe you. Tell me about it."

"What do you want to know?"

Maybe this guy, with his disappearing signet ring, had a bit of talent as a magician, but I still had a trump card up my sleeve. I'd learned a few tricks myself, over the years.

"If you've really seen it, you shouldn't even have to ask what I want to know."

He smiled. I couldn't tell if he was bluffing or not.

"Ten thousand more, that's the deal? Can I trust you?"

"I'm straight as a die," I told him. "Anyone can tell you."

Radjic's hands moved quickly, and he dropped the signet ring on the table. He was nervous. Or he wanted me to think he was, that sly bastard. I picked up the coaster and wrote on it: "Lise-Rose. September 27, 1980."

Exactly the same words as the ad.

I passed him the coaster.

"Is this what was engraved on the bracelet?"

"No idea about the kid's date of birth, sorry, but yeah, that's the right name..."

He rubbed his hands together. The ring was back in its original place, on his finger.

Gotcha! I thought. Another con man.

"...except I think it's spelled wrong. Lyse was written with a y, not an i, as far as I remember."

I felt another electric shock go down my back. Radjic had not fallen into the trap I had set him.

"OK," I said. "You've won another ten thousand. So, did you swap the drugs for the bracelet?"

"Well, if I'd known it was worth seventy-five thousand francs, obviously I would have...But no. I never took anything but cash in return for what I sold." He gave a wry smile. "Or perhaps a check."

"So, Pelletier disappeared with his bracelet..."

"Yeah."

"Did you see him again after that?"

"Never. Given the state he was in, I doubt whether he lasted much longer."

Damn!

I wrote the check without any qualms. Mathilde de Carville could afford twenty thousand francs, even if my doubts persisted. After all, the name "Lyse-Rose" had been in all the papers at the time of the crash. This might have been the easiest twenty thousand Zoran had ever made.

He looked carefully at the check, then offered me his hand.

"Thank you. Oh, I do have one more piece of information. This one's on the house."

The hairs on my arms stood up.

"What is it?"

"I just remembered. There was another reason I didn't accept Pelletier's bracelet. It was damaged, you see. The chain. There was a link or two missing."

The room seemed to spin around me. My God! Nobody in the world, except Nazim and I, knew about that missing link.

42

For once, the Paris–Rouen train was on time. It pulled up
in the station at exactly 5:29 p.m. The Rouen–Dieppe train
would leave in nine minutes. Marc had made this connection dozens of times since he first moved to Paris. Nine
minutes was easily enough time. After regretfully closing
Grand-Duc's notebook, he walked over to the sandwich
shop. There was only one person waiting in line. Marc
bought a slice of apple tart and a bottle of San Pellegrino.
Nicole would undoubtedly have prepared a feast for him
tonight, but that didn't alter the fact that he was hungry
now. It had been a long time since that ham sandwich on
the train to Coupvray.

The train to Dieppe was practically empty. Marc sat
next to the window. There were only two other passengers
in the car: a teenager, listening to music on an MP3 player,
and a tall guy who was asleep, sprawled over two seats.

Marc pulled down the small gray table from the seat
back in front of him, put his bag on it, then took out the
notebook. Only another twenty pages to go.

On the platform, the stationmaster blew his whistle.

Instinctively, Marc looked up. And he froze, his forehead to the window.

It was her.

The scrawny figure gave the stationmaster a nasty look, hissed a few insults at him, then jumped on to the train just as it was about to move.

Malvina de Carville.

For a long time, Marc fearfully watched the two doors at either end of the car. Malvina must be hiding somewhere on the train, but Marc had no desire to seek her out. He was not going to let her corner him again so easily. Right now, his priority was to finish reading Grand-Duc's notebook.

He would deal with the lunatic girl after that.

Crédule Grand-Duc's Journal

I left Zoran Radjic at the Espadon bar, almost certain that he had been telling me the truth. The more I thought about it, the more it made sense. Georges Pelletier, living in the hut on the mountainside, had been an eyewitness to the crash on December 23, 1980. He had been the first person to reach the scene of the accident. He had seen the miracle child, and he had stolen the gold bracelet, like the pathetic scavenger he was, before the emergency services arrived.

So, that meant the miracle child was Lyse-Rose de Carville. I was now practically sure of it. Practically, but not absolutely. Because, however unlikely it seemed, Zoran Radjic might just have invented his story. And for the moment, all I had was conjecture and supposition. There was still no concrete proof.

Assumptions, suspicions, coincidences...call it what

you want. I've told you everything; you know as much as I do about the case now, so work it out for yourself.

Well, there is actually one thing I haven't mentioned yet. A feeling, more than a fact. It is so much more complicated to explain a feeling than it is to describe a search of Mont Terri or an interview with a witness. To be perfectly honest, I reached the point where I believed that all the evidence I had accumulated—the bracelet, the grave, the clothes from the Turkish market, the child's eye color, her musical talent—was essentially irrelevant.

The truth was to be found elsewhere. The truth was to be found in a feeling. Or, to be more accurate, in a relationship.

Marc and Emilie.

It is time now, I think, to touch upon their strange bond. They couldn't do anything about it, poor kids. Fate had made the decision for them.

For all her good intentions, Nicole was too distant from them. She worked such long hours, including weekends, and the age difference was a factor, too. Marc and Emilie did not have a mother and a father to raise them; they no longer even had a grandfather. So, inevitably, the two of them grew closer. With their blond hair and their angelic faces, they looked so similar. And yet, they were so different...

All right, I am going to bite the bullet. I know that Lylie and Marc will read these words. I will try to be worthy of their expectations. In any case, I won't be there to see their reactions.

Marc...pale blue eyes that often seemed lost in contemplation of distant horizons, perhaps the glorious past of Dieppe and its pirates. And yet, deep down, Marc was a simple soul. The things he loved best were his home, his neighborhood, his friends, his grandmother...and, most of all, Emilie.

Marc's love for Emilie grew steadily over time, warmed by his generosity of spirit and his love of home. His was a shy, discreet, almost silent presence.

The girls in his school idolized him, but Marc was indifferent to their sighs and wide eyes. His only ambition, from the time I first met him, was to be utterly devoted to Emilie: to be her brother, her father, her grandfather. To be everything she needed. To shelter her from the world.

Emilie made him happy. She was so full of life, she made everyone happy. In a place that lacked beauty—with its abandoned factories, its gray brick walls, its filthy gutters—she shone like the sun on the beach at Dieppe, was radiant as a rainbow over the sea.

Like a lost butterfly. Or a dragonfly, if you prefer...

The music she played—airs by Chopin and Satie—turned the cramped little house on Rue Pocholle into a castle, a cathedral. And her laughter lit up the home with brightness and warmth.

When she was sad, she consoled herself with music.

She was not haughty. She was just different. Alone. And even then, not always. Emilie would cheer every muddy tackle Marc made at the rugby stadium. She would put on a pair of sneakers and run seven miles with him, over a succession of hills and valleys. Dieppe–Pourville–Varengeville–Puys.

Like a big sun, she made everyone melt, including me. *Crédule-la-Bascule*.

She had come too close to losing her life at three months

old to let a single moment of it go to waste. And she was so proud of her Marc, just as he was of her. Her tall, strong guardian angel.

Marc and Emilie realized early on that they were not brother and sister. Not really, anyway. Not like other brothers and sisters. The secret, so jealously guarded by Nicole Vitral, was out as soon as they set foot in the playground at the local nursery. Parents talk, and their children repeat those words, getting their facts mixed up in the process.

The children at the Paul-Langevin school invented a game: they would run around Emilie, heads lowered, arms spread wide, making airplane noises, buzzing around her before crashing close to where she stood. And Marc would stand next to her, like King Kong on the Empire State Building, swatting them away angrily. Sometimes he would get punished for it, but he never stopped protecting her.

Marc and Emilie were never truly brother and sister. They grew up in the shadow of a doubt.

The other kids in the playground would make fun of them, calling them boyfriend and girlfriend. And yes, they did love each other. That was very, very obvious. But what kind of love was it?

I think Marc must have begun to wonder about this when he was ten years of age. He and Emilie had been sharing a room ever since the verdict. They slept in a bunk bed: he below and she on top. When Marc turned ten, he remained in the little bedroom, while Emilie shared her grandmother's room.

Nicole did the best she could with the resources she had.

What kind of love ... ?

I have a confession to make. Not only did I wonder about

this, I tried to find out for myself. I spied on them. I armed Nazim with a telephoto lens and told him to take pictures.

It made no difference. Feelings are not always visible.

What kind of love?

Only they know the answer to that question.

I certainly don't.

Even science could not help me. This was later, when Lylie was fifteen. I am talking about the DNA test, of course.

I knew Mathilde de Carville would ask me to take care of that for her eventually. In spite of her principles, her faith. She wanted to know. It is only human. Actually, it seemed miraculous to me that she had managed to resist the temptation for so long.

I was fearful of the results. Fifteen years of investigation... what would that count for, against three drops of blood in a test tube?

Grand-Duc's words danced in front of Marc's eyes.

"What kind of love? Only they know the answer to that question."

The Pays de Caux undulated outside the window. Above, high-tension lines from the nuclear power station, which the train would follow all the way to Dieppe.

"What kind of love?"

What could he possibly have understood, that old detective with his telephoto lens? *Who* could possibly have understood?

"Marc loves Emilie! Emilie loves Marc!"

The children's taunts still echoed in Marc's ears. Like their poor imitations of a plane crashing.

Lylie, where are you?

*

Marc didn't feel like calling any more hospitals. Just one more, perhaps. Another failure.

"Marc loves Emilie..."

Who knew the truth, apart from the two of them? Who knew their secret?

Nobody.

It had only begun two months before. On the sixteenth of August.

Lylie was still seventeen.

Marc closed his eyes.

Only two months.

43

This is madness, thought Marc. Going for a run in the middle of August! It was late afternoon, but still nearly eighty-six degrees. Normandy in a heat wave.

But Lylie would not give up on the idea. She was crouched in the front doorway, tying the laces of her sneakers, as if she couldn't wait to get out. Marc sighed. Reluctantly, he took off his espadrilles and went to look for his running shoes.

"Hurry up, slacker!" Lylie teased him cheerfully.

Her blond hair was tied up in a ponytail with a pale blue ribbon. Marc loved her hair like that. It made her face look bigger, exposing her forehead. She looked like a princess. A bouncing, impatient princess . . .

"Come on, let's go!"

"All right, all right . . ."

Ever since she had won a cross-country race at school, Lylie had been running regularly. All through the spring, she had been putting in five hours a week, with Marc acting as her coach.

Marc was cursing; he could not find his left shoe.

"If you don't want to come with me..."

"I do!"

Lylie picked up a bottle of mineral water and took a swig. A drop of water rolled down her lips, her chin, her neck. Confused, Marc looked away.

He found his shoe at last and tied the laces. Lylie was wearing a tight-fitting, super-expensive Sergio Tacchini sports outfit that flattened her breasts but exposed her flat stomach and the tops of her hips. Her skin was soft and slightly tanned.

"Are we ready?"

Marc grudgingly followed her out the door.

Why was he so unenthusiastic about running today? Was it just the heat, the absence of a breeze? Or did he have a bad feeling about something? Lylie seemed almost too happy.

They ran through Pollet, crossed the ferry bridge, went along the seawall, and then climbed the steep hill to the castle.

Lylie always ran in front. Marc adapted his stride to hers. They passed the golf course and then the Ango school, with its futurist architecture, at the foot of the cliffs. Lylie mischievously waved good-bye to the school.

They now had half a mile of flat road until they reached Pourville, so they could lengthen their strides. As they rounded a bend, the view opened up before them: the hanging valley of Pourville, dazzling in the sunlight. Lylie sped up as they descended. People watched as they ran past. Men especially. They were hypnotized by the regular movement of Lylie's long bare legs. Marc acted as a body-guard, with 360-degree vision, as they ran.

He was used to men ogling Lylie, but that did not make

him any less jealous. They had crossed Pourville beach and were now climbing the Varengeville hill, the steepest and most sheltered on their run. Along this slope the most beautiful houses were hidden, with stunning views and shielded from the west wind.

Lylie toiled up the steep hill. Marc followed her without any difficulty. He stared out at the wild Scie valley in the distance. Above all, he did his best not to spend too long looking directly ahead, as Lylie's bottom bounced pertly in front of his eyes.

He was turned on, in spite of himself. Did Lylie have any idea of the effect her body had on him? One last bend and the road finally flattened out. Marc accelerated until he was running alongside her. She turned to smile at him. Radiant.

So beautiful.

Marc felt an emotion rising within him. It was far from new, but it was more intense, more powerful than ever before.

For the next two or three miles, all the way to Varengeville, the road was flat. Varengeville was the most densely wooded village on this coastline, and the shade it offered would be welcome. They ran past the Manoir d'Ango, the floral gardens in Moûtiers, in single file, for fear of cars trying to overtake them from behind.

Two hundred yards from their destination, Lylie looked as if she was about to sprint. Marc gave her a short head start. That was a mistake. Sweat was running down Lylie's bare back. The drops glistened as they ran into her shorts. Marc wished he could run his tongue up that naked flesh, taste that salty sweat.

Calm down. Jesus, calm down!

Marc accelerated, laughing as he overtook Lylie, then slowed down so that they would finish together. Lylie collapsed on the grass, exhausted. Again, Marc looked away from that beautiful body, stretched out in the sun.

He walked to the gate of the sailors' cemetery, and pushed it open. Lylie caught up with him a few seconds later. They were not alone there. There must have been about twenty tourists walking around the tiny graveyard, some of them looking for Georges Braque's tombstone, and for his stained-glass window in the church. Others posed for photographs in front of the dazzling view: Dieppe, Criel, Le Tréport... all the way up the coastline to Ault, in Picardie.

How many lovers dreamed of marrying here, in this sublime little sandstone church, set amid greenery, between sea and sky?

Did Marc dream of that?

He shook his head to rid his mind of such ridiculous thoughts.

"Shall we go back?"

He'd heard somewhere that the cliff here was receding more than anywhere else. Beneath them, the rock was crumbling. The chalk was soaked with water. One day, it would all collapse into the sea. The church. The gravestones. The sandstone cross.

All of it. Into the water, then swept away by the tide.

Lylie had drunk some water from the tap near the cemetery gates, and was already on her way.

Marc followed, like a faithful dog.

They passed a line of cars coming the other way. The narrow roadside was bordered by a carefully maintained hedge, so it was impossible to run side by side. Marc had to follow in Lylie's footsteps once more, watching her glistening back, her rounded buttocks, the nape of her neck with its tiny soft blond hairs.

Impossible.

Or was it?

Don't even think about it! screamed a voice inside his head.

Don't look at her anymore. Concentrate on your breathing, the length of your stride.

They were on their way back down toward Pourville. They passed a series of belle époque mansions, each of them a baroque fantasy. Suddenly, Lylie turned left in the direction of the Gorge du Petit Ailly, a little beach at the end of the hanging valley. Only the locals knew about this place. And yet surely there would be plenty of them there, in the middle of August. Marc caught up with Lylie again.

"Where are we going?"

Lylie's eyes sparkled. "Bet you can't catch me!"

She turned again, to the right this time. They were in a forest of willows now, no longer following a path. Barely two hundred yards farther on, they emerged from the woods and passed a little pond to their right. Lylie kept running.

They ran down toward the sea along a steep path. Cows stared at them from a meadow. It seemed as if they were on a farm, although there was no sign of any farmer. Lylie ran alongside an electric fence. Clearly, she knew where she was going. Marc concentrated and the map of the local area unfurled inside his mind. They had turned off to the north of the Gorge du Petit Ailly, so they must have crossed the farm at Pin-Brûlé and then the one at Morval. Now he felt sure he could guess where they were headed: Morval harbor. He had never been there, but had heard about it. It was one of those little coves inaccessible to tourists. A private beach reserved for the use of the local landowner, who probably never went there.

In the last twenty yards before they reached the sea, the land was crumbling. You could see the clay on the surface, running in ocher lines toward the sea. They had to cross a crater ten yards long, but it was easy to climb down and it had the distinct advantage of making the beach invisible from the field.

Lylie's feet slipped on the clay. Her legs and expensive outfit were covered in red mud. Laughing triumphantly, she stood up on the pebbles.

The tide was going out now, and there was a sandy space of about ten feet beyond the line of pebbles.

Lylie pulled the blue ribbon from her hair and it fell like a blond cascade. Marc shivered.

"Shall we go in?" Lylie asked, frowning sweetly, as if asking for forgiveness.

Marc did not reply. He was worried. That bad feeling had not left him.

"Come on!" Lylie said teasingly. "I'm covered in sweat. And the weather is so nice for a change. It's the most beautiful day of the summer."

Lylie was right, at least from a strictly meteorological point of view.

The calm sea. The heat. The sand. The silence.

Their closeness.

How could he resist?

Anyway, Lylie had not waited for a reply. Her sneakers

were sent flying onto the pebbles, and she dived into the water. Her running outfit worked equally well as a swimsuit. Marc was wearing a baggy red-and-black T-shirt and a pair of long canvas shorts. He threw his T-shirt and sneakers next to Lylie's on the pebbles.

They swam for nearly an hour. And that was all they did.

Marc began to snap out of his mood. Lylie's body was invisible beneath the gray waters of the English Channel. They swam breaststroke and crawl, side by side, happy and at ease.

Lylie had been right, as always. This had been a wonderful idea.

So what had he been worried about?

A jet of water startled him from his thoughts. Lylie laughed and splashed Marc again. He splashed her back. Lylie let him swim away, and then nimbly climbed on top of his back and pushed his head under the water. Marc did not resist. He resurfaced and took a breath of air. Lylie was six feet away from him now, still laughing.

Marc reached out and managed to grab Lylie's foot. She protested: "Hey, that's not fair!"

He pulled her toward him. When they were young, he and Lylie used to play like this every night, in a soapy bath. Marc's strong hand gripped Lylie's waist. She was as light as a feather.

"Cheat!"

Still laughing, Lylie turned around so she was facing him.

Marc's hand slid upward, to her arm, her shoulder. Gently he pushed her down, using her as a support to lift himself out of the water. Lylie's chest rubbed against Marc's stomach. Then her shoulders did the same. And then her face, eyes closed to protect them from the salt water.

Deeper underwater. Lylie's face touched the soaked cloth of Marc's shorts. By accident, almost, her mouth touched his penis.

He went hard. How could he do otherwise?

Far off, a ferry was leaving the port in Dieppe, headed toward Newhaven. A few white triangles followed in its wake—seagulls, probably, or small sailing boats. It was difficult to be sure from this distance.

Lylie and Marc said nothing. They swam slowly toward the beach. The sand was nearly dry. Lylie lay facedown.

"Shall we dry off for a bit before we go home?"

She sounded embarrassed. There was a new timbre to her voice, an adult timbre. Marc sat with his arms around his knees, staring out toward the horizon.

How long did they stay like that? A few minutes? Hours?

The ferry had disappeared long ago, and the seagulls— or yachts—had returned to the port. The sea lay flat and featureless.

Suddenly, Lylie stood up. She didn't say a word. Marc could see only her shadow on the sand. She crossed her arms and, in one single movement, removed her top. She placed it delicately on the sand, stretched out flat, as if to make it dry quicker. When she bent down, Marc could see the shadow of her small, firm breasts on the sand.

Lylie then slid her hands slowly down her waist, inch by inch, as if she were dancing, and stripped off the lower part of her outfit. It fell to the ground, like a shed skin.

Marc looked at her shadow, pigmented by millions of grains of sand. It was the same as before—same waist, same hips, same thighs, with or without the second skin—and yet...

Lylie lay down on her stomach again.

Marc waited for hours. Or minutes. He couldn't tell.

Nobody came to their aid. There was not a sail on the horizon, not a single stray tourist or angry farmer to disturb them.

Lylie felt Marc's warm hand on her lower back. It felt rough from the sand stuck to his palm. She shivered, and turned onto her back. Who else could she give her eighteen years to?

Marc opened his eyes. He was covered in sweat. Through the window of the train, an endless line of pylons was rushing past.

Instinctively, he recoiled. Was he a monster?

Marc felt the weight of the blue envelope in his jacket pocket. It probably only weighed less than an ounce, but it seemed much heavier somehow.

Were they monsters?

If he opened the envelope, he would know.

The train-car door opened, and Malvina de Carville appeared.

44

The hot water rained down over Lylie's naked body. She closed her eyes under the shower, hoping to find some kind of serenity. Or calm at least. Blindly, she reached out and squeezed liquid soap from the dispenser. She rubbed it against her skin: breasts, stomach, pubis. Then she rinsed off the soap, remaining under the shower for a long time. She was desperate to feel clean. On the surface, if not underneath.

Finally, she emerged from the cubicle, wrapped in a large white bath towel. Her wet hair dripped onto the floor. Lylie wiped the steam from the mirror with the back of her hand. She felt frightened by her own blurred reflection, as if her face had been replaced by that of a stranger. She brushed her teeth so hard that her gums bled.

She had thrown up, an hour ago, outside on the street. A young policeman had helped her up from her knees and handed her a tissue. She had wiped her face while a mother pushed a stroller through her puke. The policeman could have arrested her. He probably would have had she not implored him with her doe-like eyes.

"It's the first time, Officer."

He let her go.

She threw up again half an hour later. In her room, at the foot of her bed. There was nothing left to bring up now. She felt as sick as a dog.

Lylie came out of the bathroom.

The girl lying on the other bed in the room was obviously waiting for her to come back.

"They came and cleaned up while you were in the shower."

The girl was not even sixteen. She had short-cropped red hair and her teeth were already yellow.

"You're lucky in a way. I can't throw up. I feel like I'm rotting inside. I'd give anything to be able to puke."

This was not a conversation Lylie wanted to have right now. But Yellow Teeth didn't seem to care about that; she just wanted someone to listen to her.

"This is my second time here," she went on. "I'm a reoffender! So they're pissed off with me. They were preaching at me for three hours yesterday, the bastards."

Lylie walked to the window, and looked out. The girl was annoyed: "Don't get all hoity-toity with me. You're no different than I am."

Lylie watched the ambulances come and go in the parking lot below. She had walked the streets for three hours before she finally entered. She had even followed a funeral procession for a while. She could see the bell tower of the church of Saint-Hippolyte, but the playground of the nursery next to it was obscured by a row of houses. The laughing of the children was submerged beneath the roar of traffic. Unless they had gone back into the classroom, or gone home. Lylie was unsure what time it was. She felt so confused. What was she doing here? How was she going to endure all the hours of waiting?

"I was like you, the first time..."

Oh, please just shut up! Lylie screamed inwardly.

She had left her telephone on a shelf in the bathroom. Switched off. If only she could talk to Marc. If only he were here, to protect her, as he always had, to keep the bastards away from her.

All she had to do was pick up the phone. Marc would be there in no time.

Yellow Teeth would not shut up. "You mustn't feel bad about it. Who cares what those bastards think? If they try to make you feel guilty, just tell them to fuck off."

"Thank you," Lylie managed to say.

She stared at the large cedar tree in front of the window, hoping to see a bird or some other sign of life. But there was nothing.

No, Marc would not come. She would not call him. No one could find her here. Anonymity was one of the few things they could guarantee you in a place like this. She would not call him, no matter how desperately she wanted to. She had to leave Marc out of this.

At least until tomorrow.

Lylie turned toward Yellow Teeth. The girl could at least do one thing for her. Lylie attempted a smile.

"Could I bum a cigarette?"

But Lylie never got a reply, because the door opened and a nurse with the body of a prison warden entered the room.

"Miss Emilie Vitral?"

"Yes?"

"The psychiatrist will see you now."

45

Malvina de Carville gave Marc her inimitable rich-little-mad-girl stare, her aristocratic-serial-killer smile. She sat down at the far end of the train car, facing him. Outside, the dull landscape of the Caux sped past.

Marc did not move. Malvina undoubtedly had her Mauser to hand. The best thing to do was wait. All Marc wanted, at that moment, was to finish reading Grand-Duc's notebook. He was only five pages from the end.

The memory of Lylie, lying naked on Morval beach, came back to him. Then he thought of the list of hospitals and suppressed a shiver. He must not allow himself to be sidetracked. He should read the last pages while keeping one eye on Malvina... and disarm the crazy bitch at the first opportunity he got.

Crédule Grand-Duc's Journal

You're beginning to panic now, aren't you? You've counted the pages left in this notebook and you're beginning to wonder when you'll reach the solution to the mystery. I did

warn you not to expect a happy ending. I am no Hercule
Poirot, able to tie up all the loose ends in a few theatri-
cal minutes. I know you've had enough of me rambling
on. You're sick of my methods, the endless descriptions of
my moods, all these clues that lead nowhere. You have listened very politely to my story, but now you are interested
in only one thing. All you want to know is the results of
the DNA test. Oh, yes, Science with a capital S. The miracle of genetics. Don't worry, I'm getting there. There's no
need to panic. That was Lylie's fifteenth birthday present:
three drops of blood.

But first, there are a few minor details to be dealt with.
Nazim and I continued our search for the famous Georges
Pelletier, the homeless junkie wandering around with—
perhaps—a bracelet worth seventy-five thousand francs in
his pocket. It was Nazim who finally found him, almost
by accident. For several months, we had been combing
through the list of tramps, drunks, and dropouts who had
been found dead in the streets. Then, one misty morning
in July 1993, Nazim showed a photograph of Georges to a
community police officer in the Neiges district of Le Havre.
The guy remembered Georges vaguely. We dug up the local
archives, and found a file on our man at the police station.

On January 23, 1991, an unknown man had been found
drowned in a lake. Temperatures had been below zero for
a week before that so the guy would not have survived
more than five minutes in the freezing water, even with
more than two grams of alcohol in his bloodstream. No
ID had been found on his person, but the police had taken
a picture of the corpse. There was no doubt whatsoever: it
was definitely Georges Pelletier. Nothing in his hands or
pockets: no will, no dog, and no bracelet.

The deadest of dead ends.

I told Pelletier's brother, Augustin, myself. He seemed almost relieved. His quest was finally at an end, and he could turn the page. I was not so lucky.

Georges Pelletier had taken his secret with him. What had he done, that night, on Mont Terri? What had he seen?

Malvina's eyes were closing. The rolling landscape of the Caux seemed to be sending her to sleep. Marc guessed she wasn't used to long journeys. She kept dozing off, then suddenly waking up, searching for Marc's face in a panic. But this time, her eyes had been closed for more than thirty seconds.

Without a sound, Marc stood up and crept stealthily toward her. She was less than twenty yards away. If only she would stay asleep, for just a little bit longer...

Malvina's head was still leaning, motionless, against the blue-and-yellow headrest, her mouth curved in an almost angelic smile. Marc remembered being a child in the leisure center in Dieppe, playing a game called the King of Silence, in which he had to rescue a princess tied to a chair without being clawed by the blind dragon (a child in a blindfold). Lylie had always been his princess, of course.

Only five yards to go now. The train veered to the right, and Malvina's head tipped over slightly. Marc froze. He even stopped breathing.

Malvina opened her eyes. She was looking straight at him. But she did not have time to move a muscle: one second later, Marc's one-hundred-eighty-pound body smashed into her. His right hand covered her mouth while his left pinned both her arms together. Malvina could do nothing

but roll her eyes and feebly kick her feet. The two other passengers in the carriage—the teenager wearing earphones
and the sleeping man—had not noticed a thing.

Marc pushed Malvina toward the window. A fake crocodile handbag, like something an old biddy would own,
was placed on the seat next to her. Marc's plan was simple:
get the gun. After that, they could talk...

Holding Malvina down with the weight of his body, he
rummaged around in her handbag.

All it took was a few seconds. He pulled the Mauser
L110 from the bag and pointed it at her. Then he slowly
removed his hand from her mouth.

"So you wanted to visit Dieppe?"

Malvina pulled a face. "Yeah, I'm just crazy about
kites. What will you do if I scream?"

"I'll kill you."

"You wouldn't do that! Not to your beloved sister-
in-law."

"You think? I'm a Vitral, remember. One of the bad
guys."

Malvina sighed. Clearly, she had no desire to draw any
attention to herself.

"You know this is the last train of the day, Malvina?
Are you planning to stay the night in Dieppe?"

"Who cares? I'm a de Carville, remember. I'm not
exactly short of cash."

"It doesn't matter how much cash you have. My grandmother will still chop you into tiny pieces and feed you to
the seagulls if she gets hold of you."

"Are you ever going to stop cracking stupid jokes?"

Marc was irritated by Malvina's self-assurance. He
wanted to wipe the smirk from her face. He had to make

her talk. He needed to find some way of disturbing her, cracking her arrogant facade.

He put his hand on her thigh. Malvina recoiled, banging her head against the window.

"You're planning to stay with us, aren't you? You want to share my room…"

He moved his hand up her thigh. "Sorry, sweetie, but my balls are off limits tonight."

"Stop that, or I'll scream."

Marc's hand moved up to her mauve sweater, just below her breasts.

"You'd be decent-looking, you know, if you dressed better."

"Take your hands off me…"

Malvina's voice sounded as if it were cracking.

"Sexier, I mean," Marc went on. "If you wore something that showed off your nice little titties…"

His hand caressed one of them. He could feel Malvina's heart pounding.

"And you've got enough money to pay to have bigger ones, of course…"

Malvina's fingers tightened around Marc's right arm. Her fingernails were bitten to the quick, incapable of scratching him.

He moved his face close to Malvina's and breathed into her neck. The girl's body stiffened, and her fingers gripped him convulsively. Then Malvina suddenly went limp, as if her skeleton had melted.

Marc pushed her hand away and hissed: "Never touch me again, Malvina! Understand? Never again."

Just then, the train-car door opened and a female ticket inspector entered. She walked past them without stopping, merely glanced at their intertwined bodies and smiled before she went through into the next car.

Marc relaxed his grip and pointed the Mauser at Malvina.

"All right, enough messing around. What are you doing here?"

"Go fuck yourself."

Marc smiled.

"You make me laugh, Malvina. You're like the crazy little sister I never had."

"I'm older than you, dickhead."

"I know. Weird, isn't it? Everyone goes on about you as if you're mad, bad, and dangerous to know, but I just can't bring myself to believe it."

"Who's everyone? Grand-Duc?"

"Well, he's not the only one, but yes..."

"Surely you don't believe all that crap he spouts..."

Malvina appeared to be feeling better. Marc told himself not to get sucked in by the instinctive lack of fear he felt for her. Brandishing the Mauser in front of her, he said: "Well, he won't be spouting any more crap about you, that's for sure. But shooting him in the chest seems a little over the top. Did you kill him just because he hated you?"

As before, Malvina's body went momentarily limp. Her brown eyes opened wide. "What are you talking about, Vitral? I...I didn't kill Grand-Duc!" Then as the shock passed, her voice regained its usual irony: "I would have liked to, admittedly. But the job had already been done by the time I got there."

"Do you think I'm stupid? His corpse fell out of a kitchen closet! Your Mini was parked in front of his house!"

Malvina's pupils dilated and her eyes darted about frantically. "He was dead when I got there! I swear it! I entered his house two hours before you did, and his body was already cold. As were the embers in the hearth where his head had been resting."

Marc bit his lip. He had the feeling she was telling the truth.

Grand-Duc had clearly been dead for several hours when Marc found him. Malvina seemed sincere, and her version of events was plausible. Was he being naive, trusting this madwoman? And if not Malvina, then who had killed the detective? Lylie's face suddenly appeared in his mind.

"Why should I believe you?"

"I couldn't care less if you do or don't."

"All right. So what were you doing at Grand-Duc's house?"

"I like dragonflies. I was there to admire his collection. Just like you, right?"

Marc smiled, in spite of himself, but he kept the barrel of the Mauser firmly pointed at Malvina.

"Anyway, maybe *you* killed Grand-Duc. Your fingerprints are the ones the police will find, not mine."

What a bitch! But maybe not so mad... Disconcerted, Marc stammered: "Are you... do you know what actually happened? According to his notebook, Grand-Duc was intending to commit suicide. A shot to the head, with an old newspaper to soak up the blood..."

"No..." Malvina hesitated for a few seconds, then went on: "The old bastard probably just couldn't aim straight."

She was lying. On this point at least, Marc did not trust her word at all. Had Grand-Duc contacted the de Carvilles before he was killed? Had he revealed more to them than what was written in the notebook?

"Grand-Duc had discovered something!" Marc said, almost shouting in his excitement. "He must have told your grandmother about it. What was it?"

"Stick it up your ass!"

This was almost a confession. Malvina folded her arms and turned to face the window. The top of it was open and a slight breeze ruffled the few hairs that escaped Malvina's barrette. Marc's eyes rested on the fake crocodile handbag.

"All right," he said. "If you don't want to tell me . . . I'll find it out for myself."

He opened her handbag with his left hand, his right still clutching the Mauser.

"Don't touch that, Vitral!"

Malvina's mouth suddenly snapped at Marc's wrist, as she tried to sink her teeth into his veins. With his left hand, he pushed her violently against the seat.

"Fucker!" Malvina hissed.

She kicked at Marc's knees with her feet. He thought about knocking her out, but decided against it. She struggled against him, using all the strength left in her little body, but he was too powerful. Her head slumped back against the window, defeated.

Marc exhaled. Malvina suppressed a jubilant smile. In the struggle, a blue envelope had fallen from Marc's pocket and she had kicked it under the seat without his noticing. Now all she had to do was wait until she could pick it up. It might not be anything important—just a telephone bill or a bank statement—but, then again, it might be very important.

Marc put his hand inside the handbag once more.

"Don't do that, Vitral!" she shouted.

"Getting warm, am I?" He smirked. "What are you hiding in here?"

Marc's hand rummaged around the contents of the bag: keys, a telephone, a lipstick, a wallet (also fake crocodile skin), a silver pen, a small diary...

Malvina's hands began to shake. Apparently, the diary was something she did not want him to see. He took a closer look at it: it was not actually a diary at all, just a simple notebook, about three inches by four. Marc guessed the reason for Malvina's terror. This must be some sort of private journal.

"Open it and you're dead, Vitral."

"So talk. What do you know about Grand-Duc?"

"Seriously, I will kill you..."

"Suit yourself."

Marc flicked through the pages one-handed. They were all laid out in the same way: the left-hand page had been illustrated by Malvina with drawings, photographs, and collages, while the right contained three lines of childish handwriting, like short poems.

He suspected he was the first person other than Malvina to have read this notebook. He skimmed through the pages, stopping randomly at a page containing the image of the Crucifixion—except that the head on Christ's naked body had been replaced by that of a smolderingly handsome young man, probably a TV star Marc had never heard of. In a quiet voice, he read out the words on the page opposite:

Kneading your curves, with my rosary,
Touching your body, on the cross,
I offer myself to you

"You dirty little minx," Marc sniggered. "Is this what you think about at Mass when you're looking at the image of Jesus?"

"Shut your fucking mouth!" Malvina yelled. "You're too stupid to understand. They're haiku. Japanese poems."

"What about your grandmother? Is she too stupid to understand them, too? Maybe I should send her a text..."

Malvina frowned.

"So...either you start talking or I keep reading. What do you know about Grand-Duc?"

"Fuck you."

Marc ripped the page from the notebook, scrunched it up into a ball, and tossed it through the opening at the top of the window.

"You're right. I have to be honest. That poem was crap. Shall we try another page? Come on, let's play a game. I ask you about Grand-Duc, you fail to reply, I read a page. If I don't like it, I throw it out the window; if I do like it, I send a text to your grandma."

Marc flicked through the pages, laughing loudly. His laughter was forced, though. In truth, he felt bad about invading Malvina's privacy in this way. She had curled up like a defenseless little bird. Each page he ripped out was like a feather from her wings.

Marc stopped at a photograph of an Airbus, carefully cut out and stuck to a picture of a fireplace.

Bird of fire
Angel in hell
My flesh

"That's not bad," Marc said.

His throat tightened, but he did not want to show Malvina that he was moved.

"Except for that last line: 'My flesh.' You ought to have at least added a question mark. So...out the window it goes!"

Malvina shivered as the ball of paper disappeared into the rushing air.

"Still nothing you want to tell me, Malvina? What were you doing at Grand-Duc's place?"

"Fuck off and die!"

"As you wish..."

More pages flashed past, until Marc came to a photograph of a little girl's bedroom, apparently cut from a furniture catalog. On the right-hand page, Malvina had stuck a photograph of Banjo, the enormous teddy bear. In the middle of the room, on the bed, another picture had been superimposed: a photograph of Lylie. She was sitting cross-legged and she looked about eight or nine years old. Another photograph stolen by Grand-Duc...

Marc forced himself to read in a neutral voice:

Forgotten toys
I missed you
Abandoned?

"You bastard," Malvina whispered. "And to think I showed you Lyse-Rose's room..."

"I'm waiting..."

Malvina gave Marc the finger.

The page was scrunched up. Out the window it went.

Marc looked through the notebook more carefully now.

He had to find something that would push Malvina beyond
what she could bear. He stopped at one of the final pages.
The left-hand page was illustrated with a photograph of
Lylie and himself. It was easy to date: July 10, 1998, less
than three months ago. Lylie had just received her bacca-
laureate exam results. She had passed with flying colors,
of course. She and Marc were hugging on the beach in
Dieppe.

Marc smiled to himself. So Crédule Grand-Duc,
or maybe Nazim, had played at being paparazzi. Fair
enough. They were on the de Carvilles' payroll, after all.
And Grand-Duc had not attempted to conceal the fact in
his notebook. Except that, in this particular photograph,
Lylie's face had been replaced by Malvina's. It was gro-
tesque: that ugly, stunted little head stuck on the body of a
goddess.

Tonelessly, Marc read:

Holding your lovers
Moaning, alone
A delicious game

Malvina closed her eyes. She looked like a little mouse,
caught in a trap. Marc fought the impulse to give her
back the journal, to stand up and leave her there. In truth,
Malvina was just another victim, crushed by the accident
on Mont Terri. Just like he was.

She was a child who, waking up one morning, had
spied a monster in the mirror. A child drowning in a filthy
pool of forbidden feelings. And yet, Marc found himself speaking words more hurtful than the bullets of the

Mauser that he continued to aim at her: "Shall I keep this one, Malvina? Or send it to your grandmother?"

Malvina, staring out at the featureless landscape beyond the window, was wringing her hands so frantically that Marc feared she might actually pull off one of her fingers. Dry-throated, he twisted the knife.

"Or maybe I should show it to Lylie. I think she'd find it amusing."

He began to tear out the page. Slowly, as if in a trance, Malvina spoke: "Grand-Duc called my grandmother the day before yesterday. He was still alive then. He told her he had found something. The solution to the mystery, or so he claimed. Just like that, at five minutes to midnight on the last day of his contract! Just before he was about to shoot himself in the head, with the edition of the *Est Républicain* from December 23, 1980, spread out on the desk beneath him. He said he needed a day or two to gather evidence, but he was absolutely sure that he had solved the mystery. Oh, and he needed an extra one hundred and fifty thousand francs..."

Marc closed Malvina's journal.

"How do you know all that?"

"I listened in, on the extension. I know how to be so quiet that people don't even realize I'm there. It's a sort of gift."

"Did your grandmother believe him?"

"No idea. But she agreed to pay. She doesn't care about money. Grand-Duc had been playing her for eighteen years. One more day hardly mattered..."

"What about you?"

"What about me?"

"Did you believe him?"

Malvina's face froze in an expression of incredulity.

"What? You think it's believable, do you? Finding the solution like that, with the wave of a magic wand, just before midnight? You think that seems likely?"

Marc did not reply. Through the window, the apple orchards of the Scie valley gave way to cornfields. Malvina continued, in a quiet voice: "I went to Grand-Duc's house because I wanted to see him. I wanted to tell him to stop jerking us around. I wanted to say to him that it was over: Lyse-Rose was eighteen; she was old enough to decide for herself. You've read the whole investigation, and so have I. I know all the details: the bracelet, the piano, the ring...the solution is obvious. You said it yourself at the Roseraie: Lyse-Rose is the one who survived. Emilie died in the airplane eighteen years ago. You can tell your grandmother that. It's what you think, isn't it? And she does, too."

Yes, that was what Marc thought. Malvina was right.

"So who did kill Grand-Duc, if it wasn't you?"

"No idea. And I couldn't care less."

"Your grandmother? So she wouldn't have to pay him?"

Malvina giggled. "For a measly one hundred and fifty thousand francs? Come off it..."

"Did Grand-Duc tell your grandmother how he planned to gather the evidence he needed?"

"Yes. He said he had to go to the Jura Mountains. My grandmother was supposed to send the money to a rental cottage on the Doubs River, close to Mont Terri."

To the Jura Mountains? Was this the detective's famous pilgrimage? But why?

"What was he going to do there?" Marc asked. "Look for the evidence he told your grandmother about?"

"He was taking advantage. Milking my grandmother for every last penny."

Marc said nothing. He stood up, put the Mauser in his jacket pocket, and gave Malvina her little journal.

"No hard feelings?"

"Go fuck yourself!"

46

October 2, 1998, 6:10 p.m.

Marc went back to his own seat, silently passing the teenager and the sleeping guy. The train passed through Longueville-sur-Scie and the last apple trees disappeared in a yellow ocean of corn and colza. He would be in Dieppe in less than fifteen minutes.

Marc sat down and thirstily drank more than half of his bottle of San Pellegrino. He checked that the Mauser was still in his pocket, then shot a look at the other end of the car. Malvina had not moved. Marc took Grand-Duc's notebook from his bag and opened it. He had decided to finish reading it before the train reached Dieppe. There were less than five pages left. Everything was going so fast and he felt that he would go mad if he didn't take things one step at a time. Even if he hadn't the faintest idea where it all might lead.

Crédule Grand-Duc's Journal

Mathilde de Carville made her request in 1995: she wanted me to compare the sample of blood from Emilie Vitral with that of the whole de Carville family. I still had contacts in the police forensics department, and I was a close friend of the Vitrals. How could I refuse her? But it wasn't easy, going to see the Vitrals in the evening as a family friend, then telling the de Carvilles all about it the following morning. But never mind me, you don't want to hear about me and my troubled soul... and you are right.

Of course, I couldn't just turn up at Emilie's birthday party and ask her, or her grandmother, for a sample of her blood. My strategy was perhaps not much more subtle than that, but it worked. I gave Lylie a cracked vase for a birthday present. When it broke in her hands, I picked up all the pieces of glass and threw them in the trash, except for a few that were covered in her blood, which I secreted in a small plastic bag inside my pocket.

It was that easy. No one noticed a thing.

I received the results from the laboratory a few days later. You would probably laugh at me if I told you I felt some remorse. I am just telling you to explain why I asked my contact at the forensics lab for two copies of the results, in two envelopes. One for Mathilde de Carville, one for Nicole Vitral. I handed each her envelope.

So, they have both known the truth for three years now. Science has spoken.

I could just leave it there—with the news that I delivered the envelopes to the families in question—and make my farewells.

But I am no angel. Far from it. So, of course, I was not able to resist the temptation to look at the results. What did you think I would do? After fifteen years of investigation, with no concrete evidence? I jumped on that piece of paper the way a released prisoner might rush at a whore after fifteen years in the slammer.

*

It would be something of an understatement to say that I was surprised by the results. I was so shocked, I could hardly breathe. It was as if someone up there—God, or the Virgin of Mont Terri—was deliberately fucking with us.

In fact, I think it was the DNA test that plunged me back into depression, that sent me rolling inexorably toward the void. The result was absurd. It made a mockery of all those years of searching, reading, questioning. I wanted to throw all the evidence on a bonfire and then throw myself on top of it, for having failed to find the sorceress hiding behind this entire case.

And yet, I did not give up my investigation. Since 1995, I have kept on going, like a faithful old dog, its limbs weary, its eyesight fading, but its will to obey undiminished. Nazim gave up a while ago, to work illegally as a builder and to help Ayla in the kebab shop.

In December 1997, I undertook my final pilgrimage to Mont Terri. And there I found the last—and most perplexing—piece of the jigsaw puzzle.

So there I was in the Jura, ready for my final pilgrimage. I was looking forward to tasting—for the last time—my favorite treats: some Cancoillotte, a bite of mature Comté, and a bottle of Monique Genevez's Arbois wine. I would tread the last blades of grass, snap the last twigs, before the final plunge. My pilgrimage. My own personal Lourdes. I was exactly the same as all those Lourdes pilgrims, desperately hoping for a miracle that never happened...

It came to me during the night, in Monique Genevez's cottage. Apparently I needed to drink an entire bottle of Vin Jaune before my imagination started working properly. Mathilde de Carville had known what she was doing when she gave me eighteen years to investigate the case: obviously she had guessed just how slowly my brain works. In the morning, I went up Mont Terri with a spade and a large trash bag. For an hour, I dug a hole next to the cabin, exactly where the grave had been. Over twenty pounds of soil! I carried the bulging bag on my back like a convict for two miles. When I reached the path, Grégory— the charmer who worked for the nature preserve—gave me a lift to the cottage. The next day, I made a mess of my BMW's trunk by shoving all twenty pounds of earth into it, then drove to the forensics lab in Rosny-sous-Bois.

My friend there, Jerome, was not too happy, as you can imagine. Did I expect him to examine twenty pounds of soil under a microscope? Well, yes. I did.

Jerome had just gotten married for the third time and been saddled with another mortgage, so he did not hesitate for long when I handed him an envelope stuffed with cash, equivalent to about three months of his salary. There he was, with a PhD, and paid only about a quarter of what he could have earned as a doctor. I didn't know how long it would take him to analyze what I had given him, but I didn't care.

He called me back a week later.

"Crédule?"

"Yeah?"

"I examined your earth for you. So what do you want? The pH, the humus content, the acidity of your stupid soil? What were you planning to do with it, make a vegetable garden for your retirement?"

"Get to the point, Jerome."

"OK. It's soil, Crédule . . . Just soil."

I sighed. "That's all?"

"Yes," he said.

But there was something not entirely convincing about the way he said it; a slight hesitation. I latched on to that glimmer of hope. Credulous to the end...

"You don't sound entirely sure, Jerome."

"Well...all right, there was something. But it was so tiny...it doesn't prove anything."

"Spit it out."

"All right, all right...There are a few specks of bone in the soil. Hardly anything. Just dust, really. Nothing you wouldn't expect in a forest..."

"What kind of bones, Jerome?"

"The amount is so tiny...Scientifically, you can't draw any conclusions from it..."

I decided not to let the matter drop. Jerome was the best in the business. A genius. And he had the best equipment in France to work with.

"Fair enough. But what do *you* think it is?"

"Well, it's only a hunch, and this won't appear in the report, but in my opinion the specks are more likely to have come from human rather than animal bones."

I sensed that Jerome still hadn't told me everything. He knew about the case.

"Could you date the bones?"

"No, that's impossible. I have no idea how long they've been buried there..."

"But would you be able to tell me how old the person was when he or she was buried?"

There was a long silence.

"Listen, this really is subjective. There's no way I can..."

"Skip the intro, Jerome."

He sighed. "All right. In my opinion, these are bone fragments from a young human."

"How young? A kid?"

"You're getting warm, Crédule."

"What are you saying, Jerome? Are we talking about a baby?"

"As I've said, there is nothing definite about any of this, but... yes, I would say the bone fragments are those of a human baby."

Jesus Christ! What would you have done, in my place? Learning that, after eighteen years of investigation? What would you have done, apart from shooting yourself in the head, I mean...

Forget the last eight months. Forget the last ten days, too, during which time I've been writing this notebook. Today is September 29, 1998. It is twenty minutes to midnight. Everything is ready. Lylie is about to turn eighteen. I will put my pen back in the pot on my desk. I will sit at this desk, unfold the December 23, 1980, edition of the *Est Républicain*, and I will calmly shoot myself in the head. My blood will stain this yellowed newspaper. I have failed.

All I leave behind me is this notebook. For Lylie. For whoever wishes to read it.

In this notebook, I have reviewed all the clues, all the leads, all the theories I have found in eighteen years of investigation. It is all here, in these hundred or so pages. If you have read them carefully, you will now know as much as I do. Perhaps you will be more perceptive than I. Perhaps you will find something I have missed. The key to the mystery, if one exists. Perhaps...

For me, it's over.

It would be an exaggeration to say that I have no regrets, but I have done my best.

Those were the last words. The next page was blank.

Slowly, reluctantly, Marc closed the notebook. He drank the rest of his San Pellegrino. The train would arrive in Dieppe in five minutes. As if by magic, the sleeping guy had woken up and the teenager had removed his earphones.

Marc felt as if his brain were spinning uselessly, like the wheel of a bicycle when the chain has come off. He needed time to think about all this. Most of all, he needed to talk to his grandmother. She had received the DNA test results three years ago; all that time, she had known that Lylie was not her granddaughter. It was obvious, really: she had given her Mathilde de Carville's sapphire ring, after all.

Lyse-Rose had survived, not Emilie. That was the only thing he knew for sure. All the other questions remained unanswered...

Who had dug the grave on Mont Terri? Had the bracelet been buried there? Or was it a dog? Or a baby? But which baby? Who had killed Grand-Duc, and why? Who had killed Marc's grandfather?

And where was Lyl...

A scream cut through the silence. The scream of a madwoman.

Malvina!

Marc rushed over and found Malvina curled up on her seat, her skinny body convulsing. Her hand hung limp, like the hand of someone who had just sliced their wrist open. Malvina's eyes seemed to be begging Marc for help, reaching out as if she were a mountain climber about to fall. He looked down and saw a blue envelope, torn open, and a white sheet of paper laid out on the seat.

Marc understood what had happened. The envelope must have fallen from his pocket while he was struggling with Malvina. She had opened it and read the results. But what would make her scream like that?

Marc picked up the letter from the national police forensics laboratory in Rosny-sous-Bois. It was only a few lines long:

ANALYSIS OF BLOOD SAMPLE COMPARISONS

between Emilie VITRAL *(sample 1, batch 95-233)*
and Mathilde de CARVILLE *(sample 2, batch 95-234)*

between Emilie VITRAL *(sample 1, batch 95-233)*
and Léonce de CARVILLE *(sample 2, batch 95-235)*

between Emilie VITRAL *(sample 1, batch 95-233)*
and Malvina de CARVILLE *(sample 2, batch 95-236)*

And then, below this, the punch line:

Results negative.
No family relationship possible.
Results 99.9687% reliable.

The sheet fell from Marc's hands.

So, Lylie was not a blood relation of the de Carville family.

Lyse-Rose was dead. It was Emilie who had survived. She and Marc had the same genes, the same parents, the same blood. Contrary to all his instincts, all his convictions, the desire he felt for his sister was incestuous and wrong. They *were* monsters, after all.

47

Marc walked slowly along the port. The train station was only half a mile from Pollet. The hideous face of a Chinese Dragon scowled from the sky directly above him, as if the creature had ripped apart the clouds just to taunt him. As if his life were not insane enough already ...

He increased his pace. He could not stop thinking about the DNA test. He couldn't believe it. How could a simple piece of paper, a pseudoscientific result, be trusted above his intuition, his instinct?

No, he truly believed what his heart told him: Lylie was not his sister.

Opposite the modest yachts in Dieppe's port, each politely turning its back to the sea, the streets and bars were packed with people. The kite festival was always accompanied by an orgy of mussels and fries, the famous *moules-frites*—that could easily rival a Flemish free-for-all. Marc slowed down as he neared the ferry bridge that connected the islet of Pollet to the rest of the town. After pocketing the forensics results, Marc had left Malvina in the train car, curled up in the fetal position, apparently in a state of shock.

Long lines of noisy customers were waiting to be seated in the restaurants, but Marc was oblivious to his surroundings. He was too busy trying to suppress the blind rage that was mounting inside him.

No! Lylie was *not* his sister!

It must be a mistake. Grand-Duc must have gotten the blood samples mixed up. Either that, or he was lying. Or Mathilde de Carville was attempting to manipulate them by giving them a false set of results. Or perhaps no one was lying, and Lyse-Rose really didn't share the de Carville blood. Perhaps she was adopted, or her father was not Alexandre de Carville. Even the detective had had his doubts about that. Marc remembered the blue-eyed German who rented out paddleboats...

He crossed the bridge and walked into Rue Pocholle. He had been coming to Dieppe less frequently—no more than once a month—since Lylie moved to Paris. He reached his grandmother's house: a facade of brick and flint, just like the other fifteen houses on the street. The front garden was dominated by the Citroën van, as usual, as if the garden had been planted around it. Marc noticed the rust on its front and back wings, the dent in one door. How long was it since anyone had driven that van, if only to move it out of the yard? Although there was no one left to play in the tiny garden anymore.

He rang the bell, and Nicole opened the door immediately. Marc was enveloped by the generous warmth of his grandmother's body. She hugged him for a long time. Any other day, and he might have been embarrassed; but not today. Finally, Nicole let go.

"How are you, Marc?"

"I'm OK."

His voice said otherwise. Marc looked at the little living room. It seemed to shrink and grow darker each time he came back. The Hartmann-Milonga piano was still in its place, gathering dust between the sofa and the television set, a stack of papers piled up on the keyboard cover. Well, it wasn't as if anyone played it anymore.

The table was already set: two plates, two linen napkins, and one bottle of cider. Marc sat down. Nicole came and went between the kitchen and the living room, bringing sole fillets cooked in a sauce of mussels and prawns. A good cook, Nicole also knew how to manage a conversation, asking Marc about his studies, telling him about Dieppe, the leaflets she had to distribute, the state of her lungs, a broken gutter ("Could you take a look at it, Marc?"). Nicole was as enthusiastic and chatty as any other grandmother who missed her loved ones, but Marc replied in monosyllables. His eyes kept wandering around the room, but always returned to the same spot: in the pile of papers resting on the piano, he could see a blue envelope, identical to the one he had brought with him from Coupvray. So, Nicole must have dug out that envelope, the one she had kept hidden from him and Lylie for the past three years.

Who would dare bring the subject up first?

Nicole was telling him about some neighbor who had been hospitalized recently. Marc stopped listening and retreated into his thoughts. So, his grandmother had known the truth for the past three years. She had won her personal battle against the de Carville family. Perhaps she had given Lylie the sapphire ring out of pity for Mathilde de Carville, the way she always gave a few coins to beggars in the street...

Marc had mixed feelings about this idea of the de Car-ville family being reduced to the state of beggars. He was still haunted by the image of Malvina, curled up in shock on the train.

Nicole served the cheese. As usual, she had passed on dessert, but had proudly given Marc a Salammbô. Marc had stopped liking the weird green cakes when he was eleven, but had never dared tell his grandmother. It was the cheapest item in the bakery. So, he ate it all up like a good boy while Nicole went on about the town council and the future of the port. Marc gazed at the framed photograph of his parents, Pascal and Stéphanie, above the fireplace. They were standing, in wedding dress and suit, in front of the Notre-Dame-de-Bon-Secours chapel, under a blizzard of confetti. All his life, this framed picture had hung in the same place, on the same nail. Bittersweet memories.

Nicole brought coffee, warmed up in a pan, and poured it into two cups. She made the first move, albeit a tentative one.

"So have you heard from Emilie recently?"

"No. Well, not directly." Marc hesitated. "I think she's in a hospital or a clinic or something..."

Nicole looked down. "Don't worry, Marc. She's a big girl now. She knows what she's doing."

She stood up to clear away the cups.

Marc thought about what Nicole had just said: "*She knows what she's doing.*" Were these just hollow words of reassurance, or was Nicole hiding something?

Marc got up to help Nicole tidy away the dinner things. On his second trip to the kitchen, he stopped in front of a framed photograph on a shelf, sitting between a wooden

Oware game and a barometer in the shape of a lighthouse. The picture showed Pierre and Nicole Vitral, walking side by side in front of the Dieppe town hall, beneath a huge banner. The picture was taken in May 1968, when France was in revolt. Nicole and Pierre had both been under thirty. Nicolas, their elder son, was holding Nicole's hand, while Pascal was carried on Pierre's shoulders. Pascal could have been no more than six years old. He was waving a small red flag. Marc looked closely at the faces of his grandfather, his father, and his uncle, all of them dead now. He had no real memories of any of them. He tried to keep his voice casual:

"I'm going to my room for a few minutes, Nicole. I need to take a look at my course notes."

His grandmother, busy doing the washing up, did not reply.

Marc's bedroom was perfectly clean and tidy. Nicole continued to wear herself out, tidying a room in which Marc slept less than once a month. Marc felt as if he were rediscovering his childhood here. His plastic recorder was still on the desk: the one he had lent to Lylie and on which she had played Goldman, Cabrel, and Balavoine. The bunk beds were still in the corner. The top bunk had not been slept in for eight years now, since the day Lylie had moved into Nicole's room. Marc remembered the nights he and Lylie had spent together, how she used to like making up interminable stories. Marc, lying in the bottom bunk, would listen to Lylie's voice. Sometimes, when she was scared, her arm would reach down to him, and he would sit up in bed and hold her hand until her grip relaxed and he knew she had fallen asleep. Other times, Lylie would stay up late reading. The light would prevent Marc from falling asleep, but he never complained. You can't ask the sun to stop shining.

Their house was tiny and their family life had been crowded, but Marc felt certain that Lylie would never have swapped it for all the de Carvilles' presents and luxury. Dragonflies, after all, are like butterflies: they need a cocoon when they are young. At least until they enter the chrysalis stage...

Marc shook himself free of his memories and walked over to the closet. He did not have many clothes left here. Nicole had given away everything that was too small for him, apart from his rugby jerseys... and... and a soccer shirt, red and yellow, with the name Dündar Siz on the back. Age: twelve.

Marc crouched down and began searching through the boxes containing his course notes. What he was looking for ought to be near the top of the pile: notes from the previous year's course in European law. It had mostly consisted of learning a series of dates: when the various member states had joined the European Union, treaties, directives, elections, and so on. Marc found the binder he was looking for, and then the page. He had never been a brilliant student, but at least he was well organized. The notes were about Turkey. He remembered paying more attention to the lecture because of that. He reread what he had scribbled down: the military regime, the coup d'état, the return to democracy...

He spent several minutes checking the details. When he had finished, he closed the binder, his hands clammy, his arms covered in goose bumps. Now he understood what had rung false about Grand-Duc's narrative.

It all fit.

His grandfather had not died in an accident. He had been murdered. And now Marc had proof. But if that one detail was false, then the whole direction of the investigation collapsed...

"Marc?"

Nicole's voice rang through the thin walls of the bedroom.

"Marc? Is everything all right?"

Her question was punctuated by a fit of coughing. Marc forced himself to stop thinking, for now. He put the binder in his backpack and tidied up the other course files. Then, for a few long minutes, he stood leaning against the bunk bed, trying to control his breathing.

Nicole, her voice shaky, asked again: "Marc? Are you OK?"

"I'll be there in a minute, Nicole."

The bedroom door opened directly into the living room. The washing up had been done, and a lace cloth had been placed on the table. Nicole was sitting at the table, in tears. In front of her was the blue envelope.

The DNA test.

The one that Crédule Grand-Duc had given her three years before.

48

Marc pulled up a chair and sat facing his grandmother. He retrieved the envelope that Mathilde de Carville had given him, and placed it on the table.

Two blue envelopes. One for each family.

"I knew Mathilde de Carville had a copy, of course," Nicole said quietly. "But I don't think she knew that Grand-Duc had given a copy to me."

"You're right," Marc told her. "She didn't know."

Nicole wiped her eyes with a white handkerchief.

"What exactly did she tell you?"

Marc had no choice. This was why he had come, after all. He spoke for a long time, describing his visit to the de Carvilles and summarizing the contents of Grand-Duc's notebook, in particular the final pages: the DNA test, the detective's guilty conscience. He omitted only one thing: the fact that Grand-Duc had been murdered. For some reason, he felt it would be unfair to tell his grandmother this news so suddenly, and abruptly.

Nicole coughed into her handkerchief.

"Marc, Crédule did not exactly lie in his notebook,

but he didn't tell the whole truth either. The reality was slightly different. Crédule likes to embellish things..."

His grandmother's use of the present tense made Marc squirm.

"I was there," he said. "For Lylie's fifteenth birthday. I remember what happened. The vase that broke in Lylie's hands, Grand-Duc apologizing as he picked up the pieces..."

"Of course. You're right. But he didn't write about what happened next."

Marc went pale. "What...?"

"You went out with Emilie, Marc, do you remember? You went to Manon's house to celebrate, and you didn't return until after midnight."

Marc's hand lay on top of the torn blue envelope. He slid it around the table nervously. Nicole cleared her throat and went on: "I stayed here with Crédule. He drank a glass of brandy on the sofa while I did the washing up. I was crying."

"Crying? Why?"

"Marc, I'm not stupid. Crédule was working for Mathilde de Carville. I had always expected her to ask for a DNA test one day. It was her right. I would have done the same thing, in her place... but not like that. That pathetic little deception. A booby-trapped birthday present! Crédule was the only friend we invited to Lylie's birthday party..."

Marc felt increasingly uncomfortable. His grandmother had never confided in him like this before.

"When did you guess?"

"When I saw Emilie's finger bleeding, and Crédule picking up the broken pieces of glass. It would have been better if he'd come here with a syringe, if he'd at least been

honest about it. That was our agreement, from the beginning: I would let him see Lylie, but he had to share all the
information he discovered."

"But he did that, didn't he? He gave you a copy of the
results..."

Nicole's eyes filled with tears again.

"Not exactly, Marc. Let me tell you what happened...
I was crying as I did the washing up, and then suddenly
I came to a decision. I had just rinsed a knife. I used it to
cut my little finger. Just a small cut—but enough to make
it bleed. I wrapped a dish towel around my finger, and I
gave Crédule a shot glass containing some of my blood.
He wasn't stupid—he understood what I wanted."

"How did he react?"

For the first time, Nicole smiled.

"He was a bit embarrassed, like a child caught in the act.
But Crédule isn't a bad man. He apologized for his behav-
ior and he told me he would test the de Carvilles' blood for
Mathilde and the Vitral blood for me. And then..."

Nicole coughed again. The white handkerchief twisted
in her hands.

Marc, embarrassed, said: "Nicole, what are you trying
to tell me?"

"You really want to know? Well, it's not a crime. And
I doubt whether Crédule mentioned it in his notebook..."

In fact, Marc did not really want to know. Nicole's tears
were running down her face.

"We made love, that night. While you were out celebrat-
ing at Manon's house. That was the first time...since your
grandfather died. The only time. Grand-Duc had wanted
me for years. He was kind. He was practically the only
man who ever came to visit us. He..."

"Nicole..."

Marc stood up and clumsily embraced his grandmother, then put a finger to her lips. He could not rid his mind of the memory of Grand-Duc's corpse.

"You don't need to tell me all this."

"I do, Marc. I do need to tell you."

Nicole wiped away her tears and stood up.

"OK, Marc, maybe you're right. I don't want to bother you with the troubles of an old woman."

She smoothed the tablecloth, then noticed for the first time the state of the envelope that Marc had placed there.

"Did you open it?"

"It's a long story. Let's call it an accident, but... yes, I opened it. I read it."

"So you understand why I'm crying. Not because of Crédule. Or, not just that. I'm crying because of Emilie."

Marc felt lost, submerged by a terrible wave of foreboding. Why would she be crying because of Emilie? Surely the test results were exactly what she had wanted, all these years...

He picked up the envelope that Mathilde de Carville had given to him and passed it to Nicole. Then he opened the other envelope.

He read the letter inside.

The room began to spin around him: piano, photographs, tablecloth, sofa, television, all blurred.

The sheet of paper fell from his hands.

The DNA test result made no sense at all.

49

Malvina shifted uncomfortably on the hard, cold pebbles. The beach was dimly lit by the half-moon. This was the only place Malvina could find to spend the night. The young female ticket inspector had discovered her a long time after the train had arrived at its destination in Dieppe. The woman had been quite polite and understanding as she asked Malvina to leave the train, but her attitude had changed when Malvina had called her a "stupid whore." Two other ticket inspectors had helped her to forcibly evict Malvina from the station.

Now Malvina was having to sleep outside. Thanks to that idiotic kite festival, there wasn't a single vacant room to be had in the entire town.

Malvina had spent the evening wandering around. She hadn't even eaten, but then she wasn't hungry. She had roamed the streets for a long time, before returning to the beach. She had been waiting for the festivalgoers to disappear, along with their stupid kites and their music and their balloons and the waffles, fries, and other inedible substances sold by the Vitrals' successors along the seafront.

Finally, close to midnight, it was all over. Only a few

shapes remained hovering in the sky, tethered by long strings to stakes hammered into the ground. Malvina did not like kites. She wanted to cut all those strings so that the floating objects would come crashing down into the sea.

Cut the strings, and cut the cord that connected her to her horrible, lying grandmother.

Malvina lay on the uncomfortable, cold pebbles and tried to fall asleep.

"Hello, sweetheart! Shouldn't you be at home with your mommy and daddy? It's very late, you know . . ."

Malvina turned her head toward the voice. Three men were standing on the beach, about thirty feet from where she lay. Each of them was holding a mineral-water bottle containing an orange liquid that was, almost certainly, neither water nor juice.

"It's dangerous for you to be out here all alone, sweetie. What if some bad men were to find you?"

The tallest of the three was speaking. There was a ring through his right eyebrow. A smaller one, bald, and wearing cowboy boots, was having trouble keeping his balance. The third man reminded her of the bear Banjo.

The one wearing the eyebrow ring came closer, and the others followed. Malvina sat up.

"Fucking hell, she's not a kid, she's an old woman!" said the one with the cowboy boots. "I thought we might have found a virgin . . ."

"Well, we might have," said Eyebrow Ring. "She's not exactly Sophie Marceau."

Banjo and Cowboy Boots burst out laughing. Malvina rummaged through her handbag, then remembered with a surge of anger that Marc Vitral had taken her Mauser.

Eyebrow Ring took another two steps closer.

"Are you looking for an adventure, sweetheart? Well, it's your lucky day. Three handsome men, all for you..."

"Fuck off, you prick!"

The men froze for a moment. Then Eyebrow Ring moved forward again.

"Listen to that, guys! This one's a real little whore!"

"We're not going to hurt you," Banjo reassured her. "We just want to have some fun."

"Yeah, you're just my type," said Eyebrow Ring. "I love your look. It's fifties, right? I've always wanted to get sucked off by a grandmother." He moved closer and added: "Then again, my grandmother doesn't have any teeth now..."

Banjo and Cowboy Boots laughed loudly again. They were easily amused. They walked behind their leader, closing in on their prey.

Crawling backward, Malvina attempted to get away from them. "Come any closer and I'll kill you!" she screamed.

The three men watched with amusement as the skinny little girl crouched down on the pebbles.

"Come on, don't be shy," said Eyebrow Ring. "You know you want it..."

A second later, he heard a whistling noise and saw a shadow. The next moment, he couldn't see anything. The silver ring hung there, held in place by a scrap of shredded, bloody eyelid. A few seconds later, another stone flew through the air and hit him on the nose.

"Fuck!"

The third stone missed his mouth but crashed into his jaw.

You can kill a man with a stone, if you throw it from the right range. Malvina probably didn't realize that, but the three men did. Under certain circumstances, even the most stupid people learn quickly. It's a question of survival. They fled as a storm of stones rained down on them. Cowboy Boots slipped on the pebbles, and a stone smashed into his collarbone. Banjo was hit on the back and the neck. Malvina was throwing blindly now, rage lending strength to her skinny arm.

"You'd better watch out, you little bitch!" Eyebrow Ring yelled at her, when he was beyond range of her throws. "You haven't seen the last of us!"

"Yeah, right!" Malvina said. "I don't think the police will have too much trouble finding the guy who tried to rape me. I'll just tell them to look for an ugly, one-eyed twat."

An hour later, the wind began to blow. Malvina was cold. She stood up and rubbed her arms and legs, then walked slowly through town until she reached the train station. It was closed, of course. Finally she fell asleep on a bench overlooking the parking lot.

50

October 2, 1998, 11:51 p.m.

The Vitrals' living room was frozen in time. For an eternity.

Marc bent down, his hand trembling, and picked up the fallen sheet of paper. It looked identical to the one he had read on the train: same letterhead, same typeface. It differed by only a few words.

ANALYSIS OF BLOOD SAMPLE COMPARISONS

between Emilie VITRAL *(sample 1, batch 95-233)*
and Nicole VITRAL *(sample 2, batch 95-237)*

Results negative.
No family relationship possible.
Results 99.94513% reliable.

Marc dropped the letter on the table. Nicole did the same thing, then collapsed on the sofa.

Both families' tests had come out negative...

"What...what does this mean?" Marc stammered.

Nicole wiped a tear from her cheek, then smiled strangely.

"What a joker he is, that Crédule Grand-Duc!"

"Did you know?" Marc asked.

"No. Honestly, Marc, I had no idea. Nobody knew, apart from Crédule, of course. For three years I've been so certain that the girl I raised as a granddaughter was Lyse-Rose de Carville. I had come to accept the idea. I gave her that ring, for her eighteenth birthday. In fact, I was even glad..."

Nicole went silent for a second. She pulled at the woolen shawl she wore around her shoulders, rearranging it over her blouse. She looked tenderly at Marc.

"For you, I mean. For you and Emilie. It was so much simpler that way."

Marc said nothing. He stood up and placed the two letters next to each other, to compare them. They looked completely genuine.

"Grand-Duc must have made a mistake!" he said, his voice unnaturally loud. "Maybe he got the samples mixed up...or maybe the lab made a mistake. There has to be an explanation!"

"Maybe Crédule just gave us the results we were expecting," Nicole said quietly.

"What do you mean?"

"Only he knows which blood samples he gave to the lab. Maybe these were the results he wanted. I mean, he'd spent fifteen years investigating the case...maybe he wanted to write the end of the story himself."

Nicole thought for a moment, then continued: "Two negative tests...maybe that wasn't such a bad idea. It worked perfectly, if you think about it. Mathilde de Carville was finally convinced that her granddaughter was dead. She would never have left us alone otherwise. And I don't think Grand-Duc ever liked her. As for me, he knew I would get over the pain. When I first read that result, three years ago, I cried myself to sleep, for several nights running, but in the long term it made me feel so much better: it relieved the terrible tension I felt whenever I saw the way you and Emilie looked at each other."

Marc sat down next to Nicole and rested his head on her shoulder. He put one arm around his grandmother's thick waist and his fingers played with the ends of the woolen shawl.

"You understand, don't you, Marc? Of course you do. This meant that you weren't brother and sister. You were free. Crédule had seen the two of you together, and he loved you, in his way. He was perfectly capable of coming up with such a strategy."

She looked at the blue envelopes on the table.

"As long as the two results were never read together, his plan worked perfectly..."

Marc stood up again and paced around the room. No matter what Nicole said, he could not bring himself to believe this theory. In his notebook, the detective seemed just as dismayed by the DNA test results as they were. Although it was possible that he was lying about that. It was possible he was lying about everything.

"I'm going out for a walk, Nicole. I'll be back later."

Nicole said nothing. She wiped her eyes with the corner of her handkerchief. Marc put his hand on the doorknob. When Nicole spoke again, her voice was even shakier than before:

"You haven't asked me where Emilie is."

Marc froze.

"Do you know?"

"Not exactly. I don't know where she is geographically. But I do understand what she meant by the 'one-way trip,' by the crime she kept talking about. My God, how could she call that a crime?"

Marc felt his heart pounding again. His world had been turned upside down so many times today. Yet all the symptoms of his agoraphobia seemed to have vanished, like hiccups cured by a sudden fright.

"Call what a crime?"

In a very quiet voice, Nicole replied: "Emilie is pregnant, Marc. She is pregnant with your child."

Marc's hand lost its grip on the doorknob.

"She's going to have an abortion, Marc. That's why she's in the hospital."

Marc found himself leaning against a Dumpster in Rue Pocholle. At the end of the street, illuminated by the weak moonlight, he saw two cats facing each other, their fur on end. He wondered if they were the same cats that Lylie had chased when she was seven years old. It was possible. The same cats, but eleven years older.

Marc felt strangely calm: much calmer than he had felt a few minutes, or even a few hours, earlier. Suddenly, he could see what he had to do next. The news of Lylie's pregnancy had forced him to jettison all superfluous thoughts. The mystery of the two DNA tests could wait, and so could the murder of his grandfather. Right now, Marc cared only about one thing: Lylie, lying alone in a hospital room in Paris, pregnant, a child in her womb.

Their child.

Marc walked toward the only working streetlamp in Rue Pocholle. He had tried to call Lylie five times, but there was still no answer. He knew that calling any more hospitals would be pointless. They had to respect their clients' desire for anonymity. And Lylie would have asked for anonymity, of course.

Once again, Marc resigned himself to leaving a message on Lylie's phone, leaning against a lamppost like a drunkard serenading the moon.

"Lylie, I know. Nicole told me everything. I'm so sorry I didn't realize. Where are you? I have to be there, with you. I promise I won't try to change your mind. I'm not going to lie to you—I haven't found out anything more in the investigation. All I have is my intuition, and you already know what I believe. I know that's not enough for you but wait for me, Lylie, please. Ask me to come and I'll be there. Ask me, I'm begging you. I love you so much."

The phone message flew off into the cloudless night.

The two cats were squaring up to each other now, both hissing, as if they were about to fight to the death. And yet this was just a game: the same game they played every night over so many years.

Marc sat down on the pavement. He knew this street like the back of his hand. One day, Lylie had fallen off her tricycle here, at the very spot where he was sitting. It wasn't serious, just a graze. She'd bled a little, over the pavement, but the blood had been washed away years ago by the rain.

Marc closed his eyes.

A child. Their child.

He felt angry. Not with Lylie, but with life. With the way things were. He hated feeling so powerless, so useless.

One of the first-floor windows opened, and someone

yelled out at the cats. Marc didn't know who it was; that person must have moved here recently. One of the cats ran off. The other one stood there for a few seconds, then trotted toward Marc. Marc held out his hand and the cat rubbed against it. He wondered how many times this old tomcat had been stroked by Lylie.

Of course, Marc understood why Lylie felt an abortion was necessary. It had nothing to do with her age, or worries about money, or how a baby would affect her career. It was simply that Lylie did not want to give birth to a child born of an incestuous union. Unless her identity could be proved, definitively, Lylie would never risk bringing a monster into the world.

Marc looked up at the sky. What if he could find that definitive proof? He might still be able to stop this thing from happening.

Lylie smoked a cigarette on the balcony. She knew it was wrong, but she didn't care. Just one cigarette. Well, three, in fact. The girl with the red hair and yellow teeth was not stingy with her cigarettes. She'd given Lylie the whole pack.

Lylie listened to Marc's message. She replied with a text. There was no possibility that Marc would find her. It was better like this. She had to do this alone.

It would be madness to keep this child. Lylie knew, more than anyone, how hard it was to live without an identity. How could she possibly inflict such a punishment on her own baby?

In the palm of her left hand, she held the Tuareg cross Marc had given her. The fingers of her right hand typed out the long message she sent in four parts:

*

Marc, this will soon be all over. Don't worry, it's a simple operation. It only takes a few minutes.

I will have to stay here all day tomorrow. The doctors say they need to run some more tests for the anesthetic. Maybe it's just a ruse to give me more time to think about it...

Anyway, the operation will not take place until the day after tomorrow. But please don't worry about me. I have made the right decision. Everything will be all right.

Take care of yourself.

In his bedroom, lying on his childhood bed, Marc read the message. Right away, he tried to call her back. She wasn't answering.

He read through the message again and again. Only one sentence seemed to matter: "The operation will not take place until the day after tomorrow."

So he had one more day to discover the truth. Marc took this as a sign. All was not yet lost.

He stared at the bunk bed above his. As he lay there, an idea germinated in his mind. Only one thing was certain: all of the elements in this case were somehow connected. The murder of his grandfather, the murder of Grand-Duc, perhaps other murders that he didn't yet know about... and Lylie's true identity.

Crédule Grand-Duc had found the solution. He had discovered it just before he was murdered. He had been planning to go to the Jura Mountains, to Mont Terri. That made sense. After all, that was where everything had begun. Perhaps it was fated to end there, too.

*

At 4:00 a.m., Marc got up and put on a sweater. What did he have to lose? He had no other leads. He walked carefully through the darkness, toward his grandmother's bedroom.

"Marc?" Nicole said sleepily.

"Does the van still work, Nicole?"

Nicole rubbed her eyes and glanced at the alarm clock on her bedside table. "Umm…yes…I think so. I don't use it much anymore. And the last time I drove it, there was…"

"Are the keys still in the middle drawer in the living room?"

"Yes. But…"

"Thanks. Don't worry…"

"Be careful," Nicole wanted to say, but her words were lost in a coughing fit. She held a handkerchief to her mouth. She knew she would not get any more sleep that night.

51

The van started at the first attempt. Marc had driven it several times, but only for short distances. He was usually the one who had moved it out of the garden. Nicole had taught him exactly how to maneuver it out of this tiny, confined space, navigating by means of the mailbox and the neighbors' left-hand shutter. There were only inches to spare on either side.

The Vitrals' Type H Citroën van was one of the last of its kind to be made in France. Pierre Vitral had bought it in 1979, and Citroën had stopped production two years later. Pierre had chosen the longest model, very similar to the type of van bought by butchers in the 1970s; orange with a red, flattened nose that made it look like a big dog, two round headlights for eyes, and side mirrors on metal stalks for ears. Her big bow-wow, Lylie called it. The big, lazy bow-wow that slept outside and filled the entire garden.

Pierre had converted it himself with the help of his cousin, who was a car mechanic in Neuville. This same cousin still carried out repairs on it occasionally, so it was in good condition, considering its age and the two hundred thousand miles on its odometer. And besides, Marc had no choice: he had to believe the van would hold together, in spite of its dented bodywork, the broken windshield wipers, and the hood that did not close properly.

He checked his watch: just after four. Dieppe was sleeping. He drove through a ghost town, watched over by the kites that moved in the wind high above. The Citroën was noisy, but at least it worked. Marc didn't want to count his chickens, though: there were still nearly four hundred miles to go. Marc had consulted the map before he started, and decided to avoid Paris. He had written his route down on a piece of paper: Neufchâtel-en-Bray, Beauvais, Compiègne, Soissons, Reims, Châlons-en-Champagne, Saint-Dizier, Langres, Vesoul, Montbéliard, Mont Terri. He reckoned it would take him about ten hours to reach his destination. If all went well.

Marc drove alongside the port. All he had to do now was go up Boulevard Chanzy and he would be on his way out of Dieppe. The streets were deserted. At the end of the boulevard, Marc passed the train station. For some reason his eyes were drawn toward it…and spotted a girl asleep on a bench.

The Citroën came to an abrupt halt. Well, at least the brakes worked.

And so did the horn.

Malvina de Carville awoke, startled, and instinctively reached for one of the stones she had brought with her from the beach. She stood up, then recognized Marc, sitting behind the steering wheel of an orange-and-red van. He rolled down the window.

"You're not going to stone my old van, are you?"

"Just give me back my gun!"

"Don't worry, it's in my pocket. I'm keeping it warm for you. Get in!"

Malvina's eyes opened wide with disbelief. "You want me to help you sell fries?"

"I'm going somewhere that might interest you. Get in!"

Without letting go of the stone in her hand, Malvina moved closer. She gave the van a skeptical once-over.

"Don't tell me you're planning to drive to Mont Terri in this. It's a death trap!"

Marc absorbed this verbal punch, trying not to think about whether it might have been deliberate.

"You've never been there, have you? I bet you're dying to see it."

Malvina dropped the stone. "You have no idea how right you are."

Marc opened the passenger door and she clambered inside.

"God, what a mess this thing is! I bet we won't even make it to Paris..."

"Piss off! Anyway, we're not going via Paris." He handed her the list of towns that they would pass through.

"I've never even heard of most of these places," she said. "You'd better hope we don't break down. I think you're crazier than I am."

For the next ten minutes, they drove in silence. The road hugged the valley of the Pays de Bray, tracing long curves over the landscape.

Marc said: "Sorry we didn't invite you to dinner last night. Another time, maybe."

"Don't worry about me, I can look after myself. I made friends with a few local guys."

Another ten-minute silence. They were nearing Neufchâtel-en-Bray.

"So what are we going to do at Mont Terri?" Malvina asked.

Marc shrugged. "It's a sort of pilgrimage."

Malvina looked at him curiously. "And the idea just came to you tonight? I thought the case was solved. What else is there to say after that stupid DNA test? Dragonfly is your sister. Are you're just upset because you're fucking her."

Marc braked suddenly.

Malvina, half choked by the seat belt, said: "If you're going to do that every time I have a dig at you, we'll never get there."

A *dig*? Marc was going to have to sit through ten hours of this shit.

"I'm sorry about the seat belt," he said. "I forgot to bring the booster seat."

Malvina pretended to laugh. "This isn't going to be boring at all: you'll keep me amused with all your excellent jokes," she said sarcastically.

After another silence, Marc said: "So you believe that stupid DNA test?"

"God, no!"

"Good. Then we're in agreement."

"It's total crap," Malvina said. "I always knew Grand-Duc was on your side. Because he felt guilty. And because he liked your grandmother's tits..."

This time, Marc did not hit the brakes, but he did think seriously about leaving Malvina by the roadside. He probably would have, except he needed her. He had to be patient: Malvina would be useful. She had already given him information, without being aware of it, when she talked about Grand-Duc's feelings of guilt. And that was just the start...

They were silent for almost an hour, until they reached

Beauvais. The road sped past, empty and monotonous. Malvina leaned forward, and the stiff, dusty seat belt scraped her ear. "I'm guessing your radio doesn't work."

"Nope. But the cassette player should be OK. Look in the glove compartment and you'll find the tapes we used to listen to when we were young."

"You're kidding!" Malvina laughed. "Cassette tapes? Do those things still exist?"

Malvina opened the glove compartment. "What does a tape look like?" She turned toward Marc, her eyes sparkling with mischief.

She spent a few minutes looking through the cassettes, then put one in the player, without showing it to Marc. A brutal guitar riff, mixed with the sound of a police siren, filled the van's interior. "La Ballade de Serge K." A lonely man's nighttime drive.

Marc recognized the album as soon as he heard the first chord. *Poèmes Rock*.

"*Demain, demain. Demain comme hier*," sang Charlélie Couture in his nasal voice.

"I had a feeling you'd choose that one," Marc said.

"I didn't want to disappoint you."

Marc smiled. They were entering Beauvais. Even at five in the morning, it was a pain to drive through. They kept having to stop at traffic lights that appeared to have been designed by a sadistic government employee so that any motorist obeying the speed limit would always hit a red light.

"You're right," Marc said, between two traffic lights. "*Poèmes Rock* is the best French rock album ever written, in my opinion."

"Really?" said Malvina indifferently. "I only know one

song. But unfortunately it's not a CD, so we can't just skip to it."

"What do you listen to normally?" he asked her.

"Nothing."

As they left Beauvais, the first side of the tape came to an end, and Malvina turned it over. Finally, she would get to hear the song she knew. She turned the volume as high as it would go. The van vibrated as Charlélie Couture sang:

> *Like a plane without wings,*
> *I sang all night*
> *Yes, I sang all night*
> *For the one who didn't believe me…*

Marc shivered. Malvina, eyes closed, was singing along silently to the words.

> *Even if I can't take off,*
> *I will go all the way to the end*
> *Yes, I will play all night*
> *Even though I know I can't win*

Marc had listened to this song hundreds of times. When he was alone. When he was filled with doubts. Never with Lylie—she couldn't stand it. Once, when she was eight years old, Lylie had smashed a radio at a friend's house, just because this song was playing.

> *Listen to the voice of the wind*
> *That blows, blows under the door*
> *Listen, we're going to change the bed, change our love*

Change our lives, change the day...

Malvina was almost in tears. The harrowing guitar solo did not help. Marc stared at the horizon.

Oh, dragonfly,
Your wings are so fragile,
As for me, my body is broken...

The road continued to speed past, crossing through sad villages where—in a vain attempt to convince the government to build a bypass—signs displayed the number of deaths that had occurred there and the number of trucks passing each day. Twenty minutes later, they were approaching Compiègne. The volume of traffic began to increase.

As they exited Compiègne, Marc turned to Malvina. "We'll stop at the next town, if we see a bakery open."

Malvina looked behind her, toward the back of the van. "Oh, I thought you'd let me drive while you whipped us up some crêpes and waffles, just like your grandparents used to..."

Marc did not reply. There was no point: he'd made his decision. After all, Malvina had brought the subject up herself, in a way.

They drove into the small village of Catenoy and Marc stopped in a large parking lot. All the shops were closed, and so was the restaurant proudly displaying its forty-nine-francs menu for truck drivers. He checked that the Mauser was still in his pocket, took the car keys, and got out of the van. The parking lot was bordered by a few birch trees, their leaves blackened by the incessant diesel fumes. After relieving himself behind a tree, Marc walked back to the van.

Malvina had not moved. Marc went to the passenger door and opened it. He took the five pages he had torn from the notebook from his back pocket, and handed them to Malvina.

"Read this," he said. "It's from Grand-Duc's notebook. I think you might find it interesting."

52

Mathilde de Carville brought the lit match close to the jet of gas. A circle of blue flames lapped around the edges of the pan of water. She turned around and looked one last time at the copy of the *Est Républicain* from December 23, 1980. Then she tore off the front page, scrunched it up into a ball, and set fire to it. She did not let go of it, dropping it into the sink, until the flames had blackened her fingernails.

She had found the envelope containing the newspaper in the entrance hall yesterday afternoon, and had read it immediately. It had not taken her more than a few seconds to understand.

So, Grand-Duc had not been bluffing. He was right: the truth jumped out at you the moment you looked at that newspaper... as long as you looked at it eighteen years later.

How ironic!

They had been barking up the wrong tree from the very beginning.

Worse than that: her husband had been guilty of the

most contemptible crimes. He had killed. For nothing. And she was hardly any less guilty: she had looked the other way as he did those things. For Lyse-Rose. They had hurt innocent people. The truth would come out, eventually. She did not have the courage to face the judgment of men. As for the judgment of God...

Mathilde de Carville put her finger in the water. It was lukewarm. Linda was upstairs, in the spare bedroom. She was asleep. She had fainted in the hallway, after discovering Léonce's corpse. Mathilde had given her a tranquilizer, and then a sleeping pill. She had laid Linda out on the bed and called the woman's husband to let him know that Linda would be sleeping at the Roseraie that night. It happened sometimes, when Léonce was unwell. The husband did not ask any questions. Mathilde paid generous wages.

Mathilde opened a cabinet and took out a glass bottle wrapped in newspaper. When Linda woke up, the first thing she would do was run to the police. Mathilde had no intention of stopping her. What else could she do? She was hardly going to murder the poor girl. Perhaps it would have been better to have waited a few hours yesterday, until Linda had gone home. She would have been alone with Léonce then, as she was every evening. It would have been much simpler. But she had not been able to wait—not after she read that newspaper, and understood the truth. So many times, throughout the years, she had believed that her cause was righteous, just. And yet, in the end, the only just act she had performed was to cut short the sufferings of an old man. God had already rendered His justice.

Now it was her turn to show the weight of her own remorse. She thought of the scandal it would bring, the police in the house... but what did it matter? She wouldn't have to face it.

Mathilde's finger touched the water again. It was nearly boiling now. She sighed with relief. Soon, it would all be over. She switched off the gas, poured the water into a large terra-cotta bowl, put the bowl on a silver tray alongside the bottle and a small spoon, and left the kitchen.

After climbing the staircase, Mathilde opened the first door to her right—the door to Lyse-Rose's bedroom. She gazed at the large room, filled with toys and presents. Irrespective of how much they cost, each one—bought every year, for every birthday, every Christmas—had been a message of hope. Lyse-Rose was not forgotten. Each fragile candle flame was a symbol of the slender possibility that she was still alive. The spark. But that flame had been extinguished yesterday afternoon—forever.

Léonce had killed for nothing.

Mathilde put the silver tray on the bedside table. To get to the bed, she had to move a sky-blue, lace-trimmed stroller and step over a miniature Chinese tea set. Pushing aside the large teddy bear that was sleeping on Lyse-Rose's bed, she lay down in its place; in this bed, where Lyse-Rose should have been sleeping all these years, and where, now, she would never sleep. She uncorked the bottle and poured all the yellow liquid into the bowl of hot water.

It was her favorite. Her secret. The celandine she had kept for an important occasion.

Mathilde stirred the mixture with the silver spoon, creating an herbal tea that she knew to be lethal.

She had learned that it was impossible to murder someone with celandine. Even her husband had refused to drink it, because the taste was unbearable. That was why accidents with celandine were so rare—just one death, in Germany, according to what she had read.

Mathilde placed the spoon carefully on the silver tray and unhooked the cross from around her neck.

Even for suicide, celandine was not recommended. At least not for people without extremely strong willpower. She smiled. Mathilde was not the type of person to kill herself by swallowing a bottle of tranquilizers or injecting herself with painkillers... An easy, comfortable suicide. To her, nothing could be more hypocritical.

Mathilde de Carville grimaced at the first sip of her concoction. But then she drank the entire contents of the bowl, down to the last drop.

It was disgusting, but she wasn't going to complain.

In other ages, to atone for her sins, she would have demanded that they flog her until she died, or drive a stake through her heart, or burn her alive.

Mathilde stretched out on Lyse-Rose's bed. The bed of a dead child.

She held the cross tightly in her hand.

It would not be long now...

53

October 3, 1998, 6:22 a.m.

Marc walked around the parking lot while Malvina read the five pages in the van. He took a package of cookies and a carton of orange juice from his bag and began to eat and drink. A truck had parked about fifty yards away, and the driver was drinking from a Thermos. Coffee, probably. Marc thought about asking him for a sip.

Malvina jumped down from the van, the pages in her hand.

"All right, I've read them. Happy now? I was eight years old when your granddad died. What was the point of showing me these pages? To warn me not to sleep in this death trap? Don't worry, I have no intention of spending the night with you."

Marc did not reply. Maybe he was getting used to Malvina's dark irony. It seemed to be her only mode of communicating; she probably found it therapeutic. And maybe he did, too, after all these years of silence and taboos. Marc went back to the van, rummaged around in his bag, and then took out the binder containing his course work.

"Now read this," he told her.

"What, all of it?"

"No, not all of it. Just the notes for February 12, about Turkey."

Malvina sighed. "Give me some orange juice and a few cookies first."

Marc handed her the remains of his breakfast and watched her devour it. If she was anorexic, she hid it well.

"All right, so what is all this crap?"

She grabbed the binder, opened it at the page Marc had indicated, and pulled a face. "Sorry, I can't read your scrawl. I bet they think you're a real dope at the university, don't they? Especially compared to Lylie..."

"And what qualifications do you have, Malvina?"

"The world record for the highest number of private tutors," Malvina replied. "Thirty-seven in fifteen years. The last one didn't stay more than two days."

"So you're hardly in a position to have a go at me, are you?"

Malvina began to laugh. She dropped the empty juice carton on the ground.

"It's not my fault. I'm just too special for all those teachers. I don't fit into any of their neat little boxes...Jesus Christ, I can't make heads or tails of your notes!"

"Just read the dates. Or are you too special to do that?"

"God, you're a prick..."

"Just read it!"

"OK. 'October 1923: Ataturk's Turkey becomes a republic; September 17, 1961: the prime minister, Adnan Menderes, is executed for violating the Constitution.' What exactly is the point of this?"

"Keep going!"

"For God's sake…'Twelfth of September, 1980: coup d'état and return of military to power; seventh of November, 1982: national referendum on the return to democracy…'"

"Right," said Marc. "Now take another look at those pages from Grand-Duc's notebook. The very first lines."

"Fucking hell, you're unbelievable!" Malvina threw the pages to the ground. "Let's just get out of here. Otherwise it'll be Christmas before we make it to Mont Terri…"

Ignoring her, Marc calmly picked up the pages and began to read: "'I spent that Sunday—November 7, 1982—in Antalya, on the Mediterranean coast, a place where the sun shone three hundred days of the year. I was at the residence of a high-ranking official from the Turkish Home Office…' I'll skip the next bit. Listen to this: 'The official thought I was crazy, of course. After weeks spent chasing him, he had finally given in and consented to see me at his beach house one weekend when all the bigwigs of Turkish national security would be there. Nazim was not with me, for once: Ayla had insisted he go home. He had fallen ill, if I remember correctly…This was extremely inconvenient for me, as I needed an interpreter to explain what it was that I wanted, and it was especially difficult as the others were there to relax in the sun with their wives and were not remotely convinced by the urgency of my requests. Then again, neither was I.'"

Fiddling nervously with her ring, Malvina stared at the truck at the far end of the parking lot.

"What now?" she shouted, loud enough for the truck driver to hear her. "Shall we open up your shitty van and start making waffles for all these lardass truck drivers?"

The driver heard this. He looked at Malvina as if she

were some curious beast, then shrugged and turned around, no more annoyed than he would have been by a poodle barking at his heels. Marc stared at Malvina. Once again, the girl's anger seemed false. This was clearly just a pathetic attempt at a diversionary tactic.

"I'll spell it out for you, Malvina. The point is that the dates clash. In his notebook, Crédule Grand-Duc says that he was with all the bigwigs in Turkish national security, partying at the seaside with their wives and children, on November 7, 1982. But that was the day of the national referendum. A vote on Turkey's return to democracy. The end of military rule. Don't you think the politicians would have had better things to do that day?"

Malvina shrugged. "So Grand-Duc got his dates wrong... What's the big deal?"

"Bullshit!" Marc shouted.

The truck driver with the Thermos of coffee was leaning against his vehicle, watching the scene as if Marc and Malvina were actors in a sitcom.

"Do you want a hearing aid?" Malvina yelled at the driver, who didn't even raise an eyebrow.

Marc continued. "The truth is, Malvina, that Grand-Duc wasn't in Turkey on November 7, 1982. Certainly not in a villa in Antalya. So why did he lie about it? Why use such a crappy alibi? Because he was somewhere else of course. But where? Where could he have been that weekend? Somewhere he shouldn't have been... Why go to such lengths to make clear that he was in Turkey and Nazim was in France? Because he wanted to throw suspicion on his partner!"

"You're crazy," Malvina said. "You make me look completely sane."

Marc grabbed her by the sweater. She did not fight back. She no longer had a gun in her pocket. Not even a pebble.

"So let's just consider the possibility that our honest, kind friend, Crédule-la-Bascule, who was so in love with my grandmother . . . loyal, pure-hearted Crédule Grand-Duc . . . was actually just a mercenary bastard. A piece of shit who was asked by your grandfather to get rid of my grandparents . . . and who agreed!"

Marc's fingers tightened around Malvina's sweater. In the parking lot, the truck driver got back into his truck. They could hear the static from his radio.

On the verge of tears, Marc went on: "He lied about this. Was everything else a lie, too? His love for our family, for my grandmother? Maybe not. Maybe those things were true. It's a classic scenario, after all: the murderer overcome by guilt, trying to atone for his sins . . . And to think we invited this bastard into our home! My grandfather's killer. To think that my grandmother even . . . ugh!"

Marc suddenly let go of Malvina and stalked off into the parking lot to pick up the package of cookies and the carton of orange juice that Malvina had dropped. He took them to the closest trash can.

"I don't care what you say," he said, returning. "I know what happened that day. I know who killed my grandfather. It was Grand-Duc! As soon as you understand that, all the stuff in his notebook is exposed for what it is—hypocritical bullshit. He was a mercenary, he even said so . . ."

"It was my grandfather," said Malvina.

Marc had never heard her speak so gently.

"It was my grandfather," she repeated. "Him, no one else. After his first heart attack. He was too impatient to

wait for the outcome of the investigation that my grandmother was paying for, so he got hold of Grand-Duc
shortly afterward. He paid him a lot of money: enough
to buy a house on Butte-aux-Cailles, let's say. It had to
look like an accident. His lawyers had told him that if the
Vitrals died, there was a good chance that Judge Weber
would give the baby to us. Grand-Duc was no choirboy;
my grandfather had checked out his past. That weekend,
in November 1982, he made a quick trip from Turkey to
France. No one ever knew. The rest was pretty easy for
him."

"How did you find out?"

"I was eight years old. I didn't understand everything
at the time, but I was already spying on people. Like a
naughty little mouse, I found holes to hide in. My grandmother didn't realize until later either, not until Pierre
Vitral was dead. You can't even imagine what that must
have done to her conscience. Such a crime! How could she
confess that when she prayed to the Father, the Son, and
the Holy Spirit? My grandfather suffered his second heart
attack soon afterward. His plan had failed. My grandmother considered the attack to be divine justice, and she
never breathed a word about what she knew."

"And what about you, Malvina? What did you think?"

After a second's hesitation, she replied: "I thought my
grandfather was right, of course! It could have worked: if
your grandparents had both died, then Lyse-Rose—the
baby sister you had stolen from me—would have come
home to her beautiful bedroom at last. And you would
have been sent to an orphanage. It would have been perfect! That's what I thought."

"And now? What do you think about it now?"

This time there was no hesitation. "Same thing!"

They set off again. Malvina changed the cassette in the tape player. She had chosen this one randomly, because she liked the sky-blue color of its packaging: *Brothers in Arms* by Dire Straits. Mark Knopfler's voice alternated with the ecstasies of his guitar. Malvina was the first to speak:

"That doesn't alter the fact that Grand-Duc is a piece of shit. He always hated me; I don't know why. Maybe because he guessed that I knew the truth."

Marc was hardly even listening. He felt betrayed. How much of the detective's notebook was true, and how much of it lies?

"Three days ago, he tried blackmailing my grand-mother," Malvina went on. "With that bullshit story about a last-minute discovery. One hundred and fifty thousand francs, he wanted. Three times that if he provided her with proof! I don't know who killed him, but whoever it was did the world a favor."

Marc's fingers drummed on the steering wheel. He thought about what Malvina had just told him, and his discovery of Grand-Duc's corpse. A bullet in the chest, head in the fireplace, she had said, as if he were the victim of some macabre ritual. His face covered in blisters and ashes.

"And as for that DNA test..." Malvina continued. "We both know that Lyse-Rose is the one who survived. So all those tests prove is that Grand-Duc was a lying bastard."

An awful doubt was growing in Marc's troubled mind.

"And anyway, he was crap at his job," Malvina con-cluded. "My grandfather paid him a million francs and he couldn't even manage to bump off two old farts in their sleep..."

Marc's fingers tensed around the worn leather steering wheel. Mark Knopfler's guitar screamed out one last riff.

It was just her sense of humor, he told himself. Remember...

54

October 3, 1998, 11:33 a.m.

After five hours on the road, the Citroën was still going strong. Well, strong is maybe an exaggeration—it struggled on certain sections of highway, unable to move any faster than seventy miles per hour—but at least it was still going.

They had already played all the cassettes in the glove compartment: a compendium of 1980s hits, including Supertramp's *Famous Last Words* and Jean-Jacques Goldman's *Positif*.

They stopped at Vitry-le-François, a town surrounded by cornfields in the Champagne region, and ate at a restaurant by the side of the road. They were the only customers. Marc ate an omelet and sat thinking in silence. Malvina opted for the three-course menu—charcuterie, steak, and a crème brulée.

"She's got quite an appetite, your wife," said the owner, winking at Marc. "I wonder where she puts it all!"

Back on the road, they went through Saint-Dizier and Chaumont. The flat grain-growing plains were marked out by lines of cuestas—sudden steep slopes like the steps of a staircase, at the base of which lay wooded depressions. The Citroën van sped up each time they descended a cuesta slope, as if braking were impossible and it was just hoping for another upward slope in order to slow it down. Renaud sang "En Cloque" for the third time. Malvina and Marc had not said a word for almost two hours.

"Do you think Lyse-Rose would want a sister like me?" Malvina said suddenly.

Marc, driving through a village called Fayl-Billot, did not reply.

"You know her," Malvina said. "Do you think she'd be able to understand me . . . to accept a big sister as ugly and nasty as me?"

Still Marc did not speak. On the whole, he preferred it when Malvina stuck to her dark humor.

"I can change," she insisted. "Will you tell her that I can change?"

"Are you really sure that Lylie is your sister?"

"Of course. We're both sure of that, aren't we?"

Marc envied Malvina's absence of doubt, her determination. It was as if she lived inside a bubble that nothing could burst. Just after passing Vesoul, Marc received a text from Lylie. He picked it up one-handed while continuing to drive.

Marc, the operation will take place tomorrow at 10:00 a.m. Don't worry, everything will be fine. I'll call you afterward.

Tomorrow at 10:00 a.m. So, he had less than twenty-four hours.

Goldman yelled "Envole-moi!" Instinctively, Marc pressed down on the accelerator, but the van didn't go any faster. As the miles accumulated, the crazy theory that had taken root in Marc's brain began to gain weight and substance, seeming ever more plausible. Obvious, even.

*

Three hours later, they passed through Montbéliard. The town's roads seemed too wide for the sparse amount of traffic; huge boulevards, avenues, bypasses—perhaps as a reflection of the Peugeot factory nearby, which had, at its peak, employed more than forty thousand people. The largest factory in Europe…Less than a third of it remained operational today.

Marc handed Malvina a map, telling her she had to find a tiny hamlet called Clairbief, where Monique Genevez ran what Crédule Grand-Duc had described in his notebook as the best rental cottage in the region.

"What are we going to do there?" Malvina moaned. "You think you can get back the cash that my grandma sent to Grand-Duc?"

Marc shrugged, then checked that the Mauser was still in his pocket. Would he have to use it? Was it possible he was right, and that they had all been manipulated from the very beginning?

Malvina stopped complaining and concentrated on the map. She proved to be a remarkably competent navigator. Seven miles after leaving Montbéliard, they passed through Pont-de-Roide and the valiant orange-and-red van began to climb the foothills of the Jura Mountains: first a narrow, winding road alongside the Doubs until they reached Saint-Hippolyte, then the steep slope of a wider road.

The Citroën groaned and creaked in protest, but it kept going. When they reached the top of the first hill, they were given a glorious view of the valley below. The van then happily descended back down toward the river, through a forest of pines and gold-leafed deciduous trees.

*

Monique Genevez's cottage was impossible to miss. Only
one road ran alongside the Doubs. The chalet's pale wood
was reflected in the river's calm waters. Marc held his
breath and touched the Mauser inside his pocket once
again. He stopped the van in a parking lot opposite the
chalet. There were no other vehicles there. In this tiny village at the end of the world, time itself seemed to have
stopped. Marc was struggling to breathe, his mind filled
with the possibility that his quest might be about to end
here.

"So, are we going?" Malvina said.

"Hang on..."

Marc took out the Mauser and made sure it was loaded.

"What are you planning to do with my gun? Bump off
Mrs. Genevez?"

Marc looked at Malvina. "Do you remember Grand-
Duc's corpse?"

"Er, yeah."

"What do you remember?"

"What are you talking about?"

"You remember a corpse in Grand-Duc's house, wearing Grand-Duc's clothes and shoes and watch..."

Malvina suddenly went pale.

"A corpse, with its head in the fireplace," Marc continued. "The face so badly burned and covered in blisters that
it was unrecognizable. Right?"

"What's your point?"

"Follow me!"

They got out of the van. Monique Genevez was already
standing outside the chalet, flanked by window boxes full
of geraniums.

"Hello!" Marc called out to her. "We're friends of Crédule Grand-Duc. You know him, I believe?"

The woman's face lit up.

"Mr. Grand-Duc! Of course I know him. He has stayed here every December for more than ten years now."

"I think he came back early this year, though, didn't he?"

"He certainly did," said Mrs. Genevez. "But I'm afraid you're out of luck. He left just this morning."

Marc felt the ground shift beneath his feet. Beside him, Malvina stopped breathing. Unaware of her visitors' reactions, Monique Genevez continued in the same untroubled tone: "He was here yesterday and the day before, staying in Room 12 as usual. The day before yesterday, he stayed here most of the morning because he was waiting for the mail to arrive before he went out. And when the mailman arrived, he had a large envelope for him. But he left very early this morning, around six."

"Do you know if he's coming back?" Marc managed to ask.

"Oh, I'd be surprised. He usually only stays for a night or two when he's here. He calls it his pilgrimage, you know. He's a very intriguing man, your friend. Perfectly kind and polite—and he has a very good appetite!—but I don't understand his obsession with that plane crash. After eighteen years, I'd have thought it was time to forget about it, wouldn't you?"

Marc was silent for a few seconds. Finally he said: "Do you know where he was going?"

Monique tore a few dead stems from a geranium. "No, I'm afraid not. Mr. Grand-Duc is not the type of man to reveal his secrets, not even after a bottle and a half of Vin Jaune. Anyway, I would never ask. But I imagine he's gone back to Paris, don't you? That's what he normally does."

Though he asked Mrs. Genevez a few more questions, Marc did not discover anything else. He and Malvina went back to the van.

Inside, Malvina spat angrily: "I told you that bastard had been fucking with us from the beginning!"

Marc said nothing. He felt powerless. So, Grand-Duc *was* alive . . . but they had missed him. The last lead in this investigation had slipped through his fingers.

"But hang on," said Malvina. "If you guessed that Grand-Duc had faked his own death and killed someone else in his place, what the hell are we doing here?"

"Oh, shut up!"

Malvina clapped sarcastically. "You're a genius, Vitral. We've just done a ten-hour drive for nothing. Couldn't you have phoned first?"

"I said shut up."

"You could at least get me a room in Mrs. Genevez's cottage. It looks nice."

"Shut the fuck up or I'll shoot you right now and throw your body into the river."

Malvina looked at Marc curiously. "What is your problem? I mean, it's hardly a great surprise that Grand-Duc is a piece of shit. Why are you in such a terrible mood suddenly? And why are you in such a rush? Are you marrying my sister tomorrow, or something?"

"Forget it. You wouldn't understand."

Marc turned the key in the ignition.

"Where are we going?" Malvina asked. "Don't you want to stay here for a while?"

"No, I don't! I promised you a pilgrimage, and that's exactly what you'll get. We're going to Mont Terri."

55

Through binoculars, Crédule Grand-Duc followed the mailman's bright yellow van as it wound along the curving trail through the pine forest. It was advancing slowly, taking its time, stopping at every chalet along the route. It wouldn't get there for another ten minutes.

The Xantia was parked a mile or so higher up the hill, just before the road entered Saint-Hippolyte. Sitting in his car, the detective watched the mailman's van for a few moments longer.

Ten minutes...

Would this be the right one, at last? He had already followed seven other mailmen, fruitlessly. But all he had to do was keep going, and eventually he would have his reward. He had been searching for this Mélanie Belvoir for three days now. Apparently she was completely out of touch with her family, and her name did not appear in any phone book, electronic or otherwise. He had found no trace of her existence in any government listings. She might have married, but no Mélanie Belvoir appeared in any of the local wedding registries. So he had finally thought to question

the local mailmen. Even if Mélanie Belvoir had changed
her name, she might still continue to receive correspon-
dence under her maiden name. A mailman would know
that, especially in a rural backwater like this. A mailman
would probably know every single address on his route.

And yet none, so far, had ever heard of Mélanie Belvoir.

But there was nothing to do but keep hammering away.
Persistence was his middle name. And he did not lack
motivation. This was the closest he had come to finding
the Holy Grail, the solution to his investigation.

He thought about the precariousness of life. Four days
ago, he had been sixty seconds away from shooting himself in the head.

Grand-Duc looked through the binoculars again. The yellow van had gone around another ten curves.

Inside his pocket, Grand-Duc gripped the handle of his
revolver—a Mateba. Semiautomatic. His gun had become
practically a collectible since the American company that
made it had gone bust. He had to order his bullets from
Canada now, at the outrageous price of forty Canadian dol-
lars for a box of six. But what did he care? He could afford
it, now more than ever. Yesterday morning, at Monique
Genevez's cottage, he had received the one hundred and
fifty thousand francs sent by Mathilde de Carville.

And that was only a down payment.

What else could he ask for? Apart from a clear
conscience...

He thought again about his notebook. Lylie and Marc
would have read it by now. They probably wouldn't have
gone to his house, and discovered the corpse there. But
even if they had, he had covered his tracks. To them, he

would appear to be a victim, not a murderer. As for the rest...had he been skillful enough in his account? Would they suspect the truth? That he had been the one who tampered with that ridiculous gas pipe, one night in November 1982?

Over time, Grand-Duc had convinced himself that he had been nothing but the instrument of the de Carville family, a mere tool in their hands; that he had never wished to harm the Vitrals. And even if he had refused Léonce de Carville's offer, some other thug would have carried out the deed—and would not have spared Nicole. He had redeemed himself since then. He had become close to Nicole, and to her grandchildren. He had come to know them, and to love them. Especially Nicole. He had never betrayed them, since that first time, and he had always done his best to be impartial when investigating the case. To write everything down for them, in his notebook. Well, everything except that night in Le Tréport.

He was no angel. He had never claimed to be. But he had been thorough and meticulous in his investigation, even when it came to those DNA tests...those stupid tests that had driven him crazy, driven him to the point of suicide.

But all that was over now. He had finally solved the mystery. All he needed was to find his final witness.

Mélanie Belvoir.

The yellow van appeared around the corner and parked next to the Xantia. The mailman emerged from the vehicle. He was a fit-looking young man with long hair in dreadlocks, tied up in a red bandanna. The kind of guy who would probably have been able to do his rounds on a mountain bike, taking shortcuts across the trails.

Grand-Duc got out of the car and stood before him. "Excuse me, I'd like to ask you a question. Could you tell me where Mélanie Belvoir lives?"

The mailman gave him a suspicious look.

"Sorry. We're not allowed to give out that kind of information."

The detective smiled inwardly. He had seen the way the mailman reacted to the woman's name. He knew her. Now all Grand-Duc had to do was make him admit it. The mailman slid three letters into the nearest mailbox, then turned back toward his van.

"Hang on a minute. I'm serious. Police!"

Grand-Duc held out his business card, which indicated he was a certified private detective and was stamped with the flag of the French Republic. Nine times out of ten, this did the trick.

"So?" said the postman, not even glancing at the card. "Send my boss an official request, if you like. He deals with all the paperwork."

Great—he was clearly dealing with a real pain in the neck. Still, there was no point getting heavy with him. Not yet, anyway.

Grand-Duc sighed. "Listen, this is urgent. It's a matter of life and death. I can't tell you any more than that, but believe me, every minute counts…"

The mailman stared at Grand-Duc. "Sorry, I can't tell you anything. It's confidential. But all you need to do is call the office."

"That's not true. Mélanie Belvoir isn't listed anywhere. Not under that name, anyway…"

"Well, maybe that's because she doesn't want anyone bothering her."

This guy was a real prick.

"You have a duty to help the police, young man."

The mailman waved his dreadlocks from side to side. "Sorry, mate. I'm not the kind of guy who informs on honest folks to the police. Those days are over, you know?"

"OK, how much?"

The mailman sighed. "What?"

"How much do you want for the address? Five thousand francs? Ten thousand?"

"And you claim you're a cop?" The mailman laughed. "I don't think so."

Grand-Duc had had enough of this bullshit. The mailman had already gotten back into his van when the barrel of the Mateba touched his temple.

"I don't like your attitude, pal."

All his bravado vanished immediately. The mailman placed his hands on the steering wheel. "All right, all right, take it easy."

"So, Mélanie Belvoir . . ."

"Sorry, don't know her."

Grand-Duc pushed the barrel harder into the mailman's temple.

"I told you, this is a matter of life and death. For you, too, now. I'll let you in on a secret—I'm not a policeman. I'm a serial killer, and I go after mailmen who won't cooperate. Anyone in a yellow van who fucks with me gets his head blown off. All right? So, Mélanie Belvoir . . ."

"I swear to you, I . . ."

"All right, I'm going to begin by shooting you in the kneecap. No more trekking in the mountains for you. Cross-country skiing, mountain biking, shagging hot chicks? Forget it!"

The detective lowered the gun toward the mailman's legs.

"OK, OK!" the mailman yelled. "Enough. She took her husband's name, or the guy she lives with, anyway. Luisans. Mélanie Luisans. She lives in the next valley. Follow the D34 out of Montbéliard, take the exit toward Dannemarie, and it's the first chalet after the village. Sky-blue shutters, if I remember correctly..."

"How do you know?"

"She still gets letters addressed to Mélanie Belvoir, three or four times a year."

"There you go. Wasn't so difficult, was it?"

Grand-Duc grinned openly now. He had flushed out the final witness. And he was the first, the only one, to have done so. Even if others were to guess, by looking at that old edition of *Est Républicain*, how could they make the connection to Mélanie Belvoir? And how could they ever hope to find her, so quickly? No, he was in the clear now. Well ahead of the field.

"What...what do you want from her?" the mailman stammered.

"There's nothing to worry about. I just want to chat with her about old times."

56

Marc drove instinctively. The Citroën van was still managing, thank God! This really wouldn't be a good time for it to break down. It did its best to climb at a decent speed the snaking curves that led to the foot of Mont Terri. They passed through Indevillers, then took a white gravel path, bordered on either side by stacks of wood. Wooden signs pointed them toward the nature preserve office.

The building's facade was decorated with a mural showing a map of the Jura Mountains, and indicating the various walking paths. Next to the parking lot was a small rest area with an adventure playground, presumably intended for young, wannabe mountaineers not yet exhausted by the hikes they had done with their parents.

"It's four o'clock," Marc said. "We should be able to reach the summit well before nightfall."

Malvina gave him a sarcastic look. "What do you expect to find up there?"

"Nothing. You don't have to go up there with me, you know."

"God, you're stupid. Why do you think I came all this way?"

Inside the office, Marc bought a map of the region and a guidebook. A tall, long-haired brunette was at the cash register with a man standing behind her, touching her hand as he showed her which keys to press. With his other hand, he was brazenly caressing her bottom.

That must be Grégory, Marc thought, remembering the description of the nature preserve's resident Casanova in Grand-Duc's notebook.

Outside, Marc spread out the map on a table and showed Malvina the path they needed to take to reach the top of Mont Terri. Then he folded the map and opened the back door of the van, took out a backpack, and filled it with a comforter, a flashlight, a bottle of water, a sausage, and a few packages of cookies.

"Quite a supply of food you have in there," Malvina observed wryly.

"Yeah. There's not much space in my grandmother's house—no cellar, no garage—so she stores things in the van."

"Can I take something?"

"Help yourself," Marc said. "Just don't pack too much. You don't want your bag to be heavier than you."

"Just you worry about yourself, Vitral. I'll beat you to the top, no problem!"

Marc forced himself to laugh. He knew that there was no rational reason for the trip they were about to make: climbing Mont Terri, witnessing the scene of the crash for themselves, seeking out Grand-Duc's cabin and the grave next to it... He might find the detective anywhere, but certainly not up there. He was sinking into an obsessive spiral. The gold bracelet, the traces of human bone, the search for a homeless man who had witnessed the crash... These clues were like so many bread crumbs scattered on the ground by a sadistic Hansel. So what did he hope to find? A miraculous light that would show him the way?

Well, yes. In fact, that was exactly what he hoped to find.

They got on their way. As expected, the ascent took them a good two hours. Marc climbed quickly, and Malvina followed without showing any signs of fatigue. It was not a difficult climb: the slope was not too steep, and the path through the forest was clearly marked. As they ascended, the view below them—of the Doubs, the Swiss border, the fortified village of Saint-Ursanne—slowly revealed itself. Halfway up, they stopped to drink some water. The air was warm and slightly humid. Beneath his backpack, Marc's shirt was soaked with sweat.

They continued on the gently sloping path through the pine trees toward the summit of Mont Terri. Marc increased his pace and Malvina followed him, walking—even breathing—at the same rhythm. The physical effort was bringing them closer together, Marc thought, to his surprise, then decided that he was being ridiculous.

They came upon the scene of the tragedy with no warning.

The forest simply stopped, suddenly, as if a gang of woodcutters had cleared a narrow strip of land, about fifty yards wide and a few thousand yards long. Young pine trees had been planted, but they were no more than

three feet high, and were surrounded by a multicolored sea
of wildflowers: yellow and blue gentians, lady's-slipper
orchids, and orange-tinted arnica.

Marc and Malvina stood motionless, side by side.

No trace of the actual crash remained, apart from the
absence of tall trees. No monument, not even a marble
plaque or a sign. It was better this way, Marc thought. He
liked the wildflowers. In twenty years, the young pines
would reach the height of the surrounding trees, their
branches would spread out, and gradually the wildflowers would die away, starved of sunlight, to be replaced by
ferns and moss, and perhaps a few daffodils.

Then everything that had occurred here would be
forgotten.

Marc remained where he was, on the edge of the clearing, as if he dared not profane the site of the tragedy.
Malvina waded through the thigh-high grass. Marc's
heartbeat accelerated, and he had trouble swallowing.
He knew these symptoms all too well, even if they were
appearing more slowly than they normally would, perhaps
because of the altitude. His agoraphobia...

He said nothing. He did not move. He took deep breaths.
Malvina must have heard him, or perhaps she heard nothing and was surprised, or perhaps—why not?—she understood how he felt. In any case, she turned around. She
squinted in the sunlight, and it looked almost as if she
were smiling. A sad smile, a melancholic truce, a peaceful despair. Marc coughed. He would never have admitted this to Malvina, but the sight of her smile helped him
breathe more easily. Something about the presence of this
crazy girl reassured him, particularly here, in this secret
place that meant so much to both of them.

They must have stayed there for more than an hour. The sunlight was almost level with the treetops.

"Shall we go look for the cabin?" Marc said quietly.

Malvina said nothing. She simply followed him.

Marc had to check the map several times. They spent nearly an hour wandering through the forest, retracing their steps from clearings that all looked the same. Marc began to wonder if Grand-Duc had invented the whole thing. Malvina didn't complain. In fact, she did her best to help Marc as he attempted to decipher the guidebook. Night was falling when they finally saw the shepherd's hut, just as Grand-Duc had described it. For one brief moment, Marc hoped that the detective would be waiting for them inside. Instinctively, he touched the Mauser in his pocket.

But the cabin was empty. It was cleaner than Grand-Duc had suggested, but then he had picked up a good deal of litter, sending it off to be analyzed by his friend in the forensics laboratory. All in the course of his search for Georges Pelletier.

Had that man really existed?

Marc came out of the cabin and inspected the grave. Everything was exactly as the notebook had described it: the earth, the scattered stones, two broken bits of wood that might once have formed a cross. So, Grand-Duc had not lied about this at least. In all probability, this grave really had contained a link from a gold chain and traces of human bone.

But what did that change now?

Marc looked at his watch. It was 7:36 p.m.

He had not heard from Lylie since the text he had read in the van. He sat on a tree stump, a few yards from the hut. The sun was setting, on the roof of the world, and here he was, far from everything. Alone with a crazy girl. Although it turned out that she wasn't as crazy as he had imagined. She wasn't dangerous or spiteful either.

The game was over and he had lost. Now he would allow the painful memories to wash over him; he would wallow in morbid nostalgia in order to avoid thinking about the fact that Lylie was, at that moment, going to sleep in a hospital room. That she would have an abortion a few hours from now, simply as a precaution, because the fruit of their love might be nothing but poison.

He also wished to avoid thinking about the fact that the only person who could help him—his grandfather's murderer—was roaming free somewhere, and that there was no chance of finding him.

"It's ready!"

On one corner of a blanket Malvina had laid out the bottle of water, the packages of cookies, and the sausage.

"Quite a feast, isn't it?"

They ate in silence. The cabin was illuminated now only by moonlight, so it looked like some kind of witch's hovel. They both knew it was too late to go back down, so they would have to sleep here, together. Without ever saying a word about it, they were in agreement: this was why they had come.

To spend a night on Mont Terri.

Two orphans lost in a cemetery without headstones.

When they had put away the remains of the food, Marc took Grand-Duc's notebook from his bag and handed it to Malvina.

"You've been looking for this for quite a while, haven't you? Maybe you'll find something in there that I couldn't see."

"This is the dickhead's journal?"

"Exactly."

"Thanks."

Malvina took the notebook, her comforter, and a flashlight and went into the cabin. Marc walked off on his own, wandering through the forest, finding his way by flashlight. When he returned, the interior of the cabin was dimly illuminated by Malvina's flashlight, but the girl herself was asleep. Grand-Duc's notebook was lying open, next to her head.

Marc smiled. In spite of himself, he felt increasingly tender toward this hate-filled young woman, as if—despite being four years older than he— she were another little sister that he had to protect. Quietly he picked up the green notebook and went outside to sit on the tree stump. He turned the pages, until he reached the last one. The final lines:

In this notebook, I have reviewed all the clues, all the leads, all the theories I have found in eighteen years of investigation. It is all here, in these hundred or so pages. If you have read them carefully, you will now know as much as I do. Perhaps you will be more perceptive than I. Perhaps you will find something I have missed. The key to the mystery, if one exists. Perhaps...

For me, it's over.

It would be an exaggeration to say that I have no regrets, but I have done my best.

"I have done my best."

Marc was not seized with any new inspiration. He tried

calling Lylie, but there was no signal here on this mountainside. He cursed his own stupidity. Unable to talk to Lylie, he reread her messages, from the first to the last, the one he had received earlier that day:

The operation will take place tomorrow at 10:00 a.m. Don't worry, everything will be fine. I'll call you afterward.

Tomorrow at ten.

He felt so utterly useless.

An owl hooted. Marc pointed his flashlight in the direction of the sound, but saw only branches and leaves.

"Where are you hiding?" he asked the darkness.

The owl did not respond.

"I wonder how long you've been on this mountain, watching over it every night. Were you here when the big metal bird crashed into your kingdom, all those years ago? Did you see Georges Pelletier sleeping here in this cabin? Did you see the grave he dug, and the bracelet? And Grand-Duc—did you see him, too?"

After a while, Marc went back into the cabin. He was cold. He wrapped himself up in his comforter and lay down close to Malvina, staring up at the night sky through the holes in the roof. He had to keep thinking until his subconscious, his memory gave him a sign, a light in the darkness. He had to use every minute of the hours that remained.

Malvina tossed and turned in her sleep, emitting little noises occasionally. As time passed, she inched closer to Marc, her body instinctively seeking the warmth of his. Had she ever slept with a man before? Even next to a man?

It must be long past midnight now. Marc had not slept a

wink the night before. Exhausted, he sank into sleep without even being aware of it.

It was Malvina who woke him, crying out like a demented woman. She was standing in the middle of the room, her whole body trembling. Two skinny legs emerged from the sweater she had worn to bed, and she was hopping up and down on her feet as if the floor were made of hot coals.

"Are you OK?" Marc asked huskily.

"Yeah, yeah. Don't worry about me. I'm used to it."

She lay down under her comforter again. Marc watched her, worried.

"I told you, I'm fine!"

"Are you sure?"

"Yes! Stop bugging me and go back to sleep."

Malvina turned her back on Marc. Her comforter was touching his in a way that seemed strangely intimate.

Four in the morning. It was now or never. He had to do something, or it would be too late.

Malvina was already asleep again.

What could he do? He gazed up into the dark sky. Stars appeared and vanished, presumably hidden by invisible clouds moving in the wind. Like false shooting stars on which people would make wishes that never came true. Like the flashing lights of an airplane, confused with the distant constellations beyond. Closer. More ephemeral.

Marc kept thinking about the last lines in the green notebook: Grand-Duc's aborted suicide attempt.

Had he been bluffing? Or had he really discovered something that night, after finishing his account of the eighteen-year investigation? Some new piece of evidence that he never wrote in the notebook... Marc tried to remember Malvina's exact words, when she had spoken about this on the train. Before his eyes, the only two constellations he was able to recognize—Ursa Major and Lyra—had disappeared.

Grand-Duc called my grandmother the day before yesterday. He was still alive then. He told her he had found something. The solution to the mystery, or so he claimed. Just like that, at five minutes to midnight on the last day of his contract! Just before he was about to shoot himself in the head, with the edition of the Est Républicain *from December 23, 1980, spread out on the desk beneath him. He said he needed a day or two to gather evidence, but he was absolutely sure that he had solved the mystery. Oh, and he needed an extra one hundred and fifty thousand francs…*

Marc considered her words. If he had not been lying, then Grand-Duc had discovered the solution to the mystery in his office, next to the fireplace where his archives were burning, at five minutes to midnight. The next morning, Marc had performed a thorough search of that office, but he had not found anything apart from a corpse. Nor had Malvina. What had they missed? Marc tried to imagine the scene of the detective's suicide. The pistol pressed to his temple, the old newspaper laid out in front of him. Why had Grand-Duc not pulled the trigger? What had he heard? Or seen?

Or read?

The idea came suddenly. Of course—the newspaper! The edition of the *Est Républicain* that had appeared on December 23, 1980. This would have been the last thing the detective saw before squeezing the trigger.

What if the solution to the mystery was printed in an eighteen-year-old newspaper?

*

Marc got up quietly, being careful not to wake Malvina. He threw his belongings into his backpack, then pulled a piece of paper from his pocket and wrote on the back:

Gone to buy croissants.

Marc

He left the note on the floor, close to Malvina's head. He left the guidebook there, too, but kept the map for himself. One last time, Marc looked at the shape of Malvina's small body, lost under the oversize comforter. She would have no problem finding her way back down the mountain.

Outside, the sun had not yet risen, but the sky was beginning to lighten, the stars fading one by one. Dawn on the last day. Marc thought of Lylie, in her white-walled room.

He set off.

57

October 4, 1998, 6:05 a.m.

Six in the morning. Grand-Duc stretched out inside the Xantia. He was parked on a path where tufts of grass grew between wheel ruts, near Dannemarie, about a hundred feet from the chalet in which Mélanie Belvoir—or, rather Mélanie Luisans, as she called herself now—lived.

From that position he could easily see any vehicles coming from the village long before they could see him. See without being seen. Rule 1 of being a private detective. It had been years since he had spent a night doing a stakeout. The experience reminded him of his younger days, before the de Carville contract: all those nights he had spent watching people enter and exit casinos on the Basque coast or the Côte d'Azur. Nazim's Xantia was almost as uncomfortable as the old bangers he used to drive then.

The detective took a Thermos from the glove compartment and poured some coffee into a plastic cup. The liquid burned his lips as he sipped it.

He had time. Mélanie Belvoir was not due to return until 9:00 a.m. She was a nurse in the Belfort-Montbéliard hospital, and she worked the night shift. Yesterday, Grand-Duc had spent a long time talking to her on the phone before she finally let down her guard. He had recorded their conversation, naturally. Afterward he had spent several hours at Monique Genevez's cottage, transcribing the interview on his laptop. He had printed out a copy, which now lay in an envelope on the passenger seat next to him. All he needed was Mélanie Belvoir's signature on the document.

Grand-Duc drank more coffee. It tasted of plastic.

How much would Mathilde de Carville be willing to pay for that envelope? A lot of money, undoubtedly. A fortune. At least as much as he had earned during the last eighteen years...

Grand-Duc felt no qualms about screwing the de Carvilles for all he could get. They could afford it, after all. And no amount of money, he suspected, would ever compensate him for the burden of his conscience.

He bit his lip as a wave of guilt swept over him. This reward really ought to have been shared between him and Nazim. Not fifty-fifty, of course, but his friend would have had enough to buy a villa in Turkey. However, Nazim had refused to follow him on this. He seemed to think the de Carvilles had paid enough already, and that the case was over. Crédule Grand-Duc knew he shouldn't have raised his voice: Nazim was adorable, but he was also very nervous.

"I'll go to the police, Crédule," he had warned. "I will, I swear, if you don't leave me in peace. This whole business has been eating away at me for so long..."

"What's that supposed to mean?"

Grand-Duc had smelled a rat then. Nazim was not the type to make idle threats. The detective had demanded explanations, guarantees, and then everything had spun out of control. Nazim had pulled a gun on him, but Grand-Duc had been quicker to squeeze the trigger. That was all. He had never wanted, or intended, to kill Nazim. But it had happened, and when Nazim's head fell into the fireplace, an idea had sparked in Grand-Duc's mind. All he had to do to make his friend's face unrecognizable was to push it a little farther into the flames. He had pulled him out briefly, to shave what remained of his mustache, and to dress him in Grand-Duc's own clothes, shoes, and watch, just in case Lylie or Marc became too curious.

He had not intended to kill Ayla either, but he'd had no choice. Grand-Duc knew her; she would go straight to the police. Nazim had not taken part in the murder of Pierre Vitral, but he knew about it, and he had undoubtedly told his wife everything. It was hardly Grand-Duc's fault if Nazim wasn't astute enough to keep secrets from her. She had called him, the day before, and left several panicky messages. He'd had no choice but to return to Paris, and to tail her discreetly from her kebab shop to his house, and then to the forest in Coupvray. Which was, as it happened, the perfect place to kill her. After that, he had driven back to the Jura Mountains, doing one hundred and ten miles per hour, in order to get there early enough to follow the mailman and finally put this case to rest.

Grand-Duc forced himself to finish the contents of the plastic cup. The coffee was bitter, hard to swallow.

Nazim Ozan. Ayla Ozan.

For years they had been his best friends. His only friends. And now he had murdered them.

What a farce life was!

Yes, the de Carvilles could pay for all of that.

*

Grand-Duc checked the time, displayed in retro green digits on the Xantia's clock.

6:15 a.m.

He still had time. He was the earliest bird, and he was going to catch this worm.

58

October 4, 1998, 6:29 a.m.

Marc parked the van in a parking lot in the center of Mont-béliard. It had taken him about an hour and a half to come back down Mont Terri, then three-quarters of an hour to drive here. He had gone into the first café he could see that was open, and the waiter had given him the address of the *Est Républicain*: 12 Place Jules-Viette.

The offices were closed, although that was hardly a surprise, given the hour. But he couldn't give up on his final hope: solving the mystery of Lylie's identity before their baby was aborted. In less than four hours' time...

A metal grille on the window made it impossible for him to see inside the offices. Marc turned around and noticed three trucks in the parking lot where he had left his van, all painted with the *Est Républicain* logo. Clearly, the delivery of the morning newspapers had not yet been completed. All was not lost.

Marc walked quickly to the back of the building, where three workmen were standing in front of a warehouse entrance, loading a van with piles of newspapers wrapped in clear plastic. From a radio, he heard the cheery voice of a DJ announcing the day's horoscope.

"Good morning," Marc said to one of them. "Are the offices closed?"

He bit his lip. It was a stupid question, and he knew it. The workman looked at him and replied without even bothering to remove the cigarette from his mouth.

"You're in luck. I'll be at my desk in five minutes..."

For one brief moment, Marc felt hope fluttering inside his chest.

"Just give me time to put on my skirt and makeup, and I'm all yours."

The man's colleagues sniggered. Marc swallowed his embarrassment.

"Come back in three hours, kid," one of the men told him. "We're kind of busy right now."

"I'm sorry, sir," Marc said, "but this is urgent. Is there really no one who could open the offices for me? I just need to check something..."

"He could always ask Superbitch," one of the men suggested.

The other two laughed.

"All right, if you insist," the first man said with a sigh. He pressed an intercom in the doorway of the warehouse.

"Mrs. Montaigu? There's someone here to see you, at the warehouse entrance."

A few minutes later, Mrs. Montaigu appeared. "Superbitch" was an elegantly dressed young woman with a small waist and nicely tanned legs, but her face was pinched in an expression so severe that it seemed almost comical. Clearly the years she had spent arduously climbing the company ladder had taken their toll. A small pair of spectacles was posed at the end of her nose. She held a stack of papers in one hand and a pen in the other.

"What is it?" she asked irritatedly.

Marc tried to think quickly. What story could he invent that would persuade this unsympathetic woman to open the offices so early? Should he take out the Mauser and threaten her with it? Probably not a good idea.

"So?" Mrs. Montaigu demanded, glancing at her watch.

In a panic, he stammered: "Um, listen... I need to check an old edition of your newspaper. Very old, in fact. The edition from December 23, 1980..."

The woman managed a small smile. "I assume it must be urgent, given the look on your face."

"You have no idea."

"Maybe not, but I don't see why it can't wait until nine o'clock."

The three workmen were following this conversation closely. Mrs. Montaigu had already turned on her high, thin heels when Marc shouted: "Wait!"

She turned around, her face a mask of pure annoyance.

Without thinking, Marc told her the truth. "Please... my wife is pregnant. And she is due to have an abortion in three hours because she has doubts about the identity of her parents. I have good reason to believe that the truth about her identity can be found in that edition of your newspaper..."

Mrs. Montaigu stared at him, aghast. The three workmen had stopped what they were doing to eavesdrop on the conversation. Superbitch gave them a fierce look, and they got back to work. She then turned her furious gaze on Marc.

"So you think you have the right to prevent your wife from having an abortion, do you? And you really believe that…"

"For fuck's sake!" Marc yelled. "Don't give me a stupid lecture! I just want to look at that newspaper. All I'm asking for is a chance…"

The woman appeared to be too shocked to respond. Marc took advantage of her silence to press his point: "You remember the airplane that crashed into Mont Terri?"

Mrs. Montaigu shook her head. Not surprising, thought Marc; she would probably only have been about ten years old at the time. He had no choice but to keep going.

"The *Est Républicain* scooped every other paper in the country when it discovered there had been one survivor. A baby. They called her 'Dragonfly.' The miracle child. That baby is my wife…"

Clearly, the woman had no idea what he was talking about. She was out of her depth, and she didn't like it.

"Marcel," she said to the oldest of the three workmen, "do you remember this crash on Mont Terri?"

Marcel, who had been waiting for this moment, discreetly dropped his cigarette butt to the ground. "Absolutely," he replied. "It was the biggest event this region had ever seen. Christmas 1980. Nearly two hundred people dead…"

"And the newspaper was involved?"

"We were ahead of everyone! None of the Paris papers had the story, but we did. The child who survived. It was all over the TV by the next day. The newspaper included an article about it every day for months. I'll spare you the details, but…"

"Do you remember the name of the girl?" the woman interrupted.

"Of course. It was Emilie Vitral."

Mrs. Montaigu turned to Marc. "And you are?"

"Marc Vitral."

"Her husband?"

Marc hesitated. "Yes... Well, actually... it's a bit com-plicated..."

"What time is your wife supposed to have the abortion?"

"Ten o'clock."

"Here?"

"No. In Paris."

The woman sighed. "This is unbelievable..."

"Please... all I want to do is look at that old newspaper. I swear, if I save the life of my child, I'll make you the godmother!"

Superbitch laughed coldly. "Whatever you do, don't do that. I can't stand kids."

Finally, after another sigh, she said, "All right, follow me."

Marc was taken to a large room in the basement where the archives were kept. The room was windowless, the walls unpainted, and the only light came from fluorescent strip lights on the ceiling. Back issues of the *Est Républi-cain* were filed in wooden cabinets, classified by year and month.

Marc opened the drawer labeled *1980, December*. He found the edition he was looking for and placed it on the table in the middle of the room.

The front page was mostly covered by a large color photograph of the burning remains of the crashed Air-bus. It was a scene of utter devastation. But below this was a smaller photograph showing a baby being held by a fireman outside Belfort-Montbéliard hospital. Lylie. The caption beneath it read:

The Airbus 5403, flying from Istanbul to Paris, crashed into Mont Terri, on the Franco-Swiss border, last night. Of the 169 passengers and flight crew on board, 168 were killed upon impact or perished in the flames. The sole survivor was a baby, three months old, thrown from the plane when it collided with the mountainside, before the cabin was consumed by fire.

And that was all.

Marc spent a long time looking closely at the photographs—the faces in the background, the fuselage in flames, the trees, the snow—and rereading the caption.

But there was nothing new here at all. Nothing.

All he had found was another dead end. The very last one.

Marc sat with his head in his hands, then leaned back and stared at the blank walls. Only then did he bother looking at the other stories on the front page. Not that there was much: Sochaux's 3–1 win over Angers; a strike at a glasses factory near Morez in the Haut-Jura; details of Father Christmas's appearances in the region's villages…

And a very short piece, right at the bottom of the page, no more than a few words. A missing persons ad.

Mélanie Belvoir. 18 years old. Missing since December 2.

Next to these words was a small color photograph.

Marc almost fainted. It was impossible. It had to be a fake, a forgery.

The face of this eighteen-year-old girl, Mélanie Belvoir, was instantly and heartrendingly familiar to him. It was Lylie's face.

This was not the photograph of a girl who looked like her. It *was* her. The same azure eyes, the same cheekbones, the same smile, the same dimple on her chin. Only the haircut differed: Lylie's hair was slightly shorter.

The photograph published in this newspaper eighteen years ago was an exact replica of Lylie's current ID photo: the one on her student card, the one on her travel card, the one that Marc kept in his wallet.

It was unbelievable!

On the same page of the newspaper, dated December 23, 1980, were two photographs of Lylie: one showing her at three months old, in the arms of a fireman; the other at eighteen years old, beautiful and smiling, just as she had been the last time he saw her, two days ago, on October 2, 1998.

Was he going crazy?

Was he dreaming? Would he wake up at any moment, covered in sweat, next to Lylie?

Or, far worse, next to Malvina, in the cabin on Mont Terri…

59

The rays of sunlight shone through the holes in the cabin's roof, moving across the floor until eventually they touched Malvina's face. To begin with, she savored the pleasant warmth on her skin, then turned over a couple of times beneath the comforter before finally opening her eyes.

Half asleep, she reached over to touch the comforter next to hers. Her hand found only dry earth. Marc had vanished. Only a note remained in his place:

Gone to buy croissants.
Marc

The bastard! Next to his note was the guidebook. The message was clear: *You're on your own!*

Cursing, Malvina got to her feet. She had been stupid ever to put her trust in a Vitral. What had she been thinking? Now look at her: stuck up a mountain, on her own, with a cell phone that had no signal. Like some naive child, she had walked straight into a trap. And now there was only one solution: to go back down the mountain.

*

Malvina left everything behind her in the cabin—comforter, flashlight, food—and immediately began walking down the mountainside, eyes fixed angrily on the ground. Not once during her descent did she even glance at the sliver of morning sun that made the Swiss mountains look like the Himalayas.

One hour later, the nature preserve office came into view. A few children were already messing around in the adventure playground while their parents spent a ridiculously long time tying the laces of their walking boots. Marc's van was not in the parking lot, of course. The piece of shit really had abandoned her.

She checked her phone. Finally, a signal. She would be able to get out of this hellhole. There was a message on her voice mail. Someone had tried to get hold of her last night. Her grandmother, probably. Who else could it be? Malvina clicked on the message and was surprised to see that it came from an unknown number.

Marc Vitral? Crédule Grand-Duc?

She put the phone to her ear.

"Malvina, it's Rachel. Rachel de Carville, your great-aunt…"

Her great-aunt, heir to the Elytis and La Baule perfumeries. What the hell did *she* want? They hadn't spoken in years.

"Malvina, my poor girl. You must call me as soon as possible. Something awful has happened at Coupvray. Oh, darling…your grandmother and your grandfather have both passed away. They were found this morning, in their beds, and neither was breathing. They went to heaven together, my poor angel…"

Malvina switched off her phone. Her arm fell to her side as if the phone suddenly weighed a ton. For a long time she stared into the dark forest, newly aware of the silence that surrounded her. Then she reached for her bag. There was no time to think, cry, or even pray. She had to act. To understand. To seek vengeance. She had one sole target to focus on. A very real target and still very much alive.

Inside the bag, her fingers tightened around the handle of the Mauser L110. Vitral thought he was so clever, but he had made the mistake of falling asleep last night. She was good at pretending to be a mad girl tortured by nightmares when it suited her. All she'd had to do was grab her gun back. Anyway, that hypocrite would never have been capable of using the revolver. Unlike her.

60

"Hello, Jennifer speaking."

Marc was still in the archives of the *Est Républicain.*
His friend at France Telecom was working all that weekend. This was the one advantage he had, and he could not
afford to waste it.

"Jennifer, it's Marc again. I need another favor. It's a big
one..."

"You can ask me whatever you want. You know that
Marc."

"I need a phone number and an address. Mélanie Bel
voir. B-E-L-V-O-I-R."

"Whereabouts?"

"Try the area around the Jura and the Doubs first, then
all over Franche-Comté. And then just try anywhere in
France."

"No problem..."

Marc heard the muffled sound of Jennifer's fingertip
tapping the keys of her computer keyboard. He could no
stop staring at the photograph on the front page of the
newspaper spread out before him. The resemblance wa

uncanny, almost surreal. Who was this Mélanie Belvoir?
There had to be some rational explanation...

"Sorry, Marc," said Jennifer. "Nothing at all."

"Maybe she's unlisted."

"I tried that, too. *Nada!*"

"Shit. Are there any other Belvoirs in France?"

"Hang on..."

More muffled typing.

"Yeah. Three hundred and forty-eight of them."

"And in the Jura?"

"Let me see...Oh, that's narrowed it down. Only
twenty-three. But no Mélanie."

"Maybe she changed her name..."

"Who is she, this Mélanie?"

"Sorry, Jen, it would take way too long to explain. The
craziest stuff has been happening, but I'm in a desperate
rush. Could you try checking cancellation requests under
the name of Mélanie Belvoir?"

"How do I do that?"

"Look in the archives. You can get in through the
administrator's account and do a search on cancellation
requests—they date right back to when our records were
first digitized. That was at least fifteen years ago."

"We're not supposed to do that, Marc. I could get
fired..."

"Don't worry. I've done it loads of times. Please, Jen,
it's urgent..."

"You owe me big-time for this, Marc. I want to be taken
out to dinner somewhere *really* nice."

"Anything you want, I promise. Just do it, please."

Again, Marc heard the sound of Jennifer's fingertips
tap-dancing on the keyboard.

"OK, I want a two-star restaurant, at the very least. God knows I deserve it! I've found the woman you're looking for. She canceled her subscription with France Telecom five years ago, on January 23, 1993. At the time, she was living at 65 Rue du Comte-de-la-Suze in Belfort. Since then, not a trace of her."

"OK, Jennifer. Could you check requests for call forwarding?"

"What?"

"Call forwarding. Usually when customers cancel their subscription, it's because they're moving or going to live with someone else, so they ask for calls to their old number to be forwarded to the new one, for a few months. That's archived, too, and you can access it in the same way, through the administrator's account."

"You're unbelievable! Three stars—I want a three-star restaurant for this! And as much champagne as I can drink."

"You've got it, I promise. And Hungarian violinists if you want them…"

"I'm going to hold you to that."

The seconds of silence that followed seemed interminable to Marc.

"You were right," Jennifer said finally. "Mélanie Belvoir requested call forwarding to a number belonging to Laurent Luisans. I assume you want the address? The village is Dannemarie, in the Doubs, and the address is 45 Route de Villars. You realize this information is strictly confidential. What do you want with this woman? Is she an ex? Does it have anything to do with the list of hospitals I gave you the other day?"

Marc frantically scribbled down the address on the

first piece of paper he could find: the front page of the *Est Républicain*.

"You're the best, Jen! I'll take you out to dinner and explain then, I promise. Champagne, the works...Could you do me one last favor? Are you connected to the Internet right now?"

Jennifer sighed. "Yes..."

"Can you find me the shortest route from Montbéliard to that address?"

"Jesus Christ...Who do you think I am, Miss Moneypenny?"

The Citroën slowly climbed the road that led to the Swiss border, seven miles farther on. Marc kept his foot firmly pressed to the accelerator, but that did nothing to encourage his van. Gradually, as it moved higher up the hillside, he left the edge of the town. The road snaked around a waterfall before continuing its upward trajectory. The villages became smaller and less numerous, until the only human dwellings along the route were a few scattered chalets.

The village of Dannemarie appeared as the van rounded a bend. According to Jennifer's directions, Mélanie Belvoir's chalet was located as the road left the village, a little higher still, closer to Switzerland, just beneath the ridgeline. Marc drove through the silent village. It was eight in the morning, and there was not even a bakery or a café open. One last turn and he left the village. Marc braked and parked the van on the pavement.

It would have been madness to drive to the doorstep and throw himself into the mouth of the wolf. Crédule Grand-Duc was undoubtedly on Mélanie Belvoir's trail, too, and after years of visiting the Vitrals in Dieppe he would recognize the orange-and-red van from miles away. He might as well have driven up honking his horn.

It was cold outside. Marc walked quickly, and spotted the Xantia after the third bend in the winding road. It was hidden on a small path, just off the main road. A little higher, he could see a chalet—Mélanie Belvoir's, almost certainly. Walking on the dew-wet grass beside the road, Marc approached the Xantia, making sure he couldn't be seen in the vehicle's rearview mirror.

The detective sat calmly inside the car, a white plastic cup in his hand. Marc moved stealthily toward him. If anything went wrong, he knew he could always use the Mauser, but his plan—if you could call it that—was to take a more direct approach. Grand-Duc was nearly sixty-five years old, while Marc was twenty, fit and strong. There was not much doubt over who would win in a fight.

The detective did not have time to react. The Xantia's door was wrenched open and he was grabbed by the arm and pulled roughly to the ground. Before he had even caught a glimpse of his assailant, he took a kick to the ribs that cracked a few bones, causing him to curl up in pain. Then a second kick, to the coccyx. "Bast..." His curse was swallowed up by the mountain's immense silence.

Another kick. He managed to turn onto his back. A man was towering over him.

Marc Vitral.

It wasn't possible. How could he have found him here so quickly?

"Marc?" Grand-Duc groaned. "How did you..."

The detective spat blood onto the dusty ground and attempted to get up. Marc's foot pushed down on his chest.

"Stay where you are or I'll crush you like a cockroach."

"Marc, what are you..."

"Shut the fuck up. I don't want to hear any more of your bullshit. I've spent the last two days reading your lies. Your life, your investigation, your hypocritical soul-searching..." Marc pressed his foot down harder on Grand-Duc's chest, and the detective gasped. "Let's get straight to the point. I know you killed my grandfather. You would have killed my grandmother, too, if you could..."

"Marc, surely you don't believe..."

Marc's boot lifted from Grand-Duc's chest and landed on his face, crushing his nose and mouth.

"I don't have time for this crap, Crédule-la-Bascule."

The detective spat blood again. He seemed to be having trouble breathing.

"How did you find out? Did...was it the de Carvilles who told you? Mathilde? Malvina?"

"I worked it out for myself, believe it or not. Like a big boy."

"I...I never wanted to do it. You have to believe me. I...was just following orders...I regretted it. I was honest after that...I really loved..."

Marc kicked Grand-Duc in the collarbone. The detective rolled over, howling with pain. His bloodied hand touched his shoulder. "Please, Marc, stop this. Please, I..."

"Shut up, then. And spare me all your poetic nonsense about remorse, and love. I'm not interested in that. The only thing I want to know is Lylie's identity. The truth!"

For the first time, Grand-Duc's lips curved into a sort of smile. "So you haven't understood...not everything, at least. You still have need of my services as a detective..."

Marc raised his foot threateningly again.

"Not necessarily. It's up to you to prove that to me."

"But how did you find me so quickly?"

"I'm not as slow as you think. But stop playing for time. Tell me the truth about the DNA tests. And that photograph of Lylie in the newspaper."

"But...your grandfather...did someone sell me out or did you really guess yourself?"

"I really did figure it out myself. I already told you that! Now quit stalling..."

Marc gave the detective another kick in the ribs. Grand-Duc's body twisted up in pain, and his arm reached down past his leg. Instantly Marc realized what he was doing: reaching for his gun.

Marc thrust his hand into his bag to grab the Mauser...

The bag was empty.

The Mauser had vanished.

Images of the night before flickered through Marc's brain: Malvina on her feet, awake while he slept, supposedly having had a nightmare...but it was too late for regrets.

Crédule Grand-Duc was aiming his revolver at Marc's chest.

"You were very quick, Marc. Seriously, I'm impressed. But you let your feelings get in the way. A classic mistake. You held all the winning cards—an old man at your mercy, the solution to the mystery only a few feet away, on the passenger seat of my car, the finale to my famous notebook... Yes, what you want to know is just there, inside an envelope. A few pages that explain everything and could make me a fortune. All you had to do was reach in and take it..."

Shakily, Grand-Duc stood up. His lip was bleeding and

his beige jacket was heavily stained with blood and dirt. He could barely even put weight on his right leg. Marc said nothing. He was furious with himself. To have come so close and to fail right at the end. It was so stupid...

"You were pretty tough on me, Marc. But I guess I deserved it. In your place, I'd have done the same thing. Worse, probably..."

The detective stretched his left arm gingerly while aiming the revolver steadily at Marc with his right hand.

"Sorry, Marc, but you leave me no choice. Do you understand? You're the only other person in the world who knows the truth about your grandfather. Except old Léonce, of course, but he's hardly going to spill the beans, is he? Killing you is the last thing I want, Marc, but what else can I do?"

Finally, Marc managed to say a few words. Looking over at the Xantia, he asked quietly: "Did you say the same thing to Nazim Ozan?"

Grand-Duc shrugged. He stood gingerly on his injured leg. "Life is full of surprises, Marc. It's hard to swim against the current. Five days ago, I was planning to commit suicide. At home, all alone. Everything was ready, my finger on the trigger. Game over. Now, I've won. Yet I've had to murder two of the people I love most in the world— Nazim and Ayla. You are the third, sadly."

Marc shivered. He was ten feet away from the barrel of the Mateba, which was now pointed at his head. It would be futile to attempt to disarm the detective. If Marc moved an inch, he would be shot, he had no doubt about that. The mountain road by which they stood was utterly deserted, and it was unlikely that any passing motorist would see them, hidden away on this small trail.

"Let me explain, Marc. I was paid a fortune to murder

a couple and make it look like an accident. I was a mercenary, and I had already killed people for relatively mis-
erable sums all over the world. Léonce de Carville was
offering me more money than I had ever dreamed of. It
was an offer I couldn't refuse. How could I possibly know
that I would fall in love with one of my victims?"

If only he would shut up, thought Marc. The worst thing
was that Grand-Duc wasn't insane. He didn't even have
that excuse. Yet the words came out of Marc's mouth anyway. What was he thinking, that he could move this man?

"Listen, Lylie is pregnant. With my child. She's supposed to have an abortion at ten o'clock this morning."

The detective's revolver did not tremble.

"This was bound to happen, Marc. You shouldn't have
gotten involved. You might have lived happily ever after
with Lylie—the two of you make a sweet little couple. She
will be inconsolable. But you leave me no choice. Let's just
get it over with, shall we?"

Grand-Duc aimed the Mateba at Marc's heart, and Marc
stood, frozen, incapable of moving a muscle. Strangely, his
head was filled with happy memories of their house at Rue
Pocholle: birthday parties, Lylie playing the piano, Marc
and Crédule watching the World Cup together, the penalty
shoot-out and the Didier Six shirt...

"None of this should have happened, Marc, none of
this pain and grief. But it did, and it's no one's fault. Well,
maybe Mélanie Belvoir's... but even she thought she was
doing the right thing."

I should move, thought Marc. Throw myself at his feet
or something.

As if reading his mind, Grand-Duc took a few steps
backward, still gripping the revolver.

"We all hang on desperately to life, Marc, even when there's no hope left. That's the root of the problem. That whole battle between the Vitrals and the de Carvilles was pointless. Like all wars. It was just a misunderstanding. I think you know the truth now. They both died on that plane, Marc. Emilie *and* Lyse-Rose. They both died in the accident. I am so sorry, Marc, believe me."

Grand-Duc's finger squeezed the trigger.

The gunshot echoed across the summits in the vast white silence of the morning.

61

Crédule Grand-Duc crumpled to the ground. Blood poured from the hole in his back like a crimson spring.

Malvina stood behind him, the Mauser L110 gripped in both hands.

"Don't start thinking I did this to save your life, Vitral," she said. "I just can't stand people saying that Lyse-Rose is dead."

She let the Mauser fall to the ground. Her whole body was trembling. She wasn't pretending this time. She really had pulled the trigger, and killed a man.

"You...how did you..."

Malvina managed a nervous smile. "I'm not any more stupid than you. I had the same thought as you about the newspaper. That guy from the nature preserve, Grégory Morez, drove me to the offices of the *Est Républicain* in his Jeep. You'd already done the hard work for me. The newspaper was still spread out on the table where you'd left it, with Mélanie Belvoir's address written on the front page. I just jumped in a taxi and told the driver to drop me off where the road left Dannemarie."

Marc did not know what to say. Should he thank Malvina? Give her a hug? Do nothing at all?

He moved toward her, but Malvina stiffened.

"Don't touch me!"

She suddenly collapsed to the ground, like a puppet. She was sobbing. Marc caught only snippets of her words: "Grandma and Grandpa...to heaven, yesterday...they're gone..."

He turned away and opened the door of the Xantia. Grand-Duc had not lied about the envelope at least: there it was, on the passenger seat. Marc tore it open. Inside were four typewritten pages. He walked over to where Malvina was curled up in the fetal position, still quietly weeping. He sat down next to her and began to read out loud:

"I am going to tell you everything, Mr. Grand-Duc. I never did anything wrong, after all. I have nothing to feel guilty about. I always knew I would have to tell the truth about this one day and, now that you have found me, that time has come. I was what they call a 'difficult' teenager. By the time I was seventeen, my relationship with my parents was over. I had long since stopped going to school, and I was just hanging around, like so many other young people. My parents managed to drag me to the employment agency, and I went through a series of internships before I got a temping job at the nature preserve. It was only for a few weeks and my main task was to pick up garbage in the forest. There was me and a small group of other interns, and we were all working for Grégory Morez. He was incredibly handsome, and he could be very sweet with the girls he liked. He had this way of touching you that never felt invasive. He was more than ten years older than me. I fell in love with him, like so many others before me. We made love for the first time, in the middle of the forest, near a waterfall. After that we did it many times while I was still working there, and for several weeks afterward. Everywhere, in the most amazing places. I knew he had other girls, but I thought he felt differently about me. I thought he truly loved me. I wanted to believe all his promises. It's a cliché, really, isn't it? The stupid young woman and the old charmer…"

"What happened after that?"

"I became pregnant. I didn't realize until I was six weeks gone. By then, I was already on a downward spiral: no work, a family I hardly ever saw, and increasingly estranged from my friends. And I had this suicidal obsession with Grégory Morez. For his body, and the pleasure he gave me."

"Was Grégory the father?"

"Yes. He was the only man I had ever slept with. I told him about the baby one night, in a seedy hotel room in a suburb of Belfort, after we'd made love."

"How did he react?"

"Just as you'd expect, Mr. Grand-Duc. He showed me the door. He told me I was just a little whore who was trying to trap him. He said there was no proof he was the father and that I should get an abortion."

"But you didn't?"

"No, although I never really made a decision to keep the child—I simply let the weeks go past without doing anything. It all happened so quickly. I was still completely obsessed with Grégory. I was convinced that I could change his mind and win him back. And my life was going from bad to worse: I was living on the streets most of the time. I would only go back to my parents' house about once a week, and when my pregnancy became obvious I stopped going back altogether. I just phoned them instead."

"Did you give birth in a hospital?"

"Yes, in Montbéliard. I had just turned eighteen. I was in a bad state. The baby was very small—not even five pounds. She was born on August 27, 1980. I left the hospital one week later. I still hadn't filled out all the official forms. I ended up just dumping them in a trash can."

"It was that easy?"

"I saw dozens of doctors and nurses during the week I was in the hospital. I'm sure there must be some kind of proof that my child was born there. But who was going to check that the child was still with me, that I was bringing it up? None of my family ever knew anything about the baby."

"What name did you give her?"

"I never called her anything. I told the people at the hospital that I hadn't chosen a name yet, that I was waiting for the father. I left with my child in my arms. Within a few weeks, it was as if I had fallen out of normal society altogether. I had no connection with any of my family or friends. I slept in the street, breast-feeding my child anywhere I could. I was exhausted. I hung around with people who didn't judge me. Drunks and junkies, mostly. Sometimes I thought about going home and letting my parents look after me. Sometimes I dreamed I would take my little girl to Grégory and persuade him to help me bring her up. Even at that age, she had incredible blue eyes—a bit like mine, but even more like her father's. Sometimes I thought I would just lie down and die, right there on the pavement..."

"So why did you decide to leave the town?"

"I had no choice in the end. A teenager living on the streets of Montbéliard with a baby... you can't hide that kind of thing forever. After a few weeks, social services were after me. I knew how that would end. They would steal my daughter from me and take me back to my parents' place. Without even asking for my opinion. I should confess to you, Mr. Grand-Duc, that some of the things I did were not legal. I sold drugs, I shoplifted. I sold my body, too, more than once. So I had to leave Montbéliard, just to survive."

"And that was how you met Georges Pelletier?"

"Yes. He was like me, a total down-and-out, and he needed to get away from the police and social services, too. He thought I was cute, in spite of the mess I was in. I think he imagined himself becoming my pimp, although I never let him touch me. But we both wanted the same thing—to get away—and Mont Terri seemed the obvious place. It's close to Montbéliard, and I knew no one would ever look for me there. It was the beginning of December, but the weather was still fairly warm and we were used to sleeping outside. And, best of all, I would be close to Grégory. I imagined bumping into him, and him remembering how much he used to like me, and then seeing my daughter. Surely when he saw those eyes, I thought, he wouldn't be able to deny that he was the father. I know this must seem crazy, but... well, I *was* crazy. Grégory Morez was my only lifeline. I had to believe in him."

"Did you see him again?"

"We lived in a little cabin that we found, near the top of Mont Terri. It was cold, but we could light fires and had a roof over our heads. It was better than life on the streets.

really. I am going to answer your question, Mr. Grand-Duc, don't worry. I'm getting to it. Yes, I saw Grégory Morez. Almost every day. He saw me and he saw our baby, but he didn't recognize me. He never even glanced at me. I was no longer a sexy young girl. Life had chewed me up and spit me out. I had put on weight and my breasts were saggy. There was no sparkle in my eyes. I didn't look like the same person."

"Didn't you ever speak to him?"

"You don't understand, Mr. Grand-Duc. I felt humiliated. Utterly humiliated. Had I really grown so ugly? Had he been with other girls, since me? I finally realized that he would never touch me again, never feel attracted to me again. So why on earth would he want to have anything to do with my child? My last flicker of hope died on Mont Terri. My daughter was a millstone around my neck, and the two of us would drown together. Oh, you mustn't think that I didn't love my child, Mr. Grand-Duc. I adored her! But I had nothing left to give her. No father. No more milk. I didn't even have a name for her.

"The snow started falling suddenly one morning. It was December 22, 1980. Georges Pelletier and I tried to keep ourselves warm by building a campfire in the little hut, but I had to do everything, because he was high on heroin most of the time. He would have frozen to death if I hadn't been there. I even had to force him to go outside and gather firewood."

"And then night fell . . ."

"Yes. And the storm got worse. Pelletier was completely out of it. I don't think he even heard the crash. The whole cabin shook, as if there'd been an earthquake. It felt like the end of the world. From the door of the cabin, you could see the trees on fire, half a mile away. I wrapped up my baby in a blanket and went outside. It didn't feel cold anymore. In fact, the fire was so ferocious that I could feel my skin burning."

"Weren't you scared?"

"Not at all. It was a strange scene, unreal. Snow and fire together, and then this twisted plane lying on the mountaintop, the steel melting before my eyes as if it were plastic. I knew I was the first witness there, but I didn't realize the emergency services would take so long."

"And that's when you saw it?"

"The baby, you mean? Yes, Mr. Grand-Duc, that's when I saw it."

"Was it...?"

"Dead? Yes. Its face was all swollen and I think it must have died right away. No baby could possibly have survived in those conditions. It was hell. I still find it amazing that everyone believed the story of the miracle child... Yes, the baby was dead, Mr. Grand-Duc. And I immediately felt that it wasn't fair."

"What do you mean?"

"That it was cruel, if you prefer. A whole family would cry for the loss of that baby. It was a little girl—she was wearing a dress. So many people would grieve for her. So many lives would be ruined. And yet there I was, with a baby of my own, unable to offer it any kind of future. And she would live, but without anything, anyone, apart from me. Do you understand now what I mean?"

"I understand."

"It seemed such an obvious thing to do. The dead baby in the snow was practically the same age as my baby. I acted on impulse. For the first time in my life, I felt I could do something positive for someone, something useful. Bring a dead baby back to life, save another family from grief, and give my daughter a better future. I felt as if I was saving a life. That must be how nurses and firemen feel, I thought. And it was this feeling, which took me by surprise that night, that made me decide I wanted to become a nurse. I wanted to save lives."

"You undressed the dead baby?"

"Yes, Mr. Grand-Duc, in order to save it. I was giving my daughter a loving family, a family with a home and with money, who would never be aware of my sacrifice, who would cry in gratitude for the miracle that had saved their baby. To me, it seemed like there was almost something sacred about what I was doing..."

"But that's not what happened..."

"How could I have guessed there were two babies on that plane? How could I have imagined the consequences? I thought I was doing something good, Mr. Grand-Duc. Afterward, I read the newspapers and followed the story. The families being torn apart. The verdict. But what could I do? What could I say? Apart from saying nothing. It should have been so much simpler...I waited with my baby for about an hour that night, holding her in my arms until I heard the first firemen approaching. Then I left my daughter in the snow, in her new clothes, far enough from the plane that she would be warmed by the fire without being burned. I kissed her good-bye and ran away into the night, carrying the dead baby wrapped up in my blanket."

"Was it you who buried her next to the cabin?"

"Who else? Pelletier was still asleep, high as a kite. I dug up the earth with my bare hands. It took so long. My fingers were bleeding. Pelletier woke up and saw me just as I was close to finishing. The baby's corpse was already in the grave. I was inventing prayers before I covered the body with soil because I didn't know any real ones. Pelletier went crazy. He thought I had killed my own child..."

"And then he saw the bracelet on the baby's wrist. Is that when he realized the child wasn't yours?"

"Yes. I was so upset, I hadn't even noticed the bracelet, but he saw it right away. And it was gold, too. So we made a deal. I let him have the bracelet in return for keeping his mouth shut. He left that night and I never saw him again. I filled in the grave with soil and found some stones to pile up on top of it. My fingers were so cold I could hardly even bend them. It took me forever to make a little cross from two bits of wood. I spent the rest of the night in the cabin, near the embers of the fire. I barely slept a wink that night. Or the next night..."

"You came back to tend the grave, afterward?"

"Little by little, I began to live again. My parents were looking for me—they put that missing persons ad in the newspaper, as you know—and in the end, I returned to Belfort. I went back to school, then to college. I became a nurse. I met Laurent six years ago. Laurent Luisans. He's an orderly at the hospital. My parents are both dead: my father died five years ago, my mother last year. Laurent and I are not married, but I decided to take his name. He doesn't know anything about my past. Nobody knows. Laurent wants us to have a child. It's not too late for me. I'm only thirty-six. But I don't know...It's complicated."

"I can see that, Mélanie. But you never answered my question, about the grave."

"I'm getting to that. Yes, I did go back every year, on August 27, my child's birthday. I felt as if the baby I had buried was my own child, you see. Not a stranger's. Not Lyse-Rose. I came back to tend the grave and put flowers by the cross. One year, a long time ago—in 1987, I think—I noticed that someone had disturbed the stones. I didn't know who, but I knew that the battle between the two families was still going on. That it would never end."

"Unless someone dug up the corpse of the baby you had buried next to the cabin. A particularly stubborn private detective, for example."

"Yes. I was scared when I saw that the grave had been discovered. I was afraid that if someone dug up that baby, they would dig up my past, too. So I did it myself instead."

"Did you dig another grave somewhere else?"

"That's none of your business, Mr. Grand-Duc. What are you going to do now?"

"I don't know. Could we meet?"

"I don't see that I have much choice. I'm at your mercy. Why don't we meet tomorrow morning, at nine o'clock? Laurent starts work at five, and I finish at eight. But it takes me an hour to get home. I hope you will be discreet, Mr. Grand-Duc. I have changed my life. I have put all this behind me, and it wasn't easy. I never meant to do anything bad that night. Quite the contrary. How could I have known..."

"Known what?"

Silence.

"Known what, Mélanie?"

"That my daughter would look so much like me, when she was eighteen years old?"

It was just past nine o'clock. The mists that clung to the Jura Mountains were beginning to lift. Marc was the first to spot the little white car moving up the road toward Dannemarie. It passed them and parked in front of the chalet with sky-blue shutters. Marc noticed the nurse's caduceus symbol on a sticker on the rear window. The blond-haired driver remained motionless behind the steering wheel for a while, then finally the car's lights went off and the door opened to reveal the tired smile on the achingly familiar face of a perfect stranger.

62

Tom clenched his fists as he slept in the transparent plastic bed. His tiny chest rose and fell. All that could be seen of him from this angle were a pair of chubby cheeks and a mane of blond hair, amazingly abundant for a four-day-old baby.

Marc held Lylie's hand. She was tired. Her eyes kept closing and flicking open again. The silence in the room made a welcome change: at last she was alone with Marc and Tom.

Nicole had just left. She would happily have stayed with them twenty-four hours a day, watching over her great-grandson, but Lylie had told her, in the kindest way possible, that she needed some rest. The whole of Dieppe already knew about the baby. The first person Nicole had told was Pierre, in the Janval cemetery, but after that she had rediscovered some of the energy of her youth and gone from shop to shop announcing the good news. Marc was dreading the new influx of visitors this would undoubtedly bring.

Lylie's head fell onto Marc's shoulder. He was perched

awkwardly on the edge of the bed, but he didn't dare move. Carefully, with his fingertips, he reached out to grab the card they had received from Mélanie Belvoir. It was attached to a huge bouquet of roses.

Happy birthday, Tom! Lylie, I'm sorry I wasn't able to be your mother. Perhaps you will accept me as a grand mother. I will do my best to make up for lost time, for every thing I ruined through my silence. It's not too late. Please let me into your life, for Tom's sake, if nothing else. What child wouldn't want a thirty-six-year-old grandmother?
Take care of Marc . . .
Mélanie

So far, Lylie had refused to meet her mother. Mélanie had not insisted. Lylie had felt too confused by the prospect; she needed time. But now Tom was here, and Marc felt sure he would be the link that connected mother and grandmother.

After barely three minutes of peace, Lylie was woken by the entry of another nurse. Marc cursed inwardly, but this time there was a good reason for the interruption. The nurse was carrying a gift-wrapped package that was bigger than she was.

"It's just been delivered by a messenger," said the nurse. "Good thing we don't get packages this big every day. The card is for Father, the present for Mom."

The nurse left. Lylie stared, wide-eyed.

"Aren't you going to open it?" Marc said.

"It looks like some kind of joke," said Lylie. "Are you sure it's not going to explode?"

"That depends who sent it."

Lylie tore off the wrapping paper while Marc opened the small white envelope.

He immediately recognized Malvina's barely legible scrawl, and his heart suddenly felt full.

"Who's it from?" Lylie asked, half buried under brightly colored paper.

"A friend," Marc replied. "A very dear friend."

"Oh?"

Lylie had ripped off all the wrapping paper and was now opening the cardboard box. Inside she found a gigantic brown-and-yellow teddy bear.

"Oh, my God!" Lylie squealed. "Look how beautiful it is!"

Marc finally managed to decipher Malvina's message:

For the little bastard. He'd better take good care of it.

Marc smiled and squeezed Lylie's hand. Then he turned toward the teddy bear. "You've been waiting a long time for this, haven't you? Finally you get to meet Lylie!"

The mother of his child gave him a puzzled look.

"Lylie, allow me to introduce Banjo."